There are many paths to power...

John Flaherty—A man of the cloth . . . and the flesh. He had clawed his way to the top of two empires. Now he was fighting to stay there.

Claudine Lambaire—A stunning woman of the world, she knew nothing about her handsome lover . . . except that he meant everything to her.

Eliah Varese—A Mafia kingpin with unlimited power . . . who would stop at nothing to keep it.

Monsignore Walkman—He had taught Flaherty everything he knew about the tough, dirty business of religious politics—but his pupil had gone much too far.

Mike Wyatt—An alcoholic reporter whose life was in shambles until he stumbled on the biggest story of his career—and possibly the last.

but no road to salvation for...
Monsignore

MONSIGNORE

Jack-Alain Léger

Translated by Harold J. Salemson

A DELL BOOK

Published by
Dell Publishing Co., Inc.
1 Dag Hammarskjold Plaza
New York, New York 10017

This work was first published in French by
Éditions Robert Laffont, France. © Jack-Alain Léger, 1975

Translation copyright © 1982 by Dell Publishing Co., Inc.

Dell ® TM 681510, Dell Publishing Co., Inc.

ISBN: 0-440-15752-8

Printed in the United States of America
First printing—November 1982

For
Dashiell Hedayat

ACKNOWLEDGMENTS

The author most warmly thanks Mr. Jean-Loup Champion for the inestimable assistance he gave him with the documentation necessary for the writing of this book. In order not to endanger their holy ministry and out of respect for their personal safety, it is not advisable to thank by name the many priests and lay persons who so generously opened their archives to us or so courageously let us in on the secrets to which they were privy. We are nonetheless indebted and grateful to them all.

And thank you, too, Clem Biddle Wood, for all your excellent advice.

J.-A.L.

PART ONE

*God is a scandal—but a
profitable one.*
CHARLES BAUDELAIRE

1

"In the beginning was the Word, and the Word was with God, and the Word was God."

Michael Wyatt, dead drunk, was declaiming in prophetic tones at the top of his lungs. But he could not drown out the roar of the rotor as the swish of its blades blew down the high grass around the take-off pad of Rome's Monte Sacro Heliport. He swung his gin bottle in the air, blubbered, drooled, shouted, and laughed all at the same time. Blinking his eyes merrily against the sun, which bent in through the glass bubble of the helicopter cockpit where he had just taken the rear seat, he went on undisturbed with his Biblelike improvisations.

"He was not the Light, but He came to bear witness to the Light, the Light that was the True Light, coming into the world to light up all men."

"*Madonna santa,* what is that Americano saying?" the pilot inquired of his other passenger, freeing his ear from one of the radio earphones.

"Forget it, Tonino," Cesare Tozzi yelled back. "He hasn't been sober in three days!"

"A fine how-do-you-do! What about his news story?"

"*Ma!* . . . His story'll be the same as every other year," the cynical Italian newspaperman replied as he attached his safety belt. "It'll start, 'On this Easter day of 1975, a pious and respectful crowd . . .' or else 'a respectful and pious crowd,' and then the son of a bitch'll just copy what he filed last year!"

"Which was a rehash of the year before," the pilot put in.

Cesare nodded his assent.

The sizzling acceleration of the metal blades drowned out the laughter of the two Italians. Their American passenger tossed his empty bottle of Booths out against one of the helipad lightposts.

"Some shit! Nothing left to drink!" he announced. "Remember what Holy Writ tells us, 'There was a wedding at Cana in Galilee. And the mother of Jesus was there, and Jesus too with all His disciples. And then the wine gave out . . .'"

"Cesare, make him shut up," the pilot muttered. "Or I'll throw him off this crate. We have to take off!"

Through the turned-about earphone a voice had been droning for several moments. "ITA 402. Get ready for takeoff . . ."

"Mike," Cesare begged, turning back toward him, "try to calm down a little."

"I'm perfectly calm," Mike came back, stifling a giggle. "Calm as can be."

The exasperated pilot settled back in his seat, pointed skyward as a signal that he was ready, and said into his mike, "I read you, five on five."

The control tower went right on, "ITA 402, get ready for takeoff. ITA 402 . . ." And Mike went right on, too, "*Molto* calm."

"Calm, my ass!" Cesare Tozzi roared back at him. "You just crossed yourself a dozen times, and you don't know it!"

12

MONSIGNORE

"Shut up, for Christ's sake!" Mike answered. "Respect the day of Our Savior's resurrection!"

Irritated though he was, the pilot had to laugh at that one. As he readjusted his second earphone, the voice came through, "ITA 402, the sky is yours."

"The sky is ours!" Tonino repeated in solemn merriment. And thereupon the helicopter was airborne.

The three men were up into the immense blueness with only a single tiny cloud dotting the horizon. And there was Rome beneath them, Rome in all its noonday splendor, with its pink-tiled roofs and flowered terraces, its pines and antique monuments.

On their left were the Colosseum, the Baths of Caracalla, the Roman Forum (looking from above like a half-finished architectural mockup), and the colossal Victor Emmanuel monument: the Winged Victory atop it seemed to be whipping her team of horses to catch up with them. Before them, the Pantheon and the myriad cupolas and ocher belltowers of the Campo di Marzo, the beautiful Piazza Navona and its fountains, their waters sparkling in the sunlight. Farther on, the dull silver thread of the Tiber, the gardens of the Janiculum, St. Peter's, the Castel Sant' Angelo . . . Closer, the vast empty oval of the Piazza del Popolo and then, right beneath them, the dark blue carpet of the Pincio Gardens, the shadow of the copter scurrying over its heavy pine grove like some huge insect. Now there was the Trinità dei Monti, and the Piazza di Spagna . . .

"The Eternal City!" Mike was proclaiming, overcome with excitement.

His foot stuck out in the empty space beyond the runner of the Alouette and it amused him to see the puffs of wind swell his pants leg out like a sail. Performing a ritual that was funny only to himself, he

13

gave his blessing to Rome. He blessed the majestic ruins, the steeples, the fountains, and the broken statues that all seemed to be coming up toward the whirlybird. He blessed the transparently blue sky of early spring. He blessed everything. He was happy.

Cesare, little by little, was finally getting into the spirit. "Look! Look!" he kept exclaiming, delighted as if on a Ferris wheel in some giant amusement park. There was a rooftop with laundry hung out to dry and children waving at them, and he threw them kisses in return. Farther on he recognized the roof of his own house, on Via del Angiolotto.

"Mike, did you see that?" he called. But Mike was off again in his drunken declamation:

"In the beginning, there was a she-wolf. A she-wolf that gave suck to two kids, twins. One was Romulus and the other was Remus. But that Romulus was a guy like me. Never could get enough to drink from that she-wolf's teats. He had to get rid of his brother. So he did him in. After that, he founded Rome. Some guy, that Romulus, what?"

"*Dio mio!* What a pain in the ass!" the pilot Tonino was muttering, half amused, half disgusted. "Can't you shut him up, Cesare?"

"Why don't you throw him out? You're the pilot, after all."

"With that bunch of jerks down there on the Victor Emmanuel Bridge? They would think he was Jesus coming down from heaven again. Not on a day like this, *amico!*"

"Hey, Wyatt, did you hear that?" Cesare yelled to him. "That would be a story for you! The miracle in St. Peter's Square on Easter Day: the second coming of Christ!"

"A Christ stinking of gin," the pilot cut in.

"Subhead: Christ is a lush!"

"Hey, shut your dago mouths, you guys! You got no religion at all?" Mike protested. All of a sudden, he was turning holy on them. And maybe a little scared.

The helicopter was hovering now over the Via della Conciliazione. Before their eyes was the huge triumphant ellipse of St. Peter's Square with tens of thousands of the faithful crushing in to await the appearance of the Pope and the blessing he would give, *urbi et orbi*.

The three men fell quiet. Despite themselves, that immense crowd, both merry and reverent, impressed them. Peddlers of balloons, religious objects, and souvenirs of the Holy Year were down there pushing their way through the mass of humanity as best they could.

To the left of the obelisk, in a semicircle, they could see invalids lying on stretchers telling the beads of their rosaries. Lined up along the Bernini colonnade were young pupils of Rome's religious schools, all somberly clad, pointing up at the helicopter, and above this sea of people the hundreds of white-winged nuns' coifs looked like so many sea gulls.

Just outside the basilica there was the lush multicoloring of the Swiss Guard's uniforms, the men in breeches and jerkins with blue and yellow stripings, the officers wearing inlaid breastplates, pink-feathered crests on their helmets, immaculate ruffs, and violet breeches, saluted by the halberdiers as they went by.

"It's still too early," Cesare noted. "They're not standing at attention yet. Tonino, you'll have to circle back."

"What the hell are they waiting for?" Mike asked. "Where can they be?"

"Who?"

"Why, Urbi and Orbi," he smugly replied. "They never get here on time."

Tonino laughed so hard at that one that he could hardly hold on to the joy stick.

"What a jerk!" Cesare commented. "I treat him as if he wasn't dead drunk—and I fall for his gags every time!"

The helicopter gained some altitude. It circled around the Michelangelo dome and for a moment flew over the huge intricate pattern of boxwood, yews, and white flowers in the Vatican gardens, and over the peacocks spreading their tail feathers on its lawns. Then it made a U-turn over the old quarters of the Trastevere.

They were now flying over the ancient historical neighborhoods of Rome, with their network of medieval streets and pink roofs with antique tiles. Here and there Tonino would point out some handsome rooftop: one of those hanging gardens that are the penthouses of so many old Roman buildings.

Mike whistled in admiration. And the pilot, like a good guide who knew Rome inside out, explained, "See that one? It's the Doria-Pamphilis' roof garden."

"You're right," Mike put in. "I was invited to a garden party there last summer."

"And that one is the Orsinis'," Tonino went on to Cesare, who did not have such entrées, "right behind the Mastroiannis' house."

Mike gave a wolf whistle, inspired not by the garden, but by the beautiful woman sunbathing on a

deck chair in the raw. Cesare came right back with
her measurements, "93-56-93, *chè bella bambina!*"

"More like 36-23-36," Mike corrected him, giving
his own estimate in inches instead of centimeters.

"Wanna bet? You'll lose," Cesare insisted.

"You going down to check it out?" Mike asked,
making way for Cesare to hop out of the copter. Tonino had to warn the two newshawks to cut it out,
they were knocking his crate off balance.

"Keep your eyes on the sights," he said. "Look,
that's the Della Roveres' terrace."

"Do you know the Della Roveres too?" Mike asked.

"Sure, he's terrific. He knows everybody," Cesare
answered. "Go on, Tonino. Tell Mike about Fellini.
The maestro needed a pilot for one of his pictures . . ."

"Scouting locations for *Roma*," Tonino said.
"That's why I'm so familiar with the rooftops of
Rome. But wait, you haven't seen the best part yet.
Up at the top of the Via Gregoriana. Look—there!"
And he pointed to the roof garden of the proudly
embossed palace they were approaching.

"Oh, no! That's just too grand!" This time it was
Mike who was impressed with the opulence.

The ancient baroque loggia with the smoked-glass
bay windows had been made over into a duplex, and
in front of it was a huge roof garden planted with
dwarf palms, orange trees, rose laurels, yews, lemon
trees, and tastefully laid-out beds of brightly colored
flowers among mossy rock formations. The verdant
lawn was cluttered with old statues and white leather
chaise longues with bronze frames, reminiscent of the
furnishings of Roman Caesars. On a low table there
were still the remains of someone's breakfast served
in magnificent silver plate.

17

Then, as the helicopter circled around the high penthouse which had a prince's coat of arms on its facade, the three passengers could see a small round swimming pool fed by a cool waterfall pouring from the mouth of a porphyry lion.

Seated on the marble rim of the pool, soaking their feet in the water, a naked couple were embracing.

"What a life!" Mike roared.

The man and woman, with their backs to them, now ducked their heads, surprised by the noise of the helicopter, which cast its threatening shadow over them.

So Tonino headed upward and around the nearby belltowers of the Trinità dei Monti, to circle back over the swimming pool from the other side.

The whirring blades ruffled the blue water, and as the machine circled, practically buzzing the penthouse, the woman, slightly frightened, dived into the water, while the man stood up shouting curses at the plane and shaking his fist at it.

"Holy smoke, I know who that is!" Cesare suddenly exclaimed, beginning to stutter with excitement. "It's . . . i—i-it's Finnegan! I-I-I don't believe it! Fi-Finnegan! A g-g-guy I been ch-chasing a story on for almost a month, Mike."

"What's the story?"

The man was a magnificent athletic type, maybe fifty, give or take a little. He had just wrapped a large bath towel around his middle, to cover his erection, and now, with a wave of his hand, was signaling them to be off.

"The story," Cesare, still fascinated by the sight, finally answered, "is that I think he's a top capo of the Mafia."

"An Irishman?" Mike snorted. "How does a mick get into the Mafia?" Then, slipping one of his loafers

18

off against the runner of the copter, he let it drop into the pool below.

"That for you, Don Finnegano!" he shouted, unheard, of course, by his subject.

Inside the bubble of the Alouette they were merrier than ever, Tonino now laughing as loudly as his passengers, so that he had some trouble steadying the crate as it barely cleared the rooftops of the Villa Medici. But he finally made a half turn above the gardens of the French Foundation, and as he did so the penthouse of the Via Gregoriana palace once again came into view behind the Hôtel de la Ville. There, standing proudly with feet spread wide apart, between two of the Roman busts on the terrace balustrade, Finnegan was sizzling with rage. Awesomely handsome as a statue of Jupiter or Mars, he had his forearm raised toward the craft, and he was unmistakably giving them the finger!

Tonino, the pilot, was the first to regain his composure.

"Saint Peter's," he reminded the two newshawks as he looked at his wristwatch, "noon."

As they were crossing the Tiber, they heard the cannon boom in the distance.

When they got over the Via della Conciliazione, the sky darkened for a moment: hundreds of doves were flying upwards among the released balloons, as the bells of the church tolled thunderously. From St. Peter's Square there rose the immense ovation which always greets the appearance of the Supreme Pontiff on the balcony of St. Damasus. The cry hammered out like a slogan in a variety of languages rising toward them seemed a prayer desperately trying to break through the noise of their motors.

19

"*Il Pa-pa! Il Pa-pa! Il Pa-pa!* The Pope! The Pope! The Pope! *Le Pape! Le Pape! Le Pape!*"

The mob was shouting its holy joy and prostrating itself.

To those above it seemed as if a storm had suddenly broken over an ocean that was now dashing its waves against the pink stone shoals of St. Peter's Square.

Religious fervor drove these men and women against the unyielding line of soldiers. The tide broke against the sun-glinted breastplates and the crossed halberds of the Swiss Guard. And a few of the faithful even stood on tiptoe, reaching their arms up in the mad idea that they might get as high as the Holy Father up there, miraculously touch him on his balcony, he who was only a fragile white silhouette with an arm that trembled as it gave its blessing to city and universe.

Then, coming from nowhere, two jet fighters crossed each other up in the blue, their white jetstreams making a great cross in the sky. There was another release of doves and balloons, and beneath the Michelangelo dome the great organ pealed, reminding *urbi et orbi* that Christ had risen.

A few of the faithful, raising their eyes, saw the helicopter growing smaller on the horizon and then disappearing as the cross of smoke began to dissipate above.

2

His mussed light gabardine suit was thrown over the back of a chair. Dirty socks were strewn on the worn carpet, a single moccasin sat absurdly atop a bottle of bourbon, and stray neckties and copies of *Sports Illustrated* lay on the bedspread on the floor. Mike Wyatt looked with disgust at his room—a drunkard's den. As on every other morning, for a moment before getting up, distressed and slightly ashamed of himself, he had trouble admitting that this mess was his own room.

Could he possibly have gone to sleep last night in what he mentally termed "all this shit"? But then, when had he gone to bed? At what time? He didn't know.

Had he come directly home from the Consalvis' party, or had he dragged around at Harry's Bar or the Doney?

Had he made love to Honey Pie, or had he come home alone after simply dropping her off at her place? Could he even be sure he had gone by to pick her up when she finished her song turn, as he had promised? He couldn't remember.

Fact was, he didn't want to remember.

"Some shit!" he kept muttering between clenched teeth, as he rubbed his unshaven chin and rolled the unlighted cigarette from one corner of his mouth to the other.

The dull mirror of the wardrobe returned the funny faces he made and behind them the reflection of a curtain blowing slightly in the light morning breeze. He stretched like a cat and took a deep breath, experiencing truly sensual enjoyment.

This was the Roman spring, with its sweet smells and its luscious light fragmented by the persian blinds into grotesque shadows on the hideous prewar Brazilian, rosewood and white-painted pitchpine furniture. The morning light was so bright that it even made his oversized room, number 402 at the Royal Italia, less ugly to him.

The Royal Italia was one of those Parioli "grand hotels" that had been in their heyday back when Mussolini was invading Ethiopia—or thereabouts. Three years earlier—to the day, now that he thought if it—when he had been posted to Rome as assistant to De Vaere, Mike arrived in Rome at Easter without having had the *World* reserve a room for him, trusting to luck and his legendary charm. But both the charm and the luck let him down. He wandered for hours from hotel to hotel, only to be told "No vacancy," and this was where he ended up.

Could he ever forget that dark lobby, big as a railway station waiting room? Or its doorman in his threadbare, dirty uniform, telling him in so-called English, "Very good. You very good here. Take room by month, Signore?"

"No, no, just for the night," Mike had answered, as he appraised what looked like a horror film set, the broken-down furniture buried in layers of dust, the chipping Fascist-style murals, and the unbelievable old man grabbing his luggage with the avidity of a miser and shoving him into the elevator.

But next morning he hadn't felt up to packing again, so he stayed on. And then the next day, and the next—for three years, now. And every day of those three years as he got up he swore that this would be the day he would find himself better digs. Maybe an apartment, or a studio; all he had to do was pick up *Il Tempo* and read the want ads.

But by noon each day those dreams were forgotten. He didn't bother to buy *Il Tempo*, but instead had a few Campari-and-gins at the Rosati. Then he checked in at the office on Via di Ripetta, where he passed the time of day with the secretary, Marion, making his ritual daily marriage proposal to her, to which she replied, as usual, "We'll see about that."

Then back for a pick-me-up at the Rosati: this time, gin without the Campari. And the afternoon went by without his realizing it. At the cocktail hour he'd be at the Café de Paris, watching night fall with the anxiety that always took hold of him when the sun went down beyond the top of Via Veneto.

After that, at the wheel of his banged-up old Bel Air convertible ("I'll have to replace this one day soon, too"), he went back to the Royal Italia by way of the Villa Borghese park, drinking in the same old jazz from one of his limited supply of tapes, the Duke playing "Solitude" or Coltrane on "A Love Supreme." That was really something, man! It grabbed you down in the gonads, slithered up your back, and gave you a real thrill, turned you on, made you forget everything. A man could almost be happy that way. And he could make wild plans for what to do tomorrow. While you waited for a traffic light to change, you could write yourself a note on the copy paper in your pocket, a little list of resolutions, addressed to "Dear Mike."

There was a whole collection of such notes that he wrote to himself, childish, moving letters now stuck away in the pink-mirrored drawers of the dresser in room 402.

Dear Mike:
1. Stop drinking.
2. Join American Athletic Club; dues, ten bucks. Find good swim. Pool up in Parioli.
3. Find flat, and cleaning woman—lots cheaper.
4. Reread Balzac and Dostoyevski.
5. Get going on that g.d. novel of yours—finally.

Lotsa luck, yours,
The Other Mike

One day, reading a book about F. Scott Fitzgerald, he discovered that his favorite author also made lists of resolutions addressed to himself—and it brought tears to his eyes. Then, all excited, he had said to Honey Pie, who was lying in bed next to him, painting her toenails, "Oh, Honey Pie, listen to what Scott Fitzgerald—"

"Sure," she cruelly cut him off, "but the difference is that Fitzgerald went ahead and wrote the stuff."

What a mess life was! There was always a Honey Pie to remind you that you weren't F. Scott Fitz, or John Fitz Kennedy, or Duke Ellington, or Paul Newman, or whoever—just a lousy gossip columnist pulling down 15 g's a year plus expenses to cover the silly doings of movie stars and so-called Roman society—

the Colonnas, Audrey Hepburn, Fellini, you name 'em.

Now, though, he remembered he had to go by and apologize to Honey Pie for having stood her up last night. He'd go this afternoon, after she was awake. But first he was supposed to meet Cesare at his place. He didn't know why Cesare wanted to see him; probably some lead he had for a story. Cesare was always coming up with some new idea for a story they could do together; he was always involved in a hundred different deals, running down thousands of tips. Just the opposite of Mike. But still, he liked him a lot. In fact, maybe that was just why he liked Cesare so much.

When he opened the door, Cesare would greet him with "This story is *meraviglioso*, Mike."

Usually, of course, it was nothing of the sort. But Mike would most likely go along, just to be nice to Cesare.

Oh, well, he'd see what it was this time.

Feeling suddenly quite merry, Mike kicked off the sheet, gave out with a rebel yell, and hopped under the shower—a thin trickle of water alternately scalding hot and icy cold that came out of the rusted showerhead.

"Fucking Royal Italia," he roared. "Royal, my ass!"

He parked the Bel Air in front of the Pantheon, tossing a hundred-lira coin to the disabled veteran who was in charge of the car park. Turning the corner into Via dell' Angiolotto, he walked ahead nonchalantly on the sunny side of the street, blinking but happy with the radiant sky above the rooftops. Carefree, he hummed "Strangers in the Night" and kicked a dented, rusty Coke can that bounced along before him, clanking as it went.

When he got to number 63, he went into the old house with its rickety staircase and hopped up the steps three at a time, by now singing the words—

> Strangers in the night
> Exchanging glances . . .

—not stopping till he got to the top landing. He was out of breath, his heart was pounding, but he was visibly proud that he could still put out that kind of effort.

He knocked at the low door, noting how worm-eaten it was around the edges. "Cesare! Cesare!" he called.

No answer.

Surprised at his friend's silence, he knocked louder, and shouted again, "Cesare! Cesare!"

Strange! Still not a word from Cesare.

Cesare was never one not to show up for an appointment, especially at his own place. Maybe he was asleep.

Mike was getting ready to go down those five stories, which he would have been just as happy now not to have come bounding up, when something told him to turn around and try the door.

He gave it a shove, and it opened so easily that he fell forward into the room.

Regaining his balance, he brushed off his white pants and called out loudly, "*Ave Cesar! Morituri te salu—*" but stopped in the middle of the word. "Son of a bitch!" he said.

There was the bedside lamp lying on the floor and

throwing frightening shadows against the wall—and the knocked-over furniture, the books and personal papers strewn about, the torn material, broken glass . . .

And Cesare, lying flat on his belly on the couch. Motionless.

Mike went toward him, but he understood before he saw.

"Son of a bitch," he said again.

He touched his friend's shoulder, raised his body slightly. There was a small spot of blood right over Cesare Tozzi's heart.

An irrepressible twitch distorted the corners of his mouth, and his fingers almost crushed the second glass of gin that Tino had just poured him—or was it the third? Whichever, he had to go on drinking some more. Especially when something upsetting happened.

He was almost crazy. He could hear the ice cubes tinkling in his glass, but it did not occur to him to set it down on the counter. Through the tears in his eyes he could barely see the crummy little Angiolotto Bar, where only yesterday Cesare and he had downed a quick espresso before heading for the Monte Sacro Heliport: the coffee machine, the metal pinup girl advertising Gelati Motta, the chianti and grappa bottles, and, over behind the cash register, Tino, the owner, a red-faced, bald fat giant who looked like something out of a Plautus comedy.

Hanging on to the counter like a shipwrecked sailor grasping his fragile life raft, Mike was reliving the few mad minutes that followed his discovery of Cesare's corpse.

He had let the body back down on the couch and squatted beside it, his arms dangling between his legs.

For no good reason that he could tell, he puffed noisily, like a boxer recovering from a knockdown.

Cesare's hand, already cold in death, was lying on the rug. He raised it delicately by the wrist, to place the arm on the couch, alongside the body. Again, he didn't know why: one of the those meaningless things you do when you're upset.

Then, a pocketsize *Totocalcio* soccer magazine slipped off to the floor. He picked it up. On the dog-eared page it was turned to, two names were checked in red in the list of towns whose teams were playing: Palermo and Varese. No doubt the game Cesare had a bet on for next Sunday.

But once he started looking at it, even though it was of no great interest to him, Mike, squatting still, went on reading to the last page, not even skipping the classified or display ads. An absurd thing to do, of course, but no more absurd than his being here, alive, beside Cesare Tozzi, who had been murdered.

Who could have murdered him?

Suddenly Mike felt engulfed in a mad rage. He angrily threw the tip sheet away and then, without even feeling it coming, began violently vomiting.

Who could have killed him? he kept wondering.

"You don't feel so good, *Dottore* Wyatt?" Tino asked, and the voice brought him out of his daydream.

The man poured him another drink, as he went on reading the information in his own *Totocalcio*.

"No, I'm just fine," Mike said, slowly coming back to himself.

"Don't look so good," Tino commented.

Mike had no stomach for small talk. He was afraid he'd have to tell him that Cesare had—

But then Mike authoritatively announced to Tino, "Palermo versus Varese," as he saw the bar owner hesitating between two different matches. "Palermo versus Varese," he repeated again, in suppressed rage.

Then, throwing a kiss to the Gelati Motta girl, whom he had just knocked down in a wild crash of metal, he staggered toward the pay phone on the wall.

The police answered immediately and Mike merely said, in a colorless voice, "63 Via dell' Angiolotto! Top floor! Hurry! Emergency!"

Before the operator could ask for any further details, Mike hung up. And stood there, stunned, staring into space. His eyes were filling with tears. He was desperately trying to recall Cesare—trying to remember some happy time they had had together, some game they had played, some gag they had pulled together, an affectionate pat on the back, a smile, a laugh, a joke he had cracked.

Then, suddenly, as the siren of the Pronto Soccorso squad car sounded at the end of the street, deafening, gradually taking over completely, a name popped into Mike's head:

"Finnegan!"

3

A few years before the troops of Charles V sacked Rome, the very wealthy Zanti family, which had made a fortune in trade between the Near East and its native Greece, to everyone's amazement decided to move to the Eternal City. It would have been understandable if these slightly piratical merchants and shipowners had taken up residence, say, in Venice or Genoa, or even in Florence. But Rome was certainly no city for them.

The Zantis let people talk and be amazed. But when Giulio di Medici, become Pope Clement VII, wanted to rebuild the city which the German ruffian hordes had pillaged and more than half burned and demolished, it was not to the Colonnas, the Dorias, or the Orsinis that he turned for help, but to Eusebio de Zanti, who prodigally gave of the millions he had garnered off the backs of the infidels. In a few years Rome became the most beautiful city in the world, and Eusebio was made a duke, and then a prince, in gratitude for the services he had rendered to the Papacy.

From that day forward, and into our own century, the wealth and fame of that noble family never diminished. The Zantis furnished many generals to the papal armies, dozens of cardinals to the Church,

and even two popes: Urban IX, who built onto the
Vatican the wing that bears his name—"to house his
harem," said the scandalmongers of Rome—and the
very pious Sixtus VI, who reformed canon law, changed
the monastic rules of the Discalced Camaldolese Bene-
dictines, and died with the stigmata on his body.

Alas, his nephews, in addition to squandering a part
of that immense fortune by building sumptuous palaces, could think of nothing better to do than besmirch
his memory by holding orgies that remained famous
throughout history. Heaven was not slow in manifest-
ing its displeasure: in 1780, Maestro Abracadabra, the
then-fashionable clairvoyant, prophesied that all the
Zanti palaces would burn down within the next one
hundred years.

Six of them indeed burned before the end of a
century, but Maestro Abracadabra was still proved
wrong: the greatest palace of them all, the one that
Bernini built them at the top of Via Gregoriana, is
still there, untouched in any way by fire.

Nevertheless, struck by this strange curse, the Zanti
family went into a slow decline, losing in turn its
palaces, its villas, its lands, armies, ships and banks
and factories, giving up first its political and then its
economic power, and finally, in order to live, being
forced to sell even the innumerable art treasures it
had accumulated through the ages.

In 1965 the last descendant to bear the famous name
of Zanti was a half-crazy old maid whom neighbors
often saw wandering in her loneliness through the
devastated rooms of her palace, now teeming with
stray cats. Then some wily real estate promoters realized that this magnificent baroque building, properly
refurbished and split up into apartments of about five
thousand square feet each, might make one of the

most desirable residences in all of Rome. They were not even obliged to buy it outright: the old fool deeded it to them in exchange for a guaranteed pittance for life. Considering which, they had her declared incompetent and committed to an institution.

Six months later, as they were digging out the catacombs beneath the building to make room for an underground garage, the workers' pickaxes hit a solid block of granite. Beneath it lay the treasure of the Zantis—a whole accumulation of gold coins of Greece and jewels of Arabia.

No further advertising was needed to make the seven apartments in the palace sell at a premium: in a few hours, dazzling offers had come pouring in from the four corners of the earth. Only the duplex penthouse remained available for a few days: it did, after all, require a payment of close to two million dollars.

At any rate, two years after that underground discovery hit the front pages passersby were able once again to see the admirably restored facade of the old palace in all its splendor. It had simply been scraped clean, and its antique windows had been replaced by huge smoked-glass bay windows in stainless steel frames.

Had they been allowed into the greenery-laden entryway, they could have admired the air-conditioning vents discreetly hidden inside the lampholders and the gilt wooden angel with outstretched finger showing visitors the way to the elevator doors: two sober steel portals set inside an exuberant marble drapery dating from the seventeenth century. And then, had they gone all the way to the top, they would have seen the most beautiful roof garden anyone could imagine, and the most magnificent vista in all of Rome.

But of course they were not allowed to—unless their

arrival had been properly announced in advance and they signed the guest book under the inquisitive eye of the closed-circuit television.

Peppe, the doorman, barred the way.

Peppe was always there to bar the way. And so that none might be unaware of his eminent position, he had a fine braided cap decorated with golden letters spelling RESIDENZA GREGORIANA.

"Praise be to San Giuseppe!" thought Peppe. He was done reading "his" rich tenants' mail. One by one, he resealed the envelopes which a little earlier he had steamed open. In the morning he would deliver the letters: the Italian mails are so confounded slow. Who would know the difference?

Oh, well, the day was over, and now he could go and celebrate Luisa's engagement to Aldo. He set the closed-circuit TV and the alarm system on automatic, double-locked the door to his lodge and, the ever-present cigarette butt dangling from the corner of his lip, wended his way up the service stairway, muttering *Porca Madonnas* intended for God knows whom.

Aldo, Carla, and Luisa—now, there were well mannered people! They were real friends: Peppe was hardly visible through the smoked glass when all three, the valet, the chambermaid, and the cook, were at the door to greet him with joyous delight, "Ah, our friend Peppe! How goes it, Peppe? Hi, Admiral! Welcome, illustrious Signore Peppe!" all talking at once and drinking Asti. It turned out they were discussing the subject that fascinated them the most: the strange tenant of the penthouse. Carla was saying, "Now, that Finnegan . . ."

"What about him?"

"I wonder what he . . ."

"That blasted Yankee! I wish I knew!" Peppe said.

"Let me tell you, Aldo, he's been living up there with that girl three years now. Well, not once in all that time has there been the least letter for him. Never anyone to see him. Not once! . . . Oh, that is, except for one guy, calls himself a lawyer. Another American. Berg's his name. He comes to see him once in a while . . ."

"I'm telling you there's something crooked about him," Aldo came back. "I've always figured he must be a gangster, or a spy, or something. Yes, that's it: an in-ter-na-tion-al spy!"

Aldo stressed each syllable of those last two words with punches that made the table shake and the glasses tinkle. The women peeped like frightened birds:

"Could he be?" "A gangster, Aldo?" "He's so distinguished-looking, you know."

Peppe had to go the valet one better.

"That's what he is," he concluded, "one of those CIA guys. And his so-called servants, you know what? They're hit men!"

Suddenly, they all fell silent. They could hear steps on the stairs. Someone was on the way up.

"That's him, coming back up," Peppe mumbled between his teeth. "Take a good look. Really looks like a priest, don't he?"

The young black man was carrying a heavy cardboard box sealed with big red wax seals at the four corners. This was not the first time Peppe had seen one of Finnegan's servants come up with one of those packages, the contents of which intrigued him so.

"Secret weapons, maybe?" he mumbled.

"At any rate, you got to believe that American pays 'em well. They never let on a word," Aldo said.

"You can say that again! Never a word. No way to

make 'em talk. But it's true that Finnegan isn't chintzy when it comes to paying," Peppe went on, pausing a bit so as to get his maximum effect, "not chintzy at all: he gives a million-lire tip for New Year's!"

"What?" the others gasped.

"You heard me: a million lire!"

Aldo couldn't believe his ears. He got up, speechless, and then repeated, "A million lire?"

The women were incredulous, too.

"Oh, such a distinguished-looking man," Carla dreamily repeated. "Did you talk to your son about him, Signore Peppe? He's a policeman. He ought to know, if anyone does."

"My poor Peppino is up in Milan. Freezing to death up there in that city of madmen. My poor Peppino is still waiting for his transfer," Peppe complained. "In this goddamned country, if you don't have pull . . ."

Carla looked at him with a sympathetic smile as the bell rang once more, much more insistently this time. She finally got up, quickly gulped a last swallow of the Asti, and sighed, "Oh, it must be some fine-looking place he's got up there!"

"Ah, Signorina Carla, you can't imagine," Peppe assured her. "You can't imagine what it's like. And that woman . . ."

4

CLAUDINE LAMBAIRE:

This is the time I like best. The twilight hour, what we call *l'heure bleue*—even though everything is mauve, pink, and golden. It ought to be called the wild hour. Nothing blue about it. Evening comes to Rome all delicacy and seductiveness. The air is sweet, the sky transparent. A light little wind ruffles the surface of the pool, and the flowers emit their most potent aromas: the liliums, camellias, and hollyhocks. And the bells of the Trinità dei Monti sound the Angelus, nearby. Nightbirds flutter about the roof of the penthouse and then fly off toward the west. Over there, beyond the Tiber, the world seems to be on fire. On the Aventine Hill, the outlines of the pines stand clear against the fiery horizon.

And I wait for Harold.

I've bathed, and my body smells of the bath salts, the cinnamon soap, and the three drops of *L'Heure bleue* that I like to put on the back of my neck and both my earlobes. I slowly, softly fondle myself—first my breasts, then inside my thighs, and finally, through the thin muslin of my negligee, my Venus mound.

Harold will be home tonight.

Here on the terrace, I'm stretched out on a leather

steamer chair and Diab has brought me my favorite champagne cocktail: green lemon, sugarcane syrup, a drop of angostura bitters, and a split of pink Roederer. Yes, this is the time I like best of the whole day— when Diab hasn't yet lighted the garden lanterns or Van Dông the blue venetian glass girandoles, and you feel a little bit lost in all this fragrant darkness, alone in face of the immensity with all of Rome at your feet. And all the while, Rome's lights go on, one by one, as far as the eye can see.

I've put my favorite Barry White album on the stereo, the one that has "Symphony in White" on it. Oh, that African beat that catches the very rhythm of your heart! You wait. You wait. Something is about to happen. But then, nothing does. Not yet. Not now. It's just like waiting for Harold—somehow painful yet compelling at the same time. Almost hallucinating! But it makes you want to dance! To dance before the panorama of Rome catching fire in the descending night and lash the air with your long *Heure bleue*-scented hair. . . . It's like an intoxication. A delicious one. And then a cry . . .

After that, there's the passage where the strings play together and send off the melody, which the brass immediately picks up. The trumpets, sharp as sex urges, demanding . . . And you feel yourself whipped up in a frenzy . . .

There's Harold now! He must be down in the garage, putting the Alfa-Romeo away. Maybe on his way up in the elevator . . .

But, no! The flight of fiddles has calmed down. And quiet returns.

The number is over.

So I get up to change it. And as I do every evening,

or practically every evening, the next record I put on is another one of the Love Unlimited Orchestra, or else that simple song with Barry crooning in his deep black voice, "You're my first, my last, my everything . . ."

Sure, they're ordinary song lyrics. But there are times when they could make me cry. Night is falling on the city with all its romance, its promises of happiness to come. And up there in the sky, in the waning twilight, you can see the flicker of the lights on a plane that in a few minutes will perhaps set down at Fiumicino.

And maybe Harold will be on it.

Maybe he'll be home tonight, within the hour.

Or else, tomorrow—who can ever tell, with him? I just wait for him. I'll always be waiting. If he doesn't get here tonight, it'll be tomorrow.

And we'll make love.

"If you're able to wait for me more than half a day without wanting anything more than to wait for me, then maybe we'll be able to live together for at least a few days." That was one of the first things he told me when we met. "I'm not making any promises, you see. I won't swear to love you all my life. Nor will I marry you. But I like you—and that's that."

And I could hear myself answering, "I'm crazy about you already."

"Wait," he said, with that handsome smile that did such things to me—oh, those two dimples of his as long as slashes, his white, even teeth, his mischievous eyes!—"wait, I haven't told you the whole story. In order for things to be more romantic later, you have to give me a pledge. You have to promise—"

"We'll see," I answered sharply, feigning irritation.

Jack-Alain Léger

To tell the truth, whatever he might have asked me, I was ready to answer yes.

"You have to promise never to ask me a single question about my life, my work, or the long times I'll have to stay away from you."

I laughed and made a wide-eyed face that made him laugh too.

"Oh, la, la. You must be a very important man, then, Mr. Finnegan."

"So, you know my name, do you?"

"Sure I do," I said, trying to sound as childish as possible. "And I like mysteries, too. Maybe you're a gun runner? Or a big international spy?"

I was sorry after I said that, but I was a little stoned. Then he took my hand in his and, acting the child himself, said, "You sure guessed right off, didn't you?"

I asked him, "Where're you taking me?"

"Uh-uh," he countered. "No fair. You're asking questions already." And turning to the driver, "We can go now, José."

The doorman of Annabel's closed the door of the Rolls-Royce. José went up Berkeley Square, turned into Mount Street.

It was three thirty in the morning, in June: dawn was breaking over Hyde Park. A nice litle rain was fogging the windows and isolating us from the rest of the world, hiding us from Park Lane, deserted at this hour. We were riding into life as we rode into daylight. Without being able to see a thing. And I still didn't know the first thing about him! Not even where he was taking me. This is like one of those abductions in a romantic opera, I thought.

So I snuggled up against his chest—like a heroine in a romantic opera. And I cried. I don't know why.

* * *

Andrew and I had been dining at Annabel's after having put in appearances at two equally stuffy parties. I was feeling lousy, and the idiot was boring me to death with his tales of grouse hunting in Scotland, bear hunting in Siberia, and tiger hunting the Lord alone knows where.

"Why, you're not listening to me, Claudine," he said.

"No, I'm not," I replied, suddenly hostile. "I don't give a fuck about tigers or grouse. It all bores me shitless."

"You *can* be so vulgar at times," he complained.

"Not nearly so vulgar as you," I snapped back. "If it's good manners to kiss the hands of dames you can't sleep with and never let on that you know the ones that you do sleep with—well, then I'd rather be the vulgar little French whore I am than well mannered like your fucking British Lordship."

"Please stop using that word."

"What word?"

"Why do you insist on debasing yourself?"

"Well, what do you call a girl who screws for money in your country?"

"Very well. If you feel you *must* humiliate me . . ."

"A fine how-do-you-do," I blurted out. "Now I'm the one who's humiliating you!"

"I see you want to make a scene here, where everyone knows me," he archly concluded. "Have it your way. For my part, I'm leaving. Here! Take these five-pound notes! *You* can take care of the dinner bill. As you say, you're nothing but a whore."

I should have yelled there and then. I should have slapped him and stormed out of the place. But—go know why!—I did nothing of the sort.

Anyway, I knew he'd be coming back; it was just

a question of how long he'd take. It was just one of our usual set-tos, nothing serious. I figured he'd be back in half an hour.

So I took my temper out on the food. After gobbling down my own filet mignon Rossini, I finished his, which Andrew had barely touched. If anyone was looking at me, they must have thought I was a kook—but I didn't give a fast fuck about that. I even made a joke about it with Pipetto, the maître d', who thought I absolutely ought not to pass up the soufflé.

"*Non, merci,*" I told him. "Instead, tell me who the good-looking guy at Janet Mendoza's table is."

"I don't know, Mademoiselle Lambaire. I'll try to find out."

I was all eyes, fascinated by that man. I could feel I was falling in love with his washed-out blue eyes, with his bright smile, with those childlike dimples that set off the macho quality of the rest of his features rather than canceling it; falling in love with that somewhat prominent energetic chin, that ruddy complexion that I felt like reaching out and touching; in love with the muscular athletic build that was hidden under his elegant dinner jacket, with his square but aristocratic hands and the blond hairs that grew on them. In a word, I loved him. As if I had always known him, in all ways.

As if I had long dreamed of him, or lived with him in some earlier life. And at last, he had come back to me—even though I'd never seen him before. All I could think of now was how to get him to notice me and want me. But he was too busy entertaining Janet Mendoza's guests with his witty repartee, which I couldn't hear but which had them all laughing merrily. Not once did he look my way.

* * *

"Harold Finnegan," a voice said.

I was startled. Less than half an hour had gone by and Lord Andrew Cavenaught, Duke of Warfield and Hanlow, was back standing before me, pitiable and contrite.

"What about Harold Finnegan?"

"That's the name of that man you keep staring at when I'm not about, my dear."

"You know him?" I asked.

"By name."

"Who is he? What does he do?"

"The one who can fathom that hasn't been born yet," Andrew pontificated.

"Meaning what?"

"Some kind of adventurer, I suppose. Maybe a big businessman. Maybe just a spiv."

"Well, he looks to me to be ever so courteous, refined, and charming," I said. "And it seems that Lady Mendoza—"

"Oh, the Mendozas are only what we call upstart nobility. They're just Portuguese Jews who were knighted by Elizabeth. Elizabeth the First, that is."

"I knew which one you meant," I snapped. "What do you take me for? An idiot?"

"No, but I meant to say that since Janet has such chic friends, she can probably put up with the likes of this Harold Finnegan too."

"Sure, even Lord Andrew Cavenaught can entertain his doxy at Annabel's, right?" I said. "Isn't that what you meant?"

"You're really being impossible tonight, Claudine. And anyway, stop staring at him like that. It's quite rude. Do you think he is handsome?"

"Yes, and well mannered, besides."

"I always knew you had terrible taste."

43

"That doesn't say much for you."

"What I meant by that was that only Frenchwomen can find an Irishman attractive."

"And only Englishmen can be such sore losers. I thought you were the people who invented fair play! A good thing we gave you the syph!"

"Oh, Claudine, the things you say!"

But I figured there was no sense in talking if he could be so shocked by that word. I didn't need another scene with him.

So I let Andrew ramble on to his heart's content, and listened for the umpteenth time to the story of that safari in Kenya when the lion came at him. "Why couldn't he have gobbled you up?" I was thinking. And then my mind began to wander.

Irresistibly, my eyes went back to *him*: I wanted *him* to look over at me. I concentrated on it: Look at me! Yes, look at me, Harold! (In my mind I was already calling him by his first name.) I would have done anything to get him to turn and see me; I was ready to shout, or call out his name, or even attract his attention by throwing a bread ball over onto the Mendozas' table—even if it meant I might never again be allowed to set foot in Annabel's.

But instead I just hummed "Poinciana" along with the stereo.

No use! The people at his table were all noisily laughing and applauding him.

That was when Andrew got up and asked to be excused "for a minute." As he walked away, I watched him, while absentmindedly finishing the piece of fruit tart he had left on his plate.

And suddenly—"Don't move, don't yell, this is a kidnapping," a voice was whispering in my ear.

I turned around and felt something hard and sharp

digging into my ribs. "A gun or a knife," I immediately conjectured. But it was only a finger, at the end of a hand pretending to be a revolver: he was aiming at me the way kids do when they play.

And the kidnapper was making a delightful baby face.

It was Harold Finnegan.

"How are you going to make me obey?" I asked.

"With charm," he laughed.

I should have found him conceited and sneeringly told him so. Instead of which, his smile seemed truly disarming to me and all I could stammer was "Where are you taking me?"

"To the ends of the earth, or just around the corner. You decide!"

"Since when does the hostage have a choice?"

"Since I'm the kidnapper and you're the kidnap-pee."

"What ransom will you hold me for?" I asked.

"None. You don't think I have any intention of letting you go, do you?" he replied.

"Oh, well," I laughed, "in that case . . ."

And that was that.

Later there was the Rolls-Royce we drove off in, the day dawning over Piccadilly, the red and gold Thames, and burning away the morning haze, the sun breaking through over the pretty, hilly road in Surrey.

I was dazzled and blinking; I was yawning; I was tired but not tired; I wanted to go to sleep, but not really to go to sleep. No, I just wanted to go on riding like this till the end of the day, till the end of time, comfortably ensconced on the red leather seat of the Phantom VI, as he caressed me; with my head on his chest, listening to "Yesterday" being softly played by the dashboard tapedeck; fascinatedly watching the screen of the little computer terminal underneath the limousine bar. I had never seen anything like it: figures kept appearing and disappearing with the speed of light, bringing stock market quotations from Tokyo or Vancouver. Or else a notice that there was an urgent message for him from His Majesty the Emir of Kuwait. And at the bottom, the most routine details of everyday life: the temperature outside and the correct time, the number of the tape being played over the speakers, and the frequency on which the car telephone was operating in the area we were now in, Sussex.

Realizing how amazed I was at it, Harold pressed the red button on the keyboard. The word MEMORY appeared, and flickered on and off. Harold then typed something on the keys of the computer, and it came out CLAUDINE I LOVE YOU. OVER.

I laughed and threw my arms around him. "Oh, you!" I said.

"Not me! That was the computer. I'm going to be jealous," he replied.

"Oh, you! You!" was all I could say.

The message faded out and was replaced by a wire service bulletin giving a summary of world events during the night just past. But the word MEMORY kept blinking on and off. It was very romantic to know that the computer would remember your name along with all the other millions of facts and figures it remembered, like what the futures market was in Australia, how much foreign currency the Portuguese treasury had on hand, or the latest terrorist attack by the IRA.

The steel-blue Rolls-Royce turned onto a new road leading to the private airfield at Sutton-Haven. On the side of the road I could see billboards advertising a taxi-plane service. A suspicion fleetingly came over me, and for a second I trembled, as I thought, "You must be crazy. Haven't you seen through it all yet? This guy is an international pimp, a bigshot in the white-slave trade. He's shipping you out to Kuwait or Bahrein or someplace. In a few hours, you'll be served up in a harem, or a whorehouse."

I was scared. And yet, the fear that came over me was also making me feel an unprecedented thrill: now I was his slave. He could demand anything of me, and I would do it.

"But what about luggage? I haven't any bags," I said, slightly taken aback, as José tooled the car onto the airfield parking area.

"Who ever heard of a kidnappee taking bags along?" Harold said, as he kissed the back of my neck. And then, narrowing his eyes like Rudolph Valentino in *The Sheik*, he assured me, "Never fear, my dear! In my tent in the desert, you will find the richest jewels of Araby!"

But then, in his own voice, he added, "We're going to my place in Rome. Do you have your passport with you?"

"Yes," I said, opening my handbag. "Along with ten pounds sterling, a package of Dunhills, a lighter, an eyeliner, three Kleenexes, and a picture of my mother."

"Well, you see, you're not going off empty-handed at all!"

"Will we stop in Paris? I'd like to give her a ring."

"Yes," he said. "We'll change at Charles de Gaulle for a commercial plane. But you can call her from right here." And with that he took the phone off the hook and asked for the international operator.

He smiled when he found out he had to dial the

number of the bar-grocery in Saint-Chély-le-Marché, in the château country of Indre-et-Loire. And then I smiled when I saw the computer ask: CODE?

SC, Harold answered by pushing down a key.

SCRAMBLE?

SC, he pressed again.

When I finally got Maman on the line, I informed her I had just dumped Lord Cavenaught and was flying to Rome.

"Rome?" she asked. "Well, give me your address down there, little daughter. I'll be wanting to write you. And to send you a picture of St. Yves, so you can get it blessed. For your brother . . ."

I looked inquisitively at Harold. But he shook his head no, and typed on the keyboard: IMPOSSIBLE. SAY YOU'LL CALL HER.

"Impossible, Maman," I told her, obeying him implicitly, "but I'll call you. I promise."

THANKS, said the computer, or rather, Harold, by way of it. It was a strange feeling—fascinating, yet perverse—to feel that you were the prisoner, not only of a man, but also of an electronic programming machine that knew everything.

"That thing is God," I quipped to him, as I hung up.

"Take not the name of the Lord in vain," he replied, and I couldn't tell to what extent he was serious and to what extent amused.

Then José came to inform him that the plane was ready for takeoff.

In the jet I fell asleep, drunk with weariness, cradled by the hiss of the jet engines, tucked in like a baby by Harold, at peace with the world.

* * *

And at noon, there were the bells of the Trinità dei Monti ringing away. Harold was pushing open the double doors of the penthouse. And the servants were greeting us respectfully in the vast portrait gallery that was the entranceway.

Their master, *my* master, was taking me by the hand and leading me first into the salon, then into the library, where he had pushed aside the smoked-glass bay window. And there was the dazzling Roman summer, the roof garden, the swimming pool with its cool waterfall, and, between two antique busts on the balustrade, St. Peter's with its dome standing out in the distance, as shiny as a new star fallen from the heavens.

"Oh, Harold, Harold, Harold!" was all I could say. Harold, whom I'll always stay and wait for.

∞∞∞∞

In response to a small flat key and a three-digit combination, the sliding door of the garage rose slowly up to the ceiling, in the darkness. The headlights of the Alfa-Romeo went on, scanning the humid recesses of this strange world of the dead, picking out of the shadows a huge mutilated statue carved in very pale marble. The cement ramp ran along the catacombs and made a right turn in front of a stone sarcophagus above which a single tube of neon shaped like a long curved arrow cast its cold light on the mossy walls. The echo repeated the muffled whine of the tires sliding forward over the sticky floor. The man driving straightened his wheels with a suppressed curse. His black leather gloves squeaked against the wheel and he adjusted the dark glasses on his nose. When he reached the bottom of the incline, he made a quarter turn to be able to back his car in between a black

Bentley and a government Lancia limousine. He guided it very precisely, extremely sure of himself.

He cut off his motor and leaned over the passenger seat to reach the glove compartment, which he unlocked. Under some rags and some roadmaps, he found a pistol and took it. He slipped the clip quietly out and then back in, after he had made sure it was full. Then he shoved the weapon into his pocket and got out of the Alfa-Romeo. He could see Peppe, on the other side, washing the deputy's son's Maserati with a hose and hear him singing the *Figaro* song at the top of his lungs in his gravelly smoker's voice.

The man headed deliberately toward the elevator. The light indicator showed it was at this level. Once inside, he made faces at the distorted reflection of himself that came back at him from the shiny stainless steel walls of the cabin. He ran a careless finger up and down all the buttons, past Basement, Ground Floor, 1, 2, 3, and then pressed the top one: PH.

5

He moved slowly down the white-graveled path striped at irregular intervals by the blue shadows of cypresses. He had been drinking heavily, which made him shake and finally stumble. He was having difficulty seeing the path or his unpolished shoes, or taking in the reality all about him, the blue sky, clear air, and the fragrance of the rose laurels, as well as the funeral urns, the statues, the simple crosses standing out against the transparent sky, the gravestones, the crypts. He didn't want to see them.

His back was straight, his head held high. But his knees were wobbling. He was the only one not dressed in mourning black, the only man unshaven. And he tried to convince himself that it was out of a sense of dignity and thoughtful deference to the Tozzi family that he was not walking with them—not just because he was scared to death: scared of death and the devil snickering inside him and daring him to take a swig of gin. Just one swig . . .

He could feel the flask weighing down his jacket pocket and bouncing against his hip. It would have been so easy to dart behind a tombstone and grab a quickie. But from time to time some of the people in the cortege turned furtively to look at him, somewhat put out by the inappropriate look and hesitant step of the *straniero*, the *poco per bene* foreigner whom they didn't know. They whispered inquisitive or critical comments to one another.

"Know who he is?" asked one.

"What a *maleducato*," said another, "a bull in a china shop."

"He's not even in mourning."

"And drunk besides."

"You think it could be that Mike that poor old Cesare was always talking about?"

"You mean the American?"

And now they were staring at him distastefully, as if he had been the suspected murderer of their relative and friend.

The cortege was near the gravesite and it had not occurred to Mike to make the sign of the cross as he got close. The powerful smell of the newly dug earth turned his stomach. He disgustedly noted a long pink worm wriggling out of a clump of earth, and close to his ear he could hear a repressed sob. He couldn't tell who among the mourners was weeping. Maybe it was he.

Then a few words from Shelley's *Adonais* came to mind, as if whispered to him by an inner voice:

Peace, peace! he is not dead . . .

He couldn't remember what came after that. Maybe the inner voice didn't want him to.

Peace, peace! he is not dead . . .

Well, what was there after death? What? What could there be?

Suddenly, to the dismay of the mourners, Mike Wyatt could hear himself declaiming, full of fervor and grandiloquence, like some old Shakespearean ham:

Peace, peace! he is not dead, he doth not sleep—
He hath awakened from the dream of life.

❧❧❧❧

Somewhat later, forced to leave the cemetery because of the outraged looks of the Tozzis and their clan, he had gone back to his Bel Air 54, parked with its top down in the shadow of a tall pine. The cassette he had forgotten to turn off was still playing Coltrane's "A Love Supreme." He tried to vault over the door, the way heroes do in detective novels—but he slipped and found himself on the ground.

"Oh, shit!" was all he could say.

If he had been the hero of a detective movie, as he got up he would have noticed the black-gloved man slowly walking toward the Alfasud at the other end of the parking area, unobtrusively keeping an eye on him. He would have noticed in his rearview mirror the red sedan that tailed him after he started heading back toward the center of town and its heavy eleven A.M. traffic so tough for him to negotiate in his out-sized convertible with the worn-out brakes that he would have to trade in sooner or later.

But then, if he had really been a hero, wouldn't Marion have fainted at her typewriter on seeing him dash into the office and send his beat-up old straw hat sailing across the room as he greeted her with his customary, "Marion, will you marry me?"

Instead, the ruthless secretary calmly replied, without interrupting her typing, "Of course, Mike. I'll think about it as soon as I finish retyping this lousy copy of yours."

"When you finish retyping my lousy copy, just pick up the lousy phone and get me New York, if you please."

"Certainly, Mr. Wyatt. By the way, a Police Inspector Lambrusco called."

"Well, Lambrusco is a wine, but it might also be a police inspector, I suppose."

"He didn't seem quite as drunk as you, in spite of his sparkling name."

"What did he want?"

"Just wanted to ask you two or three questions about the late Cesare Tozzi. He'll call back."

"Is that all?"

"No. Some strange character called who wouldn't leave his name."

"An Italian?"

"I don't know. All he said was 'When you see your boss, give him this message: Remember Cesare.' "

"Remember Cesare?"

"Yep. Sounds like a Latin quote, doesn't it? Something out of Cicero maybe?"

" 'Remember Cesare,' eh? Well, Marion, it's a good thing you didn't marry me. You might have turned out to be a widow before you even got to know what I was like."

"What do you mean?"

"Well, that guy—what he said was a death threat."

"A death threat? Oh, heavens!"

"All right, Marion, now get New York on the line for me without another second's delay. And don't look at me that way: I'm still alive. And I haven't drunk all that much, either. I know perfectly well what I'm talking about."

"I didn't mean that you didn't, Mike. What extension do you want? . . . Hm, a death threat. . . . What extension?"

"The morgue—no pun intended."

"Four-oh-one-two, please," she told the New York switchboard.

"Well, we'll see what happens next, Mr. Finnegan!" Mike mumbled between his clenched teeth.

The fellow could see, or imagine he saw, the Hudson outside drowned in a haze as black as night with thousands of lights twinkling above, like a continuation of the stars in the sky. Then, below the office windows, the canyon of Forty-second Street, just coming alive at this hour, and across it the shimmering facade of a Sixth Avenue skyscraper that gave him a mirror image of the sign on the tower above his own fortieth-floor office: DLROW.

But the phone ringing on his desk brought him up with a start. It was perched there between his two stockinged feet. He picked it up.

"Is this the morgue?" a voice asked.

"No, just the night city desk."

"Jim?"

"*Jawohl, mein Fuehrer.*"

Without even realizing it, he had picked up one of those comic ballpoints with a caricature of Nixon for a cap, and was using it to scratch his balls.

"Mike!" he heard a voice announce through the phone.

"Mike Wyatt?" he asked. And then, as soon as he realized who it was, the night man started answering in a somewhat mocking, exaggeratedly affectionate way, "Why, Mike! My own Mike! My dear, dear friend! Lover boy! How good to hear from you!"

"Listen, Jim—"

"Sure, Mike, I know you've got a great story for me. What am I saying? The best story of the year."

"No, listen, you goddamn jerk. I've got—"

"I know, I know, it's the biggest story of your career," the night man roared back, "but you poor son of a bitch, don't you know that whatever time it is where you are, it's five in the morning here, and our last edition went to bed a couple of hours ago?"

"Jim, listen," Mike was yelling back, "listen. I'm trying to tell you—" Then, thinking better of the whole thing, he went on in a calmer voice, "Forget it. There is no story. No story at all, this time. I just wanted to have someone give me the clips on a guy named Finnegan."

"Finnegan, did you say?"

"Yep."

"What's his first name?"

"I haven't got that yet."

"Oh, boy, you think there's only one Finnegan in the world? You sure it isn't Smith?"

"Quit the kidding, Jim. I'm sorry I woke you. But this is on the level."

"Okay. How do you spell Finnegan? Two n's?"

"Don't worry about that: this Finnegan lives in Rome on Via Gregoriana. That ought to pin him down pretty quick."

Jim was no longer scratching his crotch with the ballpoint but writing the information on a pad of copy paper. But just to keep up his gag, he put on a Hispanic accent and pretended to be a yawning night

56

watchman, "Me no spik Eengleesh. Office she closed, Meester. You call later."

"I'm not kidding. I think this guy is something in the Mafia."

"An Irish Mafioso. Boy, you sure pick 'em!"

"Look, do your best, and get the poop for me as quick as you can."

"Okay, hold your horses. You'll get your big break yet, don't worry."

"Fuck the break," Mike said. "I just want to stay alive. Incidentally, how're Joyce and the kids?"

"All fine. How about you?"

"I'll let you know in a few days—if I'm still around. So get cracking, asshole."

"Me no asshole, señor," Jim replied in his resumed Hispanic accent, but then, just before hanging up, he asked seriously, "Have you filled De Vaere in on this, I hope? We're not supposed to be going over his head, you know. So don't try to cross him up. I don't have the feeling he exactly loves you, anyway."

"Don't worry about that, Jim! Good night," Mike said.

"Same to you, or rather have a good lunch. And try not to get yourself killed."

The night man put the phone back in its cradle and stared into space for a moment. "Nice guy!" he said to himself, as he picked up the notes he had made. "Nice guy! But who the hell'd be out for Mike? Another one of his drunken imaginings!"

He shook his head, swung his feet off the desk and swiveled in his chair, as he muttered, "Goddamn Mike!"

* * *

The goddamned typewriter wouldn't work. The carriage wouldn't return.

Mike tried hitting the machine, but it didn't help.

And while he was doing that he got his tie caught behind the platen, so that when he turned it he started to choke. He swore. The tie tore, and his typewriter table fell over, while he roared in disgust. Then the phone rang.

"Yes?" he yelled.

"Okay, asshole. Got a pencil? Here's the dope."

"Jim?"

Mike sat himself down, as he heard the voice come back, "Of course, it's Jim. Who you was expecting, the Pope maybe? You ready?"

"Go ahead," Mike said, digging a pencil out of the mess on his desk.

"We don't have much, not much at all," Jim started in, but then, as he got into it, he reeled it off at top speed:

"Finnegan. Christian name: Harold.

"AKA: Question mark.

"Cosa Nostra: Question mark.

"CIA: Question mark.

"US citizen.

"Age: Fiftyish.

"Millionaire—no question mark.

"Director and legal counsel to several Swiss companies, all more or less phonies or fronts. (See appendix.)

"Involved in the Micheli bank failure—"

"Him, too?" Mike put in.

"Helped finance presidential campaign of you know who," Jim read on. "Savvy?"

"JFK?"

"You got it, pal. If the tip is true, of course."

"Wait, lemme write that one down."

"Okay, now I'll go on. Principal residence: Rome, Via Gregoriana at the Residence Gregoriana. Also has a flat at 100 Belgrave Square, London, UK.

"Car: Rolls-Royce Phantom VI with Swiss plates—question mark.

"Now, are you interested in what we have on his private life, so to speak?"

"You better believe it, and take this part slower."

"Likes golf, horse races. Plays poker. Lives in Rome with one Claudine Lambaire, Miss France and Miss Universe back in 1960 or 61. Check that one out. Often seen at the Four Seasons in New York, Annabel's in London, and Casten and Chez Régime in Paris."

"That's Régine," Mike corrected, "n as in New York."

"I'm just reading you what it says here," Jim answered. "Below that, there are three lines in red ink."

"Okay, go ahead."

"Associates: Not known in Italy.

"Next line, Lawyer: Robert Berg. Period. A name crossed out, then a colon. Friends—question mark.

"Next line, a question mark, and, below that a name: Eliah Varese. Over."

"Varese?" Mike asked. "Varese, did you say?"

"Yeah, no mystery. He's a capo in the mob."

"American?"

"You said it, fatso. But he spends six months every year in Palermo. Got it? Can I hang up? And, listen, don't go off half-cocked. Make sure De Vaere is in on this. If you need anything else on Varese, we've got a lot. Just call me any time. Good night, sweetheart."

Jim hung up, but Mike still sat with the phone in his hand. His eyes seemed to be trying to find something in the distance. He kept thinking hard, grabbing after a forgotten name, a word, an idea. And then he experienced a sudden sense of vertigo. He started to get up.

Suddenly, it hit him, and almost unaware of what he was saying, his lips formed the words: "Varese at Palermo."

Then he said it aloud: "Palermo-Varese."

Only then did he realize he was still holding the phone in his hand. He quickly put it back in its cradle.

"Palermo-Varese," he repeated to himself, and grabbed his jacket off the back of the chair as he ran out of his room.

6

"No way I can do that! He's got a gun!"

Pressed against the wardrobe, its pointed knob digging into his back, Peppe stammered in terror as he watched the other man come toward him—hand raised as if to slap him.

"So! There it is," the man said. "First you said you didn't know a thing—that you never saw or heard anything. But you do know that he has a gun."

"Well, what I mean is, I-I-I—" Peppe blubbered.

What had he said? The cop clenched his fist, as if now to punch rather than slap him. Peppe held his elbow up to protect his chin, instinctively closing his eyes. He was scared, afraid his heart was going to stop beating. But the man didn't hit him.

Worrying about it was worse than actually being hit.

"What you mean is you've been putting us on right from the start," Babu yelled into his face, pulling his lifted arm down and leaving him defenseless, while also twisting his wrist.

Peppe began to cry. What did the bastard want from him, anyway?

Babu was a nickname, short for *il Babuino* (Baboon), which was what his partner called him. And it was true that the huge plainclothesman looked more

61

ape than man. He was a bushel of flabby muscles squeezed into too tight a tannish suit. He had a curved forehead, with hair between the eyebrows and across the nose, and through his overgrown snout he was barking, "Putting us on is what you were! Yes, putting us on!"

Peppe's eyes were open again but he could see his tormentor only through a colored fog: Babu had taken a step back and was smiling eerily—like a man who knows his own physical superiority and is getting ready to show it. Yet, it was the other one, Gigi, who now seemed more terrifying to Peppe. He too was a giant, but unlike his partner, very skinny. He had a sallow complexion, bags under his eyes, and a sullen look that sent shivers down your back. He didn't say a thing, didn't threaten in any way. He was standing still, leaning back against the door of the lodge, picking his teeth with a flat little safety lock key.

Babu started in again, hiccuping with fury, "You know very well who this Finnegan is."

"*Porca Madonna! Dio Boïa!*" Peppe was thinking. "He's at it again." For an hour now he'd been trying to convince these two godforsaken cops, trying to demonstrate to them by *a* plus *b* that he didn't know a thing about this Finnegan, that it was as if he had never seen the man. *Porco Dio! Madonna Troïa!*

"I already told you I don't know a thing!" he kept repeating.

They had come in just as he was finishing lunch. They shoved their police IDs under his nose and ever since were grilling him about Finnegan, asking him to help them, sometimes asking him to keep quiet, sometimes to talk. They were threatening *povero* Peppe who didn't know a thing, hadn't done a thing. *Ahimè!* San Giuseppe, have pity on me!

"Scum!" Babu spat at him, waving a steamed-open envelope. "You're lying! You read people's mail, and snoop at their doors, Peppe! And you search the cars they park in the garage, don't you? And get information from their servants, eh? I know how you worm it out of the servants, Peppe. So you've got to know plenty about this Finnegan!"

Under this torrent of abuse, all the poor doorman could mumble was, "That's not true. I don't know a thing. It just isn't so!"

That was when Gigi, taking over from Babu, moved in and in a very delicate voice, which he didn't raise, murmured to Peppe, "Tell me, Signore Scacciale, you have a son if I remember correctly. Right? A *carabiniere* in Milan?"

Peppe looked at him, silently, not knowing whether this sudden intimacy was a new threat or whether the man was trying to lend him a helping hand. What could he want from his son Peppino? Wasn't it enough that they were bothering Peppe? He decided to play it close to the vest. Not a word that might reflect on his son or hurt his career. So Peppe kept still.

Babu sighed in exasperation, and hissed, "You heard what Gigi said. Can't you answer him? Or is that too much trouble?"

And Peppe heard himself whisper, as if he were telling them a great secret, "Yes, yes, in Milan. My Peppino is a *carabiniere*, a sergeant."

So Gigi went on, "And you have grandchildren. You'd like to see them more often, wouldn't you? Your darling little Ciccio and Marianina?"

The big goon actually knew the names of his darlings! Rolypoly Ciccio and pretty little Nina who was going on three! A flash of hope went through the doorman's eyes, as he nodded his head and mouthed a silent servile "yes." Yes, he missed his little darlings.

"Of course, you love them dearly." Gigi was agreeing with him. "Well, I'll tell you what, Signore Scacciale. We can get your son Peppino reassigned to Rome for you!"

"Reassigned?"

"Transferred, if you prefer."

"You mean that—?"

"In less than two months, it can be done. Can't it, Babu?"

"Absolutely. Gigi and I don't lie. And we don't make empty promises."

"True? Really and truly?" Peppe asked. "Could you do that—so that, in Rome, I could see them?"

"Yes, and we could probably get him a promotion at the same time," Gigi added, while Babu smilingly chimed in with "You know, we really like your little Peppino."

"Besides," Gigi resumed, "we're all cops after all, like one big family, so—any time we can help out a pal!"

"Only, for that, you've got to lend us a hand," Babu started in again, grabbing Peppe by his braided lapel. "You help, or else Peppino Scacciale won't like it when he hears his old man is a—"

"That's enough, Babu," Gigi cut him off. "I believe Signore Scacciale has understood us completely."

Signore Scacciale was flushed with delight, though still shaken by the fright he had just been through. He sank down into a chair. He hadn't even partly understood what these cops wanted—but he had understood that it might mean Peppino could get back to Rome. And he had also understood that if he "helped," he might at last be able to satisfy his own curiosity.

"Well, then," he stuttered, "then, I'll find out, won't I? You'll tell me all about him? I want to know who this Finnegan is! After you put your—your stuff in here, I'll know, won't I? He's a swindler, eh? Isn't he? Aldo, the majordomo on the second floor says he's 'an in-ter-na-tion-al crook.' Is that it? A CIA type?"

"Right you are! Right on the button!" Babu mockingly assured him, but without arousing the doorman's suspicions.

"That's it!" Gigi confirmed. "You caught on right away, Signore Scacciale. He's CIA all right."

The light wind wafted far into the darkness the ethereal accents of Berlioz's *Requiem*. The song rose up into the night, pure, vibrant, and yet restrained. It proclaimed that heaven and earth were filled with the glory of God: Rome, sleeping among its brilliantly lighted monuments beneath the starry dome above, was so beautiful that it seemed like a bit of eternity in suspended animation.

Raising his eyes, the man caught a glimpse of the bluish glint that came from the girandoles of the roof garden. In the half-light, he could see shadows go by as they stretched between the posts of the balustrade or espoused a pedestal or the marble toga of one of the antique statues.

Hidden behind a shutter, he was trying to estimate the distance that separated the fourth-floor balcony where he was from the cornice of the palace.

"Field glasses," he muttered, and from behind the other shutter a pair of binoculars were immediately handed to him.

Through the magnifying lenses he could now gauge the condition of the stone and decide whether it would splinter under the pull of his hook. He lowered the glasses with a sigh of satisfaction and returned them to his helper hiding in the shadow.

"I'm going up," he said after discreetly crossing himself.

A black silk hood without mouth or nose holes fully covered his face. The eye slits were so narrow that one could barely make them out in the solid mass. He was wearing a mechanic's coverall of tight black twill, which bulged only where the tools in its numerous pockets made somewhat frightening outcroppings on his solid body. On his feet he wore flexible gymnast's shoes, and the black leather gloves on his hands were hard to make out in the darkness.

He heard a voice behind him mutter, "The rope."

Without turning, he grabbed it and found the roll of gray nylon with the steel snap hook on the end. He attached to it the grapnel that lay at his feet and swung it above his head before letting it fly like a lasso. Its sharp point whistled through the air but was drowned out by the music. He suppressed a grunt as he felt the hook catch and hold solidly on the cusp of the cornice.

Now he had to make his dangerous climb up to the penthouse. The wind buffeted him against the wall and the dangling rope swung him dizzily out over the gaping dark street below.

The closer he got to the roof, the louder came the serene prayer for the dead, its majesty increasing, its choruses more fervent, as if challenging him and shoving him back into the emptiness. A gust sent him sharply against one of the granite pilasters. His coverall tore and his knee got skinned. With his foot he positioned himself off the wall, but felt rather desperate: the sweat-soaked hood virtually blinded him, for the eye slits had slipped up and the seams stuck to his eyelids.

But just then, through his glove he felt the snap hook, not a moment too soon. He was at the cornice now. All he needed was to get a foothold.

Putting his main weight on the stone pillar in front of him, which his hand could get a good grip on, he righted himself. His foot slipped, he almost fell, but caught on again. Finally, he was able to make the leap —and his body rolled onto the rooftop lawn while the grapnel fell the twenty feet to the floor below, where his aide was already picking it up.

"A few points remain unclear to me," he heard someone say, quite close to where he was. "For instance, I can't see why the emir's brother has to get so many shares of HUELCO. He seems to me to be a, uh, rather flighty young man."

"Fuad?" a voice answered. "Worse than that. He's a dope."

Pulling his hood back into place, he was now able to get a better view of where he was: a few steps away from him there was a table, on which a meal had just been finished. The flames of the melted candles were dying in bluish glass holders and the wind caused the pendants of a chandelier and the crystal glasses on the table to tinkle. Three fine brocaded napkins lay in disorder over the three opulent table settings: antique porcelain set on gold plates, with gilt dessert spoons. In a fine sculptured silver pail, there was a magnum of champagne, a slight haze of frozen vapor still curling up out of it.

All of the scene was brilliantly reflected in the large tinted bay windows of the living room. But that room was in half darkness, looking like some large aquarium with an open fire glowing in it. A woman dressed in a sequined dress not unlike a mermaid's skin walked back and forth: Claudine, assuredly. Farther on, the hooded man could see a Roman bust, a leather-upholstered garden chair, and the pool lighted from below, its rippling surface casting ever-changing reflections on the penthouse wall. Closer, there was a coffee table on which sat an open case with a shortwave telephone in it, probably connected to the house system.

And right close to him, against the pillar of the balustrade that hid him, what he had taken for two statues turned out to be the two men talking—Finnegan and someone else whom he could not identify.

He had recognized Finnegan when the other man cupped his hands over a lighted match and held it out to him to light his cigar. Now lighting his own cigar, the other was a stranger to him: young, with long fair hair down to his shoulders, he wore gold-rimmed glasses, the kind you sometimes see on affected Yalies or teaching fellows of other universities. Looked like the well-educated scion of some rich New York or Boston family.

"I never would have dared," he was saying to Finnegan, who had just called this Fuad, probably the brother of the emir of Ahmat-Ahbat, a dope. "I never would have dared."

But Finnegan just took a long puff on his cigar and went on, "Yes, I assure you, he's not quite bright. When I'm in London, I play poker with them. Endlessly, at the Clermont. I always let him win, and he thinks he's a genius. Calls himself the world's champion bluffer." The other man laughed as Finnegan put on an Arab accent to say, " 'I'm the world's champion bluffer, Harold. Champion of champions!' I guess I've let him take me for thirty thousand pounds.

But he'll be the one to rid us of Farouh-Ahbat. He's the only one who can make the coup look like a palace revolution. After that, we can twist the champion of bluffers around our little fingers. No danger of his ever voting against us in HUELCO. First of all, he's too dumb for it to occur to him. And besides, the Institute retains the whip hand in all decisions."

"But someone smarter might suggest it to him."

"No, don't worry about that, Robert. Anyway, Fuad is crapping in his pants as it is: he's too scared that we might have him overthrown in turn—he has twenty-eight brothers who are all candidates to do it. Twenty-nine direct heirs, no less!"

"Then, when will the coup take place?"

Finnegan's answer was not audible, as he walked away from the balustrade he had been leaning against. The two men were walking toward the opposite corner of the terrace and the music drowned out their conversation. The intruder was now free to crawl over toward the open phone case on the coffee table.

The case was a sumptuous piece of wild-crocodile hide such as he had never seen, but the field phone in it was a type he had learned to take apart and put together at Langley, Virginia.

In his hip pocket he had the kind of Phillips screwdriver he needed, and in his breast pocket a pickup mike that he inserted in the instrument in no time.

Then he crawled noiselessly through the flowerbeds and did not get up until he was in front of the half-open door to the library. He was going to dash through the dim light from the venetian lamp held by a sculpted wood Ethiopian, but he had to jump back immediately, as he could hear the two men approaching and Finnegan saying, "Robert, I'm leaving it all up to you. After all, you've been my lawyer for eight years now."

"But what about the concessions?" Robert asked.

"Well, the concessions these, uh, Bedouins, uh, make to us must be perfectly legal. Above suspicion. Even if the name of the Institute never appears, but only my own—the name of Harold Finnegan, that is, of course."

"Excuse me for being so direct about this, John," the lawyer replied, "but how can you be sure that some investigator, some smart-aleck newspaper reporter, won't be able to trace them to you—and to the Institute —and finally to . . ."

"No, I don't think they'd be able to."

"After all, the chief of the Haraouis might talk. He might be made to talk."

"I'm afraid there'd just be no way Ali could anymore," Finnegan assured him.

The intruder held his breath as he backed away to avoid being seen while taking this all in. Suddenly, he was startled and stopped stock still—terrified. At the level of his fifth rib, a hard sharp instrument was digging into his flesh, a revolver, no question about it. But he couldn't hear anything behind him, not even a breath. Trying to keep his pounding heart under control, he turned. It was the finger of a statue he had backed into.

Fully calm again, as a properly trained secret agent should be, he walked around the stone Diana and into the large white living room, where he squatted behind a couch. There was a slight odor of marijuana in the air. On the couch that he was hiding behind, the woman lay smoking a small joint she had made. The speakers in the four corners of the room were still stereoing the Berlioz. But to his amazement he could see in a mirror hanging at an angle over the fireplace that the woman had a set of earphones on and was listening to something coming from another tapedeck. Her head was beating a blues rhythm. She'd surely not hear if he touched the phone.

This one was a very sophisticated instrument: three separate but interconnected lines with twelve extensions inside the apartment. Fortunately, this was the main instrument, the only one he could put the tap on. But getting it installed would certainly take more than a minute. He looked around him: only the heavy double curtains nearby would afford him a hiding place to work in. Provided no one tried closing them and, even more important, no one tried to use the phone while he was at work.

With a lump in his throat, he put a masked light around his head and began the delicate job. The loud grandiose music gave him relative security: if he dropped anything no one would hear. But while he was unscrewing the underplate of the instrument, one side of the LP came to an end. And at the same moment he could hear Finnegan and the lawyer come shivering back in from the terrace and slide the bay window closed behind them.

The younger man was saying, "John, I'm not afraid, I can assure you. You got out of that Micheli mess okay."

"Robert, you're the one who got me out of it," the other replied. "I know how indebted I am to you for that. That's why I want you to have a share in this killing—if we do make a killing."

"You're paying me quite enough as a retainer."

"You're too modest, my boy. You'll never get anywhere that way," Finnegan said, in feigned sanctimoniousness.

From behind the white velvet drape where he was

hidden, the man could hear him taking the record off the turntable and whispering, "And it's Harold now."

Then he immediately heard a very faint sound of a Barry White recording: Claudine had probably taken off the headphones. She laughed merrily in reply to the lawyer's "My, you're pretty tonight, Claudine." And answered in her charming French accent, "Gallant as usual, aren't you, Robert?"

The man's heart skipped a beat as he heard the lawyer, right beside him, saying to Finnegan, "I'll call him now."

This was followed by the sound of glasses clinking, laughter, and a mumble of "Cheers." For a minute or two the suspense killed him. And his cold sweat got even colder when the lawyer again said, "I'll call him now."

"Robert, you'll find it more comfortable in my office," Finnegan suggested, to his great relief.

"Will you excuse us, Claudine?" Robert said.

"Of course," she replied.

Noiselessly heaving a sigh of relief inside his stuffy moist headmask, the secret agent hurriedly reconnected the necessary wires. He could feel in his hand the clicks of the dial on the extension from which Berg was calling the number in Finnegan's office. Quickly regaining his self-control, he made a mental note of the number called—091 (the Palermo area code), then 4-0-3-0-2-9—and repeated to himself, "Palermo 403-029." He was delighted to see how good his reflexes still were and that he hadn't forgotten what he learned at Langley.

A few minutes later, the lawyer hung up. Still half-suffocated, the masked agent went back to work and in no time had installed the bug. Through a slit between two panels of the drape he took a quick glance: no one was looking his way. He lay down on the floor, placed the telephone on the rug and, pushing it gingerly with his fingertips, got it to where he could lift it and put it back on the coffee table between the obsidian Buddha and the lamp—exactly where he had found it.

Then he gauged the distance separating him from the double door, across the room. Crawling noiselessly, he was able to pass behind the grand piano and get into the entryway.

A Vietnamese or Chinese servant was coming by, carrying a tray with several clinking liquor bottles on it, and he just had time to kneel behind a large baroque dresser out of sight. Now he had to hurry. Another servant might turn up at any moment. Every additional second in these rooms, which he knew only from a diagram, increased his risk of being caught.

He quickly climbed the steps to the floor above, and slipped into a dressing room with facing mirrors which repeated his black reflection in both directions as far as the eye could see. He went through the bedroom, where he implanted a minimicrophone in the canopy above the bed, then through His bathroom, all black tile, and Hers, done in seashells; the gym; the sauna—and in each of these places his experienced eye at a glance found the best and least suspect place for a bug. He slipped back downstairs and did the same in the library, the office, the dining room, the small salon, and finally the winter garden: a thorough, precise, and professional job.

Finally, he was down in the huge galleria, the walls of which looked like some old museum. From floor to ceiling, in three tiers, and sometimes four, there were dozens of portraits of cardinals. Some were conventional likenesses done by lesser masters, while others

were sixteenth- and seventeenth-century masterpieces,
oils, gouaches, pencil drawings, charcoals, and red
chalks. All were richly framed, except for two modern
works set in thin stainless steel: a cardinal painted by
Francis Bacon, a raw-faced character wearing the
biretta against a bright orange background, and one
painted by David Hockney in an entirely different
mode, a subdued blend of suave pinks, mauves, and
lilacs.

There were also two little satirical pictures, one of
a monkey Monsignore saying Mass, and the other a
Council of Crocodiles. Then there was the portrait
of Monsignore Zanti painted by Caravaggio, an amazing gouache by El Greco, a sketch torn from a very
old catalog of holy vestments designed by Borromini,
two studies of the hands of Cardinal Galeazzo by
Guido Reni, Salvador Dali's famous *Cardinal Sodom-
ized by His Own Chastity Inside the Railway Station
at Perpignan*, a period copy of the portrait of Cardinal Richelieu painted by Philippe de Champagne,
and finally some works by unknown or unsung painters who had also painted cardinals. The subjects were
the only connecting link of this collection of strange
exhibits, and they displayed all the vanities of the
breed: the splendor of scarlet robes and frosty laces,
haughty faces peering out of chiaroscuros, the subdued
brilliance of golden crosses and jewels, disdainful
sneers revealing carnivores' fangs, and cold, dull eyes
that were enough to give one the chills.

But the secret agent was not spending his time taking in the artistic wonders of these princes of the
Church immortalized by cruel or servile painters. He
was already at the front door and trying to open it—
in vain, for the door had no visible lock, no bolt, and
apparently no hinges. It closed by some absolutely

secret mechanism and nothing happened when he turned the handle, which was apparently there only for decorative—or deceptive—purposes.

Useless. He would have to go back out the way he came in, face the danger of being seen, go back across the terrace, and climb down his rope. But the rope was no longer there: he had dropped it below to avoid its being seen. So he would just have to jump for it— and make sure not to miss the balcony that jutted out ever so little twenty feet below.

Grudgingly, he retraced his steps.

"Van Dông, did you hear the same cry I did?"

"Yes, sir."

"You think it might have been a drunk, down in the street?"

"Or perhaps a murder?" Claudine put in.

"Romantic as usual, my little French doll," Finnegan commented.

"I didn't hear anything," Berg said.

"You've been drinking too much!"

"Berg, do you want another whiskey? Van Dông . . ."

"Coming, madame."

"*Sanctus! Sanctus!*" Berg sang along with the music.

"Oh, boy, now he's started to sing!"

"We may have to take him to bed with us!"

"Maybe that's just what he'd like."

"Oh, Harold, the things you say!"

"But I'm not drunk. Not yet . . . *Sanctus! Sanctus!*" Berg kept chirping.

7

Honey Pie is a hell of a nice kid. Not all that pretty
but a million bucks' worth of charm and fun. With
her big pale-green eyes and thousands of freckles, the
girls at school referred to her as Lentil Soup, and
sometimes Rusty, but all the boys were nuts about her.
Her mouth might be a bit too big, but it was always
laughing. And what if her nose was a little crooked?

Look, before she became famous, Barbra Streisand
was no beauty queen either. Or Liza Minnelli. But
that never kept them from getting there, "making it"
in Hollywood. They were stars in spite of their
looks. And millions of men around the world adored
them.

If there was one thing Honey Pie had no doubts
about, it was that someday she'd be a star, too. She
would have her name up in lights and people would
break their necks to get hundred-dollar seats to her
Shea Stadium or Carnegie Hall concerts. Right now,
she was desperately trying to be the new Marilyn Monroe. A few months before, she'd wanted to be the new
Edith Piaf, and before that the new Judy Garland.
She'd even sung "La Vie en Rose" as the Dorothy of *Oz*
might do it. But that was throwing pearls before the
Roman swine.

On the walls of her little skylight studio on the Via

Giulia there was a collection of pictures, like geological strata, that revealed who her star of the moment was: on top of the posters and stills of Judy and Piaf she now had stuck shots of Marilyn in *Gentlemen Prefer Blondes,* Marilyn in *Bus Stop,* Marilyn in *The Seven Year Itch,* Marilyn here, Marilyn there . . . And framed on the piano, there was that last picture of her, taken on the beach at Santa Monica. The one that makes Honey Pie cry when she's feeling blue and night is falling, bringing darkness to the studio she lives in— if you can call it living when every time you move you have to walk around the grand piano that takes up the whole room and keeps you from getting around. But her concert Steinway is her one real extravagance. She bought it with the fee from a commercial she did showing "fun girls," real relaxed types, smoking mentholated cigarettes.

It was two P.M., and not quite awake yet, she was yawning wide enough to dislocate her jaw. But as she lapped up her jasmine tea the way her kitten Gary Cooper was lapping up the milk she had poured into his dish on the piano, she sat down at the keyboard and making a face into the mirror set on top of the lead sheets, began to rehearse, trying to get the same intonation as M.M. in *Some Like It Hot:*

> I wanna be loved by you
> Just you, and nobody else but you . . .

"Oh, shit!" She could hear her crazy darling Mike coming up the stairs, recognize his unsteady and eerily swaggering step that made the risers creak. She hit three chords and repeated, "I wanna be loved by you . . ."

Mike, outside the door, could hear her singing. He closed his eyes and hummed the melody as he tapped

out its rhythm with the knocker on the door that had
HONEY PIE scrawled on it in chalk. With a shout of delight, she was greeting him.

And Mike felt happy: he was clean-shaven and his
light-colored suit was almost neatly pressed. He hadn't
touched a drop yet and felt very rested. And here he
was, come to see his sweet Honey Pie.

Without getting off her piano stool, she swung
around a quarter turn, stuck out her long naked leg
and, with her curled toes, turned the doorknob.

Crazy Mike! Out on the landing, he was tapdancing
on the echoing tiles, as he continued the tune, singing
out now, loud enough to disturb the neighbors,
"Wanna be loved by you . . ."

"Now I know you're drunk. Still drunk from last
night. Where were you at four o'clock this morning?"

". . . lo-o-o-oved by you" was all he could repeat.

"Fat chance," she said. "Why the hell should I love
you, you bum? You said four o'clock at the Rosati.
Where were you?"

"I was out arresting a ring of international spies,"
Mike shot back, but then, pretending to show how
sorry he was, he got down on his knees to her, and as
she pushed him away—and in so doing banged her
back aaginst the keyboard, making the piano resound
strangely—he kept repeating "Honey Pie! Honey Pie!"
while rolling her T-shirt up over her bare belly.

Making clown eyes with delight, Mike pulled the
T-shirt off and covered her breasts with kisses, as she
teasingly held them out to him. Sliding around the
piano, she was already heading for the bed while he
was undoing his necktie and informing her in mock
solemnity: "You know, it wasn't true, what I said
about rounding up a ring of spies. But Sunday I'm
going down to Palermo, and that's on the level."

"Going for a Sicilian wine tasting?"

"For that, and also to interview one Eliah Varese."

"Who dat?"

"Dat what?"

"Eliah Varese? He the wine dealer?"

"No, he's a number one boss in the Mafia."

"Since when have you been covering people like that for your paper?" she wanted to know.

"Since they knocked Cesare off."

Honey Pie pulled Mike against the bed and finished unbuttoning his shirt, which he was taking off. She whispered, "You won't be in any danger, will you? I don't like that kind of stuff, Mike. Mixing it up with the Mafia. You sure you're not gonna be in danger?"

"No, of course not. But if this Varese had anything to do with—"

"Why don't you tell that Inspector Whatsisname about it?" she interrupted. "Inspector Chianti?"

"No, Lambrusco," Mike laughingly corrected. "I haven't told him, because I want to see where my lead takes me—find out about this Varese and a guy named Finnegan."

"I know a guy named Finnegan," she said.

"You do?"

"Well, not him, really, but his girl friend," she informed him. "Name of Claudine, an old pal of mine."

"Claudine uh . . . ," Mike answered, trying to recall her last name. He had a sudden feeling he was on the right track.

"Claudine Lambaire," she told him.

"That's right. That's the one."

"She used to be Miss France."

Mike was so excited he could hardly get the words out.

80

"That's—that's the one. That's m-m-my Finnegan all right. That's the one. Where do you know her from?"

"Oh, from a long while back. We used to do a number together at the Hit, like five years ago. Yes, back in 1970." And imitating the grandiloquent tones of an Italian nightclub emcee, she announced, *"Un duetto eccezionale e inter-naz-zzzionale: Miss France e Honey Pie!"* Then, going back to her own voice, "But she'd pick up anything in pants, so I split up with her, before it turned into a real hassle . . .".

"Then what happened?"

"Oh, a little while later, she took off one night without even finishing the last two numbers of her set. Went to London with a photographer who promised to use her as a model in this agency he was setting up. And there she shacked up with a British Lord. Lord Cava-something."

"Cavenaught?"

"That's his name."

"Now what's she up to?" Mike asked.

"Now, she's got it made. She's with this Finnegan guy. Loaded with mazuma, and handsome as a god."

"Did you ever see him?"

"No, but she told me about him. Wouldn't be my luck to find a guy like that. Not me! All I get are lushes and second-rate reporters."

Mike, who was now bare-chested, pretended to choke her for what she had said, but then, kissing her on the nose, he murmured, "Never you mind. All that's gonna change—right now."

Going back to her Italian emcee voice, she mocked him with, *"Un numero eccez-z-z-zionale!* After too long an absence from the limelight, we present the return of the famous Mike Wyatt, with the story of the year!"

81

Mike played right along, and in the same tone went on, "Aided and abetted by his well-known assistant, Miss Honey Spy!"

"Honey Spy indeed!" she gawked back at him.

"Yep, that's just what I want you to be. Tell me, do you still see this Claudine character?"

"Sure, we're still friends. We have lunch together every once in a while."

"At her place—I mean, at Finnegan's?"

"No, we always meet in some restaurant. Finnegan doesn't want her inviting her friends up there."

"He must be a strange one. Look, will you make a call?"

"To who? To him? You must be crazy."

"No, to Miss France. Get her to invite you to lunch—but try to set it up at her place."

"What is all this? No wanna be loved today?"

"Yes, sure, but after this is set."

"Okay, at your secret service, Major Wyatt!"

"Good, then get to work, 007 and a half!"

"Hey, this is the Year of the Woman, remember?"

"Fine. Then you be Agent 006."

"In Her Majesty's Service," Honey Pie saluted. "Say, aren't you carrying this cops-and-robbers business a little bit far?"

"No," Mike said. "I have to get even for Cesare."

TELEPHONIC TRANSCRIPT No. 3: Girolamo Barbieri.

DATE & TIME: Friday, 3:07 P.M.

TYPE: Incoming. Direct.

CALLER: Unidentified. Young woman. American?

ANSWERED BY: Claudine L.

ANSWERER: Hello.

CALLER: Hi, there!

A.: Oh, it's you, Honey. How are things?

C.: Can't complain. How about you?

A.: Just fine. How nice of you to call.

C.: I felt like seeing you.

A.: That's a great idea. How about lunch together?

C.: At your place?

A.: No, not here. No can do.

C.: Why not?

A.: Well, you know—Harold doesn't like it. You know how he is.

C.: Sounds like some kind of Oriental pasha.

A.: Yes, something like that. Look, darling, how about, say, next Tuesday?

C.: Fine with me.

A.: Then I'll pick you up in the car about noon. And if it's a nice day we can have lunch at Fregene. There's a new place at the beach there. That suit you?

C.: Sure, great. So long, Claudine. See you Tuesday.

A. So long to you, too, Edith, or Marilyn, or Judy, or whoever you are now. *Ciao*, sweetie!

TERMINATED: 3:08 P.M.

8

AUDIO SURVEILLANCE REPORT No. 7:
Franco Aduanello.
DATE & TIME: Saturday 5th, 10:32–10:40 A.M.
BETWEEN: Mr. Robert Berg & F.
OTHER PARTICIPANTS: ?
PLACE: Library and Office. Hallway?
BLANKS: Yes.
STATIC: Yes.

F.: . . . like in the Standard matter . . . third for
Varese, one third for the Institute—and a
third for me . . . sharing out of the HUELCO
drilling rights: fifty for Fuad, fifty for . . .

BERG: You mean: transferring the Institute account over to the AMDG's? Incidentally,
what does that AMDG stand for?

F.: What's the matter, Robert? Didn't they teach
you any Latin at Harvard?

B.: Uh . . . sure . . . I see: A-M . . . oh, *Ad Ma-
jorem* . . . whatever it is . . . *(Laughter)* Like
in the . . . uh . . . the motto of the . . . To
the Greater Glory of God, eh? *(Laughter)*

F.: . . . got through to Varese?

B.: Yes. He'll have fifteen hand-picked fully
trained men. Four of them were instructors in

Korea, six were in Vietnam or Cambodia.
And the other five are part of his Chicago
crew.

F.: But the conditions are different here. This is
Arab country and . . .

B.: Hold on! He's got them covered by three professional agitators who used to work for the
PLO. One of 'em was even Arafat's secretary,
and no one ever realized . . .

F.: . . . mean Arabs?

B.: Arabs.

F.: Great. That Varese always does things
right. . . .

TERMINATED.

GIUSEPPE SCACCIALE:

Giuseppe here! Giuseppe there! Alla time, Giuseppe, Giuseppe! How do they expect me to get it all
done? Why don't they ever give me a breather? Leave
me alone?

First, it's Babu, he says to me: "Peppe, you sure
that nobody heard me?" He busted his arm jumping
down from Finnegan's to the fourth-floor balcony,
and he cried out. I told him, "No, nobody couldn't 'a'
heard you."

But then the fat one, the boss lady from the fourth
floor, she comes down and comes rushing into my cabin
like her ass was on fire, and yells at me that she don't
understand what's going on! She got two broken windowpanes in her bathroom! And it ain't her house-
keeper's fault! Musta been me, she says. Me! Me!
Everybody always takin' it out on *povero* Peppe.
Porco Dio!

Afters, I went down to the cellar. The second cellar,

86

the one they call Domitian's cellar, 'cause they say that Roman emperor once lived here. Funny idea for a emperor, living down in a cellar! Anyway! It's down in Domitian's cellar, under the catacombs, that Gigi and Babu set up shop. So I went down there. First, I had a fall in the dark, and then, what'd I hear? Groans of pleasure, crying out! You know what I mean? Like in a movie, like one of them *pronographic* movies! The girl was moaning, "Ah! ah! ah!" Yep, long "Aaaahhhs" like that, and the guy panting like somebody getting his nuts off! So I says to myself, "What they got here now? A whorehouse?" That's all I need, Gigi and Babu, and the fat boss from the fourth floor bawling the shit out of me—and now people humping each other in behind my catacombs!

So I sneaked up on 'em without making no noise. And then I finally understood what was going on: Gigi was spying on the people. That's what it was: Babu put a bug in Finnegan's bedroom, and Finnegan and his broad—well, they were fuckin' their heads off. Nothin' more than that. Boy, you shoulda seen what that Gigi looked like: red as a beet! He was all flushed, and you could tell he had a hard on, the way he was squirming around on the campstool. I thought he was gonna fall off. But then Babu came in from the next-door cellar and he yelled somethin' at him in English or American, I couldn't understand. And I couldn't understand why they wasn't talking Italian. When he seen me, Babu made a face, and then he talked in Italian to his pal, and said, "Gigi, can't you quit going after those cheap thrills? Come on and help me get the fuckin' recorder going. You can see I'm handi-capped." He was handicapped account of his busted arm in the cast. Gigi turned the receiver off: he was all in a sweat, and trembling all over, like one of them

Peeping Tom fellows! Only he wasn't no Peeping Tom, he was a Listening Tom! Anyway, you see what I mean; I mean, you understand what I'm tryin' to say. *Porca Madonna!* It sure is complicated!

I followed Gigi into the second cellar, and there what do I see? *Watergame* in Rome! Listening tables, tape recorders, a whole layout of gadgets—as I live and breathe, *Watergame* all over again! It scared me a little. I didn't even dare ask 'em have they done anything for my son Peppino yet. Babu put the earphones back on and was filling out his reports. So I just slipped the screwdriver to Gigi and went back up where I belonged. I had the Maserati to wash, the deputy's son's one . . .

So then, who I see coming on? Aldo! The maître d' from the second floor, my good friend. He tells me his boss has been complaining since this morning 'cause he's getting interference on his radio, and he's wondering what's going on and all. So I says to him, "Y'know, maybe it's on account of what those cops they got set up in the basement. You oughta see it! A regular *Watergame!*" "*Watergame?*" he says to me. "Well, then maybe Gigi and Babu they're Americans, then. Like CIA types. What we need that for here in Italy?"

And no sooner Aldo goes out, in comes a certain Inspector Lambrusco. He shoves a mug shot of some guy under my nose and asks, "You know him, Signore Scacciale?" Never seen that bird in my whole life. What else they trying to get me mixed up in? I was wondering: When is all this gonna end? And the inspector says, "Cesare Tozzi." So that's the bugger's name: Cesare Tozzi. "Ever hear of him around here?" the cop wants to know. Hell, no! What does he take me for, the FBI or something?

Like I tell you, Peppe here, Peppe there! Everybody pickin' on me! I got so upset I almost spilled the beans to this fuckin' bigshot inspector. I almost came out and told him two of his colleagues was located downstairs. But since the two of them threatened me if I told anybody about 'em, I kept still. So then, he got very polite with me, I dunno why, and he says, "Varese? That name mean anything to you?" Varese, what kind of an ignoramus did he think I was? "I went to school," I told him. "I learned geography. I know Varese is a town in Lombardy."

"That's right," he says, "but it's also somebody's name. And I just wondered if you knew him?" So, I says, "Look, Varese is the name of a city, so that guy must be a Jew. When people are called like a city, like Ancona, or Messina, or Napoli, that means they're Jewish. And me, Giuseppe Scacciale, I don't know no Jews," I says to him. And it's true. I got no truck with that kind of people. Okay? The cop says to me, "Too bad," and before going out he tells me to be sure and call him if I ever hear about any of those people. I sighed, and thought good riddance! Now maybe I could have some peace.

Some peace! The front doorbell rings again, and on the closed-circuit I can see a guy I never saw before. I go and open, and he introduces himself: "Michael Wyatt," he says, "New York *World*." So there it goes again, Giuseppe this, Giuseppe that! What can this one want from me? Anyway, this one is a nice one. Right off, he says to me, "You don't have to cook those cannelloni, Mr. Sciaccale. Be my guest for a good lunch at the Trattoria da Mimi." And then, "I'd like you to tell me something about Finnegan." What? Him too? This is getting to be an epidemic!

Oh, *povero* Peppe! *Povero* Peppe! When will this nightmare ever end? *Porco Dio!* How long can it go on?

Boy, I wish they'd let me have a breather—but no, it's Giuseppe here, Giuseppe there, Giuseppe this, Giuseppe that! *Basta*, already!

> TELEPHONE TRANSCRIPT, No. 4: Franco Aduanello.
>
> DATE & TIME: Saturday 5th. 7:00 P.M.
>
> CALL: Incoming. Palermo?
>
> CALLER: Eliah Varese? Identifies himself as Black Fangs.
>
> ANSWERED BY: Servant, then F.
>
> ANSWERER: Hello.
>
> CALLER: Diab, I'd like to speak with the Signore.
>
> A.: This is Alchim, sir. Hold the line, I'll get him.
>
> F.: Devils!
>
> C.: Black Fangs!
> *(Laughter)*
>
> C.: I spoke to Berg.
>
> F.: What'd he have to say?
>
> C.: Everything you had agreed upon. Did you see that article in *Time* on the ICC, that your name was mentioned in?
>
> F.: Yeah, but it was my real one. Who knows enough to make the connection? And besides, that isn't the first time there's been an article on the ICC, and it won't be the last. Remember the Micheli affair? No one ever saw through it.
>
> C.: One other thing. One of the guys I got tells me that those Bedouins are well armed.

F.: Look, there's about a thousand of them, spread out over about thirty thousand square miles of desert. And the few guns they have date back to Lawrence of Arabia. Ten of your men would be enough to surround 'em all!

C.: Who was Lawrence of Arabia?

F.: An adventurer. A terrific guy. He got converted to Mohammedanism. If you ever went to the movies, you'd know about him.

C.: To Mohammedanism? So, why are you so hot for him, eh?

F.: All right. Quit the kidding.
(Laughter)

F.: Can we talk this all over Monday noon?

C.: See you Monday noon, then. It's sure been a long time, John.

F.: And just as long since I saw you, kid.
(Laughter)

C.: You'll never change, will you?

F.: Nor you.

C.: See you Monday, then. Take care.

F.: You, too, old man.

TERMINATED

9

"Ladies and gentlemen, we have just landed at Palermo. It is exactly noon, local time, and the temperature outside is 26 degrees Centigrade, 78 degrees Fahrenheit."

Gigi and Babu were the only ones on the plane who did not seem concerned by the weather. As soon as the hostess made her announcement, they automatically snapped shut the huge file folders they had been reading. Gigi helped his friend, whose arm was still in a cast, out of the safety belt and the seat, which was barely wide enough to hold him. As he got up and turned toward the rear of the cabin, Gigi caught a face that made him think: Him again!

"Buba," he whispered, "you see what I see?"

"What?"

"That guy back there, in the next to last row."

"I don't see him."

"The one that's nipping at the pint of booze he's got hidden in his hand."

"You think so?"

"Sure. He's the one we've seen twice outside the Residenza Gregoriana. The one with the face I can't place."

"Yeah, I guess you're right," Babu conceded.

"Wait a minute," Gigi answered excitedly. "I know

who it is now. It's Wyatt, that *World* columnist. That's who!"

"Wyatt? Wyatt?"

"Yeah, don't you remember? When we investigated the foreign press corps in Rome to see who belonged. Remember? For the longest time we thought he was one of our boys."

"A jerk like that? I'd be surprised. He's just a gossip columnist."

"Jerk or no jerk, he was hanging around the Residenza, and now, bingo! here he is on the same plane as us. Talk about a coincidence! Anyway, hanging out with celebs is the best cover a guy can have."

"Chance, just chance," Babu insisted. "That guy is only interested in spicy tidbits. And there's that movie producer at the Residenza—what's his name? And why shouldn't he be going to Palermo? Maybe Frank Sinatra's goin' to be water-skiing here, or maybe the Shah of Iran."

Without raising his voice, Gigi started to laugh. "That's it! the Shah or the Sha-na-na! No, I think he's here to fish in the murky waters of the Mafia," he added, in a voice that parodied someone else's.

"Say that again," Babu asked.

"Say what?"

"What you just said."

"The murky waters of the Mafia."

"That's it! To a tee! The boss!"

"Which one?"

"Colby, of course, what a question," Babu commented. "You do him perfectly."

As Mike was pushing his way out and reached their level, Gigi winked to Babu to keep still and kept him from following right behind Mike on the way out.

That way, they'd be able to tail him better, at a slight distance.

From the exit ramp, they could see him going into the arrival room and up to the Hertz Rent A Car desk.

"Il Viale Trionfale, per favore," he had already asked three passersby in his somewhat hesitant Italian. But not one had deigned to answer, or even seemed to know he was talking to them. As if he hadn't been there or hadn't spoken.

Sitting at the wheel of his rented Fiat 124 and inwardly cursing the map of Palermo they had given him, which covered nothing but the center and immediate outlying neighborhoods, Mike was finding out the hard way about *omertà,* the Sicilian code of silence. He couldn't believe that no one around here knew where this *viale* was, especially if a guy like Varese lived on it. Usually, and even in Sicily where nothing was quite as usual, people didn't name little side-streets or cul-de-sacs Triumphal Avenue. All of a sudden, Mike felt sore at the world.

Yet when the alarm had rung at eight this morning in his huge room at the Grand Hotel delle Palme, he had gotten up cheerily, delighted with the beautiful day it was turning out to be, with the sunlight streaming in through the venetian blinds. He hadn't had anything to drink, because he wanted to keep as clear a head as possible for the tough meeting he was to have that evening with Varese.

The night before, as he was running his bath, he had desultorily riffled through the telephone book that was in the night-table drawer—a typical traveling man's habit. First, you look to see if there's anyone by

your name in the town, then, without any special
order, you do the same for other names that pop into
your head. When he got to the V's, one struck him
immediately—the only phone subscriber in Palermo
by that name:

Varese, Eliah, Viale Trinofale 161 ....40 30 29

Wow! He was supposed to be a Mafia capo, and he
had a listed telephone number! Like any ordinary citizen! With a trembling finger, and forgetting about the
bath that was almost ready to overflow, Mike had dialed
the number. He figured that, if by some chance he got
one of the Mafioso's henchmen on the wire, he'd be
able to think of something to say. But he never figured
he'd get beyond the first line of defense of valets and
gardeners.

To his surprise, a feminine voice answered, saying,
"Mrs. Varese speaking, what can I do for you?"

Mike was nonplussed, and sputtered, "Uh . . . I . . .
uh . . . that is, I'd like to interview Mr.—I mean, your
husband—Mr. Varese. That is, I'd like to meet him."

"Just a minute," she replied pleasantly, ignoring his
stammerings. "I'll put him on."

Mike was completely taken aback now. Rushing to
turn the faucets off on the tub, he got back in time to
hear a voice, as pleasant and friendly as the woman's,
saying, "This is Eliah Varese. Who am I speaking to?
What was that, sir? I didn't get the name."

Of course not. Mike hadn't mentioned it. But on
the spur of the moment it didn't occur to him to try
to change his voice or hide who he was. "Mike Wyatt,
of the *World*," he said. "I'd like to meet you."

"Certainly. But what for? In what way can I help
you?"

For the briefest second, Mike thought it might be a case of mistaken identity. This Varese didn't seem to have anything to hide, and was so open, he couldn't be *that* Varese. But then, it occurred to him, both Mr. and Mrs. Varese had spoken English to him!

"Well, Mr. Varese," Mike said as an idea popped into his head, "the *World* is planning a roundup on rich and famous Italian-Americans who've gone back to the old country. You know, how they live over here. Their reasons for coming back, and stuff like that."

"Well, that's very interesting," Varese replied, "but I'm not sure you'd find *me* very interesting. I lead a very quiet life, six months in New York and six months here with my two grown children. You know, I'm only half what you might say, coming back to the old country. My real roots are in America—and besides I hardly speak any Italian at all!"

"That's just the kind of human interest stuff that our roundup is looking for," Mike said, proud of himself for being so quick with his answers and sounding, he was sure, so plausible. "You know, this isn't anything political, or sociological—just the human interest things—yeah, just the facts, sir!"

"The *facts*. Well, I know what you're driving at, Mr. Wyatt, details of everyday life. Okay. How about dropping by for a drink tomorrow, say, around six or seven?"

"Six thirty okay?" Mike said, not believing his own ears.

"Just fine. Six thirty it'll be. We can have a little chat. My wife's Italian too, but from the Abruzzi. She'll be delighted to tell you how she finds things here. And she's got quite a touch with the pasta. Maybe you can join us for a bite. We live at number

97

161 Viale Trionfale, that's the road that goes up to Monte Pellegrino."

Mike thanked him somehow, and hung up. Varese hadn't had a second's hesitation, hadn't seemed the least bit worried. Did a Mafia capo act that way with a reporter? Either this guy was a lot sharper cookie than Mike had figured, he thought, in which case he might be leading him into a trap, or else maybe he wasn't a bigshot at all, but just some underling, who was protecting the boss above him. Who could that be? Finnegan? he wondered.

There was no way of getting to Finnegan. That one lived as guarded a life as an Al Capone or a Lucky Luciano, even though he was a mick. Of course, Mike knew that, in this new generation of godfathers who are better with a balance sheet than with a gun, they pretended that everything was open and aboveboard. But this Varese seemed to be carrying it just too far.

Yes, he thought again, this was a real sharp cookie. He was laying a trap, and Mike might fall right into it. But then he thought of Cesare, and wrote his name down on the pad in front of him and surrounded it with doodles while he thought the matter through.

That was what he would do next day: As he walked into Varese's, and shook his hand, he would greet him with, "Cesare! Cesare Tozzi! Remember Cesare Tozzi!"

But Mike Wyatt read too many murder mysteries.

And just because he did, he had decided to come here in the morning and case the place, before coming back for his drink with Varese at six thirty. Wasn't that what a Raymond Chandler or James Hadley Chase hero would do?

"Yeah, but they would have found Viale Trionfale already," he thought aloud as he parked the Fiat 124 at a lookout promontory. He got out of the car, breathed in the fine smell of pines, and admired the panorama of Palermo at his feet, the Conca d'Oro with its pinkish sand beach, the Mondello Lido, the Mediterranean, so intensely, so dazzlingly blue . . .

He turned around, blinking, and there on the side of a retaining wall he saw a street sign: VIALE TRIONFALE. He'd been driving up the road to Monte Pellegrino for a quarter of an hour without remembering that Varese had said they were the same thing.

And the villa behind that retaining wall was number 161!

There was a long black Lincoln limousine with New Jersey license plates and half-open tinted windows parked outside the gate of the estate. The place looked like an old Sicilian-Norman manor, but it had probably been built around the turn of the century, with the two bastardized Florentino-Persian towers added on a couple of decades later. Tamarisks, pines, palm trees, bougainvillaeas, and laurel roses shaded its somewhat flaking lilac facade. Mike walked circumspectly up to the gate to see what he could see. The crickets stopped chirping. He could hear the dull thud of a tennis ball being lobbed back and forth: two barechested young men in dirty jeans were playing on a well-kept court next to a fine oval swimming pool surrounded by inflatable chairs and cushions.

This Eliah Varese couldn't be anybody's front man or second in command.

Mike was startled by steps on the gravel path. Two huge characters were coming toward him—Americans, to be sure. And, to be equally sure, two of Varese's hit men, or else two killers from some other gang. One of them, the bigger one, wrapped in a trench coat that seemed to be choking him, had an arm in a cast and the suspicious-looking aspect that hired killers always have in B movies. The other was just as tall, but lean and lanky, and he had the kind of sallow complexion that villains or poisoners have in the same kind of flicks.

Both of them had cold, mobile, and intelligent eyes that made his blood run cold.

He figured the better part of valor was to hightail it back to his Fiat. As he was putting the key in the ignition, he could see them through the rearview mirror: they were snooping around the limo and sticking their heads through the windows to peer inside.

He turned on the ignition and shifted into low.

Gigi pulled his hand back from where it was searching between the jump seat and the partition. Babu had just discreetly whistled between his teeth to warn him they had better get going.

They had no sooner started toward their red Alfetta parked a little farther up the scenic road, when the gate of Villa Varese turned creakingly on its hinges.

An impeccably uniformed chauffeur appeared, in the traditional gray, with double-breasted coat, jodhpurs, and black leggings polished to a high shine. Holding his cap under his arm, he held the wrought-iron gate for Eliah Varese to come through.

Varese opened the Lincoln door himself, before the chauffeur could get to it, and sat down inside with a weary sigh. "To San Frusto, on the Caltanissetta road," he said, rubbing his tired eyelids.

Then his fingers went down to his necktie and he patted the good-luck charm that hung on a little gold chain over the discreet blue and gray striped silk. It was a coral horn that added a strange note to his otherwise elegant attire. He wore an anthracite gray suit of the finest material and tailoring, a two-tone gray vest, and a smoky-gray silk shirt. Handsomely turned out, slim and tanned as he was, Eliah Varese, however tired he might be, looked a good deal less than the fifty he admitted to.

"On the road there, where the plane of the Monsignore lands, eh, sir?" the chauffeur replied in an accent as British as the cut of his master's wardrobe.

Varese did not answer. The chauffeur had pushed the button that raised the bulletproof windows before turning on the air conditioning, and in the bluish green light Varese saw his own face reflected in the tinted glass that separated him from his driver. "A shark," he thought, "a deep-sea fish, a manta ray." And he smiled slightly to himself, revealing deadly gleaming teeth.

Mike shrugged with impatience. What was that car that was blowing its horn at him and trying to pass him on the hairpin turn? A quick look into the rearview mirror revealed that it was the swank Lincoln he had just seen, with the New Jersey license plates.

That was Eliah Varese!

He no longer hesitated: he would let the long black car by, and then follow it—at least as well as his little Fiat could keep up with it.

He had no idea where he was going, or what sort of complications lay ahead, but he suddenly felt game for anything, enthusiastic and high.

He veered as far as he could to the right and signaled the Lincoln to pass. In his excitement, he didn't see the little red Alfetta that was following at some distance, beyond a wave of heat that was coming up from the pavement.

Then, as he put himself into overdrive, Mike let out a yell, "Okay, Signore Varese, this is the showdown!"

10

"Sleep, my dear Chevalley, sleep, that is what Sicilians want, and they will always hate anyone who tries to wake them, even in order to bring them the most wonderful of gifts . . ."

As he rolled into San Frusto, Mike remembered those disillusioned words spoken by Prince Salina in *The Leopard*. It was an agglomeration of some hundred earth-colored houses no one had dreamt of repainting in over a century, lying sleepily at the foot of a great baroque church that dwarfed them; great clouds of flies; garbage all over the sidewalks; a hungry donkey clop-clopping along with one unshod hoof; a few ragged children and some old men straddling their brokendown chairs as they eyed him, hostile and stubborn.

Then, a bit farther on, he saw the Lincoln maneuver with difficulty onto a steep incline that turned up toward the high rocky sun-scorched plateau they had been skirting for some time now. He pulled up in the shade of an old figtree and waited.

"*Strada Altamonte?*" the English chauffeur solemnly asked from behind the half-lowered tinted window. The child playing in the middle of the narrow steep little street did not answer the foreigner, and ostentatiously turned his back on him. An unkempt woman came running out of her hut, grabbed her two little girls, and hurried back in, slamming the door behind her. A number of shutters up and down the street were just as quickly closed.

"*Strada Altamonte?*" the chauffeur asked again of an old woman carrying a load of firewood a few car lengths farther up the street. The poverty-stricken thing looked him straight in the eye and remained silent as if she had not heard.

Omertà!

Then the rear window of the limousine quietly came down and Varese appeared, yelling obscene threats in Sicilian.

"*Vigliacca!* You piece of manure! He's asking the way to Altamonte. Can't you hear, you slut?"

The terrified old woman pointed the way.

As Mike was starting up again, he was somewhat worried to see a red Alfetta that he had already seen twice before this morning. His worry turned to panic when he was able to make out its two occupants: the two giants he had seen snooping around Eliah Varese's car. The skinny one was driving, and the one with the cast on his arm had a set of earphones on.

Mike speeded up.

"Well, the jerk finally saw us!" Babu sneered. "He's shittin' his pants, but he won't get far. Altamonte is right over there."

Indeed, as they got outside the village, Mike barely had time to slam on his brakes and find a free-standing stone wall behind which he could hide his white Fiat. In front of his half-blinded eyes, a huge desert of rocks and weeds swept by very strong winds and enclosed by a semicircle of mountains looked like a moonscape. Traced cleanly between the craters of white stones was a long straight runway, recently resurfaced.

And there stood the Lincoln, spang in the middle of the runway.

The chauffeur was inside the Lincoln, but Eliah Varese was leaning against one of its doors, smoking a cigar.

Mike felt an unreasoning fear come over him. Wasn't this the trap he had let himself be led into? Wouldn't the two in the Alfetta be the accomplices, the Mafia boss's enforcers who had already knocked off Cesare and were now going to close in on him?

"Monsignore!" Babu exclaimed, as he heard the muffled drone of a motor in his earphones.

Mike looked up about the same time: in the very blue sky, a tiny private plane had just come over the mountains. Eliah Varese, his hand shading his eyes, watched it come down toward him.

He was smiling.

"It's gotta crash!" the reporter thought, as he watched the plane get fearfully close to the ground. Then, at the last second, he saw the landing gear drop from the fuselage and the plane rolled onto the runway . . . just a few yards from the Lincoln.

Its propellor was still whirling as Harold Finnegan alighted and walked toward Varese. Eliah Varese had straightened up, tossed away his cigar, and was walking toward Finnegan, in the full glare of the sun.

When they were about ten paces apart, they stopped as if petrified. Mike saw Finnegan snap his fingers and Varese jump into the air clacking his heels together.

"Black Fangs!" Varese shouted, and Finnegan answered, even louder, "Devils!"

The echo made his war cry resound infinitely.

"Devils!" he repeated, as if defying the rocky encirclement.

"Devils!" the echo came back.

"Black Fangs!"

"Devils!"

And then Mike saw those two men, so serious looking, run toward each other like two kids, and hug as they shouted, "Oh, John! John!" "Oh, Eliah! Eliah!"

They seemed drunk with delight, as they made the plateau echo with their exclamations of "Black Fangs!" and "Devils!" which the rocks kept repeating, the better to intoxicate them with their joy in seeing each other again, and the power they felt.

It felt good—as it had in Brooklyn in 1935, on the West Side in 1940, in Rome in 1945 during the war, and in Las Vegas in 1950! It made them feel as giddy as they had that time when they knocked over the Church of the Holy Virgin, the time they danced with those broads at El Morocco, the way they'd felt when they took off at dawn on that C-47 for Korea, the way it had been when they got even with the damned pimps at the Imperator's Palace. Once more, Devils and Black Fangs were together—and their shouts made mountains quake.

The two men walked to the limousine, holding each other affectionately by the shoulder. Harold Finnegan turned and waved to his pilot that he could take off. Then they got into the car, which backed slowly for the quarter mile or so in a straight line to the edge of San Frusto and the little wall of dry stones behind

which Mike sat watching them. The improvised runway was now free: the motors of the plane roared and
it became airborne just opposite the Fiat 124, making
a swing around the bell tower before disappearing into
the blinding sunlight.

Following the Lincoln, Mike had come back to the
main square of the village, where he saw the limousine
parked in front of the local church's monumental
staircase. In the greenish light, Varese was sitting nonchalantly on a bench, delicately picking his nose, as he
watched his Irish friend make his way up the fifty or
so steps and push aside the red plush curtain over the
front door. Barefoot beggar kids were scrambling after
the coins which he had almost unnoticingly tossed to
them.

Mike turned around and shuddered: at the other
end of the square, in front of the only café-diner in
San Frusto, stood the red Alfetta. There was nobody
in it, but he thought he could make out the two giants
in the murky shadows inside the little bar, drinking
wine and chewing on some *pizzette*. He wanted to find
out for himself what was what. He carefully walked toward their car, circled it in the hope of finding a door
open—but all four were locked—and tried to read the
title on a file folder lying on the back seat.

Then he fell solidly, like a lump.

"Go ahead! Rearrange his face a little, so we can
recognize the cocksucker better next time we see him,"
Babu was saying to Gigi after having laid Mike out
with a wallop of his plaster cast on the back of his
neck.

11

"Sure—of course it was—ouch!—they were Varese's
men. You understand—it was a kinda trap they set. I
was supposed to go see him in the evening, after he
was all milk and honey to me on the phone. But—at
noon he had his toughs knock me out. A classical
trick. You find it in every Raymond Chandler novel.
Boy, was I ever a sap!"

"Well, why did you have to follow him like that?"

Honey Pie, as she spoke, was daintily taking a large
Band-Aid spotted with dried blood from his eyebrow.
Mike was biting the bullet out of pride: he didn't
want to moan with pain even though it hurt him just
to speak, what with his puffed lips, aching gums, and
all the rest of the traces Gigi and Babu had left on him.

As she tamped the wounds with disinfectant, Honey
Pie tried to soothe him, talking as if to a child:
"Ummm, easy now. There, that won't hurt . . . ummm
. . . that's a good boy!"

Mike took a swig of gin from his bottle and then
asked, "But—what'd—ouch!—what'd she have to say
about him—huh?"

"Not much," Honey Pie answered. "She's been with
him for three years now, but still doesn't know much
about him. And by now she knows there's not much
point in asking questions. He's just a mystery man.

Always traveling, and he never lets her know when he'll be back or when he's leaving again. And he has these strange servants. But she doesn't want to lose him: after all, he gives her five thousand bucks a month to do what she wants with. And anyway, I think she's really in love this time. I mean it. He's so good-looking, and lotsa fun, she says, and I gather he's pretty hot in the hay, too. She said, you'd never believe he was over fifty. Every morning he does over an hour of sitting-up exercises, and then he boxes a few rounds with one of his servants, the black one. He has a regular training gym set up in that penthouse. Mike, stop moving that way, your stitches are going to come out."

"Ouch! You think I'm enjoying this?"

"Oh, no, baby, of course not. But since you insist on being a big hero . . ."

"Tell me," he insisted, "hasn't she ever gotten any idea of what he does for a living?"

"Just once, she overheard a conversation with his lawyer, a man named Robert Berg. They were saying a lot of things about the Vatican. And Claudine thinks they must do business with the Vatican. Now, watch out, this is gonna hurt."

Mike suppressed a deep groan, took another swig of gin, and then resumed the conversation in a low voice, a phrase at a time, while Honey Pie wiped the sweat from his gleaming forehead.

"In Rome," he said, "everybody . . . everybody . . . does business with the Vatican."

"Really?" she asked. "Is the Vatican supposed to—"

"Don't you believe me?" he interrupted. "The Holy See owns at least half of this goddamned town. They have the concessions at Fiumicino Airport and had a half interest in the building of the Hilton Cavalieri. They're part owners of the Water and Gas Company, and the Olympic Village, and you name it! Don't you know that the Holy See is up to its neck in banking? It owns the Banco di Santo Spirito, the Banco di Roma, and insurance companies, and shares in God knows how many different companies—and He should know! Anyway, that's what De Vaere says, and I believe him. The Vatican has the biggest stock portfolio in the whole world. What did you think it lived on—Sunday collections?"

"Oh, I never even thought about it," Honey Pie sighed. "And besides I really couldn't care less, one way or the other." But then, seeing how excited he was about the whole thing, she added, "If you'd just keep quiet, I could take care of your lip."

"Well, Frankenstein's monster," De Vaere yelled at him, when they met at the Rosati as arranged.

At first Mike had made a point of finding it funny when people laughed at his wounds. But now, after a half hour's discussion with the head of the *World*'s Rome bureau, he was in enough pain so that he no longer appreciated being made the butt of the joke.

"You know very well why," he was practically shouting at De Vaere. "You never would have given me your okay. You would've told me it was a political story and belonged in your bailiwick."

"And I would have been right," the bureau chief said. "At least I would've kept you from getting beaten up by those two huskies."

"They were Americans. Mafia hit men."

"Or maybe two poor Sicilian slobs who work as bodyguards for Varese. Who knows?"

"You never want to believe me, De Vaere," Mike complained.

"I only believe the truth. And I don't go for your fantasies, old man!" De Vaere corrected him. And then, finishing his iced coffee in one gulp and almost choking over it, he added, "Mike, you know very well why New York keeps you on here in Rome."

The argument was getting heated.

"Sure, I know. I know! *I know*," Mike retorted with growing emphasis. "Only because I get invited every place, because I make *them* laugh, and I'm a lush, and I quote Shakespeare and Milton at *their* parties and *their* balls, and I'm on a first-name basis with Gina and Sophia and Monica and Silvana, and because Sergio calls me Piccolo Hamlet, and Federico calls me in the middle of the night to talk to me about his next picture. So what?"

He took a breather. His hands were trembling, the perspiration was running down his bruised cheeks and onto his wilted and slightly bloodstained collar. He felt as though he were about to cry. Like when you're a kid and you tell the truth, and nobody'll believe you. Finally, he went on, in a more moderate tone, "Okay, I know all that, De Vaere. But I know too that this time I'm on to something big."

"Your big scoop, as usual," the other replied.

Mike decided to ignore that. Keep calm, he urged himself inwardly; you have to impress him with your coolheadedness and determination. He resumed, as collectedly as he could:

"What I have is a sort of intuition. An inward certainty, if you prefer. I know that I'm really onto something. And besides, I want to get even for Cesare. I'll find out who Varese is, but mostly I'll find out who that other guy is, who's working under cover for him— unless it turns out to be vice versa. Yes, I will find out who this Finnegan is and what the hell he's up to—what kind of shady deals he's working. Anyway, I've learned one thing already—I've learned that he, well, he works for the Vatican."

De Vaere reacted to that as if he had been given an electric shock. "The Vatican?" he said. "If that's the case, hold everything, Mike! Remember: *No* touching the Vatican, not under *any* circumstances. You remember the Micheli affair? You remember all the headaches we got out of that? If this Finnegan is a financial adviser to the Holy See, or an investment broker for the Institute for Christian Charity—or God knows what else! If he's any of those things, Mike, for Christ's sake, lay off it!"

But Mike suddenly stood up and gave De Vaere a sarcastic Boy Scout salute, as he solemnly pronounced, "The truth and nothing but the truth, remember? That's our motto!"

He tried to smile despite the pain in his jaws, then turned and left. He felt a new courage, which buoyed him up.

Making his way with difficulty through the five rows of tables on the café terrace, he heard half-admiring kidding comments from a number of them:

"What'd you do, Mike? Mix it up with Muhammad Ali again?"

"You back from Vietnam or Cambodia, honey?"

"Mike, darling, did Honey Pie do that to you?"

"You know, you look great that way! Can I get a cover shot of you for *Uomo-Vogue*?"

De Vaere had always been jealous of Mike's celebrity among the idlers and loungers of the Roman Who's Who and the café society types at the Rosati. He watched him at length as he went toward his Bel Air that was double-parked on Via di Ripetta. The crazy character was singing, in spite of the fact that he was obviously hurting. Singing "Make 'em laugh, make 'em laugh, make 'em laugh!" no less!

12

"I've had it!" Gigi moaned, as he collapsed on the bed. He was so tired he felt racked with dry sobs that nauseated him. Babu, livid with nerves and his own eyes red too, in turn flopped like a lump, on his creaking mattress, grumbling, "How the hell does he do it, anyway?"

It was evening, and through the parted curtains of their hotel room the neon lights of the street cast strange effects. For a second, Gigi couldn't remember whether they were in New York, London, Paris, Chicago, Ahmat-Ahbat, Zurich, or Algiers. This dull motel room in Brooklyn Heights might just as well have been in any other city, or on any other continent. And it might just as well be seven in the morning now as seven at night.

Without listening, he could hear the rain pelting outside and the unabated buzz of traffic on the wet street. But the noise of a siren stridently broke his eardrums and he thought: New York, Chicago, some place in the US of A. Only in America do squad cars have that kind of siren. He had vague recollections of tailing "Monsignore" through Manhattan, staying endless hours across from La Caravelle or the Four Seasons, and then that deathly watch in the blind alley off Lenox Avenue, when every breath might have been your last.

He could remember the suspicious and hostile looks of the blacks watching Babu and him as they kept cruising in their rented Escort, over on 135th Street, back on 136th, over on 137th, back on 138th, and then back down to 135th and all over again. He could also remember a scare in the elevator at the Pierre, when the crush of people almost pushed him right into "Monsignore," unrecognizable in a leather jacket and a cap. And the time the traffic cops stopped them—but only because the rear directional on the Escort was on the blink!

Then, as in a dream, he visualized his little Maria-Pia playing on the beach at Ostia with Charity, her mother—and, fully dressed, he fell asleep on the un-opened bed, his leg with one final reflex action pushing away the tapes and files piled up at its foot.

Babu got up wearily and knelt to pick up the scattered sheets with his one good hand, the left one. With a sign of despair, he checked off another day on his cruddy-looking cast ("Only twelve more to go!" he thought), stuck his head under the faucet to get a drink of water, and flopped back on the bed, still wrapped in the old wet mackintosh with the right sleeve ripped so his broken arm could go through it.

"How does that Monsignore do it?" he repeated aloud. "How the hell can he keep up that pace?"

Thursday, 8:00 A.M., Bahrein Airport. The light was blinding already. Thirty-two degrees Celsius, eighty-nine degrees Fahrenheit on the lighted electronic thermometer, as the MEA-747 landed.

Ten minutes later, "Monsignore" was off in another plane, a private one, this time a Lear-Jet decorated with the coat of arms and colors of the Ahmats, while they had to cover the hundred miles of terrible red sands of the Harzat, finer than talcum powder, under a scorching sun in a rented jeep—in order to catch up with him at Ahmat-Ahbat.

Ahmat-Ahbat: refineries and oil fires, a sleepy city, piled up to withstand the cobalt-covered waves of the Persian Gulf. Farther on, an immense greensward of English grass, covered by the haze of the water that started evaporating as soon as it spurted from the thousands of mechanized sprinklers. And, as indistinct as if they were part of some Impressionist painting, there were the figures of Emir Farouh-Ahbat in his black djellaba and "Monsignore" wearing an elegant light-colored golfing outfit. Behind them, caddies, bodyguards, and soldiers in jungle fatigues. Gigi and he had to hide behind bushes or in the shadow of some small wood in order to record the conversation between the American and the Ahbatan chief of state. "Monsignore" insisted on playing all eighteen holes on foot, turning up his nose at the electric carts.

Then, at the royal palace, that endless banquet for three hundred. Couscouses and *tajines* served in overturned ancient Ahbatan shields, each carried by eight Nubians. Between courses, there were ritual dagger duels: "Monsignore" cut his opponent on the belly. And the latter, a son of the emir named Loucif, congratulated him before passing out. Or, at least, that's what Gigi thought he saw, from behind one of the panels of the tent that had been set up in the palace gardens. And after dessert, dancers and houris . . .

Before dawn the next day, falcon hunting in the gypsum and wormwood desert of Efharzat: a horseback ride that lasted several hours, which they couldn't get near, but later heard and recorded that it had been

led from one end to the other by "Monsignore," who
had a horse drop under him.

Friday, 6:00 P.M.: Zurich in the rain. Meeting with
bankers and representatives of the Limmat Bank and
the Crédit Vaudois at the Cercle du Parc, and then a
poker game at the Cercle de l'Athénée. "Monsignore"
hit the sack at 2:00 A.M., seven thousand Swiss francs
ahead.

Saturday, 9:00 A.M., Geneva. "Monsignore" had a
date with his old friend, the former tennis champion
Walter Greensdale. They went out for a six-mile run
through the woods. 11:30: Business brunch at the
Richmond with two characters known as "Le Marseil-
lais" and "Monsieur Armand." Leisurely afternoon:
"Monsignore" stopped in at Davidoff's to buy cigars,
and picked up two cases of Château-Margaux from the
former wine steward of the Beau-Rivage.

Sunday, 10:00 A.M., High Mass at the Madeleine in
Paris. Private luncheon at the restaurant of the Ritz
with a famous French writer, a former member of the
government. Out to Vincennes for the races. "Monsignore" was joined there by Robert Berg and the "Secretary of State" of Prince Fuad, along with a chargé
d'affaires of the Algerian government. The four bet on
Blue Muslim and lost, causing "Monsignore" to re-
mark, "Well, that takes care of our calling our operation Blue Muslim. That nag would sink it for sure."
And in the evening, supper at the Closerie des Lilas
with Cartier's female press agent.

Monday, midnight: Supper in Chicago at the home
of John Varese, financial counselor to HUELCO and—
as Gigi was to discover through one of the taps—also
to the AMDG.

The next day their subject spent two hours in a

sauna with Tom Mozza. Of course, they couldn't record anything from there, nor could they get seats later that night on the plane he took to London.

London, Wednesday, April 16th, 5:00 P.M.: Caught up with him again.

"Monsignore" was having tea with Prince Fuad at the residence the British government rents to the exiled nobleman. Fuad gave him a Matisse sketch, which he shortly passed on to his driver, José, when the latter drove him back to Belgrave Square: "The poor joker got conned with a lousy fake, a Legros or something of the sort," he said aloud, knowing the driver didn't understand a word of English.

Thursday, morning aperitif time: Algiers. "Monsignore" went swimming in the Mediterranean before having lunch with a movie producer whose next picture he was financing. Around 3:30 P.M. a DS-21 that looked like an official car drove him to an unidentified villa in the suburbs of the white city. Repeated passage of an army truck up and down the avenue where Gigi and Babu were parked made them lose the tail for a while.

Friday: Algiers—New York by way of Paris, stopping off there long enough to deposit a check at the Charles de Gaulle Airport bank. "Monsignore" had dinner at La Caravelle with a group of childhood friends. He had smoked salmon mousse, duck St.-Hubert, and iced-coffee soufflé, while Gigi and Babu had to make do with soggy rain-soaked hamburgers.

Weekend in New Jersey, at the home of one of his old pals of the Devils gang, now president of a local of the Teamsters Union. "Monsignore" made a kite for his onetime lieutenant's children and played with them on the beach for almost half the day. After taking a nap, he ran through the reports and files he had brought with him. Sunday morning, early mass at St. Patrick's Cathedral. Then, tennis and swimming with his old friend's eldest boy. But spent the afternoon reading and marking up an issue of the French journal *Études Augustiniennes* (that was the title Gigi thought he could make out through his fieldglasses), before returning to reading St. Ignatius of Loyola's *Spiritual Exercises.*

And the very next day—"this morning practically at the crack of dawn," Babu said as he thought of the dizzy whirl they were on—at 8:00 A.M. he was in Manhattan again and they were tailing him.

Early appointment at the headquarters of the First Vancouver Bank, "Monsignore" dressed in a dark gray suit and carrying a black crocodile attaché case. Then back to the Pierre, where he ordered the *Osservatore Romano* brought up to his suite along with his usual morning malted milk. Next, to meet with the financial director of HUELCO in a Rockefeller Center office, followed by lunch at the Four Seasons. Back to the Pierre by cab after purchasing a bracelet at Tiffany's and leaving his bishop's ring to be fixed, the amethyst in it having come loose.

To their amazement, when "Monsignore" went back out at 4:00 P.M., he changed to faded jeans, tennis shoes, a leather jacket, and a tweed cap, with one-way aviator's goggles hiding his eyes. The tight-fitting T-shirt on his powerful torso under his jacket made him look like a teen-ager. He ran through the rain to the orange Volkswagen he had borrowed the night before from his friend's oldest son, and took off like a blue streak. Did he know that they were following him?

Gigi was surprised and somewhat taken aback when he had seen him looking like this in the elevator.

Turning into 60th Street, he went up Park Avenue, then over to Madison at 91st Street, and on up into Harlem—125th, 130th, 135th . . .

Gigi whistled with admiration. "Hey, it really takes a pair of balls to go up into Harlem this way."

"What about us poor suckers? We got two pair, but they're not gonna help us any in this mess."

"Babu, do you see what I do?" Gigi came back. "The points in the pocket of his jacket?"

"Brass knuckles?"

"Right. Brass knucks, it is."

There was a blind alley off Lenox Avenue, with old torn mattresses and a cast-off refrigerator piled up in it. A half-unconscious junkie lay there in his own vomit. But among all this mess, kids were still playing—at war, naturally: the rusty chassis of a car being used as their Alamo. They stopped cold when they saw "Monsignore" coming toward them. "Out!" one of them yelled at him—this was their turf. But the way the honkie kept coming on made them shut up. At the end of the blind alley, a red-painted door in the brick wall led to a broken-down loft. "Monsignore" tried, the handle; it was locked. Then, limber and noiseless on his rubber soles, he climbed the steps of the fire escape two by two. He knocked at a small door all covered with graffiti, giving the prearranged signal: two long knocks, two short, one long. It opened slightly to reveal a half-black, half-Seminole Indian, who asked him in.

Gigi went up after "Monsignore" so as to be able to see what could be seen through the dusty skylight: a cruddy gym with some black boxers in training. A second Seminole, a trainer, came toward "Monsignore" and shook his hand effusively, then led him to a corner of the room where five men were having a poker game on a massage table. Along the way, "Monsignore" took a few swipes at the punching bags, left hooks that had a professional touch about them. The mixed-breed laughed and slapped him on the back in admiration. And one of the cardplayers got up to have a private conversation with him.

When that was done, "Monsignore" showed a Puerto Rican kid how to jump rope like a pro, and got so involved that he himself skipped rope for half an hour after taking off his jacket and shirt.

"How does he do it? Oh, how *does* he do it?" Babu was wondering; just a moment before he was so tired he thought he was hallucinating: the walls of his bedroom seemed to be closing in on him noiselessly.

He had taken his socks off and was rubbing the moist dirt between his toes, sighing noisily every time he heard Gigi snore for a few minutes.

Then, finding his own socks malodorous, he got up, took a tube of amphetamines out of his toilet kit, swallowed the last two pills in it, and sat down at the desk to go on typing his report with two fingers of his left hand on his trusty portable.

Geneva, April 23, 1975

RECAP OF REPORT "F"

Attention: His Most Eminent, Most Reverend
          Excellency the Cardinal Camerlengo
          and Secretary of State, Monsignore V.

Your Excellency will find attached hereto the

recap of the "F" matter, which Your Excellency did me the honor of having me investigate.

> Your most humble and faithful servant,
> /s/   Franco Aduanello

It all began with the discovery of bituminous shale deposits in the emirate of Ahmat-Ahbat by prospectors working for the HUELCO Search Department which, as Your Excellency is well aware, is a wholly owned subsidiary of HUELCO, which in turn is controlled to the extent of 51.2% of its shares by the Institute for Christian Charity. According to a projection of which a copy is held in box 83-630-30 of the Banque du Léman et Mont Blanc, where F. has a numbered account, this would appear to be the largest oil field discovered in the Middle East up to the present.

But on the one hand, the territory in which it is located is claimed by the Haraoui tribe of nomadic Bedouins (about a thousand to twelve hundred in number, women and children included, according to HUELCO's most recent educated guess), and on the other hand Emir Farouh-Ahbat has conceded to HUELCO only the right to set up drilling derricks and build refineries and pipelines but without agreeing to pay any royalty whatsoever thereafter on either the crude or refined product.

The plan, originally called Blue Muslim (?), but recently renamed Operation Golden Sand, is to unfold in three stages:

In the first stage, F. has charged Eliah Varese—about whom Your Excellency can find full details in Secret File 9A 927 of the Secret Archives of the

123

Vatican—with recruiting some professional agitators and mercenaries (cf. Appendix B of the Full Report). F. himself has made contact in Harlem, New York, and probably also in Algiers —although we are without specific information on this point—with men who will undertake to cause and lead the uprising of the Haraouis against Emir Farouh. The Haraouis have been formed into a National Liberation Movement, led by Ali-Halacem and infiltrated by two Algerian secret agents, who are on the payroll of the AMDG, F.'s corporation set up in Liechtenstein (see below).

In the second stage, F. will bring back to Ahmat Prince Fuad, exiled in London since 1971, and will engineer a palace revolution. Fuad-Ahbat is an ambitious man, but without any political intelligence whatsoever, who is easily manipulated by those around him—notably Gebe Gabo Bobu, a former military adviser in Uganda. He is completely under the thumb of F., who has gotten him to sign notes of indebtedness for a fictitious loan of $35,000,000 to be paid back in royalties, the first third of which are to go to the AMDG.

The AMDG is an Anstalt-type front company (a dummy corporation, which may have a board of directors made up of no more than one individual, as is the case with AMDG), set up in Vaduz on July 19, 1971, by F.

F. got Fuad to give him much greater concessions than Emir Farouh, including a substantial royalty of 0.23% on every barrel of crude, for HUELCO as well as for himself.

Finally, in the third stage, the army is to be taken over by Fuad and Eliah Varese's "advisers." Troops will be sent to fight the Haraoui National

Liberation Movement and Ali-Halacem will be arrested. Operation Golden Sand calls for the entire tribe to be "resettled" on a different nomadic range. This will be accomplished in part by various threats, and in part by poisoning or drying up the wells and waterholes at which its camels drink.

Your Excellency will find further details in the complete report, filed as No. 10A 002, which I have the honor of sending him through the diplomatic pouch of the Apostolic Nuncio accredited to the Helvetic Confederation.

3000 BERN, THUNSTRASSE 60.
Phone: 44 60 40
CABLE ADDRESS: NUNTIUS BERN C.H.

13

"She wanted to know things about you—how you live—what you do. You know, it began to strike me funny that she should be so nosy," Claudine was saying as she slowly sank up to her chin in the bluish foam of her bath.

Between two left hooks, as the heavy punching bag swung away from him, Harold Finnegan could see his girl friend as she talked. Or rather, see the somewhat sullied reflection of her in the large baroque Murano-glass mirror set into the mosaic of seashells.

Then the bag swung back and his gloves hit it again at the exact spot where the trademark, ST. PETER, LTD, appeared in white letters on the black leather. Probably out of some secret sense of irony, Harold Finnegan had had his private gymnasium furnished by the famous British sporting goods company of that name.

The perspiration had already drenched his T-shirt and was beginning to come through his woolen warm-up pants, but he went right on punching as he answered Claudine, with what breath he could muster, "And—uh—wh-what did you tell her?"

Claudine did not answer right away. She was gargling a mouthful of cool water. But she finally spit it out and, with a bit of hurt in her voice, sighed, "The only thing I could, Harold. The truth: that I don't know anything about you. Not a thing."

Left jab! Right! Left! Then, amused by what he detected in her voice, he came back, "That was fine, Claudine." And added, by way of encouragement to himself, "Now, left hook. Right uppercut!"

"What's that?" she asked. "I can't hear you very well. That damned punching bag makes so much noise."

"Nothing. I was just talking to myself. I'm finishing off the champ," he laughed. "Say, tell me, Claudine, what's that Honey Pie's boyfriend's name, huh? What did you say it was?"

"Mike Wyatt. He's a newspaperman. On the *World*, I think. Can you hear me? . . . Are you listening, Harold? . . ."

But Harold was no longer listening to her. While he landed a series of right jabs, he had heard some commotion behind the door, voices being raised, and Van Dông swearing at someone and protesting in his high, pipey voice: "You brute! You nasty thug! No! No, I said! Keep out! Diab, come help me! You brute! You pig! Who do you think you . . . But who are you, anyway? . . . Keep out! You have no right in here! No! Sir! Please, sir!"

Startled, he slammed the bag sideways with a violent uppercut, stood stockstill, transfixed, and caught himself just in time to duck as the heavy bag came bouncing back at him.

At that moment, Gigi and Babu, shoving Diab and Van Dông aside, burst into the gym.

From deep in her tub, Claudine could not see what was going on. "Are you listening, Harold?" she went right on asking him, irritatedly.

As he shoved the bathroom door shut, Finnegan whispered to her, "Don't move, Claudine. Stay where you are. Especially, don't try to come out here."

Then, turning suddenly on the two secret agents, he spat at them, "Aha! Mr. Gigi and Mr. Babu. So, it *was* you that I spotted in London and Algiers." And, more fiercely, "Now, what do you think you're doing here?"

Claudine, completely at sea, was calling from behind the bathroom door, "Harold! Harold! What's the matter?"

But her lover was no longer answering. He was watching Gigi, who calmly came toward him, as deferential as could be, and said, "Monsignore, I'm afraid you'll have to come with us. His Holiness wishes to see you immediately. He has called together a special vigilance meeting of the Sacred College."

Harold Finnegan let his arms droop and looked at the man as if he did not understand him.

"You'll have to come with us now," Babu said, more roughly.

And Claudine just kept calling, "Harold! Harold!"

Then the Vatican secret agent started toward the bathroom. But Finnegan, fully composed again, stood in his way and threw a punch at him, which Babu deflected with his plaster cast.

"Please, Monsignore. Please," he said.

Finnegan took his gloves off. He was licked.

"Okay. Okay. I'll come with you. But I forbid you . . ."

Gigi and Babu acquiesced without saying a word and fell in on either side of him as he walked out of the gym pulling off his sweaty T-shirt. On the threshold of his dressing room, he barked, "You'll at least let me dress by myself, won't you?"

* * *

Noiselessly, the mirrored doors closed behind him and immediately reflected endless images of him: over and over again, his muscular torso shining in the half-light, his face livid with rage, his nostrils quivering, his mouth distorted with hatred and a slight foam around its edges, his pale and terrifying gaze that kept peering back at him.

"A Michelangelo!"

Without his knowing why, the words had come back to his memory. They were the words Monsignore Walkman had spoken in the Sistine Chapel when he had shown him the great athletic Christ of *The Last Judgment*. "A Michelangelo, John. Look! See how much you look like him!"

14

"*Madonna mia!* Aldo! Aldo!" Peppe was calling.

"What is it, Peppe?" the valet replied. "You look all upset."

"Aldo!"

"Well, what is it? Say something!"

"*Madonna,* Aldo!"

"Come on, get it out, man!"

"There . . . there . . . Finnegan. You know who, you know—that Finnegan . . ."

"Yes, what about that Finnegan?"

"Aldo, he's a *Monsignore*! Nigeft—I mean Finnegan, he's a *Monsignore*!"

"What kind of a story is that?"

"And Gigi and Babu"—Peppe was trying to get the story out—"they just arrested him. Right there!"

"Arrested him?"

"Here. Just now, I tell you."

"What arrested? What Monsignore? I can't make head or tail—"

"Gigi and Babu arrested him and took him away, I tell you."

"Well, I'm not surprised," the majordomo smugly commented. "I always knew he was a swindler, a gangster, a CIA type. Didn't I tell you as much?"

"No," Peppe replied, now pleading, "you're not

listening to me. I told you he was dressed in his Monsignore's clothes. He must be a cardinal, or something like that!"

"You must be seeing things, Peppe! Have you been overdoing it with the *grappa* again?"

"Ah, *puta madonna, porco Dio*," Peppe countered, trying to make his point. "I tell you he was wearing a black cassock with red piping and a red skullcap, the kind cardinals wear these days. You know, when you see them on TV. I tell you that's just the way he was dressed: the black cassock with the red piping, a red belt, red buttons, the skullcap, and the big cross, whatever they call it, the *pestoral* one! That's what he had on!"

"Well, then, what were Gigi and Babu doing with him?" Aldo asked.

"I was talking to my friend, Mr. Wyatt, the journalist from the *World*, and I saw them coming out of the elevator. They were walking one on each side of him. Like that! And they loaded him into a long black car with little curtains in the back, you know what I mean? One of the Fiat Lungas that have six doors. And behind, I could see, it had license plates with the letters *SCV* on them."

"You mean one of the Vatican cars?"

"Yep. Wyatt couldn't get over it."

"I should think not! A Vatican car, wow!"

"And Wyatt says to me, 'Well, I'll be . . . He's a Monsignore. That's what he is: a Monsignore!'"

"A Monsignore!" Aldo whistled.

PART TWO

1

He was not thinking of anything and nothing could be read on his face. Wedged in between Gigi and Babu, equally silent, he could see the light and the blue shadow of the pines and tall linden trees pass over the windshield of the limousine. They were on Viale Trinità dei Monti. On the left were the terraces and flowered roof gardens of Via Margutta, on the right the high blank walls of the Villa Medici.

By way of the Salita Valadier, the auto was now going down toward the Piazza del Popolo, crossing the Tiber on the Margherita Bridge, and making its leisurely way to the Vatican through the midday traffic of Via Cola di Rienzo.

Only then did he start wondering what *they* knew, what *they* might have found out, and why *they* were calling him in. Since this was a special meeting, and it had been so hurriedly called, and since *they* had had him picked up at Via Gregoriana when *they* were at the very least supposed to be unaware that he was living there under the name of Harold Finnegan, *they* must be on to an awful lot of things.

It looked as though he might have to stand trial. Much as he had had to over the Micheli Affair. But what he feared most was that his personal papers might have fallen into their hands.

"Good heavens!" he was saying to himself, "can these bloody bastards Gigi and Babu have gotten anything more on me?"

What had they been investigating? he wondered. What had they found out in London or Algiers? Had they passed it on to the papal secretary of state? And if so, what? The AMDG? Ahmat-Ahbat? The coup that was being planned?

Bah! He had come through the Micheli Affair and the Holy Father had since renewed his unfaltering demonstrations of friendship to him. And besides, hadn't he already overcome greater perils than this in the past? Just thinking of the adventures he had been through in the last few days made him smile involuntarily in a way that lighted up his face. This gave him his customary look of polite but determined defiance that made people tremble and bow their heads much more effectively than threats or shouts. He had been through the worst dives of Harlem without once having felt any fear; he had fought a dagger duel with Loucif, the son of Emir Farouh, and had not feared being killed; and those were much more dangerous situations than being brought face to face with His Holiness and a few of his colleagues on the Curia.

He relaxed, slipped nonchalantly back against the seat of the car, and only then, in the pocket of his jeans, felt a blunt object digging into his thigh: in his hurry to dress, he had slipped into the first pair of pants at hand, the jeans with the brass knuckles in the pocket. He had a wild urge to laugh, but held it back: Gigi and Babu had no way of knowing what he had on under his cassock or that he had the lethal weapon on him.

As they started into St. Peter's Square, he snorted in a way that confounded his guards. Wasn't he afraid of anything, or was he trying to brazen it out? they wondered. And if so, why was he wasting his time trying to impress them? After all, they were just carrying out orders. But what surprised them most was that he didn't say a word to them, didn't try to question them, when he knew them so well for having had them under his command a few years earlier when he headed the Vatican's Secret Service.

The limousine crossed the square and was photographed by some Japanese tourists whose guide had pointed out its *SCV* license plate to them. The car stopped to the left of the basilica, in front of the half-open grille of the Porta del Arco delle Campane, the main entrance to the part of Vatican City from which the general public is excluded. The Swiss Guards on either side of the gateway snapped impeccably to attention. One of their fellows, dressed in the standard dark blue uniform, came to peer into the window and recognize the occupants of the limousine. With a gesture of respect, he waved the driver in and bowed to the car. Then he went to the wall phone in the sentry box and announced: "Barbieri, Aduanello, and Monsignore John K. Flaherty."

The Fiat slowly went on into the Cortile dei Protomartiri, where it passed Cardinal Camerlengo's black Mercedes going the other way. John Flaherty gave a start: the papal secretary of state had Father Arrupe with him. That must mean that Camerlengo was not going to attend the special meeting he had undoubtedly asked His Holiness to call. What kind of a trap could such a maneuver be hiding? And was it by chance or by design that his limousine had been made to pass the other? The two cardinals exchanged a fleeting glance of hatred and then immediately bowed toward each other with unction and feigned warmth.

The Fiat went beneath the shadow of the stone arches connecting the basilica to the sacristy. Coming out into the Piazza di Santa Marta, John Flaherty blinked in the blaze of the noonday sun. The sprinklers showering all over the greensward drowned the gardens in an iridescent rainfall. And the facade of the Palace of Justice and the Church of Santo Stefano sparkled in this silver-flecked haze.

Finally, beyond the Fondamenta and the Piazza del Forno, the car inched into the Cortile della Sentinella, crossed the Cortile Borgia, and stopped at the Cortile del Papagallo checkpoint. The three men then got out of the Fiat and walked into the Cortile di Santo Damaso, waved through by the Civil Security Service.

"The Commission meeting will be held in the Very Holy Father's library," Girolamo Barbieri whispered to Monsignore Flaherty as they neared the fountain beneath the great clock. And Franco Aduanello, glancing surreptitiously at its face, added, "In fact, it must be starting right now."

This was intended—as a deceptive kind of courtesy—to inform the cardinal that he was not presumed to be brought here as a prisoner but as one free to attend the meeting of the Sacred College, of which he was still a member. He reacted with equally hypocritical politeness: he nodded, as if to dismiss them with thanks. Face had been saved. Gigi and Babu could now withdraw.

A prelate of the Pope's household was already coming forward toward His Excellency and bowing respectfully before showing him to the elevator, the doors of which were guarded by Swiss Guards in blue and yellow striped dress uniforms. As he headed into the lift, Monsignore Flaherty saw the door close behind four of his colleagues, Monsignore Nichols, Monsignore Mc-Awkleen, Monsignore Maraîcher, and that senile old Cardinal Galeazzo-Consalvi who, despite all the recent vestimentary *aggiornamenti,* had never been able to bring himself to give up the scarlet silks and the diamond, the four-cornered biretta and the moiré *ferraiolo,* that huge cape even more flowing than the ancient ceremonial cappa. Nor had he forsworn the gold-buckled red velvet slippers that had come down to him from his great-great-uncle Hannibal, Pope Gregory XVI's secretary of state.

John had no doubt that these were the four "judges" who would shortly be sentencing him.

The official quarters of the Pope, located on the third floor of the apostolic palace, are a series of austere-looking rooms. Their walls are draped in light colors, pearl gray or chamois, and the windows have white curtains. Spotlights play on the fine frescoes above; in their reflections, the marble floors seem to shine as if they were made of ice. Here and there, some green plants add a touch of exuberance to the spare furnishings.

The library, of course, is a more human and tolerable place. Behind the desk is a tapestry taken from Raphael, and on the rear wall a Perugino *Resurrection.* In opposite corners, there are a miniature Renaissance Bible, a processional cross, and on two consoles German wood statues also from the fifteenth century. On a table laden with large quarto volumes and small prayer books, a profusion of trinkets are evidence to the fact that this is the only room of the *piano mobile* in which the Pope occasionally lives.

Paul VI was not sitting behind the desk but over to the side in a high-backed armchair which, by its very magnificence, bespoke the solemnity of this meeting, secret though it might be even to other members of the Sacred College. That morning, an oval conference table had been moved in, with five chairs placed around it and, alongside, the folding table for the recording priest who takes the minutes of Curia meetings in shorthand. The door was guarded by two officers of the Swiss Guard, resplendent in their ceremonial uniforms: purple breeches, inlaid breastplates, crested helmets with pink plumes, and the fluted ruffs that give the guard such haughty bearing.

A prelate came forward and, like the "barker" at a gala reception, announced: "His Most Eminent, Most Reverend Excellency, Tancredi Umberto Cardinal di Galeazzo-Consalvi."

Supported by a tonsured young priest, the mummified-looking old man moved up in a swish of scarlet silk and bowed before the Supreme Pontiff, who said to him, "We beg you, beloved son, take your place at the council table and may God bless you."

This kept the old man from having to bend over to kiss the Pope's pastoral ring.

"Your Holiness is too kind thus to dispense me from having to perform my most sacred duties," the old cardinal said in a quavering voice.

He took his place at the table, wondering what was inside the small carrying case placed on it, right in the middle of the red velvet tablecloth.

As he was doing so, the prelate acting as chamberlain was already announcing the names of his three colleagues who, one after the other, made their approach, bowed deeply, kissed the pontifical ring, and then each took his own seat: "His Most Eminent, Most Reverend Excellency Paul Cardinal Nichols, His Most Eminent, Most Reverend Excellency Patrick Cardinal McAwkleen, His Most Eminent, Most Reverend Excellency Jean Cardinal Maraîcher . . ."

Then there was silence: They were all waiting for Monsignore John K. Flaherty.

Through the Clementine Room, the Room of Consistories, and the Throne Room, a priest in a purple-bordered cassock was at that very moment guiding him toward the library. Along the way, John returned the greeting of another prelate who happened to be named exactly like him. This was hardly surprising in a pontifical court which had no less than six Flahertys (Anthony, Francis, two Johns, Martin, and Walter), eight Flanagans, two Finnegans, four O'Rourkes, seven O'Sullivans, and innumerable Murphys, Ryans, O'Connors, and O'Neills—the Irish Mafia, as they were sometimes derisively called. For they shared an unspoken but deep-rooted sense of solidarity. Those who lived in the Vatican were all in the same wing of the place, had the same father confessor, played bridge together, and entertained one another night after night, drinking Irish whiskey out of champagne glasses, according to a peculiar Vatican custom, the origin of which none seemed to know.

So when he saw the smile of support on the lips of this John F. Flaherty, John realized that this special meeting was already an open secret. "In the Vatican, word gets around about everything, and the sooner the more secret it is"—the words of Monsignore Walkman came back to him, and he had to repress a sarcastic smirk. He could hear himself being announced:

"His Most Eminent, Most Reverend Excellency John Cardinal Flaherty!"

John immediately bowed at the Holy Father's feet and fervently kissed the ring, saying in Italian, "Very

141

Holy Father, I fear that your urgent need to see your humble servant bespeaks some sudden misfortune."

"My very dear son," Paul VI replied, clearing his voice, "it is to God—to God and your colleagues—that you owe some clarification. Not to us."

"And I am ready to supply whatever is needed," he answered, "on any subject within my all too humble and human competence."

John then turned to look at the council table: the two American cardinals and the Frenchman were eyeing him with somewhat muted hostility, and only Monsignore di Galeazzo-Consalvi wore a timid and senile half-smile of sympathy. But in the storm that was brewing, what help could he expect from this old man with softening of the brain who, from living so long within the suffocating atmosphere of the Curia, no longer even had sense enough to know what was at stake? And besides, he was well aware that his virile good looks appealed more than a little to the latent old homosexual.

He finally got back up, crushed by it all, and went to the foot of the table, where he stood in front of the empty chair until the Pope nodded to him to take his place among his peers.

The tension in the air was almost palpable. It was the kind of hard silence that precedes the shock of combat. John looked in turn at each member of the Cardinals' Commission of Supervision of the Institute for Christian Charity. The places around the table had been meted out according to a very subtle sense of protocol, the full intricacy of which he tried to figure out, the way you try to guess what each of the players in a poker game is holding. But he had a joker that none of them could match: as president of the Institute, he was personal banker to each of them. Among the 10,552 accounts entrusted to his care, he knew exactly what each of theirs was, just as he knew their individual little corner-cuttings and their own special frauds. So he could evaluate each one mentally, going from left to right:

#63-80-46, Patrick McAwkleen: App. $27,000 cash, and $31,000 in bonds. The former archbishop of Los Angeles was a sixtyish man with a pompadour and an officer's energetic features. But his too soft, too white hands betrayed the deep imprint of his Jesuit training.

#63-89-46, Paul Nichols: App. $110,000 in stocks, some land holdings, factories, freight cars, and a thirtieth share of a tanker. How had this titular bishop, who had never served anywhere but at the Vatican, been able to accumulate such a fortune, when he came from a family only slightly better off than John's own, which meant still virtually poverty-stricken? The features of the man's face gave a semblance of an answer: Monsignore Nichols had the thin lips and high bulging forehead of an intriguer. What was worse, behind his little steel-rimmed glasses his pale gaze was enough to turn one to ice.

#63-90-00, Jean Maraîcher: Not more than $3,000 cash. The jovial native of Périgord, ruddy as the wine lover he had to be, was the only person at the Holy See who didn't care for money, certainly. He had deposited with the Institute for Christian Charity a tiny inheritance that came from his father, and added his salary to it, because, as he told John in his rugged accent with its rolling r's, "My dearrrr Flaherrrty, it's the bank that's nearest to my rrrresidence, and besides it's open Saturrrrrdays."

And, finally, Monsignore di Galeazzo-Consalvi, who did not bank with the ICC, but probably at the bank

143

in Lombardy that was run by his nephew Ercole, who had for years acted as his uncle's business representative, and was a good friend of Jack Varese's.

Which among them could have brought the case to put on the council table? And what could be in it? John was now looking feverishly at it, as if his eyes might see through its black leather.

The two Swiss Guard officers closed the doors to the library behind them and took up their positions on either side, heels together, arms crossed, stiff and motionless as statues. The young recording priest took the cover off his speedwriting machine. By a nod, the Pope instructed Monsignore Nichols to begin.

The titular bishop of Laodicea in Numidia was obviously fully aware of what it meant to be firing the opening gun. Before saying a word, he buried his head in his open palms.

Then he sighed and, out of affectation, said in Latin, rather than Italian or English, "May God inspire and assist us in the work of this special commission."

"Amen," said the other three judges, joining with him.

"Amen," came back the president of the Institute for Christian Charity. And as he closed his eyes, his hands came together in prayer.

2

"Cheap spy stories! Made-up concoctions! These are the imaginings of sick minds or have been inspired by the devil. These secret agents of ours have hatched an odious plot against my humble person!"

With these words, his fingers pointing, his lips taut, livid with rage, Cardinal Flaherty was defending himself in a voice he did not raise but which nevertheless was vibrant with indignation. For almost twenty minutes he had been subjected to a series of accusations such as he had never heard before in his life. And now he knew what must be in the file that Monsignore Maraîcher, sitting across from him, was quietly thumbing through: the most specific details of the HUELCO operations, with the plans for the coup d'état in Ahmat-Ahbat.

Gigi and Babu had done a thorough job! But how had they gotten hold of this? And what did they really know? At what point in his travels about the world had the two "plumbers" picked up his trail?

He was so angry at having fallen into their trap that he could hardly control himself. He could see Monsignore McAwkleen and Monsignore Nichols look at each other and express a kind of amused contempt for him. Suddenly, without regard for the place they were all in, he jumped up and shouted:

Jack-Alain Léger

"But in the final analysis, what am I being accused of? What kind of a trial is this, anyway? Why this special meeting of the Supervisory Commission?"

He could hear his anger echoing off the ceiling. Out of the corner of his eye he saw that Paul VI was scandalized by his vehemence. He gradually regained his self-control and, after clearing his throat and sitting down, went on:

"Most Holy Father, eminent colleagues and brothers:

"God has come to my assistance since the day you saw fit to put me in charge of reorganizing the Institute for Christian Charity. In September 1967 we were on the verge of bankruptcy. The Vatican Council, as you will recall, had cost us $42,752,000, or, if you prefer, Monsignore di Galeazzo-Consalvi, some twenty-six billion lire. Twenty-six billions that in the course of that year were to be added to the debt contracted, uh, during the preceding pontificate."

At these words, the Pope nodded agreement: He had never relished John XXIII's openhandedness or his concern for charity. He waved to John to go on with his defense.

"His Holiness and the Sacred College did me the signal honor of calling me in as consultant to the Prefecture for Economic Affairs of the Holy See. In 1968, the cardinal-prefect was able to present a balanced budget, the first one in six years. This, in spite of an increase of 54 percent of the allocations to, among others, the Sacred Congregation for the Propagation of the Faith. His Holiness and the Sacred College then expressed their full confidence in me by giving me the most difficult task within the ICC, that of managing its investments. In 1969 our profits were such that we were able to triple, yes, triple the gifts we gave to the missions. At the end of the same year, the wages of 3,127 employees of the Vatican were raised by almost 23 percent. But I hardly need bore you with all these figures.

"When I left the Prefecture for Economic Affairs and the Administration of the Patrimony to assume the presidency of the Institute for Christian Charity, I believe I had completely restored the condition of our economy. By now I have made the Institute into one of the world's leading banking institutions. So what am I being accused of?"

He let his voice drop. For a moment his colleagues could see him looking for inspiration in a feigned contemplation of the ceiling frescoes. That was one of the most famous bits of stage business in the repertoire of that consummate actor, Monsignore John K. Flaherty, but it still got to them. And no one dreamed of interrupting him.

He went on in the kind of whisper that one uses in a funeral crypt, his eyes humbly lowered:

"I would simply add that I hereby tender my resignation if that will appease the wrath of the Sacred College. A wrath which I am at a loss to understand, for I am, if I may say so, proud of not having failed in the task that was assigned me. This year the Institute's profits will allow the Holy See to distribute almost twenty billion lire to good works, to the propagation of the faith, the evangelization of nations, the seminaries, the missions, and the needy monasteries. Yes, God was with me in what I accomplished for His evergreater glory. There is nothing in this area of which I need be ashamed. And I await your judgment with the utmost serenity."

He stopped and, sitting slightly sidewise, nonchalantly leaned his left arm against the back of his chair, thus turning toward Cardinal di Galeazzo-Consalvi and seeking his approval.

But with a senile tic of his eyelid the old courtier stared coldly back at him and said in his quavering voice, "Brother, very dear brother and eminent colleague, have you lost all humility?"

"Ah, brother and most eminent colleague," John immediately came back in a tone of contained irony, "most eminent colleague, Prince di Galeazzo-Consalvi! Humility comes easily to those who are born princes! You come from a family which gave three supreme pontiffs to the Church, and you grew up in your palace at Galeazzo, your palace at Luma, your palace at Brianza, your villa at Sermionetta, your castle at San Sisto-Maggiore. Yes, you grew up there surrounded by portraits of those and others among your famous forebears: the uncles and cousins who were cardinals before you, twelve Galeazzo cardinals and twenty-one Consalvis. And when you sat down to eat, it was with silverware engraved with the coat of arms of Saint Peter."

Then, suddenly, carried away by his cold rage, his Italian gave way to English, or more properly speaking to American, to his native Brooklynese, that lowdown working-class lingo that John knew so admirably how to handle when he wished:

"No trick in being humble, when that's the case! But I came up from the slums, Monsignore! My father was unemployed, Monsignore! My mother went out to do housework—when she wasn't sick or pregnant, Monsignore! And there were nine of us kids, Monsignore! Oh, I know, Monsignore, Christian humility does order us to obey our father, to be submissive to his will. One day, just the same, I forgot my humility: one day . . .

my father came in, drunk as a lord—the very words horrify you, don't they? Well, I'll say it again: One day, my father was drunk as a lord, and he was going to kill my mother. Went after her with a broken whiskey bottle, Monsignore! My mother was screaming with terror!" John could feel the tears welling into his eyes, and he struggled to repress this emotion which was forcing him to lower his voice. He cast a distraught eye over to the young recording priest who was stenotyping away, but then felt more secure when he noticed the Pope signaling him with his eyes to stop taking notes. And he went on, barely audible:

"I was nine years old, Monsignore. And on that occasion I was not humble! I struck my own father! And I forced him down to his knees. Now I had to threaten him with the jagged whiskey bottle I had grabbed out of his hands, cutting myself in the process." He stopped and showed a scar that he still had along his thumb. "I was nine years old. And I saved my poor mother's life, Monsignore. No, on that occasion I was anything but humble. Prince—brother—most eminent colleague—believe me, I was anything but humble!

"But there was a time when Annibale-Ettore di Galeazzo was not humble either! That great soldier-monk went out to fight against the infidels and for the greater glory of God. Monsignore, can it be that you have forgotten the motto of your own ancestors—*Me alone, and God?* If you have, then I have not—for I learned it back in seminary from one of those good books of moral principles that are no longer required reading since the *aggiornamento!*"

Paul VI made a most eloquent face. He could not hide his disagreement with John on that score. After all, it was he who had engineered this change in schooling. But, although he has been somewhat manhandled by Monsignore Flaherty, the old integralist Galeazzo-Consalvi approved of his having dared say aloud what he himself was only thinking. And John knew that he could now go even further; he had them bemused.

"And then Gregorio," he went on, "Prince Gregorio di Galeazzo, Grand Duke of Theofili-Farnese, that Gregorio who had Bernini build him a marble mausoleum that put St. Peter's in hock for over a century! Was that Gregorio humble? Yes, he was humble before God, Monsignore, but not before men! The glory of his death was a present he made to God—so what did he care what men might think?

"*Io solo, e Dio!*" he said. "Yes, 'Me alone, and God!'"

He let a moment of silence go by before returning to his own defense. No one dared cut him off yet, no one dared tell him to mind what he said.

"Eminent colleague, I am humble before God, as were your ancestors. And just like your ancestors, I have no humility about me in my service to the Church. The Church has made me a prince, too, sire. The Church has made me your equal. Your peer!

"Yes, I know what I accomplished at the Prefecture of Economics as well as at the Institute. And, as I said before, I won't stand for some vulgar undercover gossip being spread to besmirch my honor as a humble servant of the Church!

"'Deliver me not over to the will of them that trouble me: for unjust witnesses have risen up against me; and an iniquity hath lied to itself.'"

"Vulgar undercover gossip, you say!" It was the sudden voice of Monsignore McAwkleen who, as if in an attempt to break the spell he felt himself falling under as he heard John speak, had half risen from his seat and protested violently. "Vulgar gossip, indeed! And false witnesses! Impudently quoting from the Twenty-ninth Psalm, which has nothing to do with the matter."

"Psalm Twenty-six, twelve," Flaherty corrected him in a honey-sweet voice, not devoid of sarcasm.

Then the former archbishop of Los Angeles, his patience at an end, turned to the Pope:

"Gossip, false witnesses? Not at all, Holy Father. But on the contrary, proofs of infamy, of iniquity"—as as he spoke, he pulled toward him the black case that so interested the president of the ICC—"proofs of such turpitude as, had we not called a halt to it, would soon have bespattered our Holy Mother Church, yes, and, much as my heart bleeds to say so, besmirched even the robe of Saint Peter himself!"

With this last verbal flourish he snapped open the locks of the case. Magnetic tapes and file folders crammed into it popped out. The table was suddenly covered with all kinds of typewritten reports. And John, completely amazed, began to guess—yet, with all his heart and soul refused to admit to himself that this could be—and he backed away, as if some ferocious beast were coming at him.

His lips formed an unspoken denial. And he fell back into his chair.

Monsignore Maraîcher took the floor.

"We are indebted to our faithful servants, Girolamo Barbieri and Franco—"

"Franco Aduanello," Monsignore Nichols cut in, helping him out.

But John had already regained his composure, and he snorted, oozing with contempt, "Gigi and Babu! Ha, *il Babuino,* the baboon, Monsignore Maraîcher! That is what they call this Aduanello! It might interest you to know that the character also eats like an ape—

at least, if you can call what he does eating. He more properly *devours* his food—ten bananas and several pounds of peanuts a day! Babu, indeed! Babu and Gigi, the inseparable pair! It's unbelievable that you should not know about these two!"

"Two devoted agents of our Vatican police," Nichols put in.

"Two devoted double agents of the CIA would be more like it! Or were you all unaware of that?"

John got up from his seat and, pointing like Christ the Avenger toward the opened case, roared, "Now, those tapes—those tapes that were probably recorded at the Institute, or at its annex on the Via Sottocolle next door—sure, they're records, transcripts, that is, of my phone conversations, no doubt—and don't you imagine that copies of them and the files before you have already found their way to Langley, Virginia? Of course they have. Stolen and sent there by our Vatican police specialists."

Monsignore di Galeazzo-Consalvi bent toward his neighbor's ear and asked Monsignore Maraîcher, "Langley?"

"Headquarters of the CIA, eminent colleague," the Frenchman replied.

"But then, that's the American secret police, isn't it? I don't understand . . ."

John had sunk down into his chair again. He could feel the brass knuckles in his jeans pocket, and the contact filled him with new drive and daring. He realized he should try as quickly as possible to win Paul VI over to his side. And with apparent serenity he turned toward the Pontiff and said, "Your Holiness must remember having put me in charge of military and police matters at the Vatican some years ago."

"Yes, my very dear son," the Pope replied amicably. "And we have not forgotten that it was you who saved our poor earthly life the day when some feeble mind tried to assassinate us in Bombay."

"Very Holy Father, you are being too kind. But I am sure the Very Holy Father will believe me if I assure him that those two Vatican agents are also agents of the CIA."

"But they are Italians, aren't they, my son?"

"Not really Italians, Holy Father. Just Italian-Americans who have lived here so long now that they have reverted to type, if I may use that expression. I found out about them at that time, just as I found out which of our Swiss Guards were on Moscow's payroll!"

"Moscow?"

At the exclamation, all eyes inevitably turned toward the two officers standing at attention by the door. But John added reassuringly, "Not those two. They are loyal servitors and valiant soldiers: Helmuth Höfflin von Brag and Jean-Louis Davos, who was the one who taught me what the guard was all about. Your Holiness owes your life more to his advice than to my own initiative."

The two Guard officers had not moved an eyelash or evinced the slightest awareness of what was going on. But their eyes were thanking John without the other cardinals being aware of the intercommunication.

The Pope in his turn nodded his appreciation to them.

But Monsignore Nichols, unwilling to admit that his colleague Flaherty knew more about the Vatican and its secrets than he who had been there so much longer, haughtily commented:

153

"If what has been said is true, if Barbieri and Adua-nello are working for the CIA, why have they not been dismissed from our own service?"

"My good colleague is perhaps unaware that that is not the way to handle double agents," Flaherty replied with an edge of sarcasm. "I hope Your Holiness will excuse my going into some of these rather sordid details," he added, turning to the Pope, and then continued, "but my brothers should know of this. When one discovers that a spy is playing a double game, the first step is to neutralize him. That is, keep him where he can do you no harm."

John, absolutely delighted to be able to offer this demonstration, wrinkled his nose and eyelids, as if he were trying to keep from laughing.

"After that," he went on, "well, you—*co-opt* or *turn* him, to use the technical term, and he becomes a triple agent.

"Perhaps my eminent colleague of the Curia never wondered where we got those fully detailed reports on how the American secret service works, which we have had at our disposal ever since I, with the help of God, was able to turn these two gentlemen referred to as Gigi and Babu."

He could feel himself getting hot under the collar again, and his tone rising.

"No, my eminent colleague obviously never did wonder about that. He simply trusted the Baboon and his sidekick and set them to spying on the Institute—and see where that has led! At this very moment, if Gigi and Babu have done their job properly, the specialists at Langley are enjoying the opportunity of going over the secret accounts at the Institute, the annual reports, and even the keys to the coded accounts. They probably now know exactly what is in account number 16-16."

"Number 16-16?" old Galeazzo-Consalvi asked in a stage whisper of his neighbor, and the French cardinal told him, "His Holiness's personal account."

At the same time, the Pope was instructing the recording priest, by a discreet wave of the hand, to strike Monsignore Flaherty's last sentence from the record.

"They now know at Langley," John was going on.

"Have no fear!" Monsignore Nichols abruptly interrupted. "Have no fear, eminent colleague. There is nothing of the sort on any of these magnetic tapes! No one at Langley will see what the assets of double 16 may be. These tapes were not recorded at the ICC, nor even at Via Sottocolle. No, these tapes all cover the activities of one Mr. Finnegan. One Mr. *Harold* Finnegan. Perhaps you've heard of him?"

"Harold Finnegan?" Flaherty exclaimed.

3

He could feel his faith falling away.

Not his faith in God, but the faith he had always had in himself, in his strength, his intelligence, his courage and clear-mindedness. For an hour now he had been fighting foot by foot against the stream of accusations coming against him, and now every word his colleagues spoke condemned him—for there was not one detail of his private life that they did not know about.

His private life? Actually, his double life. For it was this double life which, above all else, was a scandal to them.

What if he *was* involved in staging a coup in the Middle East?

"After all," Monsignore di Galeazzo-Consalvi would say, "those people are only infidels." For the Cardinal's title of nobility went back to the Crusades; and the more senile he became, the more his manner of thinking unconsciously aped that of the Dark Ages.

What if he *had* cheated on the Italian tax system?

There was nothing wrong in robbing that government of robbers, those usurpers of the Universal Church's temporal power! That was a viewpoint that Monsignore Nichols could readily agree with.

Had he associated with some of the worst sharpers in the dubious world of shady finance?

"Our presence among such sinners can only have a moralizing influence on their behavior," Cardinal Flaherty had asserted, not without some hypocrisy, and on this Cardinal McAwkleen had seconded him.

No, all of his business shenanigans, however improper in their eyes, could be justified and rationalized, and they were all casuists enough to absolve the president of the ICC a hundred times of his venial sins. But what the Vigilance Committee could not accept was that he had led a double life, had a double identity.

And Monsignore Maraîcher was quick to quote to him Matthew 6:24: " 'No man can serve two masters. For either he will hate the one, and love the other: or he will sustain the one, and despise the other. You cannot serve God and mammon,' in other words, money, wealth."

Coming slowly back from the depression that had overcome him in the last few moments, John resumed his defense in a colorless voice:

"Everything I did was done for the greater glory of Our Lord. I did it all only to serve Him. Believe me, it was not for my own enjoyment that I assumed this . . . this second skin. But in the painful mission assigned me, it seemed to me"—he turned to the Pope— ". . . yes, and it also seemed to the Holy Father . . . Well, it seemed to us that so great an end, so edifying a goal, if I may so express it, seemed to justify the means which rightly strike you as strange. . . . Yet, they are means that a Della Rovere, a Zanti, a Medici, or a Galeazzo of olden times would not have found unacceptable . . ."

"Eminent colleague," Monsignore Maraîcher volunteered, "we are living in the twentieth century, not the fifteenth or sixteenth!"

"Well I know it! But neither have I forgotten the teachings of Monsignore Walkman, my mentor to whom I owe so much. Monsignore Walkman used to say, 'Are we of such little faith that we no longer know how to defend the Church? Are we of such little faith that we are ashamed of our strength, our wealth?' "

Unconsciously, he had closed his fist as if he were about to deliver an uppercut, and it was strange to see that martial hand emerging from the red-bordered sleeve of the cassock. He went on, more vehemently still: "Well, there are the facts! I *have* led what small minds might call a double life. But that was only so as not to compromise the dignity of the Church in sordid matters of finance. It was so that businessmen might deal with Harold Finnegan, the banker and president of the AMDG, and not with His Excellency John Cardinal Flaherty, *in partibus* bishop of Aurea-Azurea in Phrygia and curator of the Institute for Christian Charity. Yes, I swear it to you: it was only the better to serve God and His Holiness!"

"And yet, you did not even have the decency to be present at Saint Peter's on the day of the resurrection of Our Lord!" Monsignore McAwkleen craftily protested.

But now the Pope intervened for the second time since the start of the discussion, and in a voice full of gentleness recalled to the bishop of Laodicea in Numidia: "My very dear son, have you forgotten what Saint Paul said to the Colossians: 'Let no man therefore judge you in meat or in drink, or in respect of a festival day.' Let us cleave to the object of this special meeting. None among us, I am sure, would even sug-

159

gest that Cardinal Flaherty is anything but a good Christian. His faith is as solid and as . . . agile . . . as his athletic body," he added with a smile, the mild irony of which was perceptible to none other than John, who thanked him with an equally subtle flicker of his eyelids.

Monsignore di Galeazzo-Consalvi, who had been dozing for a good half hour, suddenly awoke and grasped at the chance to show how obsequious he could be to the Supreme Pontiff. "I approve what His Holiness says, brothers," he commented. "After all, what have we against Monsignore Flaherty?"

"What do we have against him?" Monsignore Mc-Awkleen roared back. "Why, all the proofs are before us of the most shameful swindle involving the Institute and Flaher—well, Harold Finnegan."

"A swindle?" Flaherty asked, amazed.

"Yes, John, you heard me: a swindle! Let me tell you, Monsignore di Galeazzo, that Finnegan, or Cardinal Flaherty, if you prefer, invested the monies of the Institute in petroleum ventures in Ahmat-Ahbat."

"Of course!" John exploded. "Why should the Institute not be in on such an immense source of future profits?"

"Well, that is not what I am condemning. But now we know that you are fomenting a coup d'état in the emirate. We know that you are behind a so-called Haraoui National Liberation Movement, which is laying claim to lands—"

"—which it is historically entitled to!"

"Precisely! And we also know that, flying in the face of any known morality, you are planning to fleece the chief of the Haraouis—just as you are fleecing Emir Farouh-Ahbat, whom you plan to replace by his exiled brother Fuad—"

"That is not true! Not true at all! All I did was—"

"Double-cross still someone else, perhaps? Perhaps you were planning to betray this Fuad as well? Have you lost your mind, John? Have you let power go to your head to this extent?"

"Patrick, Patrick, you, my friend, you with whom I—"

"I am no friend to a swindler who dreams up diabolical schemes," McAwkleen came back. "Planning to supply arms to the rebels so they can help Prince Fuad overthrow Farouh—and then planning to betray the rebels by launching an army against them, an army organized by a capo of the Syndicate, the Cosa Nostra!"

"A capo of the Syndicate?" John cried out, beside himself, as he stood up and pushed his chair back. "A member of the Mafia?"

"Just what I said: a notorious mafioso! A criminal! A swindler! One Eliah Varese!"

"I forbid you to say that!" Flaherty cried. "Eliah is not a criminal! You are bearing false witness against a good Christian. And what is more, against a Jew who has embraced our faith! Eliah is a true Catholic, a benefactor who has given tens of thousands of dollars to good works year after year after year. You know who the anonymous donor was who paid for restoring the tombs of St. Donatus and St. Alphonse? It was he!"

John was at the end of his rope, and his two American colleagues were watching him with an air of scornful pity, while Monsignore Galeazzo-Consalvi shook his head and repeated in an idiotic tone, "Turpe est! Turpissime! This is shameful, completely shameful!" and Monsignore Maraîcher, waving the loose sheets from a file, was shouting, "Swindlers, crooked bankers, shyster lawyers, mafiosi, killers, and —and Magdalenes! That is the kind of people Harold

Finnegan lives with, the kind of people Flaherty lives with!"

"It's not true! Not true!" John was answering. "All of that is nothing but lies!"

He was as if drunk, intoxicated by his rage. And that was when Monsignore McAwkleen viciously waved a tape in his face.

"We have the proofs of your shameful carryings-on right here," he stormed. "Your licentiousness with a Magdalene, one Claudine, Claudine Lambaire . . ."

Terrified by all this, the Pope sat up in his seat. The young recording priest rushed to his assistance, and the Pope said a few inaudible words to him: he was begging to be helped from this room, where, he seemed to be saying, he had already heard much too much.

The doors of the library closed behind him as Cardinal Flaherty was recoiling in horror, gasping, "H-how, h-how can you? H-how could you? Oh, how abject you are! All of you so abject! To spy on people! To snoop into their private lives! Oh, Patrick, Patrick, of you I never expected this!"

His fist flew out as if he could no longer control it.

He was all over Monsignore McAwkleen, striking him on the head, in the stomach, slapping him. . . . McAwkleen fell under the blows, got up, tried meekly to protect himself, and then fell again.

While John just kept hitting him, as the other cardinals sat there, nonplussed.

Finally, the Swiss Guard officers rushed over to pull the men apart. Monsignore McAwkleen's face was puffed with bruises, his eyebrow bleeding. And John's hands were bloody, his lips foaming, his eyes wild.

Lieutenant Colonel Helmuth Höfflin von Brag had gotten a grip on him, while his aide Jean-Louis Davos was helping the archbishop up from the floor and helping him to a couch, where McAwkleen passed out.

But John, who could not get over his humiliation, broke away from the man's grasp and turned against the guard, tearing his cassock against the graved steel of the other's inlaid breastplate.

Then the cardinals saw the two of them roll on the floor, locked in a terrible struggle: the metal clanged against the marble while the coffered ceiling returned the echoes of their terrible panting and repeated the dull impact of the blows.

Höfflin's helmet rolled on the floor with a terrifying crash.

John groaned long and furiously.

Then he fell again, struck in the side by an inadvertent blow from the guard officer's knee.

Everything went black. He had fainted.

"My eminent colleague is well aware that we no longer have any prison cells. The few that were left were turned to other uses during the pontificate of John XXIII," Monsignore Nichols unctuously whispered.

Indeed, the Vatican had not had a prisoner in years. And one could count on the fingers of one hand those who had been locked up at the Holy See within the past century.

There was a Piedmontese antifascist who had been arrested in 1933 as he prepared to assassinate Mussolini. The young fanatic had been sheltered by one of his fellow townsmen, a gatekeeper at the Vatican. But the Italian police had gotten wind of the plot and had him arrested: a bomb he had fashioned was found in the quarters of the overtrusting gatekeeper.

Then, after World War II, there was Monsignore

Cipicco, a swindler who had promised some rich Italians that he could shift their wealth to Switzerland through the good offices of the Administration of the Patrimony of the Apostolic See, which was not subject to the monetary laws then in force in their country. But unfortunately, that worldly intriguing prelate simply "forgot" to effect the transfer and they were out their money.

Finally, more recently, a petty burglar was caught red-handed stealing from the sacristy of St. Peter's and was condemned to six months' detention at the Vatican.

And the detention there had as good an effect on him as it had had on the young Piedmontese atheist: the latter, while there, had become converted to Catholicism, and the thief did not want to leave at the end of his sentence, for he found the food too good and the view too appealing, looking out as it did over the gardens of the Belvedere.

But once he was released, that last cell had been converted into a garage, with its bars taken out.

"But we must find a place to lock him up," Monsignore McAwkleen was now insisting, aquiver with his unfulfilled desire for revenge.

"You are right," Monsignore Nichols agreed, "but don't forget that there hasn't been any trial. At most, all we can do is hold him for safekeeping—"

"And for medical assistance," Lieutenant Colonel Höfflin von Brag presumed to chime in, contrite as he was at having wounded His Eminence John Cardinal Flaherty.

"Yes, yes, of course, for medical assistance," Monsignore Nichols acquiesced, irritated at having to be reminded by a Swiss guard of the demands of Christian charity. "But, tell me, Colonel, don't you people have a disciplinary guardhouse, or whatever you call it?"

"The Punishment Room, Your Excellency, or sometimes it's called the Room of Pain."

"Yes, that's it. Down in the cellar of your barracks, isn't it?"

"Yes, Your Excellency. But in point of fact, we've not had to use it for several years."

"Oh, it saw plenty of goings-on in the last century!" chuckled Cardinal di Galeazzo-Consalvi, interrupting them.

The officer gave His Eminence a cold stare, which was meant to quash any such dishonorable insinuations. What Monsignore di Galeazzo-Consalvi was referring to was the widespread rumor that at the end of the nineteenth century this Room of Pain had been the scene of sadomasochistic orgies in which the Swiss Guards used the old torture implements as tools of pleasure—undoubtedly a tale without any foundation in fact. And Helmuth Höfflin von Brag was too upright a person to lend any credence to it. He went on: "I hardly think that room is presently suitable to accommodate His Excellency Cardinal Flaherty with the respect and honors due him. But we do have at the barracks a sort of apartment in which the officers sometimes receive guests and put them up. Might I suggest to Your Excellencies that we might—uh—lend it to Monsignore Flaherty for the night?"

"You are of good counsel, Colonel," Monsignore Maraîcher thanked him. "That is how it shall be done. Tonight, Flaherty will be the guest of the gentlemen officers of the Swiss Guard."

"Their prisoner," Monsignore McAwkleen corrected him, barely above a whisper. "*Our* prisoner!"

165

4

Where was he?

And why was it dark all around him?

He kept trying to remember the sequence of the day's events. He could see that trip in the long black Vatican City limousine, wedged in between Gigi and Babu, who in his present feverish state seemed even huger to him than they actually were. He remembered a prelate leading him through the apostolic quarters to the door of the Pope's private library. He saw himself seated facing that black case with contents that intrigued him: hideous celluloid snakes that uncoiled from it and writhed over the bloodred velvet table cover.

Then he had a picture of himself striking the lieutenant colonel of the Swiss Guard. And he understood.

He felt desperate.

He was dying of thirst and wanted to pray, to beg pardon of God, for he suddenly felt oh! so weak and so afraid of dying. But no word came to his lips. They moved but made no sound.

He sat up, wiped the sweat from his brow, and breathed noisily. He *had* to find something to drink; that, before anything else.

He got up, felt his way along the walls toward what seemed to him a half-open door. His fingers touched a switch, and the light went on, blinding him, but it also made him want to cry out with joy: he had just regained his senses. He knew where he was now, in a reception apartment of the Swiss Guard barracks.

He went to a washbasin sealed into a recess in the wall and took a long drink of water right from the faucet. Then he doused his face and looked about the room he had been brought to. It was a fine, large vaulted room, with a big bed in it, a lectern, an old gilt-wood table with a Bible on it, a missal, and—he wondered why—a pontifical directory. There were also two baroque armchairs and a faldistory, one of those huge armed prie-dieus of the kind reserved for princes of the Church. All of it spick-and-span with a good smell of polish. Facing the bed there was a pious picture in the worst possible kind of cheap taste: the martyrdom of St. Sebastian in greenish, bituminous colors. Awful! was his reaction. But at the same time it occurred to him that he was suffering the same fate as the saint in the picture: his body was pierced through with arrows, shot through with fever.

He had his wits back now, and with them his courage. He had been able to make his heart stop its wild thumping. And there was a new ardor about him. Still somewhat unsteady on his feet, he went toward the low door that was half hidden by a pillar of the vault and tried to keep from breathing: behind the sculptured-wood panel two natives of the Canton de Valais were whispering between yawns in their slow Swiss drawl.

He was under guard! But his jailers were Swiss, and the Swiss revered him since the days when he had been bodyguard to His Holiness Paul VI, his "holy gorilla," as they jestingly referred to him. He knew how brave and loyal they could be; this gave him hope. These were not the sinister employees of the pontifical police force; they were soldiers. With their help, he would be able to get out.

He cleared his voice and called, "Hello, out there! What time is it?"

"Nearly two, Monseigneur," they humbly replied.

He thanked them, went back to lie down, and had no sooner done so than he heard the bells of Santo Stefano ring twice, followed immediately by those of St. Martin of the Swiss, and then the tolling of St. Peter's.

He tried to picture Vatican City asleep, all lights out except those of Radio Vatican, which is on the air all night for the whole world to hear, and probably those in the little office the Pope had had set up for himself on the fourth floor of the apostolic palace.

John was filled with compassion as he thought back on that night last summer when the Supreme Pontiff had kept him so long at his side for company because he could not face the prospect of another terrifying night of insomnia. The cardinal and the Pope had discussed theology at length out on the little terrace behind the high walls that he had had built outside his room. It was hollow-sounding, almost like a well, with a square of starry sky visible above: John had been struck by the quasi-"metaphysical" austerity of this place where Paul VI sat up on the beautiful summer nights when he was not at Castel Gandolfo. He had mentioned the fact, and the Holy Father had answered, somewhat enigmatically, "Well, isn't that the way Dante described purgatory?"

John could still see himself, sitting on a couch and listening to the *Agnus Dei* while His Holiness, who kept none of his staff on duty after ten P.M. checked over the available supply of bottles. There were over a hundred, sent to him by the various convents and monasteries around the world that practice distilling.

"Which Chartreuse shall we honor?" he had asked somewhat jestingly, before pouring them some gentian liqueur.

Later in the night they had gotten around to questions of protocol and ritual, and John had brought up sacerdotal vestments. Although he had recently made them as simple as possible, the Pope showed how interested he was in the subject, and in one of those outgoing movements that so surprised persons admitted to his intimacy, he cried out, "Flaherty, have you ever seen my wardrobe?"

An amazed John had followed him into a large closet off his bedroom, where he was shown a wide variety of cappas, mozzettas, copes, miters, surplices, capes, farraiolas, and birettas, and a splendid panoply of velvets, furs, silks, embroidery, laces, and jewels, such as he had never imagined could exist anywhere.

Then he saw the Pope take down from a hanger a lace alb with fluted white silk velvet in front, and heard him say in a voice broken with contained emotion, "This is the alb I was ordained in. It was made from my mother's wedding gown. I still sometimes wear it when I say Mass."

John then thought that his mother, Mrs. Flaherty, had probably not been married in the kind of white dress that the wealthy Signora Montini had worn: his mother went to church in her everyday dress, mended and carefully ironed. But then he regretted this un-Christian lack of charity. He told himself the Holy Father must indeed feel lonely if he let himself go to such unseemly demonstrations of friendship—and he felt compassion for him.

170

"I feel as if I were a prisoner in the Vatican," Paul VI had said to him, as the night was coming to an end.

And now, was not he also a prisoner in the Vatican?

How long would they keep him here? How long would he have to remain within these four walls, listening to every sound in the night? Counting the stars in every pane squared off by the bars outside his window? Counting the wounds on St. Sebastian's body in the awful picture, the only bright red spots in the horrible mud-and-stagnant-water-colored daub? And thinking and rethinking his regrets and remorse?

Exaltation gave way to depression, depression to exaltation. He heard the quarter hour sound, and then the half. And later he wasn't sure whether it was three or four o'clock that Santo Stefano had pealed.

Then he became aware of being hungry. He had had nothing to eat since yesterday morning, when they came to arrest him in his gym. And at that sudden recollection, he clenched his fists, instinctively, and all thought of repentance vanished.

"I have trampled on them in my indignation, and have trodden them down in my wrath, and their blood is sprinkled upon my garments, and I have stained all my apparel.

"For the day of vengeance is in my heart, the year of my redemption is come."

How these verses from Isaias, which he had thought were forever buried deep within his soul, now ran through his head! He remembered them as well as the first time he had learned them. And he longed for times past.

A nightingale lighted on the window bar and sang of the breaking dawn. For a second he imagined the bird was caged in the whole universe, while he himself was outside it.

His faith in God returned with his faith in himself.

Then he turned out the light and lay down completely in the dark, in order to be alone with his trouble and chew upon it, the way you chew on a crust of bread through your sobs when you are a child.

Bread! Nice fresh rye bread and corn bread from the Jewish bakeries on Knickerbocker and Graham avenues, its warm aroma mixing with the smells of gefilte fish, and honey, and rock candy at the corner of Siegel Street. And farther on, oh! yes, when he went as far as Johnson Avenue, to pick Eliah up at the Vareses', there was the Italian shop that sold apple turnovers and in summer cherry ices. Right next to the five-and-dime, where you could get toy revolvers so realistic-looking that once he had scared a cop with one. And just beyond, the *salumeria* with its spicy Italian pepperoni and pepperoncini that you munched on as you went toward the corner of Meserole and Oak Street, that the Jewish kids called *Kack* Street, Turd Street.

And after that, India Street, down in Greenpoint, with Moe Lou, the tattoo artist. That was the name of the tattooer on India Street: Moe Lou. Right down near the East River docks.

It all might have been a jungle, but it was *his* jungle! His home! His country! His turf!

His and the Devils'.

John felt himself shiver as these memories came back to him, and only much later, when day had broken, did he finally fall asleep.

5

The old man started yelling again and poor Ma cried, and the twins vomited everything in them all over the bed he and Willie slept on, and Maria had hysterics, and Ryan who had "borrowed" his belt just for the afternoon, he said, wasn't home yet. Well, he wouldn't get off any easier just 'cause he tried to outwait him, and all. . . . What a jerk that one was!

And then, as if all that wasn't enough of a mess, the truant officer came—the cockeyed one!—and told his folks that he'd played hooky and beat up Mr. Hathaway, and all. And it wasn't even true. He never *beat up* no Mr. Hathaway. All he done was land a fist on his ass, just hard enough to show him who he was talkin' to.

So he slammed the door, disgusted with the whole unfair business. He went downstairs, sliding down the banister all the way, yelling "So long!" and thinking "You never gonna see me no more"! And disappeared into the night, keeping to the middle of the street, but always on the side where it was darkest.

Like a lone wolf.

It was cold enough to freeze the balls off a brass monkey, but he didn't give a fuck! He was on his own turf, here in the street, in Williamsburg! It was his bailiwick—the Devils made the law here!

He owned the street, and swaggered down it, whistling the Irish sea chanty his old man would croak when he got drunk as a lord and all, meaning every night around six o'clock:

> Let me go there, Ma!
> I'll cover ye with lace
> And chocolate, hoo-ha!
> Ma, there's work in that place!
> I'll come back carryin'
> Girls for the marryin',
> One for my brother,
> One for me . . .

What a lotta crap! That's what the micks sang who wanted to cross over here! 'N' the poor bastards never knew all there was in America was unemployment! Nobody told 'em about the Depression, the crash, Black Thursday, and all that there. Or how in Williamsburg, every Friday, Monday, and Sunday was just as black too!

The song was a lotta crap, but he hummed it with such defiance that it scared the shit out of the yellow-bellies on Stagg.

They heard that and they knew John K. Flaherty was on the loose.

He dug his fists into the pockets of his cheap little corduroy jacket, patched a thousand times. He had a red scarf around his neck, over the white undershirt that Ma washed every day. His cap was pulled down over his eye, and the "overhauls" he'd gotten when he was eight, threadbare now, barely came below his knees—Jee-suss! was he ever freezing! But on his

174

feet he had his own brogues, the ones he had fitted out with razor blades and sharp nails, and Ma was not allowed to touch 'em, not even to give 'em a shine!

Well, everybody in the neighborhood—especially the momma's boys—knew enough to keep out of his way when he went up Graham toward Greenpoint. Yeah, this was his turf all right! He had earned the leadership of it with his fists, his feet, his knife, sometimes even his teeth. He always laughed when he thought of the day he bit the ass of that old kike on Siegel Street because he yelled at him for swiping three pretzels! The kind of Yid that wore one of them black hats and the curls on the side.

It cost some hard knocks, and some blood, and some busted teeth, but block after block, house after house, he had conquered his share of Williamsburg. And he knew every corner of it, every hiding place. He could 'a' gone through it with his eyes closed and known where he was just from the smells, if he'd 'a' been blind like poor old Wee, who sold licorice and gumdrops over on Meserole. He'd 'a' known he was on McKibben from the special smell of matzos and kosher meat. Siegel, from the fish and honey. Then suddenly, when ya went across Johnson Avenue, it smelled of tomatoes, and basil, and oregano: this was wop town. At the corner of Montrose there was a high blank wall and someone had chalked on it:

REMEMBER SACCO AND VANZETTI

Prob'ly two ball teams, but he never did find out which one won the game! Next door, there was Rossini, the Black Hand guy—a bastard who took a cut from everything the poor people in the neighborhood earned. But he was the one who organized those operas, too—the ones Ma used to sing in, in the old days. By now, she cried so much, Ma, she lost her voice.

A little farther, on Ten Eyck, there was the mission where the bums lined up for free soup. They didn't know that all you had to do was slip in from behind, and *screw you!* to be first in line for the "Rockefeller special." At number 84, there was a yard, and you had to keep a sharp eye out, account of the fire escape. Sometimes one of those son-of-a-bitch Black Fangs would be hiding on it. So you had to pretend you didn't see the shitass and then—just when he dropped, not a second too soon or a second too late—you ducked sideways and let him bounce on the pavement! Whammo!

Once in his young life John had ventured over the bridge, into that holy of holies, Manhattan, all by himself. He had wandered up Broadway from the Lower East Side, and gotten onto Fifth Avenue. Then, around Times Square, he had seen the big movie houses with the cutouts of beautiful girls in front of them, throwing kisses to you—even bigger than the movies on Flatbush Avenue. And the ushers and doormen outside, with enough stripes to be full generals and all. And banks and jewelry stores and department stores and limousines with chauffeurs driving them and all!

It was just too much!

But he had also seen the soup kitchens, and the cops breaking up a demonstration of the Workers Alliance in Union Square. He'd even fought it out with some of the bums who asked him to parade with them. Boy, if a guy only knew the ropes, he didn't have to be peddling apples: he could have the Packards and Rolls-Royces, and the platinum blondes like Jean Harlow,

176

and live in hotels where guys dressed like Civil War generals bowed to you when you went in or out.

He returned all dreamy to his own side of the East River. And for the first time in his life he knew Williamsburg was not The Whole World. How tiny, how wretched, how lousy it all was! He wasn't king of anything important. His turf was hardly big enough to be called a reservation.

Well, he'd have to spread out. He'd have to lead his Devils on the warpath again, rub out Eliah Varese's Black Fangs once and for all. They were trying to move closer to Waterbury Street. He'd have to put a stop to that! And now he heard that a new gang, called the Barracudas, was beginning to stake a claim to South Bushwick.

At twelve, John F. Flaherty was a head taller than most of the others his age, but a head shorter than most of his henchmen, who were anywhere from fifteen to seventeen. He called them lieutenants, and under their orders they had scouts, lookouts, and sentinels. Not to mention his two secret agents, two smart little ten-year-old Jewboys, Abe and Jesse. These two kept him informed of everything that went on in all those streets where he made the law—the law of the Devils!

Tribal neighborhoods in Williamsburg were so clearly marked off that going from one street to the next was like changing worlds. From Flushing to Grand Street you went from the Jew neighborhood to the Italians', and then you ran into the pigheaded Irish. Johnson Avenue was the dividing line between Italians and Jews. That was where the Varese family lived, and as if to show they belonged on both sides, their house was the only one that jutted out from the even rows. The Flahertys, too, lived in a kind of no-man's-land, a blind alley off Stagg, halfway between the Irish and the Italians. John's old man came from the Ould Sod, but Ma was a Nabouletan'. "Unstable household due to excessive ethnic and cultural differences," was the way John had seen the social worker from Relief write it in her report—not the truant officer who was cross-eyed, but the walleyed one who had one eye out toward Long Island while the other seemed to be taking in the Statue of Liberty. Ethnic differences, my ass! What was unstable was that the old man was a drunk and out of work, and Ma had her hands full with nine kids in two rooms, so she never got a chance to get out of the house. Anyway, there wasn't all that much difference between guineas and micks, all of 'em wouldn't wipe their asses without getting the priest's blessing. Or give up their liquor or wine, and to hell with Prohibition!

The Black Fangs, who blackened their front teeth to look fiercer and live up to their name, came from Humboldt, and the two gangs fought it out at the corner of Johnson. The leaders, Eliah and John, had command posts behind garbage cans under a porch. They waited until the others had fought it out before they came out to meet. They had an unspoken code of chivalry, like two feudal lords at war: they would appear at exactly the same moment, and meet exactly halfway, to have their duel—with each one's men encouraging him from a proper distance, to make everything even.

They fought till first blood, then each one went back to his own side after saluting his worthy opponent, and marched off with his own bloodied henchmen, who kept scaring passersby with their bloodcurdling shouts of "Devils!" or "Black Fangs!"

Except when the rumbles were cut short by a police siren approaching from Graham Avenue. Then Devils and Black Fangs would make a united front against the flatfeet. And the harness bulls didn't always come out on top, either!

But once they were gone it would be back to ringo-levio again.

The only person who could keep them apart was Father Killarly. He was the pastor of Holy Virgin, and the only "civilian" they were scared of: he was a red-headed giant who had been a football lineman, with hands bigger than hams, a thick neck, and pale Irish eyes, but in his black suit and Roman collar he was a holy terror.

He'd appear from nowhere and come right up to them in the middle of the intersection. Then he'd take a swing at Eliah while his elbow was shoving John in the solar plexus, and he'd yell at them:

"You lousy little bums! Cut that out! Don't you know that God doesn't approve of knives? Lemme have those now, and quit your stalling, Eliah! and you too, John!"

The strangest part was that Eliah did as he was told—and so did John. Without a complaint.

They might have jumped him, or even just threatened him—and maybe he would have gone away. But it never occurred to them. Father Killarly just naturally seemed to make everybody obey. No one had ever seen him really get sore. Even the people in the neighborhood who didn't belong to his church all agreed that he was "a saint." And John agreed with them, even though he expressed it differently: "That Father Killarly, he's sure got balls!"

* * *

179

One day John was getting high on ether with Tex and Billy, in a basement on Stagg Street, a few doors from where the Flahertys lived. Even at this distance, he could hear his old man, Patrick Flaherty, yelling his head off—but the sounds came to him through a cold, blue, slightly nauseating haze.

"I think I'm gonna heave," he told his lieutenants, who laughed about it, without really knowing why.

"You guys shut up!" he yelled at them, afraid they were making fun of him.

But just then Jesse and Abe came in with hot news: The Barracudas were shaking down some of the momma's boys in front of the drugstore.

"What?" he asked, suddenly sober. "Say that again!"

"Like we said, they been staked out near the drug store since this morning. They even grabbed Bad Bull and made him cough up!"

This was too much! Until now, the Devils had had an unspoken agreement with the Black Fangs, that left them the little streets to the south, Varet, Cook, and Debevoise. That way, he knew where they were and what they were doing. But never, so long as he could remember, had any Devil or Black Fang been made to pay protection. Only guys who weren't in their gangs were subject to blackmail. And now the son-of-a-bitches had taken one of his own scouts and put the screws on him.

That was a declaration of war. And if that was what the Barracudas wanted, it was okay by him.

Then Tex and Billy reminded him that there were twice as many Barracudas as Devils—especially since they took over the Knickerbockers. John was waving that objection away, but yet he was delighted when the two little Jewboys went on to say:

"Oh, another thing: Eliah Varese said he wants to

180

see ya! He told Mimi and Salsa. I think he's had it up to here with them Barracudas too, and he wants to make an alliance with you to beat the shit out of 'em."

"Wa-a-a-ll," John stalled, "maybe that's not such a bad idea. I always knew that Eliah was no dope. But he'll have to make it a fifty-fifty deal, and you let him know I'll meet him at Humboldt and Johnson, as usual. But no blackjacks and no switchblades. Jess, tell Salsa to tell him. And Abe, you go write on Varese's door, in chalk: *OK, Noon, the 25th.* He'll understand."

He'd known Eliah Varese for so long, and fought him so many times, that he had often wondered why they went on fighting instead of going partners. Come right down to it, John liked Eliah better than any of the guys in his own gang. And he was pretty sure Eliah felt the same way about him.

They were the leaders of two gangs, and the members of both were the same—a bunch of losers. What difference did it make that some called themselves Black Fangs and the others Devils?

They got together Christmas Day at noon.

The streets were icy and shining in the sunlight. Houses were garlanded and festooned for the occasion, and the neighborhood reflected the Christmas spirit, in spite of the lean years. At Humboldt and Johnson, a group of Salvation Army girls were caroling "Noël! Noël! Noël! Noël! Born is the king of Is-ra-ël!"

The advent of the Devils frightened them away, and they were barely out of earshot when marching feet were heard on Humboldt, followed shortly by the warcry, "Black Fangs forever!"

Twenty paces apart the two armies stopped, at the same instant, at a signal from their leaders.

Everything went silent. They all held their breaths, but the hatred between the two gangs was so thick you could cut it with a knife.

Then John and Eliah took three steps toward each other, signaling their men to stay where they were. And like an actor in a B western, Eliah ceremoniously opened his right hand and let his knife drop to the ground, while showing that his left was empty too. With a smile that left the Black Fangs speechless, John raised both of his empty hands as well: he had never really doubted his enemy's loyalty, and had come unarmed.

They took three more steps toward each other.

And then, all of a sudden, as if by agreement, their two voices rang out in an accord that neither one of them would ever forget, as long as they lived: "Flaherty! Varese! Varese! Flaherty!"

The war between them was over. They had just made sure of that. They were looking at each other, clapping each other on the back, and punching each other's arms in friendship, as they yelled to their men:

"Well, Black Fangs, join with the Devils!"

"United forever! Devils, what youse guys waiting for?"

Not a thing! The two gangs were fraternizing as if the corner of Humboldt and Johnson wasn't the place where for years they had regularly fought it out.

One day, maybe, just beneath "July 4, 1776: Declaration of Independence," history books would read, "December 25, 1937: Peace Treaty of Williamsburg."

John Kevin Flaherty and Eliah Mosè Varese didn't seem to think that was an impossibility.

* * *

With their two armies joined together, they were able to extend their influence to the ends of the known world: to the south, they made short work of the Barracudas, on the east they made themselves felt in Maspeth the next week, and even ventured north into Greenpoint. Eliah and John were now respected wherever they went.

They became inseparable. Such good friends that they began to wonder what they ever saw in the creeps who were their lieutenants. Devils and Black Fangs didn't mean a thing to them anymore: they were just a bunch of losers who were handy to have around once in a while, but who would grow up to be ordinary workingmen, or more likely unemployed, like their old men. Unless they became hoods, soldiers or point men in the Mafia if they were Italians, pickpockets, crooked bookies, or pimps if they were Irish. And sooner or later they'd get nabbed by the bulls, unless some rival gang took them for a ride before that.

But not John and Eliah; they were different. They had a wealth of ambition, and they were smart and intelligent besides.

They would "get theirs," as they solemnly assured each other, when they could be seen spending whole days together in Greenpoint, near the docks, swapping their dreams of power and glory. They'd "get theirs," no matter what they had to do to make it.

Eliah was already getting in on some pretty big deals, through mysterious "contacts" he had. Deals that he went in on alone, without tipping John wise. He even knew Pinelli, the caporegime who ran the neighborhood.

One January morning, three weeks after the Peace of Williamsburg, Rossini, the head of the Black Hand, was found in his home with his throat cut, his head hanging over his blood-soaked piano, with the score of *La Traviata* in his hands. There was panic in the neighborhood. There were rumors of the kind of gang war that had decimated Montrose five years before. Everybody stayed doggo.

But a couple of days later, as the two of them were going a couple of rounds in Mr. Romeo's gym, John had mentioned the incident to his friend, saying, "Boy, everybody's scared shitless in Williamsburg since what happened day before yesterday and all." And by the proud look in Varese's eyes he sensed that his friend knew more than he was telling about how the tenor had been done in.

John didn't approve of this way of getting ahead. Too risky, he thought. And besides, although he wouldn't have been able to put it into words, he felt that the gangster days were over. There had to be a better way out for a poor kid from Williamsburg, whose old man was an unemployed professional drunk and whose old lady went out doing housework. There had to be some other way to make it.

He had even once suggested aloud "studying for something." But Eliah had come back, "Studying is for pansies and jerks!"

"Well, listen, you poor bastard," John replied, "didn't you hear FDR on the radio yesterday? He said—"

"FDR! my ass!" Eliah cut him off. "Who you think he's kiddin'? He says whatever he wants, and jerks like you believe him!"

"Well, it's not that I believe him, but . . ."

But they would spend their whole days together, going over how impatient they were, in the streets down near the East River, streets with names like Huron, India, Java. And in Buddy's Bar, where they'd

184

get drunk on beer and make the world over. Or the little red brick house, with the after-hours club where they could forget they weren't masters of the world, during one of the jam sessions, when Negro musicians came in and played variations on "If I Get Lucky."

If they got lucky! In Java Street there was a whore-house called Mrs. Moore's, where sometimes they both "got lucky," with a little Jewish girl who took them both on at once at a combination rate. Once when John asked her why she charged them only one and a half times the going rate, she answered, "Because your friend doesn't have a lace curtain!" But then she quickly changed it to, "No, not really. You're both nice kids, and I like you. You're nice and polite, and one of you is tall and dark and the other one tall and blond." And as she said it, she would lean toward one and then the other, kissing them each on the back of the neck, and wondering out loud why they had to come and pay her to put out for them when they could probably hump some of the prettiest women in the world, and maybe even get paid for it, besides!

"Well, it's because you're a nice kid, too," John told her, deeply moved. "You're one of us, Sarah. Understand?"

"Besides," Eliah asked, "can't you just picture us as gigolos?"

The young girl said you could tell Eliah Mosè Varese was Italian when he said a thing like that.

"Well, I'll make you an honorary Devil," John told her, as he kissed her on the bellybutton.

"Oh, a Devil? Is that what that means? I was wondering why you had that tattoo."

A few days before, John had had a two-colored tattoo done on his right arm muscle by Moe Lou, a toothless old skinflint nicknamed the Pirate, who ran a small "candy store" on India Street. Actually, his main business was next door to the shop, in the shack where he lived and sold sailors and longshoremen coke right off the boat and untaxed cigarettes, and dispensed his own special salve that was guaranteed to cure the clap. He also did tattooing.

"I want an upside-down cross, with flames coming up on both sides of it, and written underneath: *I'm a Devil*," he told Moe Lou, as he stripped his shirt off and straddled the chair with the armrest for the tattooee.

"Gonna hurt," the old guy muttered, while he cleaned his needles and pens in alcohol and filled the pens with india ink.

"Leave it hurt," John said, tough and uncaring.

But he had to grit his teeth when he felt the fiery ink slip under his skin and run into the flame-shaped scarifications that The Pirate had just drawn on his arm.

From that day forward he was indelibly marked for what he was: A Devil.

"Goddamn Devil and goddamn Black Fang!" Varese sighed cynically when they came out of the whorehouse and walked through the icy night toward the drydocks, so menacingly dark despite the bluish oily glints here and there.

"Goddamn Devil!" John echoed. "To think we haven't got a dime between us. Didn't even have enough to give Sarah a nice tip. Or enough to have her for the whole night!"

"Listen, baby, we gotta pull one off together."

"Pull what off? You got any ideas?"

"Yes, I have," Eliah told him.

"What we gonna grab? The Statue of Liberty or the

Empire State Building? Or we gonna sell the Brooklyn Bridge?"

"No. Listen to me. You ever been inside the sacristy at Holy Virgin?"

"Why you wanna know? You been in there? Since when you go to Holy Virgin and not to *shul* with your parents?"

"Take it easy, nuttin' to get excited about. Lemme tell you. Sure I still go to *shul*—that is, when I feel like going. But one time Salsa dragged me into Father Killarly's church, and he said, 'Take a look, Eliah. Lookit all that stuff in the sacristy!' You know, that's what you Catholics call the place where the priests change their clothes. Where they keep all their stuff for the services."

"Yep, I know all about it. I was in there when little Tommy got baptized last year."

"Well, di'n't you notice?"

"Notice what?"

"The crosses, and the vases, and all that schmear of gold stuff with precious stones in 'em."

"Hey, whatsamatta you?" John protested. "You think I'm gonna rob the Holy Virgin? Some idea! Why not go and steal what they got in your *shul* instead?"

"First of all, 'cause there's not much there to swipe. And besides, they keep it all locked up. But in Father Killarly's joint, everything's wide open. You can help yourself and bye-bye baby. No one's the wiser . . ."

"Could be," John agreed, "but I ain't pullin' no job in no church."

"Whatsamatta? You got cold feet or somethin'? You t'ink you gonna burn in hell?"

"What the hell you think I am? Of course not. But just the same—"

"I don't know what's the same," Eliah insisted. "You a Devil or not? That's all I wanna know."

"Looka my arm. Does that make me a Devil, huh? What kind of a friggin' Black Fang are you?"

"Okay, then?"

"Sure, okay. But on one condition. Afters, we knock over your place, too, the *shul* on Knickerbocker. No reason just to take from the church. Gotta be fair, after all."

"Fair is fair, all right. I dig you, kid. Okay!"

"And after that, how about the pagodas?"

"We won't forget them," Eliah agreed. "We'll go into Chinatown and knock them off too."

"Right! Chinatown!"

And arm in arm, laughing merrily, they headed toward the end of the pier and the dark waters of the East River.

6

Mrs. Rossana Flaherty wrung her hands as she sobbed and then grabbed the policeman's jacket to beg him to listen. He had arrived at their home to take John, her big boy, to reform school. In the opposite corner of her kitchen, the social worker and the truant officer, Daisy who was cross-eyed, and Minnie the walleyed one, were doing their best to keep Maria, the twins, and Alice quiet. All four had run under the kitchen table and were screaming like banshees. The old man, Patrick, had his chair tilted back against the sink, and looked on as if he didn't understand. In the bedroom, Willy and Ryan were singing a disrespectful song about the police.

But the cop remained determinedly polite and even a bit haughty. He was looking right into Mrs. Flaherty's sad Italian eyes and saying, "We got no choice, Mrs. Flaherty. Today your John's just a thief. But tomorrow he might kill someone. We have to teach him a lesson before it's—"

"No, no!" she interrupted. "Please give him a break!"

The officer had to raise his voice to make himself heard.

"Your John's a smart boy, Mrs. Flaherty," he said in his Irish brogue. "And he's got guts, too, in his way."

189

"Oh, yes, Officer, lotsa guts. You should hear him stand up to his father."

"But I'm afraid it's gone too far already. And if he keeps loafing around in the streets . . ."

He was trying to reason with her. He felt sorry for the poor woman. But her sobs just got louder. Rossana Flaherty was in hysterics and shouting in a hoarse and broken voice.

"No, no, please, Mr. Officer. What'll happen to me without him? Without my John? He's the one who protects me when his father beats me. You can't take him. He's my firstborn. What'll become of me without him? I need him—to protect me. That old man'll kill me!"

And as if to prove she was not lying, Patrick Flaherty suddenly jumped to his feet and started yelling, "Can't you shut your trap? Shut up, you dirty dago! Listen to what the man's saying. A killer—that's what your John is, a killer. Like Paul and Ryan. Like all his goddamned sisters and brothers. You hear me? Shut your goddamned trap!"

He was threatening his wife, and the officer had to come to her defense. "Mr. Flaherty, please!" he was saying.

"Don't give me no Mr. Flaherty," the drunken man replied, shaking all over almost as if he had the d.t.'s. "Forget the Mr. Flaherty. I had all I can take of this shit, and all them tears. Just gimme your paper. I'll sign it. And then you can lock the good-for-nothin' up and throw away the key, for all I care. To hell with him. Just get 'im the hell outta here."

The officer was still insisting, "You know, we're just doing this for his own good."

But by now Patrick Flaherty had opened the window and was addressing the world at large: "You heard

me! To hell with him! Him and his slob of a mother!
And all the rest of those little bastards! To hell with
'em all!"

Way down on Stagg Street, where he was hearing
this outburst, Father Killarly crossed himself and
prayed for courage. He had to get the little hood away
from those wild people; it was God's will. But by the
same token, he couldn't leave the boy in the hands of
the police and their so-called system of justice. In a
reform school or a juvenile prison, John would be cor-
rupted much more seriously than ever he could be on
the streets of Williamsburg. This was what he had to
prove to the officer and those social workers. He had
often helped them in their job, but this was no ordinary case.

John wasn't just another one of the loafers whose
souls were Father Killarly's concern, as their behavior
was the concern of the authorities. No, he wasn't one
of those unfortunates. John was handsome as are all
special people, and in his eyes shone the light given
only to the Chosen. For all the evil things the boy had
been known to do, the pastor of Holy Virgin was sure
that deep within John's heart there was true natural
goodness. He had great intelligence—unfortunately so
far never put to any good use—as well as great kindness. This had been revealed to the father more than
once. But John had never known how to show it toward anyone except his ma.

Yes, John, he was sure, was touched with divine
grace.

And Father Killarly was a Jansenist: he believed in
predestination.

"To work!" the Father exhorted himself as he
turned into Stagg Alley. But just as he was about to go
up the steps to the Flahertys' tenement, he saw John

191

suddenly appear from nowhere—and saw him turn back when he heard the shouting from the apartment window as he spied the patrol wagon parked just a short way down on Stagg.

John was adept as a gutter cat silently going through the cold darkness, but Father Killarly was already upon him. He grabbed his wrist and twisted it behind his back.

"Killarly!" the boy exclaimed, in a cry of pain.

"Yes, Killarly, it is!" the priest replied, pushing him up the stairs. "Father Killarly to you! Come on! Come along, you ne'er-do-well! Upstairs. Right now!"

"Father, please! Father!"

"You're coming along with me, brat!"

"Father!"

"Sure, 'n' now ye're askin' fer me pity," the priest said, suddenly sounding like a vaudeville Irishman. "But don't ye think I know 'twas you who stole into me sacristy this afternoon with young Varese?"

"Oh, Father—"

"And don't ye think I know ye sold those precious chalices to that fence, Moe Lou? I know iverything therr is to know, young Jawn!" And with those words, he kept shoving him up the steps, using his fists and feet to force him along.

Finally he opened the Flahertys' door and drove the missing delinquent right into the officer's arms.

"Well, 'n' thanks be to you, Father," the latter said.

But Patrick Flaherty was already grabbing at his son as if to choke him and yelling, "Murrrtherer!" while Father Killarly jumped between them and Mrs. Flaherty, throwing herself at the pastor's feet, sobbed, "Oh, Father! Father! I'm so ashamed! My son—stealing from the church. Oh, Lord! Please, Father, pray God to forgive him."

She was out of her mind with worry and pain, and it showed in her eyes. The priest, keeping calm, helped the policeman to get her up and seat her on a chair.

"Get hold of yourself, my daughter," the Father said to her. "I've come here to take charge of John. I don't want him sent to reform school or to jail. He will make good for those chalices and crucifixes he stole, and I will withdraw the charges against him."

John looked at him, amazed. The charges were going to be dropped! So the cop might as well beat it, and the social workers too. His eyes went to Father Killarly in thanks, as his hand began signaling the other intruders to make themselves scarce.

Then, without changing his tone, the Father added, "As of Monday, John will be enrolled at the Immaculate Conception Seminary. I will see to it that my friend Father McIntyre gives him full Christian supervision."

At first the words didn't penetrate. They were just words. But then, all of a sudden, John was thunderstruck. So—that was it! He was being offered a deal by that double-crossing father: seminary or jail!

He made a leap for it, but the cop grabbed him and pinned him against the door, while Father Killarly, still in the same serene tone, said, "Broughton, this is an intelligent boy, a plucky boy, and an ambitious one. I know that within him his greatest desire is to do good. He can change, I assure you. Broughton, let me lead him back into the path of righteousness. The Lord willing."

John was now terrified and looking for a way out. All he saw was his drunken father sitting back against the sink again, out of this world; his sisters and brothers fighting on the bunk beds in the next room; and the two wrong-eyed women helping his mother, one

193

with a glass of water, the other with a handkerchief. The priest meanwhile was still talking, and his words came through somewhat scrambled to him.

He was now speaking barely above a whisper to the cop, saying, "Let me get him away from these awful family surroundings. Look at the poor people! How can John learn goodness among them? But I tell you he's a smart lad. And being in jail would only make a harrdened crriminal of him!"

The policeman looked somewhat doubtful, so Father Killarly clinched his deal with, "Just give me a year, Broughton. That's all I ask. Give this boy to God for one year! If faith—yes, I said, the true faith—doesn't save this boy and make a new man of him, you know he'll be back in your hands soon enough."

He turned to John and looked meaningfully at him before adding, "Then I'll file new charges against him for larceny, and you can have him—John, are you listening?"

John had lowered his eyes. He was beaten. This was the first time in his life that he had been forced to give in. But the full weight of it only hit when he heard his mother, who had come back to herself, exclaim, "*Mamma mia!* My boy will be a priest!"

7

He was like a sleepwalker, his eyes cast down on the white, red, and black tiles of the endless gallery that led to the "beginners' classroom." He merely followed the sound of the footsteps lugubriously preceding him: the prefect of discipline in his big hobnailed peasant shoes walked deliberately on, as befits a cleric imbued with the holiness of his ministry and the dignity of his person. John wasn't even looking at him; by now he was virtually hypnotized by the pattern of the alternating tiles beneath his feet.

He felt humbled in spirit as he was humbled in fact by having to wear the black uniform they had given him, so much too small that it was bursting at the seams from the moment he got into it. He might be only fifteen, but he was as big as a man, and as a man well above average in height and weight, with his broad wrestler's shoulders and his athlete's chest. His deep regular breaths were a challenge to the skimpy cut of a blouse intended for children who merely sniffed humbly at the stale air of their chapels and classrooms but never inhaled and exhaled the way you did at a gym or down on the docks. The cheap material called for tight, pinched gestures of piety, small penitent steps.

And there was even worse mortification: the prefect

of Studies had told him that, considering his academic record, he would have to be put with the twelve-year-olds.

Yet ever since Friday, when it had been determined that he would be enrolled, John didn't know why the idea of running away had not once entered his mind. He hadn't even thought of protesting against the grotesque idea that the leader of the Devils, the lord of Williamsburg, was going to a seminary.

It was almost as if that awful look that Father Killarly had given him, when he first caught sight of him in Stagg Alley, had broken his will, tamed him forevermore.

As he thought back on it later, he realized it wasn't the look that had done it so much as his feeling of being a sinner, that strange feeling, at once horrible and delightful, which had given him such a charge when he was actually stealing the treasures of Holy Virgin.

Varese had stood guard in the transept of the church, while he sneaked into the sacristy. There was really nothing to it: just open the glass-fronted cases, which weren't even locked, take the religious objects displayed on the shelves, throw them into the big duffel bag his half brother Ryan had brought back from the Navy, and go out the back door, onto Meserole, where no one would notice.

All it took was a few moments and a cool head.

In the greenish half-light of the stained-glass windows, the treasures glinted the way a pirate treasure trove glints against its deep-sea background among the seaweed. John noted that that was what it was like, and it fascinated him. And then suddenly, on seeing so much silver and gold and so many precious stones

196

all there for the taking, he had felt a shiver run through him, and he had stopped short—as if paralyzed by some fear he couldn't comprehend.

He was stealing from God, it seemed to him. He was damning himself forever.

He shivered uncontrollably.

But he was plenty proud of daring to risk damnation. It kind of intoxicated him. Hadn't he had it engraved on his very own skin that he was The Devil? Didn't that mean that all he was ever to do from now on was evil? And to do it with joy?

Then another thought occurred to him: if there was this much wealth here, in a simple church in the slums, a poor parish with nothing but penniless wops and micks for parishioners, what kind of wealth wouldn't there be, say, at the archdiocese of Brooklyn? Probably millions in gold and diamonds and all. And at St. Patrick's on Fifth Avenue in Manhattan? And the New York archdiocese? Or the one in Washington? And how about over in Rome, where the Pope lived, as he remembered?

When he had finally made a clean haul of everything and had rendezvoused with Eliah outside on Meserole, his friend didn't know what to make of it when John announced: "Eliah, you're wrong. The mob is not the place to make it. You gotta be a priest!"

But, after that, the crazy idea had left him just the way it had come.

Yet, he didn't kick, or resist, or even drag his feet or try to duck out when Father Killarly had come for him on the next Monday morning to take him on the bus to St. James Place and enter him in Cathedral College of the Immaculate Conception Preparatory Seminary.

Only, as he went in through the great dark door, for the first time in his young life he had to fight to keep the tears back.

Father Killarly had introduced his "lost sheep"—which was how he referred to John K. Flaherty—to his friend Father McIntyre. The prefect of studies was a man around forty, with a very short crew cut and the deeply etched features of an ascetic who forswore meat and fish by way of self-purification. But the most striking thing about him was the icy stare, the more terrifying because his right eye was made of glass and didn't move with the other.

He preached at John and told him his sins would land him in hell. He also wanted to know if he had any illness, but answered himself without waiting for the boy to reply: "Looks to me like he's got the build of an Apollo. Let us hope his strength and good looks do not lead him into vanity."

Then, lowering his voice, the father asked whether he had ever "abused" himself.

"Abused myself?" John asked, taken aback.

"Yes," Father Killarly put in, trying to dispel the embarrassment, "Father McIntyre means did you ever—"

"Jack off and all? Is that what you mean?"

The two clerics exchanged a look of dismay. The prefect of studies wondered whether his friend Father Killarly had not let sentiment get the better of him: Were there really indices of possible redemption in this bravado-filled little hoodlum who admitted such things without shame, though without pride either?

"Of course, I jack off like anybody else," John was saying. "And I fuck, too. I mean, I slept with a girl already."

"That is something you will answer to the Lord

for, and to the spiritual director you will shortly select," Father McIntyre barked with finality. This conversation was getting too explicit to suit him.

Then he asked Father Killarly what kind of grades the young sinner had gotten. The pastor of Holy Virgin was almost ashamed to show him John's report cards and transcript. The prefect of studies ran his eyes over them disgustedly and then sighed, "Father Killarly, just what do you think we can make of such a dullard?"

"Why, a good Christian and a good student," Killarly answered, deliberately ignoring the rejection in his friend's voice and refusing to admit that John might not be accepted.

"Very well. Let's find some kind of uniform for him until the diocese provides a scholarship so we can dress him properly."

And with that, Father McIntyre summoned the prefect of discipline so the rest of the formalities could be taken care of.

John's fate had been sealed.

8

Summer finally came, and with it the dog days: those terrible hot New York days when the blacktop of the streets begins to soften and at noon the horizon disappears in a haze of heat waves, and everyone says, "It's not the heat, it's the humidity." Behind the high lugubrious walls of its inner yards, deep as wells, the seminary was suffocating. Its atmosphere was supercharged with nervous tension and an aggressiveness nearing the breaking point.

At class breaks there would be very short, very violent altercations: over nothing, two kids would suddenly come to blows and hit each other mercilessly before the virtually indifferent eyes of exhausted monitors, from whom the heat had driven out any urge to keep them in line.

"Vacation isn't far off," the more cynical among them commented.

It was the tenth grade's shower day.

This was the day that was most distasteful to John: the showers were where hostility most came into the open. The naked bodies, or the smell of sweat and dirty clothes and the humidity, or something, seemed to unleash the kids and their monitors in the big white-tiled concrete room. All the evil that a bunch of

young seminarians might be capable of here suddenly
overflowed, and on each occasion the onetime gang
boss of Williamsburg was subjected to humiliations
that probably no one else would have taken without
either trying to get even or going mad.

When he first entered Immaculate Conception, and
was put into the twelve-year-old class, John had
thought the high jinks in the shower were just the
result of those younger kids' envy of his unusual
strength. The monitors had taken a dislike to him immediately, because of his good looks and his open
face, and the seventh-graders had quickly understood
that any time they provoked him into any outburst, he
was the one who'd be punished. "It won't go on like
this," he had sworn to himself when he made up his
mind that he'd be first in marks as well as size—a decision he came to practically the day after he got there.

But when he was promoted to the eighth grade in
mid-April, to ninth early in May, and a couple of
weeks later into the class that was largely his own age,
he noticed that the hazing and practical jokes, instead
of diminishing, only got worse, and some of them now
turned clearly violent, which was much more painful
coming from these bigger boys, even though he was
still taller than most of them.

The topper was, while they were waiting their turn
to step under the shower and work up a lather, to trick
John into taking his left hand off his right muscle,
where he always kept it in order to hide the blasphe-
mous tattoo that dubbed him a devil. They would
pinch him, throw spitballs at him, slap him, or kick
his rear, punch him on the left arm or the back of the
neck, or even sometimes on the jaw, in order to try to
get him to let go of his tattoo and hit back. But John
would hold still for anything they tried, livid with

rage, tensing his muscles, gritting his teeth, and refusing to bat an eyelash, even when they called him yellow, and chicken, and sissy. He almost threw up with repressed anger, but he held it all in.

This June morning, being next to the last in the column of twos waiting to get under the shower, his neighbor had set about clipping the elastic of his shorts so they would drop to his ankles when he tried to move up. Behind him, the last two were digging deep scratches in his back, and up forward in the line, the ringleader of the class was passing the word that from now on he would be known as No-Balls Flaherty.

As the word passed up the line, laughter broke out. John bit his lip but reacted no more than if he had been a statue.

Suddenly, Morrison, the meanest of all the monitors in everyone's estimation, yelled, "Flaherty, what kind of trouble are you starting again?" and grabbed him brutally by the ear, pulling him out of line and dragging him under a cold shower which he turned on full force.

This was too much. John had had it, and roaring like a wild animal, he turned on the monitor and knocked him down.

There was blood on Morrison's head, for it hit the shower faucet before he went down—but the sight of blood reawakened an old instinct in John that overwhelmed him, making him quiver with delight, as if in a fit of madness. He was now unrestrainedly punching and kicking the groggy monitor, who was not much more than a helpless puppet lying on the shower floor.

Around him all the fellows were screaming in terror, but no one dared try to stop him and no one thought to call another monitor.

One of Morrison's eyebrows split like a ripe fruit, his jaw sagged, his nose broke . . . and the cold water kept running and washing the blood away. Yet John kept right on: he seemed drunk, out of control, and still, without realizing it, he was calling on the Lord. "Christ! Christ! Oh, Christ!" he kept repeating as if this might somehow save him.

Finally, exhausted by the very violence of his fit, John fell to his knees and his forehead hit against the soapy floor. He started vomiting convulsively before breaking into sobs, as he moaned, "Christ, oh Christ!"

However much he hated to admit it, Father McIntyre came to the conclusion that his friend Father Killarly was right: one had no right to lose hope. The ways of the Lord are impenetrable indeed, and a miracle could take place anywhere, at any time—even in Brooklyn, 1938.

This young John K. Flaherty, the hoodlum from whom he had expected nothing but trouble or worse, had started practically overnight to work like a madman, and in not much more than two months had made up the ground that a few weeks before the father had felt to be lost beyond repair. He had indeed been touched by divine grace.

Several times, at confession, Father McIntyre had to admit to his special interest in this student, and several times he was told such favoritism was un-Christian. But John's thirst for knowledge was so evident, and the way his intelligence awakened and progressed from day to day was so satisfying, that it made up for many a concern and many a regret. John had been transformed: the butterfly had emerged from the cocoon.

But now this shower incident!

"Oh, Lord!" the prefect of studies said to himself, "oh, Lord, could I have been so mistaken? Lord, was it not Your intention that this boy be saved? Or if it was, what got into him this morning?"

He sat behind a large old desk, on which there were only a Bible, a book in a black paper wrapper, and a bronze pietà, in the semidarkness of the huge velvet-draped library which he used as his office. With his one good eye he was studying John's distraught face as the boy kept his eyes on the well-waxed floor in what seemed to be sincere repentance.

"John, my son," he finally began in a voice broken by emotion, "I just don't understand. We were about to congratulate you on the magnificent results you have achieved: the term will be over in less than two weeks, and even though you enrolled halfway through the year, this month you are first *cum laude* in Latin, as well as in history of religion, and among the top of your class in English and literature. You have done so well in everything, and your fervent faith and devotion to services have been noted by all. Just yesterday I was talking to the bishop, and Monsignore said he would be here in person to congratulate you at the year-end ceremonies. Meantime, he asked me to give you this fine volume of the Epistles of St. Paul, in recognition of your accomplishments.

"John, what could have happened to make you do so terrible a thing? What demon got into you? Do you realize you nearly killed poor Morrison? When I saw him in the hospital, he told me he would have to have an operation.

"Come, John, speak to me. Answer! Why? Lord, oh, Lord, why? John, what ever were you thinking of? I'm asking you this not as a priest, but as your friend. Tell me, son."

But John did not answer. And while Father McIntyre could tell that he was close to tears, he also knew the boy was much too proud to shed them. He merely swallowed hard and his Adam's apple bobbed up and down, so fascinatingly that as he watched it the father lost his train of thought.

"Tell me, John," he was saying, "did you—I mean, have you—that is, God: have you confessed this to Him?"

The boy nodded yes. And McIntyre, trying not to admire his masculinely handsome face, lowered his eyes to ask, "Is there something troubling you? Tell me. Is it the flesh? Do you sometimes have concupiscent dreams?"

John blinked no. And the clergyman raised his voice just the slightest bit: "Speak to me, son. As you see, I am not sitting in judgment on you. I am offering you my love, which is great, as you know."

Finally, without looking up at him, John began confiding, barely above a whisper:

"Father . . . when I entered here in February, the boys gave me a very rough time . . . because I was so ill-mannered . . . because I didn't know anything. Nothing but how to fight and all. Sorry, see, there I am saying 'and all' again. I forgot."

"Go ahead, son, just tell me what's in your heart—and all."

"Father . . . I felt so humiliated that I decided I had to work harder than anybody else. I had to be first in everything—and now I hope God forgives me that sin of vanity!"

"He will, son, He will."

"Father . . . you were good enough to look after me.

206

You taught me faith and hope and charity and you helped me so much that I was able to make up for all those years I had hung out in the streets.

"But, Father," he finally exploded, all his repressed hurt coming out, "now they're taking it out on me because I'm at the head of the class, and proud of it. And because, as Our Lord taught, when they hit me and taunted me, what I did was turn the other cheek. For that, they said I was guilty of the sin of pride. They said that I was affected!"

"Oh, John! John!" Father McIntyre said, getting up and going over to comfort the boy, "John, my son."

But John pulled away from him and, reverting to his Williamsburg intonations, hissed at him:

"I'm not your son. I'm the son of Patrick Flaherty, an unemployed bum, and Rossana Flaherty, a domestic servant. And I've turned the other cheek for the last time.

"Let me leave this seminary. It's no place for the likes of me. I wanna get out of here, even if it means I have to go to jail. To the cooler, as we call it, Father. To the cooler for having robbed a sacristy. Father, you can see I'll never make a good Christian. People like me, people like my kind, they never make good Christians. And not all your faith, your hope, or your gosh-darned charity won't be able to do anything about that! Father, people like us, from Stagg Street, and Meserole, and Montrose Avenoo, we're just damned, Father. Damned, didn't you know that?"

McIntyre, on the verge of tears, was imploring him, "John, please, my boy, please! John, have pity, please!"

And then suddenly, with an energy born of despair, he grabbed the boy's arm, threw the library door open, and dragged him down the stairs toward the tenth-grade classroom. He burst in there without knocking and harangued the students, who had respectfully hopped up from their seats when they saw who it was.

Turning toward the teacher, who felt just as reprimanded as the twenty-eight boys who were desperately trying to find some book to look at, he added, "Brother, what has been going on here must stop. John Flaherty has been abused and taunted ever since he enrolled with us at the beginning of the semester. From now on, I want him to be held up as an example, to be respected, and loved. Our own bishop, His Excellency Monsignore Molloy, only yesterday commended him to me for how brilliant his work has been, and as evidence of his esteem inscribed a copy of the Epistles of St. Paul to him."

Boys and teacher bowed their heads, overcome by such a tribute.

Came the end of the term.

The day before, John asked and received permission to take the gym and track tests that he had missed because of all the time he had put in on more academic studies.

Without preparation, John equaled the best times anybody in the school had made, and his academic awards were now coupled with commendations for phys. ed.

After the ceremonies, Bishop Molloy gave him an accolade. Sitting in the back row of the auditorium, Rossana Flaherty was sobbing, alongside Eliah Varese, who was holding his arms aloft in the manner of a boxer who has just scored a knockout. It seemed to him that, with John as their champion, the slums of Williamsburg had just carried the day.

When he finally had him to himself and asked John and Mrs. Flaherty to be his guests at lunch at a French restaurant on Washington Avenue, Eliah whispered in his ear, "Say, did you see what the bishop came in, kid? A Caddy, no less?"

"What you talkin' about?"

"I tell you, I seen him, with a chauffeur, in a long black Cadil-lack!"

"You kiddin' or something?"

"No. On my word of honor. One of those great big whitewall jobs!"

"Well, I'll be— You hear that, Ma? The bishop, he's got a Cadillac!"

"I heard, darling."

"And how about you, Eliah? Where'd you get the dough to take Ma and me out to a joint like this?"

"That," Varese answered with a knowing air, "is the little secret of Eliah Mosè Varese!"

It was certainly a glorious, glorious day. With dessert, Ma and John tasted champagne for the first time in their lives. It tickled.

When school reopened that fall, all the troubles of the earlier months were a thing of the past. No longer scorned and taunted, John was now one of the seminary's heroes.

What really did it for him was when the other fellows found out what he did on his days off. He didn't go home to be with his folks or bury his head in books, but went out on the town with Eliah, and his old Devil friends, Tex, Billy, Jesse, Abe, and even Mimi and Salsa from the Black Fangs! He would go and mix it up in the square ring at Mr. Romeo's gym, where Bee Killing Kid came to train! There was even a rumor that sometimes he and a friend went to get their ashes hauled by a pro named Sarah!

Good law-abiding boys always being utterly fascinated by those who break the rules and get away with it, John became the focus of devotion at the school, second only to the Savior. Some of the boys referred to him as Mr. Immaculate Conception, 1939—or, off the record, among themselves, as The Cock of the Seminary.

9

His tear-drenched eyes were sore from lack of sleep, he was almost overcome with nausea and in the bluish haze of incense in the nave of the chapel he could barely make out the celebrants in front of the altar or follow the ritual of the ordination mass. All that existed for him in the universe was his faith and a few colored spots—red, white, purple, and gold —which moved about softly in the mystical penumbra of the chancel, broken only by the gleam of the great cubistic stained-glass windows through which came slanting yellow and orange stripes.

But he could still hear the archbishop's sermon echoing beneath the concrete arch.

Mystically, John was transfigured.

Looking toward the right transept, he made out Rossana Flaherty, flanked by two of her Stagg Street neighbors; all three were weeping noisily as only Italian women can.

After the ceremony, the new priests retired to the sacristy to greet their families, according to custom. Ma knelt before him and offered her forehead to be blessed. His first blessing went to her: he took her in his arms and held her there for over a quarter of an hour, unable to master his overwhelming emotion.

Then he suddenly whisked out of the sacristy without anyone seeing him go, not even his mother, whose eyes were closed.

And on this fine feast day of St. Peter and St. Paul, there was Eliah Varese proudly driving his open roadster up Fifth Avenue, celebrating in his own way the advent of summer and the glory of the scantily clad women. He announced his joy by the loud tooting of the car horn. It was a special patriotic horn that played the opening notes of "The Star-Spangled Banner": Eliah had had it put on his Lincoln as an extra, for he didn't think the expensive car was jazzy enough by itself—although the purple Zephyr 40 with its maroon and gold trim had a salmon pink folding top and bright red upholstery.

"Chic!" he would say, throwing a kiss like Ed. Pinaud in the ads, whenever he glanced into the mirror and saw the smile that made him look so much like the new bobby-soxers' idol, Frank Sinatra. "Latins are *not* lousy lovers," he would mutter in self-reassurance.

And he was on his way to Yonkers, to pick John up at St. Joseph's—because an Eliah Varese didn't have to worry about gas being rationed. Not with his pull. Eliah knew everybody worth knowing, not only Salsa's old man and Rossini's brother, but even people as important as Fiorello LaGuardia, whom he had once been introduced to.

At a stoplight he honked his star-spangled horn at a Red Cross girl who was taking a collection, shaking the coins in her tin can to attract attention. "Do you take folding money, doll?" he asked. There were rolls of money in several of Eliah's uniform pockets. He fished a twenty out of his pants pocket, and making a semblance of a plane out of it, he launched it toward her. Grabbing it out of the air, she gave him a delighted smile and a big "Thanks, Lieutenant!"

Taking off at the green with screeching tires, he let out a piercing cowboy yell, with a "Yippee-yah-yay! Make way for Lootenant Eliah Mosè Varese, folks! Lemme through! Lemme through! Gotta go pick up John K. Flaherty!"

John buried his head in the sink full of cold water. Then he straightened up again, half choking, and dabbed at his eyes with a more or less clean spot of the roll of toweling. Looking in the mirror, he frowned: you could still see that he had been crying. His eyelids were still red and swollen. So he turned the water on again and stuck his head under it, letting the cold water run right down on his eyes.

Once that was done, he quickly got out of his vestments, which he rolled into a bundle that he threw into a broom closet where the seminary's cleaning women usually put their old rags. And he carefully took his infantry lieutenant's uniform from the shelf where he had stashed it before the ordination ceremony.

As he was getting into his shirt, he felt his pectoral and abdominal muscles, made big biceps with his folded arms, and twisted his face into various kinds of beguiling smiles and seductive glances. Once dressed, he ran his fingers through his hair and let them dawdle on his tonsure, while a frown settled over his face. "Oh, shit!" he mumbled, but then he tried various angles until his overseas cap had hidden it entirely.

"Well done, Flaherty!" he congratulated himself. "A masterstroke, Lieutenant."

And turning toward the latrines, he opened his fly and whistled a tune as he urinated, satisfied and obviously pleased with himself.

Eliah's car was parked outside St. Joseph's, and he sat on the hood, smoking a cigar and beating time against the radiator with his heels. He was looking into space. Until he suddenly came to as he heard John's voice shouting, "Devils!"

How, he wondered, had that crazy guy sneaked up on him without his hearing? But he jumped down and immediately replied, "Black Fangs!"

They embraced, and he said, "John, oh, John!"

"Eliah!"

"Here you are at last, my John!"

"Oh, Eliah! At last is right, Eliah!"

10

They kept punching each other on the arms, still too emotional to say very much. They were together again, at last—for the moment, that was all that counted.

Finally, Eliah, stepping back and looking his friend over, exclaimed, "My God, a sky pilot!"

"Heavens, a pimp!" John snapped back, taking a friendly swipe at Eliah's jaw.

"The bugger still remembers how to fight!" Eliah quipped, as he ducked. "Who ever heard of that kind of a priest before?"

"A Black Fangs with clean teeth," John jibed back. "A real disgrace! I bet you sold out to Colgate's! You're a regular Frank Sinatra!"

"Look who's talkin'! A Devil with a tonsure!"

John instinctively put his hand to his head to see whether it showed. Eliah could see he had touched a sore point, and wanted to apologize, but John shrugged and burst out laughing.

"Come on, forget it, smartass! It'll grow back in a couple of weeks. And besides, by then I'll be in North Africa."

"Morocco?"

"More likely Algiers. But it could be Morocco."

"Well, then, kid, lemme start by takin' you to El Morocco tonight."

"El Morocco?" John asked. "You allowed in there? You sure you can afford it?"

"Sure, whaddya think? A few nights ago, Betty Grable was there, and I danced with her."

"Aw, quit your kidding."

"I ain't kiddin', kid. Me and you'll have dinner, with champagne and the works, and then: El Morocco."

"Well, step on it!" John said. "That fathead of a Spellman's liable to see me. Let's get our asses out of here—in a hurry!"

Eliah understood when he saw the archbishop of New York going toward a long black Cadillac, its liveried chauffeur leaping out to open the door for His Excellency and obsequiously help him into the back seat.

Eliah took off like a bat out of hell, and didn't slam the door on his side till he was a hundred yards away.

Then the two young lieutenants, delighted at having made it safely away, yipped their cowboy yell. Life was sweet.

They barreled down toward The Bronx and Manhattan, the wind whipping against their faces, as they made faces like cartoon characters, singing the words to a show tune called "Money! Money! Money!" that blared from the radio.

John was reminded now of the title of Fitzgerald's book: *Tender Is the Night.* And good, and fine, besides. Intoxicating. The last night in June! And you could forget that somewhere over there a war was going on. Manhattan was not blacked out, only dimmed, and there was no air raid drill this evening.

They had had lunch rather late, with cocktails and champagne to go with it. Then they had gone into a movie house to see *Four Sons,* but they quickly decided they didn't need that kind of heroics, so they ambled over to see *Gone With the Wind.* And they had a huge all-black ice cream soda in the kind of ice cream parlor they used to wish they could go into when they were kids.

Now Eliah was parking the car on Fifty-fourth Street, just a few doors from El Morocco.

As they sat in the car, slightly the worse for drinking, waiting to catch their breaths—as if they had run here from Brooklyn Heights instead of riding—Eliah grinned like a clown and whispered to his friend, "John, can I touch your balls?"

"What?" John gasped, looking at him in amazement. "You gone queer on me or something?"

"No," Eliah replied with feigned embarrassment, "but in Sicily, where my Pa comes from, they say you touch the balls of a priest it brings you luck. And you're the first priest I was ever able to ask that."

John burst out laughing, as he twisted his index finger on his temple: Eliah was nuts, but for real! Wanting to grab my balls! he thought. Then, in a fit of ill temper as drunks are wont to have, he lashed back: "Can't you can that shit for a while? You're giving me the willies! Priest, priest, priest! Is that all you can find to say? I know fuckin' well I'm a priest, you sorry son of a bitch."

A contrite Eliah mumbled an apology and then hid his head in his arms folded over the wheel, waiting for the storm he had inadvertently unleashed to pass.

After a moment of embarrassment, John, seeing how
upset his friend was, started to laugh again and all
was forgotten. "Okay! Here's to your future success,
Eliah!" he shouted, as he grabbed his hand and guided
it down to his crotch. "Or, rather, to our joint success!"

"To us, John!" Eliah replied, seriously.

"The two of us!" John said.

Eliah, both ashamed and amused, tried to pull his
hand back, but John kept a solid grip on his wrist,
and kept saying, "Black Fangs and Devils together
forever!"

He finally let go and Varese, convulsed with laughter, pressed down on the horn that played the national
anthem, to the delight of passersby who answered,
"Oh, say, you can see . . ."

In the midst of the shouts and singing, John whispered, almost as if he were talking to himself rather
than to Eliah, "Black Fangs and Devils! Listen, kid,
if you want, we can always keep it like that. Always
you and me against all those others. . . . You know
what I mean? Makes no difference that I'm a priest,
as you keep saying, kid. This was just my only way
of making it. Some day I'll even be a bishop—that's
what I swore when old Father Killarly forced me
into that seminary. And at that time, I didn't even
have the faith! Except in myself. You know what I
mean?

"Well, lemme clue you in on one more thing,
kiddo, and then we can go and get drunk at El
Morocco. At the seminary I got straightened out on
a lotta things about politics and economics, too.
Theology wasn't the only thing I studied there. I
know all about who the Heptaic Gneneumaist
Stylites were and why they were condemned for

heresy at the First Council of Nicaea, but I also know that the Catholic Church is a business, and I mean Big Business—the biggest business in the world. So big it makes A T and T, and Ford, and all the Rockefellers look like pikers. Uh-uh! Don't look at me that way, I didn't flip my lid. What I'm telling you is straight, the *emmis* like you say. The Church is a government for one thing, and it's a business too. A terrific, unending, solid business, solider than any bank you can name. And you know why? Can you tell me, Eliah, pal?"

"No, but put me wise before you get too drunk to make any sense."

"Okay, because it's a system that's built on the same rules, and the same setup, as the Mafia. Same kind of rigid chain of command, same kind of self-perpetuating leadership, same infallibility of the God-father—only they call him the Pope. And the same kind of vow of silence, the *omertà*."

"Look, John, old boy, you better change your tune, or I'll end up thinking you turned into some kind of fuckin' saint!"

"Well, I'm sorry. I know this must all be a bore to you. The thing is, I think they're right. How do you like them apples? They're like the Mafia, except they never killed anybody, they never even fired a shot in anger. So that shows you how much sharper they are, don't it? You saw Monsignore Spellman in his Cadillac this morning. You wanna know the difference between him and Lucky Luciano? He's never been in the jug, that's all. He's too smart for that. But when it comes to tricky deals and underhanded jobs, he could teach old Lucky plenty."

"Really?"

"And how! He's workin' some racket more often

than not. And if you knew the annual income of the archbishopric! Well, sometimes, kid, it beats the shit out of me. I get depressed over it and wanna cry. I wish I was still as simpleminded as when Ma made me an altarboy. Isn't there any way to make it, to get to be first, without having to be crooked about it? Or do you think I'm just being a sap, and getting it all mixed up? Maybe I'm confusing morality and stuff that don't have a thing to do with morality.

"You know, nothing is really good or evil in itself. Deep inside me, I know that. But it's so hard always to stick to your own ideas, to be an individual—you know what I'm trying to say?—to remain true to yourself each day and never conform to what they want. Does that make sense, kiddo?

"Okay, I know, I'm boring the shit out of you with all this. You don't give a damn for any of it. Why don't you tell me to shut my trap?"

"No, John, I listened to every word you said. When I hear you go on like that, I feel like all of a sudden I got smarter too."

"We've had enough philosophy for a while. Let's go to El Morocco. Let's head for champagne, and Betty Grable, Joan Crawford, Lana Turner, Rita Hayworth —and you name it!"

They danced all night, and drank, and made love, the way you dance and drink and make love when you're twenty—as if you were eaten with suppressed rage and desperation.

At the cloakroom they were greeted noisily as all uniforms were in those days. Eliah insisted that John must take half the money he had on him, and he stuffed wads of it into his jacket pockets. John found that very funny, and only went through the motions of refusing. But at first he just sat at their table getting systematically drunk, and Eliah thought he wouldn't dance at all: "The poor kid *has* turned into a priest," he concluded.

Eliah was eyeing all the society ladies about him with a somewhat blasé air, and finally clicked with one of the bar girls, a slightly vulgar but entertaining brunette wearing a bolero and a long flouncy skirt split down the front, like Carmen Miranda wore. She was humming "Brasil" along with the band, while Eliah whispered sweet words in her ear, telling her about his pal Flaherty, saying how nice it would be of her if she asked the poor kid to dance, and not to take no for an answer 'cause he's very shy and sorry for himself.

"He'll say no at first," he told her.

"You said he was shy?" the girl finally exclaimed, between chomps on her wad of gum. "You must be kiddin'! Just look who that handsome brute is with!"

And turning around—I'm a son of a bitch!—the amazed Eliah—I'm a son of a bitch!—saw his friend dancing cheek to cheek with a beautiful blond actress. "I'm a son of a bitch!" he finally said aloud. She was the one broad everybody at El Morocco dreamed of getting next to, even if only for one dance.

And John was petting her bare shoulders and bending his head over the gold lamé straps of her evening dress. He seemed ecstatic, his eyes half closed, smiling and crying all at the same time. . . . Sometimes, too, he would whisper something in her ear, which made her laugh and then brush her lips against his. The lights were going out at the tables and the overhead lighting was dimming to a soft blue. A muted trumpet, heartrending as a sob, was vamping "Moonlight Serenade."

* * *

When at last they left, among the last to go, day was breaking pink and gold over Fifth-fourth Street. Everything shone as if it had just been washed, the chrome on the cars and the windowpanes of the buildings.

Staggering exhaustedly, they made their slightly chilly way over to Broadway, where they drank strong black coffee at the counter of a drug store.

Then John went to St. Patrick's Cathedral to pray for an hour, while Eliah went to get the baggage he had checked.

He came back to pick his friend up in the car and drive him down to the Battery.

John was blinking in the light of the rising sun, when he heard his name called: "Lieutenant John K. Flaherty."

Eliah gave him a quick embrace, and after that did not look back at him. He didn't want his friend to see that he was on the verge of tears.

John was taking it all in stride.

11

It was a biblical night—clear and calm as a nativity in an unsophisticated religious book, with an infinity of stars. And the sea was utterly still.

Ashore, through a strange phenomenon of astral reverberation, the golden limestone of the grandiose ruins of Paestum shone softly in the darkness. The columns of the Temple of Neptune stood out clearly in the half-light, a sacred, supernatural halo about them.

"Oh, Lord!" John sighed before so much beauty and the imminence of battle. "What matter the day or time . . ."

In this simple effect of light breaking through the shadows he saw a manifestation of the Maker's presence, and he felt suddenly at peace, reconciled with the world, and happy. What mattered "the day or time," or even the place?

Against the horizon to the north, large cruisers and destroyers lay at anchor twelve miles out, behind fields of underwater mines, and the stars above were one with the milky way of floodlights and storm lanterns playing on the water. Just as if nothing unusual were going on, the Salerno fishermen were out on this fine night, their barks sliding noiselessly

across the water among the hundreds of landing craft
—LST, LCVP, LCT, LCL, and amphibious DUKW—
the whole overwhelming armada assembled for Operation Avalanche.

It was 0330 hours. The men lined up close together
in the LCT watched the shore come closer, and with
it their baptism of fire.

They were smart in their new battle dress, chin-
straps already holding their helmets secure, on orders
from Lieutenant Flaherty. Faces tense and lips tight,
from time to time they exchanged a few meaningless
phrases to counteract the dull fear growing within
them. John liked to listen to their accents: most of
them were young Texans about to get their first taste
of combat after a brief layover at Oran. One of them
was playing "Deep in the Heart of Texas" on the
harmonica, and John could picture his blue eyes
shining through his tears in the dark.

"Hey, cut it out! That stuff gives me the red ass,"
a sergeant called. "Play something else, Howard."

But John motioned to him to be quiet and said,
"You go right on if you want, Howard."

Then he saw another GI, held up by two of his
buddies, vomiting over the side. "Open his collar,"
John ordered. "Can't you see he's choking?"

He caught everything. But the closer they got the
heavier the silence around him grew. He was surprised at not sharing the men's ever-increasing nervous-
ness.

Did I become hardened at the seminary? he wondered.

No, on the contrary, he felt exalted. He was just as
aware of the impending danger as the others, but as
in all other situations in life, he reacted "differently."
He knew he was fully trained and perfectly equipped:

He was carrying a Garand M1 and knew its characteristics and nomenclature as well as he knew the Gospel. He could take it down or put it together with one hand, blindfolded.

And going into combat held no terror for him, as he was not afraid to die. It was more like a sport, and all he could feel was the headiness of the long-distance runner who knows he's at the top of his form.

But he also had a duty to the men, which he could not overlook. He was, after all, a lieutenant—a lieutenant and a padre.

The harmonica was now intoning a muted "St. Louis Blues,". and John thought nothing could have been more appropriate. This was a moment of longing and nostalgia.

Then, without warning, on a brief command from the barge captain, the landing ramp, loosed of bolts and cleats, slowly began to lower in a deafening screech of metal against metal.

Directly below them the black and oily water was barely moving with the slightest of swells. Five hundred paces ahead lay the lighter line of the beach named Blue for this operation, although now it seemed more like several stripes of alternating green and purple sands.

John led the way, his rifle high over his head, as an example for his boys to follow. The water came up to his waist, and his combat boots sank into the sand underfoot.

"Make it snappy," he called. "Soggy bottom."

Struggling against the undertow, he advanced slowly. When finally he hit the beach, he fell but immediately got up again. Turning, he saw the men still far behind in the water.

"Come on," he yelled to them. "We'll be in Rome tonight, if you hurry!" And then laughed at his own private joke: Rome, indeed!

He bent down and picked up a handful of sand and let it run through his fingers. "John K. Flaherty in Rome," he mumbled to himself.

But his reverie was interrupted by a German voice calling in English over a loudspeaker, "We've got you covered! Come forward with your arms up and surrender!"

His watch showed 0352 hours. The Battle of Salerno had begun.

Like so many other palaces on the Amalfi coast, the Palazzino delle Muse, a delightful villa built early in the nineteenth century on the heights above Sorrento, was now a Fifth Army hospital designed for the recuperation of serious casualties. It stood among groves of orange trees and pines, laid out in terraces overlooking the Bay of Naples.

On fine February afternoons, when the sun was bright, the wounded awaiting return home for discharge could be seen resting on cots in the gardens. Their war was over, and the joy of living gone forever: their last rumble had come to a bad end. Now their only consolation was a view of the world's most beautiful panorama: Capri, looking like a wrecked ship on the lapis lazuli sea, and, facing it, a plume rising above Vesuvius—while they fingered their Purple Hearts.

Sergeant Jim Butley, twenty-one, from Dallas, who lost his right leg in the Battle of the Rapido, was out there now, talking hours on end about Lieutenant Flaherty, to anyone who was willing to listen.

MONSIGNORE

JIM BUTLEY:

I was with him the night he cut that kraut officer's throat. I was with John, or maybe I oughta say the padre. We all called him that at first, that or Reverend. But mostly as a gag. 'Cause the stupid fuckin' supply had put an ID tag over his pocket that said Rev. John K. Flaherty. But he was one good looey. And we didn't make fun of him for long. One day that stupid fuckin' O'Connor—another Irishman, but a real pain in the ass—I remember, it was at the bridge over the Sele, two days after the landing, and the lieutenant he asked me to have the guys get a move on. That goldbrick O'Connor started in pissing and moaning, and then all of a sudden he whispered—loud enough for everybody to hear—"Oh, my achin' back! Sky pilots in the army! Who needs 'em? All they do is fuck everything up!"

Everybody laughed, and we turned toward the padre, 'cause he heard it too. Well, all that John did was he joined his hands like at Mass, and lowered his eyes, and walked over to O'Connor, saying "Now, now, brother," as friendly as you please. And then, whammo! He lets O'Connor have one in the puss.

Boy, oh, boy, you shoulda seen that! Knocked him off his feet. None of us guys knew he was a boxer. He was a priest and all. But then he grabbed him by his shirt and pulled him up. And asked him if he was all right. "Yuh, yuh, yuh," was all Bobby could say. He had a split lip and it was bleeding plenty. But John yelled at him, "Say 'Yes, Father,' when you talk to me!" and let him have another wallop. This one was a real pro's uppercut, and O'Connor was out cold.

After that, nobody ever fucked around with Padre John no more. You know, he coulda brought O'Connor up on charges; he was an officer, after all. But not him. He even got real friendly with the guy and started to teach him how to box. You can believe it or not, but he's an honest-to-God padre. But every time they mixed it up John whipped the other guy's ass, even though the bastard had been a tackle on his school team back in Houston.

Man! that John was powerful, and you never felt scairt when you was around him. Seemed like he didn't give a damn about nothin', not about life and not about death. No sweat! Always out front, and when things got tough he wouldn't even hit the dirt. Just full speed ahead!

But I'll tell you, that night that we was on patrol in the park of the Royal Palace at Caserta, it was scary enough to give you the shits!

The two of us was lost, it was so dark there, under the trees. We'd been tramping around for three hours and could hear shots fired now and then. But no way to locate those fuckin' Nazis—prob'ly not more than a squad of 'em—or to know what they was up to. And the two of us, poor suckers, thought our guys was still right behind us.

Then, around midnight, with the moon coming up, there was this burst of machine gun fire, much longer and much closer. And another. And another. I threw myself down behind a hedge. John just squatted for a minute. I could see the moon reflecting off his helmet, and wanted to tell him to duck down, but I was too scared to get a word out. And then, all of a sudden—nothing.

We couldn't hear the guys any more. The machine

gun stopped, and the two of us was there alone freezing our balls off in the dark.

Then John says to me, "Don't move, I'm gonna do a little recon over there." And I was alone, for maybe a quarter of an hour. Scared shitless! My fingers was getting stiff on my BAR. And I was sick of the whole fuckin' business. All I wanted was out—any place, as long as it was out! I says to myself, "That fuckin' padre just ran out on you," and figgered I was prob'ly the world's biggest sucker, 'cause anyway, in the woods where we was, he wouldna found me even if he was trying.

Then I saw something coming toward me in the dark, and I raised my weapon to get ready to fire.

But John could see in the dark—like a cat.

From as far away as he could make me out, he called, just loud enough so I could hear, "Cut the shit, Butley! It's me, the padre."

Believe me, I was in a cold sweat. It was a close one, and that was the only time I ever called him Father.

I called out, "I'm right here, Father."

He was all out of breath. I could see it steaming in the moonlight, and he says to me, "Well, we're at the end of the park. I spotted the Nymphs Basin, on the right, maybe five, six minutes away. The Fritzes must be on the other side, on that hill, behind the lookout point and the waterfall."

So we figgered the other guys in our patrol musta hid out in the Tea Pavilion, a fancy kinda building with columns, and angels, and all that jazz, kinda like a little White House, behind us, where the two pathways crossed.

That's why we didn't hear 'em coming on anymore behind us.

John didn't get sore or nothin'. Fact is, I never heard him chew the guys out. He was always as calm as could be and he'd have a little smile always on his lips: maybe that was the one thing gave him away to be a priest.

But that night, he was really gung-ho. He says, "Ahead?"

And like the dumb jerk I was, I says, "Right on."

I didn't feel so cocky, but I figgered with the padre with me, what could happen? He was so sure of himself.

One day, he had showed me where he kept his trench knife: along his ankle, inside his boot. And he carried another knife that sure wasn't government issue—a Fright Silver Special, it was called—it hung from the same chain as the little gold crucifix around his neck, under his shirt.

He took it out of his blouse, and I could see the blade glint in his fist. Then we started walking again silently, holding our breaths. The moon was making scary shadows between the trees and John's face changed colors, sometimes greenish, sometimes purple. An owl hooted in the night. A crazy hare darted out between my legs. And then there we was on the grass alongside the canal to the basin. Right out in the open!

We hit the ground and started crawling toward the water, but the machine gun fire started in again and drowned out the croaking of the toads. Then we heard some guy scream like his number come up, and the padre, right next to me, began reciting, "Our Father, who art in heaven, hallowed be thy name," and so on. But I stopped him. "Padre, can't you stop that?" I says. I was much scairder since he started that Lord's Prayer, so I says, "Shut up, won't you, Padre?"

230

I thought maybe he'd slug me across the mouth or somethin', but instead he just smiled. And shut up. Then he pointed to a big white marble statue—Apollo, he called it—that was shining like neon in the moonlight. And he nodded to tell me we could find shelter behind its pedestal.

So we crawled over to it. . . . That's when I started in to scream!

All of a sudden, a man's arm popped out from behind the statue's arm, and there was a guy with a knife in his hand, jumping down on John and yelling, *"To-o-o-ode!"*

I froze with fright. And just closed my eyes.

When I looked again, John had busted the guy's grip on him and was rolling in the grass, with his hands around the German's throat. I got up and ran toward them. I picked up his gun. But they was grappling so you could hardly tell them apart. One single cloud of steamy breath rose up from the both of them. I tried to grab an arm or a leg, but I couldn't, and John accidentally kicked me in the face.

So then I couldn't see nothing no more. Until I seen a knife blade . . .

John was on top of the other guy. The German was pinned face down. John was shoving his knee into the guy's ribs and twisting his arm, and I heard a bone crack.

The guy let out a squeak like a stuck pig. And then it was over. The jagged end of the Fright was driving into his flesh—right between the SS insignia on his collar and the strap of his helmet. His blood gushed out like a fountain—all over John's hands and face and into his eyes . . . but he wasn't giving up: with his two hands he was still driving the knife handle into the torn flesh. It was like butchering . . .

The SS guy gave one final dying jerk. His legs twitched.

Then John rolled the body over: he slipped his other knife up out of his boot, and drove it into the guy's heart, to make sure he was done for quick. And more blood poured out, in spurt after spurt.

Boy, all I could do was turn away and puke, all over the grass and even some on myself.

I was crazy terrified, like in a nightmare. There was this moonlight that was so white, and these toads croaking in the water and this SS corpse laying in the grass. And there was John, squatting in front of it, wiping his bloody hands on his combat blouse and laughing at the whole thing.

And when he finished, he began to sob out loud.

I guess John was like a little bit crazy, too. But he always hung in there. He was always calm and composed, like nothing never got to him. And never prickly with the guys, never chewing their asses. You wouldn't believe how much they liked him. But then, once in a while, he'd get a hair up his ass and he'd take it out on the captain, and even once, at the Trocchio, on the colonel.

It was at a briefing session, two days before we was gonna cross the Rapido. John figgered it wasn't possible to get across the Rapido without a massacre, and he yelled his head off at Keasey, calling him every fuckin' thing under the sun, and threatening to write to his congressman that he was just a murderer.

"Murderer!" he was yelling, and we could hear him all over the camp, and the funniest part was this here Keasey he was a real good Catholic, and all he kept answering was "Father! Father!"

And John shouted back, "Father says shit for you! And so does the Lord! You're just a poor incompetent slob trying to get a promotion over the dead bodies of as many GIs as possible. You're a lousy butcher!"

"Father, please," Keasey answered. "Flaherty! Get hold of yourself! Flaherty! Padre!"

"Flaherty pisses in your eye. And if you think he's gonna give you Communion tomorrow morning, you got another think coming. I said and I say again that it's madness to try to get across the Rapido in the state it's now in. Our commando raid the other night should have proved that even to you. If worst comes to worst, I'll call for a congressional investigation, 'cause I know this has to be a disaster."

"Father!"

"If a single one of my GIs gets killed, it'll be on your conscience, Keasey."

"Father!"

"But I'm not so sure you got a conscience. And I assure you lots more than one of 'em will get killed tomorrow."

And John wasn't wrong. Everybody knows that we was sitting ducks in the Rapido. All that fog and slush and this Bailey bridge they built right opposite a kraut mortar emplacement. And the other bank, a solid bed of mines!

When day broke we knew that trying to cross was just asking for it. But orders is orders. John was running from one guy to another, with his lips foaming and tears in his eyes. He held us back as long as he could without giving Keasey the right to blow his brains out for insubordination, which he could perfectly well have done.

Finally, it was my turn to start across the pontoon—and that's when it blew up. I seen this torn-off leg flying before my eyes, and only later I realized it was my own—when I was already down in the freezing water, drowning along with a dozen other wounded GIs.

John was the one who saved my life, and the life of maybe ten more like me. He threw away his gun and gear and dove in after us. He swam over to me and pulled me back to shore, and that's when I went into the coma.

But I heard afters how he dove back in time after time, dragging back two or three guys at a time who couldn't find a footing, or others who was caught under the wooden girders and was screaming for help.

There was just one GI he couldn't save: that was Howard, the harmonica player. When he jumped from the bridge, he impaled himself on a broken beam and his guts was spilling out. He was dying slowly. So John climbed up over the debris to put him out of his misery with a bullet in the brain.

But his pistol jammed, so he put his hands around poor Howard's neck, and finished him off, and the guys on the bank they told me later they could hear him saying over and over, "*Requiescat in pace! Requiescat in pace!*"

I guess he was delirious.

The Fritzes was shooting again, and the water was popping with bullets all around him, so the guys yelled, "Padre! Come on back, Padre!"

When he did get back, he had Howard's harmonica in his hand and he was holding it clear of the water.

And later when what was left of the battalion had got back to camp, he spent the whole night walking around between our pup tents, trying to get enough notes out of that mouth organ to make it sound like "St. Louis Blues."

Some of the medics they tried talking him out of it and giving him a sedative, but he fought back and slugged a couple of 'em. They heard him cursing God, and Jesus Christ, and all kinds of saints they never even knew existed. They thought he flipped his lid for good.

But I didn't see none of that. While that was going on, I was on the operating table. But they told me that the next morning they found him kneeling in a field not too far from camp. He was shivering with the cold, but he was smiling and happy, because he finally succeeded in playing "St. Louis Blues" on that fuckin' mouth organ.

12

No one was quite sure just what Monsignore Walkman's job was in the Fifth Army. As bishop of Reno he was not officially an army chaplain, although he had long acted as such with the 36th Division. He donned his vestments only to say Mass on Sundays, the rest of the time wearing the uniform of an infantry colonel. A World War I hero, he had not been ordained a priest until 1924. From his military past he retained a certain amount of stiffness in bearing. His forceful features and cold eyes were more those of a soldier than of a clergyman. At times a mysterious black Lancia limousine with *SCV* plates, or—after the fall of Rome in June 1944—an army jeep, would come to pick him up at the Ascanio Palace in Naples, where he made his office. And when he rode off, he was dressed in full episcopal pomp: the purple cassock with its capelet setting off on his chest the darker tone of the Purple Heart he had earned when severely burned on the Somme in 1917; the skullcap and the belt with its prune-colored silk fringe, and embroidered lilac gloves; a moiré ferraiola with a clasp of chiseled silver chain; medals of the Order of the Golden Spur, the Pius, the Order of St. Sylvester, and *Pro Ecclesia et Pontifice;* and, of course, the pectoral cross and amethyst ring on his finger.

Along with this regalia, he assumed a sudden kind of unction, a sweetness of tone and manner as surprising to those who knew him as a soldier as it would have been to see him charge into the crowd of worshipers at St. Peter's brandishing a drawn saber. Those who observed this sometimes referred to him as Monsignore Jekyll and Colonel Hyde. It was John K. Flaherty who was credited with having coined the phrase.

Apart from the general staff, which knew he was President Roosevelt's secret contact with the Holy See, young Chaplain Lieutenant Flaherty was the only one aware that on those days Monsignore Walkman went to the Vatican. Before Rome was in Allied hands, the *SCV* registration of the limousine had been his safe-conduct through the enemy lines. After early June of '44, of course, he no longer needed to be so secretive about it.

But, as he told Father Flaherty, who had become his protégé, this did not make his mission any less perilous. Any number of ambassadors accredited to His Holiness, as well as secret agents, including those of the OSS, would have given a lot to know what went on within the four scarlet-draped walls of the discreet little parlor in the Borgia Tower where the Pope and Monsignore Walkman met without other witnesses.

Which—as the bishop of Reno cynically added—was really just as well. He would not have relished the idea of any newsmen or Russian spies overhearing the wild plans for peace and realignment of alliances which Pope Pius XII and his secretary of state, Monsignore Maglione, from time to time thought they could get the United Nations forces to accept. That would have been a fine scandal—even to the most devout of Catholics! And the Vatican would certainly have looked ridiculous—especially since it had not come up smelling of roses after the way it played footsie with the Nazis.

In the papal secretary of state's word, the German army was now "the only possible rampart against atheistic communism." So, according to his plan—which the Pope fully endorsed—the main aim was "to free the soldiers of the Wehrmacht in the West from Anglo-American *pressure*"—that word being used deliberately to stress how weak they considered the Allied counterattack to be—"and then to create a rapprochement between the Western democracies and the Axis powers for a common fight against bolshevism."

"Nazism," the Holy Father would add, "will come out of the struggle greatly weakened, and the Anglo-Saxons, having suffered so much less, will then have no trouble in doing away with the Hitler regime, if indeed it does not collapse of its own accord. That way, all three totalitarianisms will be overthrown: atheistic communism, Hitler's neo-paganism, and what is left in our country of Mussolini's fascism."

For Pius XII never used the conditional but always the future tense, so firmly convinced was he of the correctness of the political theories the Lord vouchsafed to him. In a like manner he referred to Italy as "our country," not because he was Italian by birth but because he was one of those who never quite became reconciled to the fact that the Holy See had been stripped of its pontifical states.

One evening, as he was meeting with Myron Taylor, President Roosevelt's official envoy to Vatican City, he again outlined to him these same confused ideas for the tenth or eleventh time. It was the only occasion on which his legendary courtesy failed the onetime chairman of the board of U.S. Steel. In a quite impatient and irritated voice he explained the situation to Pius XII.

"Why, Your Holiness can't mean that!" he expostulated. "Our primary enemy is Nazism. And we will fight to our last drop of blood if necessary in order to wipe out that awful tyranny. Does Your Holiness really think that American soldiers or the American people would understand it if the President now came to them and said that all they had suffered and sacrificed had been in vain, and they were now to join hands with the Germans?"

"The American people!" the Pope muttered in exasperation. "What do we care about them?" For at times like this his infirmities and stomach pains made the Holy Father forget all about Christian kindness and serenity.

"But they're the ones who have sent me here, Your Holiness!"

"Didn't it ever occur to you that you might be excommunicated?"' the Pontiff shot back, in desperation.

To which the Protestant Taylor, completely taken aback by this venom in one he had so long considered his friend, answered, "Surely Your Holiness knows that that happened long since!"

Later on, there were other meetings—with Taylor, and with Tittman. But General Mark Clark thought it would be a good idea to send a Catholic, preferably a leading light of the Church in America, as a representative to the Holy See. Such a man might better be able to roll with the punches in dealing with the man whom every Catholic priest must look upon as his only true and authentic sovereign. Not, of course, that Clark expected much to come of such diplomacy, but he certainly could not brush the Vatican aside, nor could he afford to ignore it, when the Italian clergy were so precious a source of information on enemy troop movements.

Monsignore Walkman was the ideal choice. The bishop of Reno was skillful, sharp, devious, cynical, very savvy about American politics, an ardent Democrat, and yet a close friend of the Pope's. Besides which, he was a soldier of long standing.

John had been apprised of this the very first time he called on his superior prelate, when he came to prostrate himself at his feet and confess to him the very un-Christian feelings he had had when he killed the Nazi officer in the park of the Reggia di Caserta. He had accused himself of not having a true vocation for the priesthood, told how involved he could get in action and violence, and begged the bishop to allow him to renounce his orders without being driven from the Church.

"If you abandon me, Monsignore," he had pleaded with him, "I shall be lost forever."

But His Excellency had explained to him that his scruples were "just childishness," and that he was indulging in "ridiculous angelism."

On the other hand, this young fighting chaplain was so attractive with his youth, his handsomeness, his intelligence and bravery—and he had been recommended to him in a confidential letter from Cardinal Spellman, to boot—that the bishop fought inch by inch for two hours to get him to give up each and every one of those decisions of his and forget his overwrought contrition.

"Now, listen to me, you stupid mucker!" the Monsignore snapped. "All that is just talk. Listen to me, John." And the latter was surprised at his new tone of voice. "You're just acting like a kid who thinks he can be a saint. The Church is a trust. Not just a sacred trust, but a profane trust, too, as much a trust as United Fruit, or A T and T, or General Motors.

"That surprises you, eh? Well, it doesn't make much difference whether you're selling cars, or bananas, or phone communications to a whole country, on the one hand, or working for the country's spiritual salvation, on the other. You're a priest: that means you've got a franchise from heaven. Just like the local Buick or Ford dealer. You're selling people good seats on the Lord's right hand, like a ticket broker.

"All the rest is just second-rate self-pity! It's just stupid Jansenism, or irrelevant angelism! Your personal problems, your moods and soul searching don't mean a thing to the people who come into a church to pray. What they expect from you is for you to help save them—that and nothing more. In going to confession, in taking Communion, they are making a contract with you—you're the seller. When they buy a refrigerator or a radio they don't give a damn whether the dealer had a good lunch today or slept well last night. They want value received for their money and a guarantee that they can return the thing or get it repaired if it doesn't work right."

"Well, that's certainly putting religion in a new light. And maybe you're opening my eyes for me," John hissed back in disgust. "St. Ignatius never thought of it that way, when he listed all the spiritual exercises. No, sir, he never thought of salvation as a service to be sold through a proper marketing campaign, nor of the Gospel as a Sears Roebuck catalog with God as the purveyor of a better brand of household appliance. When Father Killarly got me into

Immaculate Conception, I never knew he intended for me to become a traveling salesman!"

Whereupon, aquiver with indignation, he walked out of the tent which was the bishop's field office when the American camp was just outside Caserta that winter.

But His Excellency had not taken offense at the rudeness of this hotheaded Irishman. He was much too impressed by the unusual strength of character the young man showed at his age, and he wrote Monsignore Spellman to say what a great future he saw for this "bucking thoroughbred." Besides, he felt the young chaplain probably returned his admiration and would be back before too long to apologize for his intemperance.

And he was not wrong. John came back soon, and after that very often, to discuss his doubts with the bishop of Reno.

So the latter was able to watch his development and help him gradually get rid of what he called "all those childish choirboy notions."

In early spring the Texas Division was sent to the rear for R&R after the effort it had put out at Monte Cassino.

In Naples, the Ascanio Palace was one of the rest areas where battle-weary GIs could sleep their heads off between clean sheets and have a few days of perhaps not so clean fun before going back into action.

The baroque palace with its richly decorated halls now turned into barracks was a sight to see. The handsome wall sconces were being used as clothes racks, and the statuesque Dianas and Venuses sported overseas caps or blouses that there was no place else to hang.

On the main floor, a jeep was parked in a large silk-print-draped parlor. The Corps of Engineers had brought dozens of statues of Greek lads, discus throwers, Apollos, and the like, in from the park to protect them from vandalism and stored them in a hall of mirrors across a gallery from this parlor. Reflected by the mirrors, they constituted an endless crowd of handsome male nudes, apparently appealing to Monsignore Walkman, for it was there that, strangely, he had set up his desk, a small folding field desk, in front of which he sat in a luxurious Empire-style armchair, once the throne of Joseph Bonaparte.

It was in this hall of mirrors that John was seeing His Excellency this morning.

"Excellency," John begged, "I can't function as a priest anymore. Please, please, release me from my vows, and have my ordination annulled, or whatever it takes."

Monsignore Walkman stood up, trembling with rage. "Oh, so that's it now, is it?" he thundered. "Starting in again, are you, John? And violating not only your holy vows, but your word to me as well. You promised me on the Sacred Heart of—"

"I can't, Monsignore, I just can't go on," John interrupted, in his distress forgetting his duty of respect to the bishop and his senior officer. "You know my weakness! Monsignore, I am not worthy of serving the Lord—not the way I enjoy fighting."

Monsignore Walkman slumped back down onto the Bonaparte throne, and when he spoke again it was in a milder tone.

"John, you're breaking my heart! Have you forgotten everything I told you, no more than three months ago? The time you came to confess that so-called crime of yours? John, you know that man was an SS monster! He wasn't a human, but an SS—a beast, John. The Angel of Darkness! What do you think you are guilty of? Do you think St. George or St. Michael felt no elation when they slew the dragons?"

John, barely able to contain his ire, reverted again to his Williamsburg accent, as he retorted, "Awright, enough already! I know about them, and about St. Dominic, too. And the popes who were condottieri! But does a man have to kill to become blessed?

"Won't you understand? Won't you see, Monsignore? 'They have ears and hear not.' You won't listen, will you? No, that's not it, you just *don't want* to hear or to understand. I'm a cheater, Monsignore! Yes, that's it—my vows are just . . . just a fraud!"

"Fine, another fit of angelism," the bishop answered with a sneer.

But John went right on, as if he had not heard. "I went into the seminary to get away from prison. I took orders to get away from the gutter. I'm just a priest out of opportunism, Monsignore. And it was out of opportunism that I agreed to be your secretary when I get out of the army."

"You're fooling yourself, John! You're wallowing in self-contempt! That's just another face of pride. And the more contempt you express for yourself, the more sincere I can see your faith to be. And I also know what you were feeling during that disaster at the Rapido."

John was stubbornly shaking his head in contradiction.

But Monsignore Walkman, pushing his desk away, got up again and resumed his tirade. "No, don't try to interrupt me, you little twerp! There's nothing to get your bowels in an uproar over."

John was taken aback by the bishop's sudden vulgarity. But Monsignore grabbed him by the zipper of his fatigues, and wouldn't let go. Now he too echoed his origins: "Whaddya think? You lousy sap, you're not the first snotnose little priest I've had to take to task! But you're going to be the first priest in the new Church that I'm dreaming of—no, that is, the Church I'm building! You'll be its first bishop—its first cardinal! All the others, John—the McKays and Joneses and Rossettis, the De Santises and Ryans, all of your schoolchums—well, you know what they're like just as well as I do! Nothing but a bunch of sugar candy saints, up to their eyes in piety—so they can't see anything else, and they haven't got wise yet. They're the ones who are betraying Our Lord, they who maybe haven't killed anybody—but what they want is a humble, weak, weepy Church. A Church that people ought to be ashamed to belong to.

"And what kind of priests would it have? Poor stupid slobs, sissies and momma's boys, as we called them when I was a kid in Cicero. 'A contemplative Church, Monsignore,' that's the way that lumpin' fathead Father Humphrey described it to me just yesterday. Contemplative, indeed! Old Joe Stalin is gonna march in to destroy what little Hitler still leaves standing, and these idiots want us to genuflect before his tanks—and *contemplate!* Stop them with prayer? My ear!

"Communism is on the march—and materialism—and all these old fools expect to stop it with is prayer! When they're not saying, like that s.o.b. De Santis, that they can't see any difference between democracy and tyranny—because, well, they practically say because their kingdom is not of this earth!

246

What crap! What impudent, arrant, nauseating crap! They spit on what they call 'the temporal.' As if 'temporal' was some kind of a four-letter word! Well, if that's the way they feel, why the devil did they become priests? Why in Heaven's name aren't they Trappists?

"Let me tell you, John, m'boy, they're the criminals, not you! They're the traitors! They're the apostates! They're the ones 'but the blasphemy of the spirit shall not be forgiven.' "

As if he had used up all his energy, Monsignore Walkman slumped against the pedestal of the Farnese Hercules, and then, after catching his breath, he resumed in a loud stage whisper, like the consummate actor he was, "John, our Church must be strong, stronger than it ever was. Our Church needs men like you!

"And, yes, I know how great a sacrifice I am asking of you."

The bishop of Reno stopped. John wasn't quite sure how to take all this, and finally dug a crumpled cigarette out of his fatigues pocket and lit it just to have something to do. The lighter made a loud snap in the silent hall.

"Are you going to take Communion this morning?" His Excellency asked, coming back down to earth.

"Yes," John said, and then, "oh—uh—Monsignore," as he pinched the light off the end of his cigarette according to the GI rules.

The bishop smiled in mild deprecation, and said, "Smoking is not food. Didn't you know? You haven't broken your fast. Nor I mine."

Then he got up, patted John affectionately on the back of the neck, and said, "Come on, John. Come and say Mass with me. That Father Humphrey is really no good at it at all. He just doesn't have your knack for presenting the Eucharist—all thumbs, we used to say in Cicero. But first you'd better get shaved, son."

13

It was dawn at last. The foothills around the camp took on a bluish cast in the dissipating darkness. The ocher stones of the cathedral of Anagni were turning pink and gold, as were the medieval walls in the sunlight rising far to the west. A beam filtered through a slit in the tent, oblique as the divine light in religious images. It gave a strange glow to John's face, his eyes fighting to stay closed. In the distance, the waning sounds of celebration could be heard, the last notes of an indistinguishable samba. But he had to fight against sleep, for Monsignore Walkman would shortly be coming to take him to Rome, where he was to be introduced to the Holy Father.

All night, alone in his tent, lying on his camp bed, he had kept repeating the sacred name like a prayer, "Rome! Rome!"

While the men celebrated, to the extent that they could in wartime, he had to turn a deaf ear to the dancing and drinking. Alone with himself, he had to prepare for his private audience with the Pope as for a sacrament.

He tried keeping his mind on his breviary. But out there they were having fun. GIs forming conga lines or snakedancing to the accompaniment of the jukebox borrowed from the officers' mess. Carmen

Miranda singing "Tico-Tico" or "Brasil" and Xavier Cugat's maracas in the warm summery night called to him to take it easy, to join in the fun.

And John sat up, started to relace his boots. He was giving in to temptation. Why not go out and flirt, maybe even made love, like the others? Monsignore Walkman would never know.

But it was not on account of Monsignore Walkman that he needed to be strong; it was on account of himself. He had to overcome his own weakness, not give in. And as he fell back on the bed, each time he obstinately murmured again, "Rome!"

The thin lines of his little breviary danced before his eyes. He could no longer see the text before him.

Then, in the warmth of the night, there had been a hard sad moment for him. The sambas and mambos were over, and on the main square of Anagni the local band was playing romantic dance tunes that the guys had called for.

"Moonlight Serenade," "Lili Marlene," "In the Mood" . . . songs that were popular—or had been at the start of the war—recalling so many sentimental memories.

John had raised a flap of the tent, looked at the clear blue sky, on this the shortest night of the year, and tears had come to his eyes. The horn player sounded like Glenn Miller and the languid sounds of the brasses spoke of a romantic love that would never again be his. For a second he thought back on that night Eliah and he had spent at El Morocco. And even back to little Sarah in Williamsburg.

And then, right near him—"Lord, take pity on my weakness!"—he heard the laughter of girls being tickled, exciting daughters of Campania that some of the soldiers had brought into camp through the secret passage that John knew all too well, beneath the ramparts of Anagni. He closed his eyes and could feel their hands in his, the hands of some young brunette named Aurelia, or Carla, or Maria-Pia.

But, no! He was alone in his sleeping bag, racked by insomnia. And his hands trembled when he wiped the sweat from his brow. Two outlines were suddenly thrown on the tent, like a shadow play, and he heard the slightly intoxicated Italian girl murmur the few words of English she knew, "Me love Bobby," while O'Connor came back in equally broken Italian, *"Bob moltissimi amar Lucia!"*

Then, as Lucia laughed even louder, the sergeant had put a finger to his mouth and whispered, "Let's go over there."

"No, me love very Bobby," she tittered.

"Shush! You'll wake the padre. He's asleep right in there."

The padre! Angry and humiliated, John could have cried; he clenched his fists till his palms bled. Padre, indeed!

But then, as every other time, his anger quickly gave way to dreams of glory and brilliant revenge. What did he care, after all? What if they called him Padre and snickered? Some day, every one of these Bobby O'Connors would kneel before him. The way they had in the ring—but now to revere him. And they would humbly lower their eyes, and devoutly kiss his episcopal amethyst, his sparkling cardinal's ring, the burnt topaz given him by His Holiness on the morning of his election.

Yes, one day he would be another Walkman, another Spellman, "Monsignore" John Flaherty! He would be a cardinal, perhaps His Holiness's camerlengo—or even His Holiness himself!

The first time Monsignore Walkman had taken him to the Vatican, just a few days before, in the first of the Raphael rooms he had told John of Correggio as a boy seeing the master's frescoes for the first time and exclaiming, *"Anch'io sono pittore!"* (I'm a painter, too!)

And John had replied, *"Anch'io sono Monsignore!"* Then, ashamed of so un-Christian a display of pride, he had asked His Excellency to forgive the words that had slipped out. But Monsignore Walkman had said to him, "Your pride is not a sin, my son. God loves the ambitious too. And the Church, nowadays, needs men like you. The Church needs priests who are fighters. God wants a Church militant."

In the San Damaso Gallery, as the bishop of Reno spoke those words like a prince of the Renaissance Church, John felt himself growing even more ecstatic over all the treasures on display: the jaspers, onyxes, porphyries, stamped velvets, brocades, laces, and gleaming precious woods! He felt like the Stagg Street kid whistling when he saw a Cadillac go down Montrose Avenue. He had trouble keeping from yelling.

"Come on, John. Let me show you the Sistine Chapel, now that you've seen the library and the treasures. I want you to see the great athletic Christ that Michelangelo painted on the wall of the *Last Judgment*. Do you know that you're built just like him? That you look like him?"

Then Monsignore Walkman pushed aside a red velvet door curtain and John, going up the three steps leading to the chapel, gave vent to an exclamation in which amazement joined with a kind of beatitude and sacred fervor. He was thrilled: yes, this was *his* Church, too!

In the semidarkness he made out huge prophets with their strongmen's torsos, statuesque Sybils whose glorious nudity was only half hidden by their transparent togas, terrifying angels more powerful than antique heroes, all of triumphant humanity swept up in the anticipation of an even greater triumph, the afterlife.

Then, still peering into the shadows, John raised his eyes to the *Creation*. He studied its somewhat earthy colors, its beauty of motion. Head thrown back, he felt slightly dizzy; he shuddered and his hand opened without his willing it. He was half stretching it.

He was stretching it as Adam stretches toward the hand of God in the fresco.

Three steps away, Monsignore Walkman stood warmly observing him and stretching his own hand in turn like Michelangelo's God.

John vaguely felt as though he were being watched. His hand slumped to his side, and his eyes looked down toward His Excellency. At that moment he knew a secret pact had just been sealed between them. He knew they would remain side by side, the master and his spiritual son, in all the battles they were preparing to fight for the greater glory of God.

Monsignore Walkman had just raised the flap of the tent in which John was asleep fully dressed, his breviary lying on his chest, and he was merrily calling, "Lieutenant Flaherty! We're off to Rome!"

But John did not respond, and the bishop had to go into the tent, shake him by the shoulder, and wipe the perspiration from his brow. Then John woke with a start, repeated the last word, "Rome," and switched to "Oh, excuse me, Monsignore, I just dozed off!"

Tottering exhaustedly, John knelt to kiss the episcopal ring while His Excellency was saying, "John, your matins . . . Now get shaved. We're due to leave at seven thirty. And need I remind you that this is your saint's day?"

Then, as his protégé dragged slowly off toward the showers, he called, "And put on a clean uniform. That one is pretty rumpled."

"I slept in it, Excellency," John replied. "The only other thing I have to wear is my battle dress."

Walkman laughed. "Well, His Holiness will certainly be impressed by that. Wear it, by all means!"

He walked out of the tent to watch him go. But inwardly he was asking the Lord to give him the strength to tear his eyes away from the handsome youngster now shirtless and pulling his T-shirt up over his head—now strutting bare-chested through the morning light . . .

"Well, it's Monsignore!"

"Yes, Walkman."

A few Catholic soldiers, staggering home dead drunk from the revelry, nevertheless recognized the bishop and knelt to get his blessing, ashamed at having been so loud and seeming so merry. He bade them get up, spoke to them for a few minutes, reminding them of the greatness of John the Baptist and then asking where they had fought, what life in camp was like, whether they had left a girl behind back home, and how they had enjoyed the feast of St. John in Anagni.

In a short time, John emerged from the showers,

bathed and clean-shaven. The cold water had done him good and he was walking almost upright. But His Excellency got a laugh from the GIs around him when he mocked, "Just look at that simpleton! He's not wearing his medals! What will His Holiness think, after I told him I was bringing a hero to meet him?"

Rome!

Rome was a holiday, and John, harassed and sleepy though he was, was gaily laughing at and with it. Little beggar kids swarmed all over the jeep, sticking their hands out and rhythmically repeating a refrain that they had apparently found to pay off in the twenty days or so since the Allies had marched in: "*Gomma! Cio-cco-la-ta-a-a! Sigarette-e-ee!* Coca-Cola!"

But they were a bit overawed by the presence of a Monsignore in the military vehicle. They jumped back to try to grab their share of the chewing gum and cigarettes that the driver, Sergeant Ralph Hoover, tossed to them. John had already emptied his pockets but encouraged them with, "Go to it! See that one there! Grab it, kid!"

It was like trick or treat back in Williamsburg on Halloween, and he loved it.

In front of the Colosseum he had seen French, British, and American soldiers, as well as Arab riflemen, strolling with Italian girls, having their pictures taken by the souvenir peddlers or getting their shoes shined by the *sciuscià* boys. In the ruins of the Forum, a kilted Scot was the object of extra curiosity, the kids dancing around him and trying to lift his kilt and see what was underneath as if it were a game of blindman's buff.

On all sides the merriment was intoxicating, the

feeling of freedom made you want to sing and dance. Before getting into the city proper, as they went by Cinecittà, they had also seen a gaggle of rampaging GIs dressed up in costumes stolen from the movie wardrobe department which had been torn open by a stray shell. Alongside Via Tuscolana, a tall Negro wearing a Madame Pompadour outfit, powdered wig under his overseas cap and paniered gown over his ranger's boots, was tottering drunkenly along, proclaiming to the world, "De wah's ovuh!"

Yet, near the Vatican, on Via della Conciliazione, you could see it was not. The jeep had to make its way between barriers of sandbags and rolls of barbed wire. In St. Peter's Square, the Swiss Guards had traded their picturesque Michelangelo yellow and blue uniforms for combat fatigues, and all the windows of the pontifical palace were covered by blackout curtains. The police who pulled away the saw horses at the Porta del Arco to let their jeep into Vatican City were armed with submachine guns. The Holy See was one huge armed camp.

But while they were making obeisance to His Excellency the Bishop of Reno, a black Alfa-Romeo came out in the opposite direction, forcing Sergeant Hoover to go into quick reverse.

"Volodenko!" Monsignore Walkman whispered, as the luxury car passed them. John could make out someone inside, half hidden behind a copy of the *Osservatore Romano*. "Who's that?" he asked.

"Stalin's envoy, Volodenko," the bishop said. And there was just the slightest trace of hate on His Excellency's mouth.

Then, collecting himself, he tapped the driver's shoulder, as a signal to move forward again. The pontifical police had resumed their military bearing and were announcing, "His Excellency the Most Reverend Monsignore Walkman.

In the Cortile del Papagallo, even before Sergeant Hoover had turned off the ignition, a Swiss Guard officer came forward to do the honors to the envoy of the Fifth Army. The sun glinted so on the man's finely chiseled armor that John had to avert his eyes as he helped Monsignore Walkman to alight. Prelates, chamberlains, and Palatine Guards were rushing to welcome His Excellency whom the prefect of the bed-chamber personally greeted at the foot of the grand staircase in the Court of San Damaso.

Seeing a Sister of Mercy of the Order of St. Martha, the bishop of Reno quietly said to her in Italian, "Sister, would you show Father Flaherty and this young soldier to the eating quarters? I think they're both famished."

Turning to John, in English: "After lunch, I'll come and get you to present you to His Holiness. The audience is set for two P.M. But you look pretty sorry, m'lad. Try to perk up a little. I told him I was bringing a valiant soldier-priest—and you look like some anchorite just in from the desert."

"I'm dead tired," John confessed, looking like a scolded child. And then, along with the sergeant, he followed after Sister Teresa, slightly overwhelmed by the ceremonial and the vastness of the hallways and galleries that led to the Anone kitchens.

He was indeed famished, but more than that he was parched. It had taken them almost six hours under a scorching sun to cover the thirty-five-odd miles from Anagni to Frascati and then to Rome. At several places the road had been cut by recent artillery barrages, and the jeep had to make detours through improvised paths and open country. Nothing could be more depressing than the Roman countryside: ash-colored fields, shapeless hills, ruined aqueducts, ageless mausoleums. And all over the melancholy landscape the recent battles had left their traces: wrecks, a burnt-out jeep, a self-propelled gun turned over in a ditch, a bombed farmhouse with the sun glinting off the glass strewn in its garden, a tall burned pine standing alone in the middle of a field churned up by the bombs . . .

As they went through villages, from the first sight of the flag on their jeep kids would come yelling," *Americani! Americani!*" And then, as they saw Monsignore Walkman, they would be surprised, and scatter like a flight of sparrows. Why should there be a Monsignore in a U.S. jeep, with his big hat, his cape, and his purple cassock all covered with dust? What was he doing with American soldiers? Could somebody be a Monsignore and an American at the same time?

When their parents came out of their houses to see what was going on, they showed the same kind of slightly antagonistic surprise: working-class Italians of the period felt very warmly toward their liberators but fiercely hated the upper clergy, which had been much too chummy with the Fascists. A wave of anti-clericalism was sweeping the country.

At Frascati they attended Monsignore Valuzzi's Mass purely out of duty, for it was well known that the bishop had been a great admirer of Mussolini's. And while there, Monsignore Walkman and his young protégé had gotten a thorough taste of that scornful curiosity and been subjected to a few manifestations of insolence they were not prepared for. As they entered the suburbicarian Duomo, they had been hissed, and a woman dressed in black even tried to push them around as she shouted into their faces, "Down with the clergy! Fascists! Death to the priests! Fascists! Down with Christ!"

John was too shocked to comprehend, and clenching his fists, asked, "What is she saying?"

"Just blaspheming, son," Walkman told him. "This country is revolting against Christianity. That's what happens when the Church, as it did here, plays the game of the Fascists instead of defending democracy."

John could have cried. He, the slum kid, being accused of being a rich Fascist by this poor woman who reminded him of his mother! Had he gone back on Williamsburg, on his people? For the second time in his young life, he was ashamed of being a priest. The first time had been during that horror at the Rapido, when he had been unable to save Howard, the harmonica player, unable to do anything but finish him off.

My Lord, he whispered to himself, how long will it take me to become a total cynic—or a saint? Which, after all, amounts to the same thing: both cynic and saint are equally indifferent. Well, when will I learn to be indifferent?

But Ralph, who was a Protestant, had not gone into the Dome, and the kids had clustered around him: While the two priests were taking Communion, he was handing out chewing gum.

John was mortified. Wouldn't St. Francis of Assisi have given sweets to the kids rather than go to pray? he wondered.

Then, subconsciously, his thoughts went back to Eliah Varese and their dreams of fortune and glory, and he wondered: Oh, Lord, how long till I become a cynic—like Monsignore?

* * *

As they were going into the cool Anone refectory, the sergeant whispered, "I'm dying of thirst."

"We'll get something to drink," John reassured him. "In just a minute." He too was feeling faint and the Sister of Mercy who smiled so kindly at them with eyes lowered hardly seemed in a hurry.

Finally, after ten minutes or so, she brought cool bottles of wine and water to the table where they were sitting. John joined his hands and mumbled a quick grace as he reached for a bottle. At last, something to drink!

But just then a prelate came rushing in, bowed to him, and said in halting English, "Brother, it please His Holiness you breaketh bread with him. Do me honor of following."

John rose in surprise and Ralph had to help him extricate his feet from the bench. The whole room was swaying around him as if he were hung over, and he could hardly bear the sound of the cool water being poured.

The determined step of his guide made a lugubrious sound on the marble floor. They descended a short flight and then the chamberlain showed him through a low door.

The blinding light of noon rushed into the hall. John had to close his eyes. He took three more steps onto what looked to him like a lawn, and then he was completely dazzled: over there, beneath a bower of bougainvillaeas, he could see a frail white silhouette, phantomatic, floating visionlike, in some sort of mystical levitation.

And then he passed out.

As he slowly came to, he could hear within a confusion of murmurs Monsignore Walkman saying to the Supreme Pontiff in Italian, "He has been under fire for a week, and hasn't slept for the past three nights. What the army expects of these young chaplains is simply superhuman. And this one, Your Holiness, is certainly a hero, if not yet a saint."

"Well," Pius XII answered, "they are soldiers of God, in their own way." Then, laughing, he added in fluent English, "We have already noted that the priests who come out of your seminaries are more valorous and—perhaps because they play American football?—built more solidly than those from other countries. Look, this one is something like Caravaggio's Saint Paul, the one in the antechamber of the Borgia Tower."

Finally, John opened his eyes and prostrated himself at the Pope's feet before feverishly kissing St. Peter's ring. Pius XII blessed him and softly said, "Rise, my son. We know what suffering you have been through. It is our pleasure for you to break bread with us along with His Excellency Monsignore Walkman, who is also very dear to us. Besides, you must regain your strength."

Sister Pasqualina came and put His Holiness's medications on the table and poured into a glass the bismuth he had to take before each meal. Then, while the three men recited the Benedicite, two other nuns began to serve the Pope's favorite dishes: eggs, lentils, polenta with a bit of whitefish, ewe cheese made by the Carthusians at Empoli, and fruit compote.

Lest his protégé fall to too ravenously, Monsignore Walkman had forewarned him with a threatening glance. But Sister Pasqualina—irreverently referred to within Vatican circles as Mrs. Pacelli or even the

Popess—saw to it that the interesting young man was well served with everything, and John was able to eat and drink without false shame or affectation.

Only when he began to feel full did he realize the honor that was being done him. And that this was a moment among moments.

And he discovered that this time, instead of feeling the obvious sense of triumph that he had experienced every other time that he won out over the fate to which his origins had seemed to doom him, he had a sense of warmth, a new kind of serenity—which transported him—indeed, almost went to his head.

The thought that he was still so vulnerable made him feel stronger and happier, so that, for a moment, he felt tears in his eyes.

The Pope and Monsignore Walkman had resumed their talk.

Suddenly, as they started discussing the thorny question of the infiltration of the OSS into the Vatican's secret service and the fact that Monsignore Mortini was said to be a double agent, Pius rattled off in Latin, *"Num licet nos coram puerto isto colloqui?"* ("Can we talk in front of this child?")

The bishop of Reno smiled. "Very Holy Father, we also teach them Latin in our seminaries. And what is more, this child is soon to be a member of the secretary of state's staff, isn't he?"

"Yes, indeed, he was recommended by Monsignore Spellman to poor old Maglione, whose health gives us more concern with each passing day. But he was well enough to sign the *nihil obstat*. We believe he expects to make him a corresponding secretary for our secret communications with America, in the beginning."

"If it please the Lord and Your Holiness!"

"So be it, if that is Our Lord's will. As for us, we see no objection and therefore add our own *nihil obstat.*"

14

Nihil obstat. Nothing now stood in the way of his working and making his career in the Curia, since the general staff of the Fifth Army, on the recommendation of Their Excellencies Monsignore Spellman and Monsignore Walkman, had put him on detached service so that he might remain at the Vatican instead of going on in the ETO. (The intelligence people on General Clark's staff thought that they would thus have a most precious informant for the OSS, which was infiltrating both the Congregations and the Papal Secretariat of State.) Nothing, that is, except the fierce jealousies, the ideological struggles, the partisan hatreds, the anti-Americanism that was professed by all the princes of the Church who were still so "old European"—all of that, plus the subtle interplay of the various factions, camarillas, juntas, and patronages which, hidden though it may be, runs through the sheltered life of feudal courts. And the pontifical court was ancient régime, if ever anything was.

"I'm not doing you any favor by shoving you into the Vatican," Monsignore Walkman had confessed to John. "Indeed, it is more a test that I am putting you to. You'll be like Daniel in the lions' den: they'll all be out to destroy you, and I'm afraid your character is too strong to put up with their meanness.

You will have to learn how to bend—so as not to break. Or else, in everything, at all times, be first and best.

"Never forget this: You're an American, and like every other one of us, you stand for only one thing in the eyes of these Romans: Money. Dough—no use mincing words about it. They need us to finance their big-money deals. We're so rich, you know! But to these exquisite Europeans, who are so refined for being heirs to two thousand years of good manners, I am and you are—you will always be—someone from the New World, and *therefore*, a savage, a democrat, and an illiterate. As they see you walk over the fine carpets of their offices, they will think, That imbecile can't tell a mozetta from a mantelet. He doesn't know when a cardinal is supposed to don the purple. He probably doesn't know the difference between the Farnese Hercules and the Galeazzo Apollo, or between Guercino's St. Sebastian and any of the pietistic artifacts in the Papagallo rooms."

"Well, they'll soon find out," John retorted. "I know the purple is worn for Advent, Lent, and Ember Week. I know the Galeazzo Apollo is in the Barberini and not the Consalvi Palace. I know that Guercino's painting in Montini's . . ."

"Monsignore Montini's!"

". . . in Monsignore Montini's antechamber is just a vulgar copy done in the eighteenth century. I know that—"

"But that's just what I don't want you to know, you poor dear fool!" Monsignore Walkman cut him off. "John, you must not know all that. You'll have to learn to keep your knowledge to yourself or they'll eat you alive. It never pays for one of us to appear more familiar with the ins and outs of protocol than an old courtier or to have any real knowledge of sacred art. Remember—you must be uneducated, vulgar, and pigheaded! As wet behind the ears as the lowliest of Texas cowboys. Because did you know that that's how Tardini refers to us?—*the cowboys.* Well, if you don't want to upset these Monsignoris, you have to be one of the *cowboys* and just as simpleminded! Do you get my meaning?"

"Yes, Your Excellency. But—"

"No buts about it. Unless you think you can turn out to be so brilliant a genius that they'll put up with anything the minute they recognize you're His Holiness's coming favorite. In that case, you have to be so brilliant that—"

"I will be! I am. You've told me so!"

"You poor child," the bishop shook his head. "You will have to confess that sin of pride. And I, mine of imprudence . . ."

"*Paccavi,* Monsignori. Please forgive me."

"I am not your confessor!" the bishop of Reno exclaimed, rolling his eyes to the heaevens like a ham actor, as if to take God as his witness. "Alas! I fear me that you'll never be anything but a *bruta figura,* as they call it here.

"But, first of all, I want you to get rid of that wildly healthy look of yours, your athletic fitness, your sauntering walk . . ."

"Didn't you say I was supposed to be a cowboy?"

"Oh, John, stop trying to irritate me. You're too quick on the draw, boy! I'm warning you, you'll never last long here, if you go on that way. They're wild animals, I've told you a thousand times. You'll have to beware of every one of them, and be most wary of the ones who act friendly toward you. In the Vatican, they can do you in with a hug. Oh, you may shine all right for a while, but one day when you're off your guard the surrogate will ask you, offhandedly, with the subtle, knowledgeable smile of an old aesthete: 'Tell me, my dear son, what are your thoughts about Father Legrand's last essay in the *Études Thomistes?* Don't you think he comes a little too close to the Varangian heresies condemned by the Council of Trent?' "

"And I'll answer that I see nothing Varangian in what Father Legrand says, but rather some overtones of the condemned writings of Aurelian the Samosatan."

"Very good," Monsignore Walkman conceded, unable any longer to hide the boundless admiration he felt for his young protégé. "You know a lot more about that than I do. I never even heard of that Samosatan. Besides, I've always wondered where you got so much information and how you'd been able to read so many books in so short a time. You're only twenty-two, you don't have a doctorate in theology, and yet you'd be able to give lessons in erudition to Cardinal Tisserant. I'm wondering whether you won't be wearing the purple before me. Do you at least know how many corners there will be on your biretta?"

"Yes, three, Monsignore. Since I have no doctorate, I will never be entitled to the four-cornered one."

"Oh, this child scares me!" His Excellency exclaimed, in unconcealed delight, once again lifting his eyes to the heavens. "Who can say after this that the Lord does not perform miracles? A little hood from the slums of Brooklyn who one day will rank as a prince of the blood and take precedence over ministers and ambassadors. Which I'm sure you were aware of. As far as protocol is concerned, a cardinal is no less than the son of a king . . ."

"Alas, sir, I must admit that I was so little unaware of it that, in my vanity, I sometimes daydream of a king or queen writing me, and addressing me, as is customary, as 'Dear cousin'."

"*Optime!*" Monsignore Walkman replied, as if addressing the Lord. "If this one is not a Monsignore within ten years, it'll only be because he was thrown into some *in pace* of the Inquisition. My fears for him have grown smaller. But perhaps, on the other hand, they should be worse: so brilliant that they'll doubtless kill him unless he becomes *papabile*."

"Well," John replied with a childlike face that delighted His Excellency, although he could not admit it, "well, if Monsignore is just good enough to make me his vicar or give me some parish in his diocese when they bounce me out of here—say, Las Vegas. I think I'd like that. That is, if my bishop, Monsignore Spellman, is willing to incardinate me to you."

More moved by this statement than he wished to show, the bishop of Reno gave a First Christian's embrace to his protégé. And in doing so, blessed him, while John, aquiver as he was before going into battle, mentally shouted, "Okay, Vatican, here I come!"

During that whole endless summer of 1944, when Europe was dying so it might be born again, Monsignore Walkman guided him through the pontifical city and showed him its hidden dangers, its shoals, as he put it, "like an old sea wolf breaking in the new boy at sea."

What a strange universe it was—so strangely preserved from the *Sturm und Drang* of the outside world. Thousands of years old and yet like a musical-comedy kingdom, but still so powerful and rich in the eyes of the world!

History seemed to have passed it by; its two or three thousand inhabitants seemed to be awaiting nothing but the afterlife, despite all the engrossing activity they were involved in.

And John, who found it hard to bring his athlete's demeanor and his carefree look into harmony with the devout and submissive attitudes of the young prelates around him, considered it to be a land of the living dead—nowhere more so than in the Lipsanoteca.

This is the huge room of the apostolic palace that has bookshelves and drawers crammed with the remains of all the saints of Christianity: ashes, teeth, bits of bones, shriveled peeled-off skin, solidified pus from wounds, traces of fossilized stigmata, spots of dried blood, unspeakable dusts. . . . The day he went into this capharnaum he found there an old man who, in the dimness of the overhead lighting, himself looked like some relic: he was carefully making up a small packet with some clipped nails and a mummified toe.

"For a new basilica in the Belgian Congo," he explained in a dying voice to John, who felt he was viewing something out of a horror story. "According to our canon, every new church must have a reliquary when it is consecrated. Look, my son, at this fine toe of St. Edme of Ascoli that I am sending them."

John backed away in disgust when the clerk offered him one of the anise biscuits he was munching on while carrying out his careful sorting of the sacred remains.

The old men devoured by infirmities, the young prelates with their honeyed voices, the hypocrites, the scornful princes around him all seemed like nightmare characters out of a Hieronymus Bosch painting: one-eyed, humpbacked, prognathous, deformed, crooked. Yet here too were the guardians of the world's highest civilization, the last witnesses of a world which soon would disappear, with all of its erudition, its manners, its culture and its wit, the last inhabitants of a country where a text written in Latin can be printed in Ptolemaic Egyptian with the hieroglyphics of the Seventh Dynasty, where one could tell a Noble Guard's rank in the hierarchy merely by gauging the angle at which he bowed in returning the salute of a halberdier, or consult Dante's writings in his original drafts.

All of the West was here in this Vatican.

Early in September, John finally got an office of his own: a tiny room up under the eaves of the apostolic palace, but one he could lock. He was in charge of compiling the secret mail exchanged with the United States and doing summaries of the conglomerations of news, both important and insignificant, that daily crossed his desk: Monsignore Montini was not slow in recognizing the initiative he showed in going through this material, or the conciseness of his notes. And he told him so.

"The other secretaries load me down with reports I could never find time to read. But you have a statesman's turn of mind. Already!" said the man who in 1963 would become Paul VI.

"Do you realize it's somewhat foolhardy of you to appear so intelligent at your age? That is something one is not often forgiven for in the Vatican. Do you have a protector, at least?" And then he added, cunningly, "Don't tell me God or His Holiness."

"Monsignore Walkman has returned to the States," John answered. 'I no longer have anyone protecting me here."

"Well, we'll have to see what we can do about that and find some support for you here," His Excellency the Surrogate whispered with a knowing look.

News of his extraordinary good luck had scarcely gotten around when John found himself the object of the worst kind of petty jealousies; he felt he would suffocate if he had to spend the rest of his life within these Leonine walls. He had to get out as fast as possible where the air was breathable. So he rented a small apartment in town, on Via Margutta, a place to go to after his day's work was done. He filled it with books and supplies that he bought at the Vatican market as well as the army PX, since he still held officer's rank. He also joined the interallied sports club, which had just set up a fine gym on the Via Ludovisi, and decided he would go swimming at Ostia after Mass every Sunday that he was able to.

Thereafter, as soon as six P.M. rang on the clock in the Cortile San Damaso, he was off down the stairs, through a hidden corridor that led to the Swiss Guards barracks by way of an underground passage, and ran out of the Vatican through the St. Anne Gate. In the washroom of a café in Via di Porta Angelica he would get out of his cassock and into his lieutenant's uniform, reappearing with the black robe rolled under his arm, unrecognizable to anyone who had just seen him in his office at the Curia.

Then he hopped on a bus that took him toward Piazza del Popolo, toward life, as he happily visualized it. And he would stand on the platform with the wind in his face, humming, "Money! Money! Money!"

The young prelates who hung around the antechambers long after office hours in the hope of coming by some favor and having their devotion noticed by the Monsignori whom they fawned upon nevertheless went right on calling him an opportunist and a brown-nose.

Word of this got back to Monsignore Montini. One day, as he voiced his surprise about it in front of some of his devotees, a surly Jesuit father insinuatingly replied, "Yes, Monsignore, an opportunist. And devilishly clever about it! Making no effort to ingratiate himself with anyone at the Vatican is the most impressive way to do just that, isn't it? He probably wants people to take him for a saint!"

That evening, John was torn to bits for two solid hours in the red-silk-draped rooms of the Secretariat of State, while he was in his little whitewashed room on Via Margutta, writing a letter to Eliah Varese. He was feasting on a double C-ration and a tall malted milk. As he tried to remember the name of one of the Devils and licked the jellied gravy from his fingers, his eyes caught sight of a postcard Monsignore Walkman had sent him, which he had thumbtacked to the wall: It was a picure of Daniel in the lions' den.

15

Sitting on his windowsill in the Via Margutta apartment, he was listening to the American Forces Network broadcast of Toscanini's recording of *La
Bohème,* while the autumnal twilight of Rome darkened. Looking out into the descending night, he felt
suddenly at peace after a tough, disappointing day of
trying to defend the American viewpoint on democracy before a council of the Secretariat. At peace as
after having experienced a loss—serene. Chewing
gum (one of the minor delights which like so many
others was forbidden by an unspoken rule of the
Vatican), he was humming the tune he had so often
heard his mother sing when she played the role in
the local amateur performances put on by Rossini,
the head of the Black Hand. Now, for the first time
in his life, he really understood the Italian lyrics.

The room was by now quite dark, and all the furniture was disappearing into one gloomy mass. He shivered, and tried not to think depressing thoughts.
There was no moon as yet, but the evening star was
brightly reflected in his wardrobe mirror.

Then, suddenly, the music stopped. The streetlight
went out. And he heard a cry of pain in the hallway.

He started: three days before, a partisan had been

found lying in a pool of blood on the stairway, his throat cut by Fascists. But this time it was a woman moaning outside his door.

Grabbing his revolver, he ran to the door and opened it.

"Who's there?" he asked.

"Excuse me."

As luck would have it, the light came back on just then, the music gradually picked up, and he saw the girl crying like a baby over her skinned knee: in the darkness, she had tripped two steps below.

"Damned power failures!" he muttered, and went to help her, picking her up and carrying her in to place her on the small couch in his dining room.

"Just wait there," he told her, as he turned a lamp on and kicked the door shut. "We'll be able to take care of that. Surely nothing is broken. But please stop crying."

Then he realized he had spoken to her in English, and he repeated what he had said in Italian. But she smiled through her tears and reassured him, "You can talk American. I understand it a little." Her accent was so atrocious that he in turn smiled reassuringly at her.

They were both embarrassed and stared at each other for a moment. He had quite forgotten about going after mercurochrome and a bandage. He was looking at her: under twenty, tiny and fragile as an undernourished little girl of the slums, yet radiating health and merriment, and nattily, almost smartly, dressed. Pretty rather than beautiful. In fact, very pretty, John noted mentally. Something of Judy Garland about her. Coal-black hair, very dark laughing eyes, uneven dimples that made her look irresistibly mischievous.

"Who are you?" he asked timidly, but with enough hesitation in his voice to make it suggestive.

"Well, you know—the neighbor who just hurt her knee."

He blushed, suddenly coming to, and mumbled, "Of course. Let me get what I need to bandage it. Then you can tell me . . ."

"My name is Georgia."

He was so flustered by it all that he broke the bottle of mercurochrome he was trying to open, spattering it on Georgia. She jumped up, saying, "Oh, my! Oh, my!" as he tried awkwardly to apologize for being so gauche. But her "Oh, my!" was not caused by what he thought.

Glancing up at the canned goods on his shelf, she was going on, "Oh, my! Oh, my! So many things to eat! How lucky you are!"

He burst out laughing and watched amazedly as she pounced on some fruit cookies on a plate on the table. She was devouring them as though she hadn't eaten for days, and mumbling through her full mouth, "Milk . . . oh, condensed milk . . . Could you open a can for me? And canned meat—that's corned beef, isn't it? . . . Oh, and chocolate . . . and peanut butter . . . and real sugar. That *is* real sugar, isn't it?"

She did not quit until she had consumed half a pound of Spam and three K rations left over from his last tour of field duty that John had never turned in.

"I was hungry, oh, so hungry!" she sighed as she flopped on the couch.

"I never would have suspected it," he laughed.

"Really?"

She wanted to thank him, but at this point all she could do was burp.

"Very romantic," he commented, as he sat down beside her.

She giggled, and he looked sweetly at her. "Well, that's that," she said. "Yes, it is," he answered.

The first act of *La Bohème* was ending, and he turned off the radio and returned to sit next to her.

There was a brief moment of embarrassment and then suddenly their arms were around each other, their mouths were glued together, they were caressing each other, then whispering, he in Italian, she in English, "Oh, my love, my love—*Mi amore, mi amore!*"

16

Georgia held on to the closing red curtain as she bowed to acknowledge the audience's applause at the end of her song. She could feel her knees buckling under her and thought she might fall. She knew she could not hold back her tears. Because she had sung the rather banal song in such a heartfelt manner, the audience of American and English officers, and the few Romans who attended the nightclub, were giving her an ovation. But all she could see was a colored haze from which arose applause that was too loud, "bravos" and "encores" that scared her. She tried to see John, but could barely make out the gold-mirrored columns, the tables with pink tablecloths, the opaline lamps, the flags of allied armies stuck in the middle of bouquets made up to match the Italian flag's colors: lilies, red roses, and greenery. She smiled mechanically to her audience, her whole body tensed.

Then, finally, the curtain closed; it was dark; and she was able to cry.

She had known for several days now. One evening he had just had to let her know. He could not go on forever hiding the fact that he was a priest, that that was why he worked at the Vatican and got his supplies there. In his eyes, it was a sin of omission to keep avoiding the subject, and each time they met he promised himself he'd have the courage to tell her . . . well, to tell her "tomorrow."

He made up his mind to tell her the very day when Monsignore Walkman, back from America, walked in on him at the Secretariat as he was quickly putting his things away so as to steal back to Via Margutta, to the studio that Georgia lived in, so much like the lovers' nest of *La Bohème*.

"Georgia, Georgia darling," he had stammered. "I have to . . . uh . . . I have to . . ."

And the minute the word was out, she had been revolted, as if he had humiliated her. A priest! It was worse than if he had said he had been two-timing her from the very first night.

"A priest!" She had cried with rage and shaken as if she were going to throw up. And run away. For three days she didn't go home or near the nightclub, where they didn't know what to make of her absence. He had looked for her everywhere, and finally in despair, one morning when he heard a shoeshine boy singing Rodolfo's main aria on the street, he had even contemplated suicide.

But then he had gone to confess to Monsignore Walkman, who told him, "I knew all about it, you poor wretch! Did you really think no one would spy on you in the Vatican? Why, this place is worse than a crabs' nest, it's a den of holy-water freaks! I got written reports about you every two, three days, and I even know that *her* name is Georgia Scott professionally, but she's really Giorgina Olivieri, and she lives on Via Margutta in the same building you do, and sings at the Notte Bianche."

"Oh, Father," John had exclaimed in mortification

at having been found out. "Can't you see that I'll never make a good priest, nor even a good Christian? I told you that long ago." Then, self-deprecatingly, "Like a dope, I fell right into their trap. Don't you see? I don't have the very first qualities needed to get along as a priest: I don't know how to brownnose, or how to be a talebearer. . . . I don't have those sublime Christian virtues. I'm not a voyeur, and I don't like picking through garbage pails." He stopped, and then resumed, now quite coldly and full of respect. "Your Excellency, I know that ordination is for eternity, that my vows are irrevocable and I am dooming myself to damnation. But I've made up my mind. I have to leave the Church."

But with his usual cynicism, the bishop of Reno had shouted right back at him. "You poor stupid jerk! Forget it! You're not quitting! Not after what Monsignore Montini said to me about you this very morning: 'You know, he'll go a long way, that young Flaherty, my dear Walkman.' Not after I heard Sister Pasqualina repeat that His Holiness—who, just between us, can really murder Latin when he gets going—found your work *optimissime.* I thought I had made it clear to you once and for all: you are allowed all the delights you wish; and they will be forgiven, as they were to Paul on his road to Damascus. But what is not permissible is passion. Have all the good times your little heart desires, my boy. You're not the only one in the Vatican who likes a good time: they'll shut their eyes to it. First of all, because they expect you to shut *your* eyes to *their* escapades. Rome is a village after all; everyone knows everything. And the prelates who go in for what they call *la dolce vita* all hang out at the same two or three nightclubs, two or three houses of assignation, always the same ones. You can go bay with the wolves if you like, drag yourself through the mud—but no lasting relationships, you understand me, John? No relationships that leave the kind of wounds one doesn't get over, or lingering regrets. Just remember the words of that very subtle casuist Monsignore Chiarini: 'Loving a woman turns you away from Christ; loving all women gives you a surfeit of the flesh, and brings you back to Christ.' "

"Some fine kettle of slops!" John muttered, exhausted, before he began to sob.

For two hours and more Monsignore Walkman preached to him, reasoned with him, parading every resource of his very Jesuitical intelligence. And when he left him, the Monsignore had no qualms or worries: he knew he would win out over the boy he already privately, and affectionately, referred to as "my young rebel" and "my intractable child."

That evening, while John was praying on his knees on the cold tiles of the kitchen, Georgia had come back to the Via Margutta, pale and upset, repentant, one might have said, and they made love with a sort of desperate fury, an ultimate climax of all their senses. And at dawn they thought of dying together, in each other's arms. But curiously enough, it was not he who pulled back at the last moment; she who with childish ardor referred to herself as "the only real atheist in this whole goddamned country" suddenly discovered she was afraid of burning in hell.

And John had seen in that a sign of God, and in the veriest depths of his unhappiness it had made him strangely happy.

Well, it was that fugitive, unnameable feeling that he was trying so hard, but in vain, to make her share, now that he was sitting on the stool in her little dressing room, unhooking her black velvet bodice while she took off her stage makeup. The mascara had run from her eyelids, and her tears, now black on her cheeks, mixed with the powder and the pink base, making her look tragic and clownish at the same time—and very vulnerable, too. He wanted to protect her, to take her in his arms, but she was obstinately fending him off. She would not abide his forever changing the subject and refusing to answer the one question she had told him was crucial: "The Church or me?"

Every time she repeated it, it irritated him. But much as he hated her for it, he loved her. He loved the torture she was inflicting on his poor lost soul. And while he was just as upset by it all as she, so far he had been able to hold back his tears: penance after penance, he had become toughened.

"I just can't, Georgia," he would whisper to her. "I can't give it up. That's impossible, my poor love."

He searched her sobbing lips, hoping for some word of encouragement, for some sign, some little smile, no matter how weak, that might have helped him, saved him. But she left him to his trouble, alone with his awful decision. And half hiding his face behind his hands, wiping his eyelids weary with sorrow and insomnia, all by himself he had to go on trying to justify himself, to make her understand.

"Georgia, I can't drop out, my love. I tried too hard . . . yes, I dreamed too long . . . of this revenge! Because that's what it is—my revenge against the street I was born on, Stagg Street, poverty, my nine brothers and sisters, my poor old lady who kept getting beaten up by my lousy old man—God rest his soul! Can you understand that, my love, my Giorgina? *Gina mia?* You do understand, don't you? You're something like me; your childhood wasn't so different from mine. Even if your mother was an actress and your father was stage manager in a touring company—and even if they loved you. You were born in the Trastevere, Gina, just as I was born in Brooklyn, both of us *on the wrong side of the river,* on *our* side, the side where the outcasts live. You tried to fight your way out of it by singing, and me by becoming a priest. How else can I explain it to you? I was a poor slob, a nothing. And the Church turned me into an educated, intelligent, strong person. I washed away the humiliation.

"Anyway," he ranted on, "it would be a betrayal, a foul, a low blow. . . . Because at first I didn't really have the faith, Georgia, I just pretended to. It was the only way to get picked up out of the slime. So I played their game. I prayed and all that, made out like a saint; in fact, I even overdid it a little. But in time faith came. It was a little the way Pascal says, you know, 'Dull yourselves, kneel down, and soon you will believe'."

She started to say something, but her hoarse voice broke in a hiccup. John was visibly upset and took her in his arms, but she still fought him off and her pink muslin dress tore. And she began to pummel his chest.

"Georgia," he kept protesting, almost in tears himself, "Giorgina, *Gina mia,* I had no choice—no choice—no choice . . ."

"Well, then, go away!" she shouted as she burst into violent sobs. "If you don't want to choose, then get out! Go! Don't ever come back! Get out, now, John! Quick!"

She let her head fall to the glass top of her dressing table, totally overcome by her fit of hysterics.

Helpless, John watched her wring her hands and stifle the roars of a wounded animal in the handkerchief that she was biting till it tore.

It was too much for him. He too would soon be sobbing; he ran out, terrified, and kept bumping into the walls of the corridor that swayed before his eyes.

Then he heard a terrifying noise. But he did not turn back. Georgia had just upset the antique porcelain wash basin he had given her that very morning.

"Oh, Lord! Have pity!" was all he could say.

17

As he repeated "Oh, Lord! Have pity!" the storm that had been brewing since early evening finally broke. John wandered through the Piazza Navona, unmindful of the rain beating down on him. Soaked, sobbing, and his face contorted by nervous tics, he moved slowly along, his fists dug into his jacket pockets. He seemed to have gone crazy. For an hour now he had been walking the streets of Rome, in the dark, paying no heed to the MP jeeps speeding by without ever blowing a horn or blinking their lights.

He had gone first to Piazza Navona, because that was where Monsignore Walkman was staying, in one of the palaces of the Holy See. When pulling at the bell chain brought no response, he started yelling, "Open up! I wanna see Monsignore Walkman!"

Wild-eyed and beside himself, he kept kicking at a marble pillar without even feeling the pain in his foot, as he shouted, "Monsignore! Monsignore!" But no one answered.

Finally, a light went on in the doorman's lodge, and a sleepy Italian voice called, "Who's there? What do you want?"

"I wanna see Monsignore Walkman," John obstinately repeated in English.

All the doorman could understand was that this

was probably something for that American bishop.

"*Madonna!* In the middle of the night!" he protested.

"I gotta see him," John begged. And then, suddenly realizing he was talking English, said in Italian, as he kept drumming against the window shutter, "*Voglio vederlo!*"

"You crazy or something?" the old Roman insultingly asked him. "Something screwy in your head? You crazy 'Murrican! You gonna break my shutter. Anyway, your Monsignore, he's not here."

"Where is he?"

"Went away this morning."

"Went away?"

"Yes, off to inspect the Bologna front."

Oh, Lord, have pity!

Now he was alone; everyone had abandoned him. So he had gone back, even more depressed than before, toward Via Margutta, wondering why he was heading that way. Was there anything there for him?

A light in the studio? What studio? Oh, yes . . . the one Georgia lived in. He repeated "Georgia" to himself, as if the name no longer had any meaning. Then he remembered: Georgia—the girl he had loved. Oh, Lord, have pity! The girl he still loved. Yes, Georgia must be there, in her room, up there—and she must be crying too!

"Georgia! Georgia!" he yelled at the top of his lungs.

And immediately the light went out. "Oh, Lord!"

John was drunk with fear: Someone had grabbed him by the shoulder.

"What is it?" he barked.

A Negro MP was asking him, "Somethin' wrong, Lieutenant?"

Did they think he was acting crazy? Well, he was. All of a sudden, he let out a shout, broke away from the soldier, and ran.

He didn't slow down until he got to Piazza Colonna, on the Corso. Lord! What was happening to him? He was not going totally out of his mind, was he? At times he would laugh aloud, when he recognized a monument: the Pantheon, the Fountain of the Four Rivers, Sant' Andrea della Valle . . .

Pacing up and down the Campo dei Fiori now, he noticed the rain had stopped. He was somewhat more in control of himself. But at the same time, he was all the more conscious of his unhappiness, and he was beginning to shiver in his soaking uniform.

Bits of happy memories popped into his mind. As he walked down the Via Giulia, he remembered walking there with Georgia—when she wore a little organdy cape and sang "Moonlight Serenade" while he kissed her on the neck, and life was happy.

He kept on roaming, his teeth chattering. He dreamed that he was dying suddenly, struck by lightning in the middle of the street. But the thunder was far away now and the lightning barely lit up the Janiculum.

He started onto the high paved sidewalk of the Ponte Sisto and, halfway across, stopped to look down into the dark waters of the Tiber, listening to the powerful rumble of the river and cooling his head against the wet railing. The blood was beating against his temples, surging up from the depths of his conscience, obsessively repeating, "Damned. . . . You will be damned!"

But when was it that he had first experienced this poignant feeling of irretrievable fall, this endless damnation? Was it the morning he was ordained, or earlier, on that afternoon when he had gone in to rob the Church of the Holy Virgin? Or that time he got his arm tattooed?

"Damned!" he softly repeated to himself. And tears came to his eyes—bitter, yet soothing.

That was when he heard a jeep behind him, with someone in it singing out, "Georgia on my mind. . ."

Well, damned he was, and damned if it wasn't the voice of Eliah Varese—which he recognized in an almost unbelieving burst of ferocious elation.

He wasn't dreaming, and he wasn't crazy, much less damned. That was old Eliah in person driving the jeep. Eliah in his Air Force uniform and two Italian girls, whores no doubt, with him.

Eliah jammed on the brakes as he wildly shouted, "John!"

"Oh, Eliah!" John staggered toward him, hands extended, like a blind man. And the fact was, he could hardly see through his tears. Eliah had jumped from the jeep and run to him, and they were hugging and repeating each other's names—just like in the old days back in Williamsburg.

Finally, Eliah pulled back, looked into his friend's face, and asked, "John, what's the matter?"

"Nothing, nothing! Everything's just fine," John pretended, in a voice that belied what he said.

"You've been crying, kid," Eliah said.

"No, of course not," John replied with irritation.

The two girls still in the jeep were calling to Eliah, "Who is that, Varese?"

They were looking John up and down, both interested in him and laughing aloud. They were two or three sheets to the wind. Finally, Eliah turned back toward them and called, "All right, shut your traps. This is that John Flaherty I was telling you about!"

While he kept slapping John on the back to buoy up his spirits, the girls were commenting from the jeep, "Say, he's good-looking all right!"

"He's the priest, isn't he? Looks like he was crying. *Poveretto!*"

"Sure is a pity, a good-looking guy like that being a priest!"

"You know they say it's bad luck to turn a trick with a priest. Antonella says when she finds out she's got one, she won't let him pay her."

"Well, I'd pay my own money to fuck a guy that looks like that. What do I care if he brings me bad luck? It'd be worth it, 'cause I think he'd send me right up to heaven!"

"Oh, Simonetta, you shouldn't oughta say things like that. You'll get in trouble. With Him—you know, the one up there!"

Seeing that John was beginning to relax, Eliah started to laugh. "Man, oh, man! Just think! Bumping into you like this!"

"What are you doing in Rome?" John asked. "Where'd you liberate the jeep?"

"Mum's the word! That's a little secret between me, myself, and I," said Eliah Mosé Varese, putting on the usual slightly burlesque air of mystery that always delighted John so.

"Never one to miss a deal, are you?" John said. "But I think I can figure it out. At the Secretariat of the Holy See, we know about things like that—all about the deal the government made with the Mafia, and how they're using Lucky Luciano . . ."

"Hoo, hah! What are you dreaming up? Kid, it's much less complicated than that!" And leading him over to the jeep, Eliah went on, "Hop in, you god-damned Devil. Lemme tell you all about it. Lemme tell you how somebody who wasn't born yesterday can make a killing—selling back to the American Army a lot of junk that was given to the krauts by those bastards in the Vatican, beggin' yo' pahdon, lootenant, suh!"

"The Vatican?" John asked.

"Sure, Mike! Whaddya think? You don't know everything that's goin' on, even if you do work up in that cesspool up there. Just lemme clue you in, brother. And you ain't seen nothin' yet!"

"The Vatican, you say? The Vatican was supplying the Fritzes?"

"With weapons and food . . ."

"You gotta be kiddin'!"

"Don't you believe it, pal. Take the word of Eliah Mosè Varese for it: arms and supplies."

"You mean, they gave 'em to them . . ."

"Yessirree! You heard me. But now the wind's changed, bubby, and they was just waitin' for some smartass guy like E.M.V. to step in and take the crap off their hands, so there wouldn't be such a stink in the nostrils of the world. Y'know, as far as Mark Clark and them is concerned, get it? There was a pretty penny to be made on the deal, and since I'm in like Flynn with you know who, it's all mine for the taking. You could even be in on it, fifty-fifty, if you want, you lousy stinking papal secretary."

John was flabbergasted. He was getting ready to sit down on the back of the jeep, but the two girls grabbed him and hauled him down on their laps, laughing gaily as Eliah Varese took off like a shot, mumbling, as if to himself, "John! Of all people, good old John!"

Bells were tolling away, calling the faithful to early Sunday Mass. He opened his eyes. He was naked, lying in a narrow bed under the eaves in a small room that at first he did not recognize. The walls were draped with threadbare cheap red plush, torn and dirty. An officer's uniform was thrown over the back of a brokendown chair along with a pair of silk stockings.

Above him an old whorehouse ceiling mirror reflected Claudia's nude body, lying nestled against his in a gutter of the worn old mattress. She was sound asleep, the sheet covering her legs and the bottom of her belly. The venetian blinds let in the pink autumnal morning light and the stripes of light and shadow danced on her overmadeup prostitute's face.

John got up and rubbed his scalp vigorously as he repressed a yawn.

"Claudia," he murmured, finally realizing whom he was with.

Delicately, he brought the sheet up over her breasts so she wouldn't be cold. Then he leaned over and whispered into her ear: "All the delights you want, but no involvements: that's what Monsignore said."

But the girl was sleeping so soundly she didn't hear him. So he threw her a kiss with the tips of his fingers.

Then he slipped into his trousers, still moist from last night's rain, and opened the blinds. The light came streaming into the room, which opened onto a pretty flowered terrace, the roofs of the neighboring houses, and St. Peter's not far away. Now he remembered that Simonetta and Claudia said they had a little penthouse in an old building on the side of the Janiculum. He stepped over the sill and walked out, blinking and shivering a little, but inexplicably happy deep within himself and light of heart, full of a sudden gaiety that surprised him.

Eliah, also bare-chested, was leaning back against the railing and taking visible pleasure in the morning's first smoke.

"Well," he said in answer to John's mumbled Hi, "did you get a look at that?"

During the night, the sky had been washed clean by the storm, and St. Peter's was now resplendent under the first rays of the sun. Some birds were chirping gaily in a cage. A light fresh breeze made the flowers dance in their chipped pots.

John stretched and yawned broadly, cracked his knuckles and flexed his muscles, then, apparently addressing the wild blue yonder—or, perhaps, the Vatican—said, as he punched the air, "Well, well—you haven't heard the last of me—over there!"

Eliah turned to look at the panorama and topped him with, "You haven't heard the last of *us. Us,* John! You're not running out on me, are you?"

"Of course not, kid, I'm with you all the way," John grumbled, and then added in mock solemnity, "Remember—we swore an oath to each other, long ago. So, tremble, vile minions!"

The two friends clapped each other soundly on the back several times and then formed their hands into play guns as they shouted:

"Black Fangs!"

"Devils!"

They were now laughing wildly. Hugging each other and jumping around like two kids playing cowboys and Indians. Then John, a bit out of breath,

said, "Kid, you know what? Well, Monsignore Walkman . . . he promised me . . . my first parish . . .
whenever I'm fed up with staying here . . . you know
where it'll be?"

"Nope."

"Las Vegas!" he blurted out.

"Las Vegas?" Eliah laughed.

"Las Vegas!" John repeated, doubling over with
laughter.

"Las Vegas! Las Vegas! Las Vegas!" Eliah sang out.

And then Simonetta, who had just awakened, saw
the two of them dance a burlesque and mildly
hysterical tango together, while John improvised
words for it:

> Las Vegas! Las Vegas! Las Vegas, brothers!
> That's where I'll go if I have my druthers!
> The Vatican's a crummy enchilada,
> Like the Sacré Corazón
> Or Immaculada Concepción,
> The Vatican's a crummy enchilada!
> So I'll just take Las Vegas, Nevada!

18

When, later on, he thought back on the twenty-five years or so that took him from his little office up under the eaves of the Secretariat to the board of directors of the Institute for Christian Charity—from the black cassock of a novice priest to the cardinal scarlet—John would claim that it was during this terrifying night of November 1944, when he had wanted to die, that his fate had been decided. It had determined his destiny—and made it a great one.

He was indeed "damned," as he so often repeated to himself with no little amount of bravado or silent complicity, interpreting it to mean that he was condemned to live a life he had not chosen. That being the case, he was making the most of it. And he was doing right well at it, for if he had not made the choice, he himself had been chosen—by God. Yes, he alone among the millions and millions like him. Therefore, wasn't he justified in seeing his fate as sealed by divine will?

Not every little slum kid from Brooklyn gets to be a prince of the Church, to go to Rome and there be given the most important and most absolute of all temporal powers: the power of the purse. In a way, he was damned just *because* he was chosen, and he

knew it. He was the Chosen here on earth though he
might not be in Heaven.

But some day, he was sure, he would also enter into
a state of grace. "He who ever strives to outdo himself," Goethe somewhere writes, "is the one we can
save."

Chosen. Damned. Neither angel nor beast. But not
a simple human among suffering humanity, either:
he had promised himself ever to outdo himself, and
he was going to keep that promise. He would never
be heard to complain of the fate that was his. On the
contrary, he would put it to use with a slightly
haughty kind of aristocratic detachment: he would
make it his game. "You can't change the rules of the
game," he said to himself. "You either play or you
don't; and if you do play, you have to play by the
rules." Elegance appeared to him to require impas-
siveness, humility before one's fate. To be sure, he
would forever carry within his deepest self an un-
healed wound named Georgia, but none would ever
know him to be bitter, cynical, or disillusioned. This
was what he had decided, with a sublime effort of
will which, all things considered, was "most Christian."

His faith, which was very real, whatever one might
think, he would live up to with a kind of contained
rage, as if it were a fight. "The way a man fights,"
he concluded, "the way Muhammad Ali fights: suit-
ing the means perfectly to the ends, and with that un-
challengeable superiority, that 'calmness of the strong'
which in his case is not just a stupid appearance of
self-confidence, quite the contrary, but the fact that
he knows he can call his enemy names, that he can
rave and yell how scared he is louder than the other

guy, rather than try to hide it. In brief, knowing how to be mad. And to keep your madness in check."

Thus, Monsignore John K. Flaherty was at times heard to swear at God; but it was out of humility. He was caught up in the *game,* and like any great player out on the field, he forgot himself—in which he was that much closer to his Lord. His superabundance of nervous energy gave him a kind of spiritual immobility. His constant travels and his delight in physical danger and violent sports brought him closer to the serenity of the stylites, those anchorites who steep themselves in prayer perched high atop a column all day long in the heat of the desert sun. Every excess thus became its opposite: "He who has sinned greatly will be more surely saved than the occasional sinner."

God does not like the soft or the tepid. Those who dare put his power and his glory to the test, and defy him at the risk of being damned, are dearer to him than those who are devout merely out of conformism or cowardice. So John was earning his salvation by being a prince of the temporal church. By throwing himself bodily into the worldly whirlpool, he was the more Christian in spirit, that is, just simply Christian.

Don't all roads lead to Rome? What matter how, as long as he got there? "He who ever strives to outdo himself . . ."

Chosen and damned at the same time, neither angel nor beast. Nothing affected him because everything hurt his extreme sensitivity. He could steal from businessmen, swindle them, but where the meek were concerned his pity was sincere because it grew out of affection, not condescension. "My great strength," he was always fond of saying, "lay in getting out of it without ever forgetting it." He had doubts, yet he pretended never to have any: that was his quite un-Pascalian way of playing the game and playing it better than anyone else.

The game was the key word to his character, the whole meaning of his life. It was all a game to be won. Existing on this earth did not mean hiding your face and blinding yourself while awaiting a better world to come, but on the contrary always looking the adversary square in the face and getting the best of him without ever hiding your own fears, your own inner hesitations. The fascination with evil, the temptations of the Fall, on the one hand, and on the other jejune quietism, narrow little angelism—these were the two shoals between which you had to steer your course with open eyes. *Open eyes* were the operative words. For beyond was salvation.

The game was just beginning.

In three years at the Vatican he had learned the rules of that game among games, power. The Church forced him to be an opportunist? Well, he was paying it back a hundredfold. He had very quickly learned the vulgar Machiavellianism current in the chanceries, the art of saying a thing while suggesting the opposite, the way to oblige someone while doing him a disservice or, on the contrary, really helping while pretending it was nothing. Icy courtesy, unbounded use of the weasel word and the double negative, a gift for the little enigmatic phrase or the expression that has become ambiguous from overuse: soon he knew all the ropes of being a cabinet man, even the way to revise the written report of a conversation so as to take over the other person's good ideas and stick him with the dirty end of the stick, the appearance of having said nothing but stupidities throughout the colloquy. By then he was held in high enough esteem to be entrusted with the most difficult of negotiations, and allowed to settle matters which before his time had been only within the province of the surrogate or the secret offices of the father general of the Society of Jesus, whom Vatican circles knew as the Black Pope.

The Bureau of American Affairs of the Secretariat was at the time extremely active. For the Holy See was going through difficult times: Togliatti's Italian Communist party had a majority and it looked very much as if Italy might go over to the side of the Soviets with the first free election, "which will also be the last," according to Monsignore Walkman's dire prediction. What the Vatican had to do was to transfer to the U.S. the huge sums it had invested in the peninsula under Mussolini and in that way shelter a part of its real estate holdings by converting them into liquid assets. But at the same time, it could not afford to bend the laws of the international market place too violently, nor especially could it take the risk of ruining the still-unstable economy of Italy, for that would most certainly have led to just what the Pope most feared: power to the "Bolsheviks."

Discreetly selling off the properties in Rome and Milan, and making secret purchases in New York, Chicago, or Philadelphia, "laundering" money through Mafia connections, these were the tasks assigned the Vatican financiers. Monsignori Walkman and Spellman—*Propaganda fide et dollaro,*" as Monsignore Tardini wittily dubbed them—were the artisans of this new "American policy." And Father John K. Flaherty was their Mr. Handyman. Who could ever have suspected that young giant with his open look and his childlike smile? Who could doubt the word of the "cowboy"? The tall naïve blond lad was just a simpleton in the eyes of the outsiders who dealt with him. What is the Church thinking of, sending us kids that are so easy to screw, when always before we've had to reckon with Jesuit double-dealers?

John was having the time of his life. In the country where the shady *combinazione* is the rule, "the big Yankee boob"—Monsignore Tisserant's affectionate nickname for him—was already a past master of the *imbroglio*.

The life he was leading at this time was in every way what it had been for young priests of the court under the pontificates of the Pignatellis, Barberinis, Pamphilis, and Aldobrandinis: "balls, luscious private suppers in gallant company, duels, and orgies," according to reports brought back in the century of the Enlightenment.

Nothing had changed in Rome: John got invited to receptions and soirées, where he met the descendants of the great patrician families whose names dotted the history of the papacy. He went to endless teas given by social Monsignori and was often asked to be "the fourteenth guest" at aristocratic dinners where prelates' careers could be made or ruined, where the odds on the *papabili* were computed, and where to this day plots and whispering campaigns against this or that cardinal are hatched. Then, after midnight, there were the drunken binges in which he drowned his boredom and sadness, the kinky sex connections, the whole wild *dolce vita* that was to make him forget Georgia while following Monsignore Walkman's precept of "all the delights, but no involvement."

Increasingly disgusted by his own excesses, he was beginning to experience self-contempt.

Suddenly, in the middle of the scorching summer of 1947, he began to hate Rome. At the Vatican, the growing paranoia of Pius XII was making life intolerable for the prelates and young secretary-priests. Sister Pasqualina, no longer only called Mrs. Pacelli or The Popess, but now more often, The Kapo or Sister Hitler of the Angels, sowed holy terror among His Holiness's subjects. Anyone meeting the Supreme Pontiff in the hallway had to back away, no one was supposed to come closer than three meters from his desk, one was not to turn his back on him after bidding him farewell, one must not fail to bow when passing in front of the door to his quarters—even in his absence. It was a modern replica of the suffocating etiquette of the court of Louis XIV under the "reign" of Madame de Maintenon.

One morning, in the wee hours, after a much too bibulous supper where he had been bored to death, John had picked a quarrel with young Prince Boccanera, known as Baby, who, for no other apparent reason than his drunkenness, had started insulting the masses of the poor. "Bums, hoodlums, and moochers is all they are, my dear Flaherty," he had assured him in his prissy tone.

"You're looking at one of the sons of those bums, hoodlums, and moochers," John had testily replied, as he swung his forearm against the other man's stomach. Then, snarling, "Well, come on, where is the famous bravery of the Boccaneras, the Black Mouths, eh? I know a lot of Black Fangs who maybe never went on the Crusades but can stand up for themselves a lot better than you. Sure, they're bums, and hoodlums, and maybe cutthroats, too, but they're not afraid to defend themselves, *Prince* Boccanera!"

They finally had to be separated by bystanders, and

Baby ended in the emergency room, pretty badly marked up.

That created one heck of a scandal, with consequences that were all too predictable. While the Boccaneras might not have been as powerful as once they were, they still cut plenty of ice at the Holy See. One word from them could ruin John's career, wipe out his newborn ambitions. So he was smart enough to beat them to the punch. At eight that morning, he very gallantly had his confessor inquire after the health of the prince, and at ten he cabled Monsignore Walkman, who shortly before had gone back to his diocese. At noon he asked for and received an audience with Cardinal Spellman and had the good sense to tell him the whole truth and nothing but the truth, before humbly requesting that he be incardinated to the bishop of Reno.

The next day, following a brief farewell interview with Monsignore Montini, who expressed his sincere disappointment at the sudden defection of so promising a young cleric, but said it all with a very knowing look, the surrogate handed him a cable that had been sent from the U.S. the night before, and had been opened even though it was personally addressed to FATHER JOHN K. FLAHERTY, ON DISTINGUISHED DETACHED SERVICE TO THE HOLY SEE. Unlike the wordy address, the message itself was brief. It just read: LAS VEGAS.

The prospect of Las Vegas brought John back to life.

That was for him all right: hot dogs, milk shakes. Cokes, hamburgers, skyscrapers, high-pressure advertising, real (American) football, Hollywood, TV commercials, cars—cars by the thousands and millions that from his plane window looked like ants on the magnificent highways built under the New Deal. In a few years, that road system had truly made the United States united. By night, he had flown over Nebraska, Colorado, Utah; here and there the cars in the darkness were like glowworms on the long ribbons of asphalt. But tiny as they looked, these were real American cars, twice the size of those Italian bugs! And there were man-sized service stations, too, and grain silos as tall as cathedrals, and bridges, and stockyards—the Promised Land, God's country. How far poor wretched Italy seemed from him now!

Finally, after a quick stop at Salt Lake City, they flew into Las Vegas, and he was ready to jump for joy—especially since Eliah Varese had just moved there.

And on this fine September morning of 1947, Eliah had his chauffeur drive him out to the airport to greet his old friend with their old familiar slogan. The other landing passengers were amazed to see two grown men throw their arms around each other with repeated shouts of "Black Fangs! Devils! Forever!"

John added, happily, "Together again! Tremble, vile minions!"

Later, in the Cadillac taking them back to Eliah's bungalow high above the water level of Lake Mead, he guardedly explained to John the kind of business he was in since coming to Nevada. Listening to the way he worded it all so uncompromisingly, John couldn't help saying, "Listen, kid, you're the one who shoulda been working at the Vatican. Talk about a Jesuit! You take the cake!"

Still later, over the very old Bordeaux wine that he drank iced, Varese, after dismissing his Filipino houseboy, whom he more or less suspected of spying on him, put his proposition to John without beating about the bush:

"Say, how about we go partners? Nothin' to keep you from being a priest and still helping me—being my adviser."

"Well, that's not so easy," John said with an amused sigh. "I might start right off by telling you you're committing a crime. Did you hear that, Eliah? A crime!"

"Whatzat? What crime?"

"Putting a gorgeous 1923 Château-Laffite into a champagne bucket like that!"

"And why the hell is that a crime? I like it cold."

"Listen, kid, you wanna be a success in business, you're gonna have to learn to drink red wine room temperature. Like it or not! That's the way it is!"

"Oh, John, you're always good for a laugh, see? That's just why you oughta become my partner, you could clue me in on all like dat. And gimme some good ideas."

"Ideas, my ass! Look, old pal, you really think I haven't seen where you're coming from in the last two hours? This dear country of ours has laws that make churches and religious communities tax-exempt enterprises, doesn't it?"

"Ummmm . . ."

"So, if I'm the pastor of Holy Trinity Church, and the good friend of the great Eliah Mosè Varese, president and chief executive officer of EMV Inc., a corporation doing some kind of business that no one knows too much about—well, is that it?"

"Okay, kiddo! You got the drift of it," the youthful mafioso exclaimed.

"Yeah, sure. But what do you take me for? John K. Flaherty wasn't born yesterday, you know. 'That young fellow'll go far'—Monsignore Montini himself said so."

"Then, you see, that explains why I think it oughta be fifty-fifty."

"Well, you don't let any grass grow under your feet, do you? I can see now why you got the Caddy, and the chauffeur, and the houseboy, and all, so fast."

As he said this, John got up and went over to pull the handle of a slot machine that stood in Eliah's living room. It came up three bold 7's, and a rain of dimes poured out of the jackpot.

"See," Eliah called to him, "right off the bat!"

John himself took it for a sign from heaven: this day was intended to be the start of his personal fortune. But he would not have been Father John K. Flaherty, S.J., if he hadn't gone on to add, "Well, if that's the way you want it, I may consider working with you, my dear friend and con man. But in that case you'll have to move the one-armed bandit out of your living room and get rid of all this positively crappy fake rustic furniture."

"You crazy or somethin'? It set me back twenty-five grand to fix dis place up."

"Well, Eliah, just remember this: most people will only judge you by appearance. The day you get that through your noodle, you got it made: Ap-pear-an-ces. Got that? When you do, you'll be king of the mountain."

John's lessons did not fall on deaf ears. In a few years, Eliah Varese was indeed king of the mountain in a good part of Las Vegas. And the pastor of Holy Trinity didn't find his parish work very time-consuming. His bishop had not been backward in explaining to him that "here people only go into a church to pray to Saint John or the Holy Virgin to make them win at twenty-one or dice. And they only come to confession when they've contemplated suicide after going for broke and crapping out!"

So the power behind the throne of the president of EMV Inc. was able to devote most of his time to the business, his own and Eliah's. In the spring of 1950 both of them were independently wealthy. John, it is true, only had half as much as Eliah, for he lavishly gave to charitable endeavors and spent a fortune improving Holy Trinity, the most prosperous church in the diocese.

When people asked where all the money came from to do so much work on the building, he would say, "Well, gamblers, you know, are very generous when the collection plate is passed. They're all superstitious. And they still have the old pagan idea that God will return threefold at the tables whatever they put into the plate or the alms boxes."

Once in a while he was also not above lending a hand to Eliah when the latter was in what he called a "hassle." Like the time Varese almost got knocked off by a gang of pimps and decided to wipe them all out, once and for all, so as to "clean up this fuckin' dump," as he put it.

There was a real fight to the finish, but in the end they won out. The pimps disappeared, and John had the satisfaction of saving a dozen young prostitutes from the degradation of the sidewalks.

19

Well, if he was neither angel nor beast, was he chosen or damned?

Damned, without doubt—because spending so much of his time at the secret board meetings of EMV Inc. and the rest in his parish simply bored him stiff. His financial success and the largess he was able to distribute were not enough to keep him happy. He no longer felt it was any great achievement to have raised his mother and sisters out of their old poverty and seen to it that all of his brothers got educated or learned a trade or both.

He was rich now—richer than that Bee Killing Kid, that boxer who, when he was twelve, had seemed to him to be the richest man in the world. And yet he was unable to define what he was missing. Deep in his heart there was that frustration that to him spelled hell on earth.

"Oh, Lord, what has happened to me?" he would pray. "What has happened to me?" Yet he had the resources of meditation and charity and reading, the resources of an education which Varese didn't even suspect, but his friend was not half as bored as he. He collected abstract paintings and rare editions of Church Fathers; he translated the Bible from Hebrew, which he had once again started studying; he staged concerts of sacred music at Holy Trinity and engaged the world's leading musical artists to perform. But none of that could truly overcome his deep-seated quiet desperation, free him from his melancholy.

Was this due to some unsatisfied lust for power, which came over him when he had exhausted all the pleasures that money can bring?

He was not yet thirty.

Damned—or perhaps chosen. For just when he had lost all taste for everything and was ready to retreat to some very strict monastery, he got another chance to run the dangers of war and devote himself to serving others: Korea.

The day after the UN resolution the American Council of Bishops suggested to John that he reenter the service as a chaplain for the Marines serving there, arranging for him to switch from the Army to the Corps. Varese, even though in a position to avoid recall as a reservist, volunteered too, without waiting for the Air Force to call him up. Perhaps, as usual, he already had some shady deal cooked up over there, or it may have been that he preferred to put more distance between himself and the owners of the Imperator's Palace, who had recently been giving him a hard time. Whatever the reason, he was delighted to have another crack at flying.

In some strange way, the serenity that John had been tempted to seek in a monastic retreat he found on the deck and in the holds of the carriers he served on, the *Badoeng Straits* and the *Sicily*. For life here, as there, left no room for improvisation or invention; everything was regulated as carefully as in a ballet. There was perfect fitting of the means to the ends, complete forswearing of free will, and an imperative feeling of necessity at every moment of the day, all of which had something very sacred about it. This new life was in a way almost mystical, and he lived it to the fullest, in fascination, sometimes almost in ecstasy.

When the war was over, he came back to the United States, a bit more disillusioned still, yet even more fervent in his faith in God and in himself. There was still something he had to prove to the world; he still had to win, still had to come out on top.

But what he did first was something that gave the Council of Bishops pause: He went into a strict Benedictine monastery in the Mexican mountains and stayed there for two months to find himself again, to regain his serenity, and toughen his will, and to pray, locked up in an *in pace*. This monastery of St. Benedict was the only one that had survived the terrible antireligious persecutions that had shaken Mexico some fifteen years earlier. To take a retreat there was a supreme act of piety, and he knew from reading about it of the existence of its *in pace* that dated back to the days of the Inquisition. He found out it had never been destroyed, even though it had not been put to use for two centuries or more. It had not been destroyed—or rather, had not been filled in: this dungeon was in fact nothing more than a well. It was a hole dug in the rock that underlay the cloister buildings, about thirty-five feet deep, and barely six feet wide, lighted only from the opening above into which in olden times they cast the unfortunate relapsed heretic. Once a day the monks lowered food and drink to John through this opening—stale bread and a pitcher of water in a basket at the end of a rope—and he sent his toilet pail up by the same route.

John had himself locked in there one December morning.

Among the remains of oldtime prisoners who had perished there and never been seen again, he dug himself a sort of litter. He was so tall that he could scarcely stretch out in this tomb.

Then he buried himself in prayer, screamed entire nights long, and mortified himself. He thought he was going crazy, but each morning a monk would look down from the top of the well and say softly to him, "Come back up, brother. What is it you still think you have to prove?"

And John answered with the arrogance of Diogenes in his barrel: "Brother, be good enough to get out of my light. It's dark enough down here without you."

He came back out the morning of Shrove Tuesday. Carnival was going full blast in Cuernavaca. Skinny, unshaven, hirsute and filthy, he walked out into the dazzling light. He tottered, and fell, and got up again—and he was delirious with joy. Around him firecrackers were going off and Bengal lights burning. A hand organ was playing "La Cucaracha." Children wearing masks and men dressed as skeletons were doing a kind of dance of death in the street. A small toothless old lady, hideous as death itself, grabbed his arm and yelled in his face, "Gringo! Try my delights."

These "delights" were in fact small orange blossom popovers. But the old hag's basket was also full of sugar candy skulls, crossed legbones made of marzipan, and for a second John thought he was still down in the *in pace* and hallucinating.

"My God, it can't be!" he muttered.

312

"Delights! Delights!" the old woman was calling. "Try my delights!"

"Oh, Lord, take pity," John moaned. But then he started to laugh—for he realized that these delights were nothing but pastry.

He was so short of everything, felt so weak and helpless, that he asked an acrobat who was doing contortions as he passed the hat among the spectators, "Say, can you tell me where I can find the United States consul?"

He immediately realized how silly it was to ask the acrobat the question, but before he could turn away, the man answered, "You no find heem today, *amigo*. Yanqui consul, heem a *borracho* like you. He drunk last night, with Eengleesh consul, I betcha."

And then, deafened by an explosion of firecrackers beneath his feet, John resumed his wandering, half aimlessly, but half amusedly, too. Little by little he felt the crowd's merriment take hold of him, and he sang along with the rest of them. They clamored at him, "Hey, gringo, sing with us! Join in the chorus!"

Dancers were passing bottles of tequila and mescal from hand to hand. One offered him a bottle in the shape of a cross. He took a swig from it and shivered, burned by the fiery liquid running into his empty stomach. He let out a shriek and joined in the dance, which promptly turned into a farandole.

At the end of the esplanade, facing the blinding sun, a big amusement park Ferris wheel was turning and turning. John laughed broadly: he suddenly saw its endless rotation as a symbol of human existence— and of his own in particular.

"Hey, gringo, dance with us. Join the chorus!" the voices shouted at him.

* * *

He was alive again. Like Antaeus touching earth, in the depths of his dark *in pace* he had once again regained control of his original strength, hardened his invincible will.

Never again was he to know doubt. Now he knew what it was that he had so long sought after, so darkly pursued.

It was power.

20

In the spring of 1952 he met again with his "evil spirit."

Since he got back from Korea, Eliah had been living on Long Island, in a fine house built in the twenties. Made of pink marble and modeled after the Petit Trianon, it was not far from the home of the Corleone family, in which he had so many friends —as well as enemies.

John had now asked his archbishop, Cardinal Spellman, to incardinate him to the bishop of Brooklyn. Father Killarly had recently died, the victim of a stray bullet when he tried to intervene in a street fight. John was given the "plum" of his parish. Local boy makes good!

He could not describe how it felt now to be the priest in the sacristy of the Holy Virgin, where fifteen years earlier he had committed the crime that was to change his whole life. Nothing had changed here. There was the same subaqueous light as on the day of that theft, the same mysterious sheen of light refracted through the newfangled cheap religious stained glass. But suddenly, stepping back and looking at them as if he had never seen them before, he realized how perfectly awful those stained-glass windows were, how perfectly awfully pietistic.

And talk about treasure! The treasure that had once seemed so overwhelmingly impressive to him was a few bits of battered tinware, a little gilt-copper metal-work, and some phony gems. Now he understood why Moe Lou, the India Street fence, had given him and Eliah such a pittance for the pyxes and crucifixes they had brought him. The fact was, John had risked eternal damnation for fakes, for cheap imitations! And that cruel mortification chastened him as much as all that he had undergone in the depths of the *in pace*.

Now he could certainly feel he had expiated his sin.

So the first act of Father John K. Flaherty, when he took over from the young vicar who had been temporarily handling the parish, was to head for Manhattan, for Fifth Avenue and Tiffany's. And there he ordered thirty-five thousand dollars' worth of religious ornaments for his church. He brought in Renaissance designs to be reproduced in the jewelers' goldsmith shops, and with a sureness of taste and a knowledgeability that made the craftsmen sit up with admiration, he suggested how they might stylize and modernize the fifteenth-century Italian masterpieces.

In so doing, he felt, he was washing away the humiliation. He was redeeming himself.

His second act—this one lay, not religious—was to organize a luncheon after his first Sunday Mass. The guests he invited were his lawyer, his accountant, Eliah, and their banker.

He informed them that he had decided to liquidate all his holdings in Nevada and reinvest all his money back here in New York—back home.

* * *

On Friday, September 20, 1959, at nightfall, on the thirtieth floor of the J and F Tower, John was in the offices of the Prima Bank, looking out through the boardroom windows at the sun setting across the Hudson. It was pink and gold, and translucent. It was, he thought, like a moment of eternity arrested forever.

In the distance, birds were flying at top speed in front of the lighter mass of a string of purplish strati lengthening out toward the horizon. Everything was shiny and bright. Beneath that sight, neon lights were going on one by one, and then, all of a sudden, all the street lights at once, hard though they were to make out from so high.

His vacant stare turned toward the other end of the oval table on which the very bright light of a stainless steel lamp made a glare: Eliah Varese was sitting there, his back to the sky and its diffused light crowning him, as he impatiently drummed his fingers on the glass tabletop.

Their eyes met. They quickly exchanged a little smile meant for themselves alone: that old bore of a Monroe (unfortunately one of the biggest stockholders in EMV Inc.) was treating them and the nine other board members to his semiannual tirade, which went on endlessly in that hesitant monotonous voice of his, that so irritated them.

"Lady and gentlemen," he was saying, "in any deal we make we must consider not only its financial advantages, but what I would call, don't you know, its moral aspects as well."

At that moment an executive secretary came noiselessly into the room and, leaning over John's shoulder, whispered, "Monsignore Walkman is on the phone for you from Rome."

He got up hurriedly, smiled and nodded his apology to the speaker and the assembly and, looking troubled, started from the room. He knew, he could feel what it was.

His own office, right next to the boardroom, was paneled in teakwood and gaboon mahogany, decorated with Pollock, Jasper Johns, and Albers abstractions, and indirectly lighted. There was an English leather couch in front of a fine Rauschenberg. He let himself down into his swivel chair. He was elated; he felt like shouting. He *knew*, he could *feel* it . . .

The secretary whispered to him, "Number two on the red line." But he did not pick it up immediately.

He wanted to savor this moment; he let his eyes wander unseeingly over the framed pictures in the empty spaces between blocks of books on his bookshelves. There was a drawing of Georgia singing at the Notte Bianche; an old snapshot with a corner missing of himself working out at Mister Romeo's gym; another, this one overexposed, of Varese and him in their military uniforms clowning for the camera; a postcard from Cuernavaca; a recent picture of his mother on her seventieth birthday in the garden of the house he had given her in Southampton; one of St. Peter's in Rome; and then him again, in a tux, at some great affair, blinking into the flash; and finally, a portrait of Pope John XXIII inscribed to him.

He settled firmly into his chair and turned to look out the window. The sky was aflame now, as immaterial and triumphant as in an apotheosis painted by Tiepolo. He took a deep breath, made his wild heartbeats quiet down, picked up the phone, and said, "Yes, Your Eminence?"

"John," he heard, "the Vatican needs you, m'boy."

PART THREE

1

He awoke with a start.

He was not looking up at *Daniel in the Lions' Den* in his room on Via Margutta, but at a terrible cheap print of St. Sebastian, which he did not immediately recognize.

There was a knock at the door: *"Monseigneur! Monseigneur!"*

The drawl of the Lucerne native made him suddenly realize where he was: in prison, in the Swiss Guard barracks.

"Entrez," he answered, getting up and wiping the sweat from his brow with a corner of the sheet.

The young halberdier, now without his weapon, threw back the bolt—John learned thereby that he had been locked in—and entered, saying, "Your Eminence's food tray."

As he set it on the table, he whispered, "If Your Eminence so desires, a Sister of Saint Martha can come and serve it to you."

John mustered all of his cardinal's unction to reply, "That will not be necessary, my son, but if you were to stay and keep me company . . ."

"I may not, Monseigneur," the Swiss guard immediately replied. "Against the rules."

John smiled with obvious sarcasm. "Rules?" he said.

321

"Why, don't you know that I used to be, uh, the recruiting sergeant? Yes, that's the word for what I was—when his Holiness John XXIII wanted to beef up the force at the time of the Council."

"Monseigneur, all the guards who knew you, uh, still are sorry you left us. You did so much for us."

Modestly waving away the compliment, John put his hand on the young fellow's shoulder, in a gesture of rough, manly fellowship.

"Well, I was a soldier, too," he said. "I was an infantry captain once, and a marine chaplain in Korea."

Then, frisking the very full blue and yellow breeches of the young guard's uniform, he outlined the revolver hidden in the thigh pocket, and commented laughingly, "That Michelangelo was certainly a genius. He even foresaw the invention of the extra-flat revolver."

The young man was both amused and intrigued. But with a shake of his head he informed the cardinal that he now had to leave. His Eminence extended his ring hand, and the guard knelt and kissed the ring.

While giving the lad his benediction, John sighed bitterly.

"So I'll eat alone," he said. "The first prisoner here in—what? Twenty years, I guess. Yes, it's twenty years since last we had to use our prisons. A happy country, this!"

The Swiss guard lingered at the door. He was sorry that Cardinal Flaherty had to be alone, he who was supposed to be so proud, so strong. Now he seemed humble and weak to the lad, as he asked him quietly, lost in his own thoughts, "What is your name, soldier?"

"Gunther, at Your Excellency's service. Gunther Aescher."

"Gunther?" John said, as if he were about to ask him to do something but had not yet made up his mind.

"Yes, Monseigneur?"

"No, nothing, my boy," John answered, dropping his idea. "Love God, my son, and go in peace."

Gunther bowed to him, quite puzzled, and closed the door behind him.

But as soon as the guard was out, John took off his skullcap with irritation and roughly unbuttoned his cassock. Then he tossed all his sacerdotal vestments onto the faldistory, and stood in jeans and T-shirt, a Holy Year T-shirt with a picture of the *Pietà* on it, and a simple Italian confession of faith inscribed beneath: *Lord Jesus, I believe in thee.*

The outfit was somehow typical of Cardinal Flaherty, and he still had his pastoral cross around his neck.

At the table he saw that they had sent him eggs scrambled in cream, a rib of beef that must have weighed a pound, mixed fresh vegetables, a sweet, fruit, a tall glass of milk, and a pot of coffee.

Well, he smiled to himself, this had not come from the kitchen of the Sisters of St. Martha but from the galley of the Swiss Guards, probably the best mess in the world along with that of the Marine officers at Quantico.

His nightmares of the past night had already dissipated. He was no longer in pain, no longer afraid. He sat down and went after the first dish that seemed appealing to him. He drank a mouthful of milk and triumphantly smacked his lips.

He knew now that he would get even; it was just a matter of time.

Violent explosive noises. Halberdier Gunther Aescher had gone through a door into the firing range of the barracks.

Dressed in athletic warmup suits, their ears covered with protective gear, a few of the Swiss Guards were shooting at human-shaped targets passing before them at the far end of the concrete shooting boxes. At times the targets come in bunches, and in the blink of an eye they have to pick out the ones wearing cassocks or just a simple cross, which must not be hit. An electronic scoreboard records their hits in green quartz and gives them an overall mark, on a scale from 1 to 10; their misses come up in red and are marked from -1 to -10. Getting a red -10 is what the Swiss Guards call "knocking off His Holiness."

Gunther walked through the room with its stench of cordite, looking indifferently at his comrades' scores. But the last of the sharpshooters turned toward him, pretending to take aim at him, and yelled, "Hands up!" followed by a more serious "How's Flaherty?"

Once over his surprise, the young Lucernian made a face.

"Listen," soldier Franz Hackmann said to him, "if you're on watch tonight, tell him when you see him that as of this morning we've renamed a green 10 'making a Flaherty.' "

"You think he'll get it?"

"Of course! He's the one who set up this range, just like the one the CIA has at Langley."

"Oh, I didn't know that! What a man! You think he'll be cleared?"

"Quicker than you think. Flaherty tops 'em all."

The sharpshooter emptied a full clip in one blast while the halberdier, hands over his ears, called to him, "I'm going out to the guardroom."

The ogival vault of that huge room was supported by a double colonnade. Its shutters were closed, and the semidarkness was striped with bands of a dramatic light that fell from small circular bull's-eye windows, a golden light such as one sees in oldtime paintings. It glinted on the metal breastplates and helmets and the leather body harnesses laid out on the tables in the shadow. Two bare-chested men from the Canton of Vaud were playing dice, the well-waxed handles of their halberd pikes stuck into their rings, and steins of full-headed beer alongside them. This scene out of a Caravaggio was reflected in the great steel door of the refrigerator when Gunther Aescher closed it after having gotten himself a can of Coca-Cola and smartly snapping the tab off it.

He unhooked his spattered doublet, sank sighing down into a large club chair in front of the television set, and pressed the remote-control button.

The sound came on first: ". . . of the assassination of the emir," an announcer was saying, followed by the sound of a shot.

Then the picture: On the steps of the palace at Ahbat, where he was waving to the crowd acclaiming him, Farouh could be seen falling as he clutched at his belly. He was dead.

2

Paul VI arose from the table, assisted by the two young priests, his usual dinner companions, with whom he enjoyed talking theology while eating. Sister Luisa was busily turning on the television set and smoothing the cushions of his favorite armchair so he might sit in it.

"We've dallied somewhat over our dinner tonight," he commented. "The evening news is already on."

And indeed, against a background of very dramatic music, the voice of Sergio Telmon, the anchorman of RAI's *Telegiornale,* coming on, was already well into his subject: ". . . funeral of His Majesty Emir Farouh-Ahbat was the occasion for renewed confrontations. In the fighting that took place, some forty persons were reported killed."

As the picture came clear, they could see behind him a picture of the emir and some still pictures of the funeral and the street fighting. Then, as he moved away, the background began to move.

"In the north of the country," he was saying, "full-fledged fighting broke out again this morning between the government forces and Haraoui rebels."

Now there were war scenes on the screen: tanks rolling across the desert in a huge cloud of dust, exhausted soldiers trudging along a path of white

sand, and oil refineries set afire by aerial bombard-
ment. Then, as the adagio was replaced by a funeral
march, there were corpses lined up on gravel dunes,
a burnt-out armored vehicle, hundreds of army boots
left behind in a disorderly retreat, and a parachutist
who had been taken prisoner and could not hold
back his tears as he went by the camera.

The announcer, over, was saying, "In a statement
sent to the UN, Ali Fahdi, head of the Haraoui National Liberation Movement, accused the CIA and
the Mafia of what he termed aiding and abetting the
emirate's shock troops. It is independently reported
that the directors of HUELCO have formally denied
allegations that the oil company, which supposedly
has interests in this part of the world, fomented this
conflict."

The Pope then saw a picture of himself appear on
the screen.

"The many urgent appeals for a cease-fire have
now been joined by an exhortation from His Holiness Paul VI. In a press release this afternoon, the
Supreme Pontiff deplored, quote, the criminal madness which has overtaken this wretched earth, unquote. He added, quote, just as is the case every time
there is fighting anywhere, each of us must feel in
the depths of his own soul his own share of guilt,
unquote."

Sergio Telmon was on again in closeup, while behind him a view of St. Peter's faded into a typical
shot of Buckingham Palace. "Now," he was saying,
"we will call in our London correspondent, Sandro
Paternostro. Can you hear me, Sandro?"

"Yes, good evening, Sergio Telmon. At noon today,
in a suite at the Dorchester Hotel, Prince Fuad held
a press conference for over fifty journalists from all

parts of the world. In his opening statement, the brother of the late emir said he was ready to return home immediately. Asked by a BBC man when he might be leaving, he said, quote, powerful friends whom I am not at present at liberty to name are preparing the way for my return, which is what the great majority of my beloved countrymen hope for, unquote."

His Holiness had had enough and impatiently motioned to one of the two young priests with him to turn the set off.

At the same moment, Sister Luisa came into the dining room and whispered, with eyes lowered, "Very Holy Father, I must tell you that the Reverend Father—"

"Shhh! No names," he interrupted her as discreetly as he could, indicating by a flicker of his eyelids the presence of the two young prelates with him. Then, in a barely audible whisper, he added, "We will see him immediately. Have him wait at the chapel door."

And His Holiness went out to say his rosary first.

The mysterious religious man with whom he had an appointment was a Jesuit father in his forties who, due to privations and penances, looked older than his years. He was frighteningly thin and all the taller for wearing under his shiny old cassock a hobnailed hairshirt which forced him to stand absolutely straight. Along with this he had the swarthy complexion of a Spanish hermit, thinning hair, deep lines in his face, black rotting teeth, and wild eyes—the very incarnation of a mystic painted by El Greco.

Through the door of the Holy Father's private chapel, which was ajar, he could see the bas-relief sculpted by Enrico Manfrini, portraying the Pentecost with the apostles kneeling before the Holy Virgin, among them John XXIII, Paul VI, and the Patriarch Athenagoras; the whole thing slightly disgusted him, as being somewhat overworldly and intended to feed secret vanities. It occurred to him that in other times this Manfrini might have been burned at the stake, or at the very least thrown into a dungeon, and this idea seemed to cheer him up. It was with good reason that the Reverend Father Francisco-Javier Olivares de la Huerta de Isunza y Pacaÿe was known behind his back, by the few who were aware of his existence at the Vatican, as The Grand Inquisitor.

He gave a start on hearing His Holiness's light step sound on the marble floor and quickly turned to kneel in obeisance.

"Get up, my son," the Pope said to him in French (for it was in this language that the noble Castilian had been raised by his governesses and tutors). "If we summoned you here to meet with us far from any witnesses, it is so we might find out the truth and the full scope of this, uh, disaster. Please, we beg you, spare us nothing. Come right to the point. We wish to know all."

The Jesuit seemed possessed of a white rage that was eating away inside of him. He could hardly contain himself before his sovereign.

"The fact," he began in a hoarse and colorless voice, "the fact is, Holy Father, that we can no longer hide that we are the major stockholders in HUELCO. And that HUELCO can no longer deny that it is indirectly—or perhaps, alas, even directly!—responsible for this war. The fact is that the UN will be convening a special meeting in"—he peered at his wristwatch, the band of which bore his family's coat of arms—without doubt, the sole self-indulgence in this austere monk's existence—and mentally figured the difference in time zones—"in three quarters of an hour, Holy Father. And we have every reason to believe—"

"Well, let's see," Paul VI cut him off, slightly annoyed by the prophetic tone Father Olivares was using to him, "let's see what we can do to counter the most pressing dangers—without doing anything to offend the Sacred College or the Secretariat."

The Spaniard hesitated to answer.

"Well, say what you're thinking, Francisco!" the Pope said.

"We could cover up," the Jesuit sighed in disgust, as if the words themselves hurt him as they came out.

"Meaning what?"

"This Eliah Varese—the swindler—Monsignore Flaherty's friend. He had the nerve to get in touch with Monsignore Razzi. And he offered to buy up all the Institute's shares in HUELCO in the name of a Zurich company. And by a purchase contract predated seven months back . . ." Indignation was choking him, and he had to take a deep breath before stating, "At that date the HUELCO shares had hit rock bottom. And this individual wanted . . ."

"You mean wants, don't you?"

Father Olivares shuddered at having been understood without having come right out, and bit his lips.

"He wants two hundred thousand dollars, uh, for supplying the fake contract covering the transaction, and his filing costs, and whatever else."

Paul VI, deeply amused, emitted a dry little laugh.

"Oh, very good! Very good indeed! Too good for words! *Stupendo!* . . . What it amounts to is: First, this character got us into this mess, and now he's offering to be our savior!"

The Spanish monk, somewhat crestfallen at the Pope's mocking reaction, regretfully went on, "Of course, we would be cleared."

"We *will* be cleared," the Pope corrected him. "For, of course, Monsignore Razzi said yes!"

"Well . . . uh . . . that is," the unhappy Jesuit stammered, "he was waiting for the decision to come from higher up, Very Holy Father."

"Ah, yes," His Holiness replied, "that sounds just like Monsignore Razzi's well-known Christian humility."

While the Holy Father looked benevolent indeed, Father Olivares stared coldly at him with eyes that betrayed all the suppressed hatred the rigidly devout man he was felt for such offhand manners, unworthy in his eyes of a Pope. In a very low voice, savoring in advance the way he was about to squelch this unwonted lightness of spirit, he hissed: "There is worse, Holy Father. Monsignore Razzi has told me that Flaherty, that is, His Eminence Cardinal Flaherty, was the only one who knew the secret code to the Institute's computers, in particular the ones at Via Sottocolle, which he had altered in '73. He can, uh, tamper with any of our personal accounts, if he wishes. And Monsignore Razzi is afraid that, uh, well, he is afraid we may have to call on Monsignore Flaherty so as to be able to get hold of the two hundred thousand dollars the Institute has to turn over to this Varese."

But his anticipated bombshell proved a dud. Paul VI answered in a detached and apparently very calm tone, "Yes, we know. That's what Monsignore Nichols also thinks, and he feels we may not be able to *depose* him as readily as the Sacred College had hoped, nor even to *suspend* him. Indeed, he has already appointed a commission to see by what artifice of our

Most Holy Canon Law we may be able to *censure* him without *suspending* him: kind of a *mezzo termine*.

"This whole affair is most heartbreaking to us," he sighed, shaking his head, a moment later.

He had just realized that his utterly sensible and serene words had shocked the half-mad mystic. But he could not keep from asking him one last question before dismissing him.

"Tell me, is what Monsignore McAwkleen claims a fact? Is it true that the Institute for Christian Charity sends five million lire a month to that, uh, that Mary Magdalene, that Miss France?"

The Spaniard muttered icily, "The wench is carried under the heading of *Miscellaneous Charities*, may God forgive me."

Then he knelt to kiss the ring which the Pope held out to him by way of dismissal.

"Tomorrow morning our coded instructions will be transmitted to you by the sacristan whom you know," the Supreme Pontiff said. "Go, and may the Lord be with you."

The Jesuit left as he had come, by a hidden stairway known to only half a dozen persons in the Vatican.

"May the Lord be with you," the Pope repeated.

But the penitent was already beyond hearing: as he walked down the stairs he felt with ineffable joy the hairshirt which was tearing his skin off. And the nailheads laid out before and behind in the form of a cross bit into his chest and back; he was near passing out with enjoyment, deaf to anything except his own secret ecstasy.

"Be with you" came the echo off the bare stone vault.

And then, in order to feel even greater pain than before, and thus a greater voluptuous enjoyment, he hurried and jumped with joined feet two steps at a time.

Now he could feel the blood running down the small of his back and over his ribs, down onto his belly, sticking to the twill of his shirt, finally seeping through to the yellowed material of his old threadbare cassock.

"Oh, Lord, may my joy be everlasting," he murmured to himself.

3

10:35 A.M.: Alitalia's Palermo–Paris DC-9 #AZ111 landed at Rome's Leonardo Da Vinci Airport.

Unbuckling his safety belt, Eliah Varese suddenly realized it must be three years since he last traveled on a regular commercial airline. His secretary, Leo Carter, had taken his buff leather case and was preceding him down the aisle toward the exit. Eliah now in turn got up from his seat, one hand stifling a mild yawn while the other played with the good-luck charm dancing on his pearl-and-smoke-gray striped tie. His eldest son, John Kevin, who sometimes acted as his bodyguard, fell in right behind him. But none of the other first-class passengers would know that the serious-looking businessman and the carefree adolescent were related to each other or even had any connection. John Kevin was wearing down-at-the-heels tennis shoes, a clean but faded pair of jeans, a "Hawaiian" shirt, and a marine jacket bought at an army and navy store. Over his shoulder was slung a large sports bag with a decal of a scuba diver on it.

Without exchanging a word or even a sign, father and son separated in the arrival hall just as Leo Carter said, between closed teeth, "He's here."

A long-haired tall blond young American, wearing black slacks and turtleneck, came smiling toward

Varese, saying, "Boss, the Mercedes is ready," while John Kevin was off hailing a taxi.

"Monsignore! This way. Pstt! Monsignore!"

But Father Francisco-Javier Olivares de la Huerta de Isunza y Pacaÿc, looking at his watch with the coat of arms and sighing aloud "Eleven o'clock! Where can he be?" did not hear the sacristan of Santa Cecilia dell' Aventino calling to him from the shadows of the transept, "Monsignore!"

Rather, in the ray of sunshine slanting through the bell turret of a side chapel, Father Olivares was watching a moustached old lady tiptoe toward the holy water, glancing furtively in all directions. Wondering what she was up to, he moved over toward her and saw her dip a silver cup into the stone shell and then drink the water she had taken from it, as she hid behind a column. "What impious, superstitious ways these local people have," he grumbled to himself. He knew that they believed that the holy water from Santa Cecilia dell' Aventino was a cure for rheumatism. He was about to call her on it, when he finally heard the sacristan's thrice-repeated "Monsignore!"

Father Olivares, livid with rage, advanced on the rolypoly old man, scolding in a voice quite inappropriate to the inside of a church, "I've told you a hundred times not to address me in that way. I'm your brother, Anselmo, your brother!"

"Yes, Monsignore, uh, I mean, Brother," the terrified sacristan replied.

"Well, do you have anything for me?" the Jesuit asked in his guttural Castilian-tinged Italian.

"Right away. I hid it behind the tabernacle, Fa— Brother."

"Good. I'll go get it," the monk replied. Then, feeling the pain from one of the nails in his hairshirt get sharper, he added, "Tell me, Anselmo, do you still have any of the antiseptic salve you make from the dust in the reliquary?"

"If you come back tomorrow, I'll have some, Brother."

As he went back out into the dazzling sunlight, the monk was thinking that this means of communication between the Holy See and him was indeed strange, if not actually dangerous; but then, he argued with himself, the apostolic palace was known to be bugged all over and crawling with spies. One can never be too cautious.

Dreamily, Claudine Lambaire, having taken just a few puffs from her tiparillo, crushed it down into the marble ashtray perched on the edge of her tub and stretched out in the scalding amber-scented water of her bath. She shivered. On her baroque dressing table she could see the time on the digital clock, 11 59 00, and for a whole minute she was fascinated by the constant change of the seconds, until it read 12 00 00.

At just that moment, Diab called from outside the door, "Mademoiselle?"

"Yes, what is it?" she asked in an irritated voice.

"It's for you, Mr. Berg."

"On the phone?"

"No, mademoiselle, he's here."

"Robert? Well, then, show him in."

She jumped out of the tub, grabbed a great terrycloth robe off a rack in the gym, and once she was dry slipped into a white satin dressing gown with a black collar, that had gold lettering on the back, reading:

HAROLD FINNEGAN
THE KING

As she closed it about her, she ran out into the entry gallery.

"Oh, Robert, Robert, I'm so glad to see you!" she exclaimed. "He's been gone for twelve whole days now. And not a word. It's just awful!"

She threw herself into the arms of the young lawyer and suddenly burst into sobs.

Trying to console her, Berg murmured, "Don't worry, Claudine. Eliah Varese'll be able to find him."

"Who," she gulped, "who is Eliah Varese?" Then she collapsed into a large baroque armchair facing the portrait of a Renaissance cardinal who appeared to be looking scornfully down on her.

"Well," Robert Berg began quietly, "I see there are two or three things I'll have to fill you in on, Claudine. Let's go into the living room, shall we? We'll be much more comfortable there."

With the top of his Bel Air down, Mike Wyatt drove along, humming "Solitude" to himself and beating time on the car door. In the middle of a phrase, he stopped the beat in order to stick out his hand: he was turning left onto the ramp of the belt parkway known as the Raccordo Anulare. The only remaining trace of the beating he had taken at the hands of Gigi and Babu was a slight dark puffiness over his right eye. He could see it as he glanced into his wide rearview mirror.

"That son of a bitch has been riding my tail for over a quarter of an hour now," he commented to himself. "Shit, man! Is the faggot trying to cruise me, or what?"

He slowed down so that the Innocenti-Cooper that had been following him all the way from the Parioli would have to pass him. The driver was a young man in a wild-patterned shirt. Once the little red car with its Venetian license plate was ahead of him, he could see a decal of the Deepsea Divers' Club on the rear window—and then it sped away.

"That jerk is in a hurry to go and get drowned," he said aloud, as he watched him pick up speed and, after working his way into the left lane of the belt parkway, disappear from sight in a few seconds. "Maybe he dives for sharks in the Grand Canal!"

As he drove into the Tivoli, he had already forgotten him. But suddenly, just as he was parking his convertible alongside the baptistery of the little church of Sant' Andrea dell' Orto, his eye caught the red splash of an Innocenti-Cooper standing in the square, across from the bell tower: same VE plate for Venice, he noted, and same decal.

"Passing strange," he commented inwardly. Then, with his characteristic flipness, added, "Strange indeed that the sharks haven't eaten our gondolier before now!"

"Signore Wyatt?"

He turned. It was the pastor of Sant' Andrea, calling him cordially from the church steps.

"Oh, hello, Father," he answered.

"I see you're punctual. It's just three. Good. Now just wait till you see what I've found for you. Come on! I don't think you'll be disappointed. I got all the information you wanted—and quite a bit more, besides!"

Putting his hand on Mike's shoulder, the white-haired old priest beckoned him inside the church.

When Monsignore Razzi, dressed in a coal black business suit and a midnight blue necktie over a sky blue shirt, got out of the taxi in front of the Excelsior, it was 6:15 P.M. A bellboy helped him turn the heavy revolving door. Despite his "anonymous" getup, the concierge recognized him as soon as he got into the lobby. Coming toward him and greeting him respectfully but as unostentatiously as possible, he said, "Good evening, Your Excellency. I've put you in room one eleven, one flight up."

As he said this, the concierge slipped his own passkey into the prelate's hand. The bishop thanked him and went toward the elevator, to go up one story.

This did not escape the notice of a fashionably dressed young lady reading the *International Herald* in an armchair in the lobby. With a sudden urge to powder her nose, she threw the paper down on a coffee table in front of her. In the middle of the mirror inside her mother-of-pearl compact there was a kind of wiremesh circle into which she whispered, "He's come, and he's alone."

After looking around Room 111, Monsignore Razzi carefully felt all the cushions of the armchairs and finally decided it was best to sit down on the bed.

A knock on the door brought him back to his feet. He could hear a key turning in the lock, and opening the inner door to step into the vestibule, he was amazed to see Eliah Varese make a deep bow, get down on one knee, and devoutly kiss his episcopal ring, as he said, "Ah, Your Excellency!"

In the sweep of his headlights, under the pale moonlight, there were two blank walls before him and, immediately after them, a chipped roadsign reading OSTIA 2 KM, which glowed eerily in the darkness. "This is the place," he said aloud to himself.

At the wheel of his Innocenti-Cooper, John Kevin

Varese slowed down before riding out on the esplanade. "A fine place to set a trap," he mused. Unconsciously, his hand went to the bulge in his jeans where his gun was. At the far end of the deserted terrace facing the sea, he made a U-turn before killing his lights and his motor.

He was not really afraid. His father had taught his brother, Eliah Junior, and him to be serene and self-controlled. Eliah Varese Senior, no longer treated them as children but as partners and friends. John Kevin had been close to the top of his class at law school, and Eliah Junior, who was following in his footsteps, would soon be ready to join the team. "With marks like that, who's ever going to believe that you're really good goyim?" their father would sometimes, teasingly but admiringly, say to them.

John Kevin smiled as he thought of that sentence, which the old man had repeated only a week ago when he was filling them in on the troubles that John Kevin's godfather, whom he had been named after, was in. "We'll have to play this close to the vest," he had later added for John Kevin alone. "You know, these Vatican operators are what you might call sharper than sharp. You got no idea, John. But then again, you might—you *do* know your godfather."

The young man felt the gun on his thigh once more and felt safe. He rolled the window of his Innocenti halfway down, took a deep breath of the good salt air, and tried to see into the darkness while he listened to the sound of the waves breaking below. Then he closed the window again and turned on the radio.

"It is midnight," the announcer was saying. "That ends our newscast. Good night."

He turned the dial, looking for some music, but on another frequency he heard: "Those close to Prince

Fuad have also denied that the CIA was involved in parachuting mercenaries into Haraoui territory" and bitterly noted that all the Italian he had so excelled in at Harvard made it easier for him to read Dante in the original that to be sure he understood what the newscaster was saying.

That was what he was thinking when the long-expected black Lancia appeared. At the wheel of the inconspicuous sedan with Milan license plates sat Father Olivares de la Huerta de Isunza y Pacaÿe, who identified himself by blinking his lights. The young American, by way of reply, turned his on too.

The car came to a stop a dozen yards or so in front of his. The cleric got out. He was dressed in mufti, but with his black turtleneck and dark gray suit he still looked quite markedly ecclesiastical. He had a worn attaché case in his hand. John Kevin, seeing him walk toward him, blinded now by the glare of his headlights, thought he was a scarecrow of a figure with his long gangling body, his emaciated features, and wild eyes.

He worked the gun out of his jeans pocket and with the end of it opened the passenger door of his Innocenti. But as soon as the Jesuit started getting in, he hid the gun quickly, killed his headlights, and took the man's hand and kissed it respectfully, as was befitting with a dignitary of the Church. The Spaniard seemed both shocked and taken aback, but made no comment. He sat back in his seat and opened the case.

With only the ceiling light on, John Kevin could see the carefully piled stacks of hundred-dollar bills, banded with sealed strips of paper bearing the coat of arms of St. Peter's and the words ISTITUTO PER LA CARITA CRISTIANA.

4

"Two weeks this morning," he said aloud, as he sighed.

Since learning that Eliah Varese had double-crossed him, John was furious, and now felt doubly frustrated at being penned up in the Swiss Guards barracks. Why had Eliah made that deal with Razzi? Didn't he trust him anymore? Or think he would be able to get himself out of this fix? And why had he pocketed all the profits from the takeover of the HUELCO shares without offering him his usual share?

When he was first locked up, John had felt pretty well resigned about what had happened: being kept in here had a certain usefulness, he was well aware. At least here no one was going to murder him; he would not have to be on the lookout every minute of the day. And under the protection of the Swiss Guards whom he knew so well, he could continue his intrigues and even—though to a lesser extent—carry on his own business.

He had established so many secret ties, done favors for so many functionaries of the Curia—from the top prelates to the least important underlings—bought the allegiance of so many Vatican clerks, in the fifteen years since he first came to work here! With the passage of time, he had built himself a real following, the "clientèle" of a cardinal-prince of the Renaissance, a shadow army whose efficiency he had seen at the time of the Micheli bankruptcy, and whose faithfulness had served him well during the trial that followed. To set up a network of informants and correspondents, and find dependable messengers to take his coded communications outside the City walls, had taken him only a few days, in some cases a few hours—and he had known that was how it would be.

.Wasn't he, after all, the most venerated of all the Monsignori, the one whom the small fry of the Holy See referred to simply as Monsignore, without having to identify him beyond that, "our own Pope," as one of the young underlings in the ICC had told him he was called, one evening when he was complimenting the young man on his work in the Via Sottocolle office?

He would not be wanting for helpers—that he knew. In fact, perhaps his helpers' enthusiasm would be what was most dangerous for him: they might be too open about it, too imprudent. And yet, being immobilized here would also be his strength, for it would in a way force him to find new devices, to put up better with adversity, to outdo even himself.

But today he was getting near the end of his rope; he was impatient. He *had* to find out why Eliah had acted as he had. He wanted to be sure that the secret report brought to him with his breakfast was indeed true. He wanted to talk to Eliah in person and confront him with it.

Was it possible that Eliah *had* double-crossed him?

This question would leave him no rest. Sitting on the floor, his back against the faldistory, his knees drawn up under his chin, John was wracking his brain.

A knock on the door brought him out of his daydream and quickly to his feet. Halberdier Franz Hackman came in and respectfully bowed before him.

"Your Excellency."

"Franz!"

"You *do* recognize me then, Monseigneur?" said the Swiss, both flattered and surprised.

"Of course. Wasn't I the one who recruited you in the Valais? That was back in '62, before the Council, wasn't it? I had just been made a bishop."

"Yes. And the very next evening . . ." Franz smiled at the recollection, but hesitated to say what it was that amused him so. Finally, he resumed, "The very next evening, if Your Eminence remembers, you took me and the other new recruits out to a night club, and —uh—"

"Oh, that's right," John laughed. "That was the year, wasn't it? I'd forgotten."

He now remembered very well his midsummer trip into the Valais mountains. A few months before the opening of Vatican II, Monsignore Cicognani had thought it would be a good thing to beef up the strength of the Swiss Guard. No less than twenty-four hundred fathers were expected to attend the Council, with an equal number of secretaries, half a thousand observers and experts, plus a hundred-odd envoys and diplomats, to say nothing of the accredited press: no question but that the personal safety of the Supreme Pontiff would require better protection.

So John was sent to do the recruiting from among the practicing Catholic Swiss families who had traditionally been supplying the guards for almost five centuries: they were to be a group of some thirty handpicked men. The usually high criteria of selection were for this occasion made even stiffer: minimum height of 5 feet 11 inches, athletic build, iron constitution, and true distinction in interscholastic sports competitions. The onetime Marine chaplain from Korea thus found himself crisscrossing the most hidden valleys of the Four Cantons and the region of Zermatt in the stifling August heat. But crowded though the mountain villages were with summer visitors, the immense black limousine with the *SCV* plates did not go unnoticed by the locals, who had of course been alerted by their parish priests. And when Monseigneur alighted, resplendent in his purple garb, the curious gathered in the squares before all the churches.

Everyone seemed to want the signal honor of serving His Holiness: John was more moved by such devotion than surprised. How great the prestige of the papacy must still be for these young marriageable men who were making a good living as mountain guides or ski instructors to want to volunteer for five years of the celibacy and strict discipline of barracks life at the Holy See!

Finally, after a week spent in giving blessings to hundreds of the faithful who came to kiss his episcopal ring, and in drinking a countless number of toasts while refusing an equal number of invitations to luncheon, in transmitting the blessing of John XXIII to the priests of every one of the villages in which he stopped, John had collected eight young recruits in the Valais.

The next evening, in Lausanne, where he had stopped for a breather before going into the canton of Lucerne, the privileged fief of the Swiss Guard since the days of Pius IX, he suddenly decided to put on street clothes and go on a bender with his "draftees," most of them young peasants who knew nothing of city life. And what an evening that turned out to be! At midnight, His Excellency could be seen doing a burlesque boogie-woogie on the dance floor of the cabaret where he had wined and dined the future halberdiers of the Holy Father.

"Sure, now I remember, Franz," he was telling the young man now, "you were the first one who shouted, 'Boy, that's some joker of a bishop!' or something of the sort. Yes, you—"

"I'd had too much to drink, Monseigneur," the guard cut in by way of self-justification. And he blushingly added, "I hope you've excused my lack of respect."

But John went right on laughing, saying, "No need to apologize, my son. I'd tied a pretty good one on myself that night!"

Then he turned serious, and asked, "Franz, tell me what they're saying about me at the Vatican."

Franz shook his head, stalled, afraid to commit himself.

"Come on, tell me, tell me," the cardinal insisted, beginning to feel a mild irritation.

Then the soldier, whispering as if he were ashamed of the words that were coming out, said, "I've heard, uh, heard the word 'excommunication' used. They said you were to be excommunicated, Monseigneur. I'm so sorry."

"Excommunicated?" John gasped.

Excommunicated! So, that was their game!

He slumped on the faldistory, as if thunderstruck. Before him, the soldier was smiling apologetically, with his eyes lowered, as if he felt himself somehow responsible for all this.

Excommunicated!

But John had already regained his wits, and standing up again at his full height, nostrils quivering, lips set in hatred, he blurted out, "Bah! Just a rumor! One of Razzi's imaginings!"

"Monseigneur," Franz replied, reassured by the return of His Excellency's habitual composure, "Monseigneur," he repeated in naïve delight, "the Swiss Guard—well, sir, you can count on us!"

John clapped him affectionately on the shoulder and said, "Thank you, Hackman. I know how loyal all of you are."

Very discreetly, turning to the side as if to keep from being seen while making sure that he was, the man from the Valais took a handkerchief out of his breeches pocket, and in so doing by deliberate inadvertance let his gun fall out on the cardinal's priedieu. John, who had seen this maneuver coming, knew precisely how to play the innocent.

He went on, in the most natural tone, "And has there been any news of the war among the emirates?"

"As of yesterday, Monseigneur, no newspapers or TV have been allowed in our barracks, not even the *Osservatore Romano.* And all passes have been canceled."

"Well," John commented derisively, "then they must be afraid that Kuwait or Qatar may come over and attack our little ramparts. Do we have enough boiling oil and molten tar to pour down on those infidels? Are all our arquebuses at the ready?"

"With Monseigneur's indulgence," Franz answered, both incredulous and shocked, not knowing quite what to say, "I'm just an ignorant fellow. Truly, I have no idea what connection there is between the Holy See and—"

"That's high-level politics, my son," the cardinal

answered in a conspiratorial tone. And then, more seriously, "Or perhaps they wish for you to remain in ignorance. But tell me, Franz, how can you remain loyal to an excommunicate?"

"Oh, Your Excellency, we all know that you will be able to defend yourself. Davos, our lieutenant, he says, 'They can't do nothing to Flaherty, uh, that is, to Monseigneur Flaherty. They can't do nothing to him. He can beat them all.'"

"Isn't he angry with me for having roughed him up a little, that time I fought with Höfflin?"

"Oh, no, Monseigneur. Just this morning, we were talking among ourselves, and you know what he said? 'Some day, Flaher—uh, I mean, Cardinal Flaherty will be Pope. He'll be the first American Pope.' And, you know, there are a lot of graffiti on the hallways and on the walls of the courtyards: *Evviva Flaherty! Down with Razzi! Down with Nichols!* There's a real big one sprayed on the wall of the Cortile del Papagallo, that says *John XXIV.* There's been a team scrubbing away at it all morning. And in Cardinal Villot's antechamber there's even one in rhyme. Let me try to remember it:

> Your days are numbered, Montini,
> And the French gangster is *fini.*
> It's time for Irish liberty:
> Our real Pope is Flaherty!

"Pure doggerel," John commented with pretended scorn. But he could barely hide his smile of satisfaction. "Come now, Franz. Lead me not into the sin of vanity. I'm not sure it's even right for you to kiss my ring anymore."

"To me, you're still Monseigneur, my lord," the

Swiss guard exclaimed, falling to his knees and fervently kissing John's hand.

"No, just the humble servant of our Lord, my son," he replied. "Love Him as I love Him, son, and peace be with you."

Franz got back up. John dismissed him with a smile, but at the same time handed him several envelopes that were on the table. Then, thinking better of it, asked, "How can you do it, if you're all confined to quarters?"

"Never fear, Your Excellency," Franz replied, with a bit of offended pride. "We even know of several chamberlains who are still devoted to you."

The door was barely closed when John seized the revolver.

With childish glee, he took imaginary shots at all the recesses of his cell, at the furniture, the stone columns, kneeling, squatting, turning, as if he were assailed from all sides, feinting, getting back up, and finally aiming, behind him, at the big vulgar St. Sebastian.

At the last minute he had to restrain himself from pulling the trigger.

5

John Kevin Varese turned off the transistor set that was hanging from a clothes peg above his workbench. The noise was keeping him from concentrating. And what he was doing had to be done just right: the slightest error in assembly, and the whole thing might blow. He'd get it first, and then Leo. And Joe, who was asleep upstairs.

"Oh! That goddamned Ahmat-Ahbat war is all they can talk about! Why don't they shove it up their ass?" he said to Leo Carter, who was opening the valve of an oxygen container alongside him.

They were working in the shop that Joe Jeffrey had lent them: a low cement room, half underground, getting its daylight from narrow loopholes of bullet-proof glass. This was where Eliah Varese's Roman representative and strong man kept the isothermic suits, flippers, masks, and spear guns for his summer diving club. If the police had searched the place well, they would have found, in addition to a ten-day supply of canned goods and bottled water, cases of ammo hidden inside diving bells, automatic weapons with silencers carefully placed inside a compressor, and bulletproof vests under the waterproof jackets hanging on the racks. But Jeffrey had well-placed connections in the S.I.D., the Italian counterintelligence force, and on the three occasions when they came into this cellar to investigate, the cops did not look very deep or very hard.

"It *is* beginning to be a pain in the ass," Leo answered indifferently, after they had been listening for a few minutes to the ticking of an electronic chronometer. "Make sure the safety catch is on. I'm going to set it again."

"Don't worry. I've seen to it. You'll see, old man! It'll be total destruction—a regular Hiroshima! And no trace of the bomb afterwards. The jerks can look high and low. This one has the Varese trademark, Pat. Pending! Just a big gust of oxygen—and whaaam!"

"How long do you figure it'll take after the shock absorbers are depressed?"

"Maybe ten seconds—just long enough to close the car door. Even the IRA doesn't have anything like this."

"Ten seconds? Okay."

"Okay."

He was asking Marion once more whether—for Christ's sakes—she wouldn't make up her mind and marry him. "Especially now that I'm gonna be in the dough, with this new scoop! Real dough!"

"Sure, why not?" his secretary sarcastically agreed. "Just show me your last bank statement and give me time to think it over. I'll try to get to it this afternoon, when I finish the typing."

"I like that! A real golddigger, aren't you?" Mike replied with feigned offense, superemoting like a silent-flicker ham. "The lady wants to see my bank statement! Because she doesn't trust me! Me, her very own boss! Really, you're a disappointment to me,

Marion darling. There's no romance in you at all."

"I know, I've been told that before," she came back, and added slyly, "but there isn't any in your bank either. Did you know they just phoned *darling* Marion a little while ago to have *darling* Marion tell her boss that's he's overdrawn by nine hundred and some dollars. That's the kind of real dough you've got!"

"What?" he demanded.

"Yes, that's the fact, but darling Marion isn't such a dope. She told that nasty old UC Bank that it surely wasn't *Signore* Wyatt who wrote all those rubber checks, surely not her sober, careful boss, Mr. Wyatt."

"Uh, what's that? What do you mean by that?"

"Sure, Mike, I know. How could I not know? Listen, Mike, I hope you don't mind my saying so, but—uh—sometimes I'm really sorry for you. Last night, in your office, you kept swearing while you were reading those damned reports on Flaherty and the ICC."

"Which reminds me," he blurted out, "that I found out in there that my fuckin' bank was half owned by the fuckin' ICC."

"Whoa, what kind of 'fuckin'' story is that you're telling me?"

"It's no story at all! Listen, Marion. Can you picture this? It's crazy! Like a poor slob, you give your money to a teller in some bank in New York, or Chicago, or Baton Rouge, or wherever, and God knows—yes, in this case God *does* know—where it ends up: those bastards at the ICC end up with it in their till. For the *Carita Cristiana*, I suppose. Charity, my ass! But if they give me too much of a hassle, I've got enough on those little darlings at the UC Bank to tell them where to get off at. All it'd take is a couple of lines in the *World*. Nine hundred dollars! Phoning about an overdraft of nine hundred bucks! Nine lousy hundred dollars!"

He went out of the girl's office without closing the glass door behind him, and grabbed his straw hat off the hook on his way out. He was all the way downstairs before he stopped mumbling about the "nine lousy fuckin' hundred bucks"!

Now, once more, the devil was at his ear, claiming he was "dying of thirst"!

So in order to buck himself up at the same time, before going to the home of the "Monsignore," Mike stopped for a Campari and gin at Rosati's. Then a gin without the Campari at the Café Greco, on Via dei Condotti, right at the foot of the Spanish Steps—a hundred of them at least that he would have to climb. "Just think," he was sighing, "Via Gregoriana is all the way up there at the top."

And when he was halfway up, damning the "nine hundred lousy dollars" for the fiftieth time in as many variations, he stopped to catch his breath and suddenly thought of a line in *Pierrot le Fou*, that French film of the sixties that he had liked so much: "Ah," the hero cried, "what a dismal five o'clock!" and then tried to commit suicide.

"What a dismal five o'clock!" It was a wonderful line. Behind his laughter, Mike could feel tears.

Just then, the Trinità dei Monti tolled six P.M.

After the long climb he was finally at the Residenza. Peppe was sitting outside his lodge and gave him a knowing wink, as he mumbled between toothless gums, "She's up there! You can go up. And I wish you luck!"

Mike paid him off with a five-thousand-lire note

folded in eight, and bowed deeply to the imbecilic-looking statue of a cherub standing guard beside the elevator's iron doors.

"Hello!" Mike said affectionately, patting its rounded belly. He got into the elevator and, after clowning as if he didn't know which button to press, opted for the penthouse.

12:10 P.M. Little Maria-Pia Barbieri had not come out of school with her classmates. Charity, her mother, wild with worry, went to the teacher. "Signorina! Signorina! I don't see my daughter. Where is she?"

"Why," the surprised woman answered, "you sent for her yourself this morning. Your brother came, around ten or ten thirty . . ."

"My brother? I have no brother! I don't under—oh, no! . . . I . . . I . ."

She was speechless with terror. Her haggard eyes filled with horror. She hung desperately to the teacher's arm. The teacher was also turning pale. They both understood.

"Oh, my God! Maria-Pia has been kidnapped!"

In the splendor of late afternoon, it was even finer than he had imagined when he had flown over it in the helicopter on Easter Sunday. Golden reflections danced on the water of the pool, nightbirds flew over the terrace of the loggia, the flowerbeds, lemon trees, orange trees, and potted azaleas gave off even more intoxicating fragrances, and against the pinkish horizon all of Rome seemed ablaze with the setting sun.

A black servant brought out a garden chandelier and lighted the candles stuck in their glass holders. The crystal drops hanging from its arms tinkled softly in the twilight breeze. Mike was so delighted that he almost forgot the purpose of his visit. He mixed some Campari into his gin and sipped, holding the icy feeling under his tongue.

The sound of footsteps on the stone edge of the pool brought him back to reality. Claudine had returned from the bathroom, where she had gone to take off her makeup, ruined by her tears. Two streaks of eyeliner still darkened the bridge of her nose, and her eyes remained clouded. Before sitting down she once more looked distractedly at the pictures on the rolling bar: official portraits of John K. Cardinal Flaherty in his purple robe and ceremonial cappa.

"I—I—just can't believe it," she said, sniffling. "It's just too—too—"

"Didn't you ever suspect anything?" Mike asked gently. "Never smelled a rat? After all, the servants are deacons of the International Seminary."

"I couldn't know that! Harold never—"

"But what about that gallery of portraits of all the cardinals?"

In a sudden fit of anger and vulgarity that seemed to come as a surprise even to her, she shouted back, "I have a girl friend who collects antique madonnas. That doesn't make her a virgin!"

"I can understand how upset you are."

"And now I understand," she went on, aggressively, "why Honey Pie was so eager to see me and asked me all those questions about him. You're in a filthy business, Mr. Wyatt."

"Well, what about Finnegan? Or, rather, *Monsignore* Flaherty—Cardinal Flaherty? Isn't he in a dirty business? A killer who—"

"I forbid you to say that!" she spat at him.

But Mike had risen with some effort from his leather deckchair, and went on, "Yes, a killer! Who murdered my friend Cesare Tozzi, or at the least had him murdered by Eliah Varese! After all, he is a *Monsignore*, so he probably doesn't do it with his own holy hands! But he did have him murdered! Yes, he was responsible for it, you hear?"

"That's not true! Not true! Harold could not possibly—"

"Harold Finnegan!" the reporter came back, sarcastically. "So refined, isn't he! So handsome, elegant, athletic, intelligent, so strong and polite, so well educated, and pretty great in the hay, from what I heard you've said."

"Oh, you *are* beneath contempt!" she hissed.

"That fine rich man who was keeping you? No, I'm not talking about Harold Finnegan: he's a perfectly respectable gentleman! But what about his other self: the president of the Institute for Christian Charity? The Vatican's secret banker? *Monsignore* Flaherty? His Eminence John Cardinal Flaherty? Your ordained lover! That one would and didn't hesitate to—"

"Enough of that! You're lying, Wyatt! Plain lying! And what's more, you're drunk! This is an outrage—you don't even know what you're saying! You're just a nobody, a rat, an earthworm. And as soon as he knows about this, Harold will crush you like the worm you are. He's strong! You said so yourself. He's intelligent, and rich, and athletic: he'll smash you to a pulp, you hear me? And if he doesn't do it himself, Eliah will!"

"Ah, Eliah Varese, his fine mafioso buddy!"

"What the hell do I care? What the hell do I care if Harold is really Cardinal Flaherty? It doesn't shock me in the slightest. How does that grab you? I'm even prouder to belong to him, now that you've told me. Hah! That's something you can't understand, isn't it, you poor slob? Well, you think I'm a whore, don't you? Okay, I am. I'm a whore and proud to be fucking a Monsignore, if you must know! Your little tart of a Honey Pie could never do as well!"

Mike had backed away, slightly frightened and not too solid on his feet. He poured himself another shot of straight gin and downed it in one gulp. But she was pursuing him. She grabbed the glass and screamed like a fury, "I never gave you permission to drink *my* gin, you lousy freeloader! This isn't your home, you know, it's Cardinal Flaherty's! . . . Now, get the hell out of here, you drunk! Get the fuck out, you hear me? I've seen all of you that I can stomach.

"Diab! Van Dông! Van Dông, come on and show this 'gentleman' out!"

"Well, now," Inspector Lambrusco was saying, "let me have the whole thing again, but slower, please. First, your name?"

"Marion Mason," she answered. "I'm an executive secretary, an American citizen."

"Not so fast, please, not so fast . . . . Er-i-can citizen. You must excuse me. My assistant isn't here, and I'm not very fast on the typewriter."

"I work for the *World.* I'll spell that: W-o-r-l-d."

"Yes, I know, Signorina. I took English in school."

"I'm sorry. Would you like me to type it for you? It'd go faster that way."

"Impossible. Against the rules."

"You're right. Anyway, you have an Italian keyboard, so I'd probably get all the letters wrong. But I'm in a hurry. I have to get home and fix dinner. I live over on the Salaria, that's pretty far out."

"Now, you were saying it was at—"

"A quarter to six, or maybe ten to six. I was closing up for the day."

"And these two masked individuals broke into your office?"

"Exactly."

"Just where were you when they came in, Signorina Mason?"

"I was looking for my shoes in the closet," she told him. "You know, I always type barefoot."

"Does that make it go faster?"

"Yes, in a way. It's easier to feel the pedal underfoot. But those damned Remingtons don't have any recall."

"You're a very amusing young lady!"

"Thanks, but we can leave that till later, if you don't mind. I have to fix—oh, incidentally, can you tell me how long you have to cook tortelloni? Oh, you don't know? Too bad! Anyway, as I was saying, my back was to the door when I heard it slam shut. First I thought it was my boss coming back."

"That's Michael—Michael—"

"Wyatt. W-y-a-double t. I thought maybe he forgot something. But then I heard them say 'Don't move. We've got you covered.' And then one of them grabbed my wrist and dragged me out into the office at gunpoint. There was even a silencer on his gun."

"Ah, you know about things like that?"

"Of course. You think I never go to the movies? Anyway, the other one asked me, where does Mr. Wyatt keep his files? No use resisting in a case like that, is there? So I showed them. They looked through all the files, and the drawers. But what struck me about them was that they were rather well bred. I mean to say, when they were done with a file they put everything back in order, didn't throw it all over the place like they do in the movies. At one point the one who must have been the boss even bawled the other one out because he was wrinkling some papers. Anyway, when they left, all they took was a big notebook that Mike—I mean, Mr. Wyatt—used to make notes in. Oh, and a report on the Institute for Christian Charity. But they were very sore! The one who must have been the boss said, 'Shit! it's not here!' And then, like I already told you, they cut the telephone wires and tied and gagged me so I wouldn't be able to call for help right away. The cleaning woman found me like that. But you know that already."

"Now, just what did they look like?"

"I told you already: both very tall and slim."

"How tall would you say?"

"Oh, six foot three or four."

"How tall is that?"

"I guess about one meter ninety centimeters. They spoke with an American accent and their voices seemed young. But that's all I can tell you, Inspector. They each wore faded jeans, a sailor jersey, and gloves, and had black hoods over their faces. Boy oh boy! did they ever scare me! You know what I mean? Those silk skimasks, or whatever, that you see on cycle riders, the kind that hide the whole face except the eyes. And over their eyes they had dark skiing goggles."

"What kind of shoes did they have on?"

"Sneakers, blue with red stripes."

"Anything else? Now, think it over. Anything worth noting? I don't know what—maybe a twitch, or the way one of them walked maybe—what we call 'identifying characteristics'?"

"Oh, yes!" she suddenly recalled. "I did notice one

thing: they were both wearing big divers' wristwatches on big strong bands. You know the kind of watch I mean, with I think they're called bathymeters in them."

"That's right."

"Okay, then, they were real professionals' watches, with this depth gauge on the band."

"I must say, Signorina Marion, that you are a most observant young lady. That last detail may be of immense help to us."

As she left the police station, hurrying to be home on time for her date, Marion was thinking, "Some machos, these Italian types like Lambrusco! They just have to talk to you and it's like they were copping a free feel with every word."

6

"You're not listening to me, De Vaere," Mike said.

"Yes, I am. I'm all ears. You were talking about Korea, how he came back from Korea, where he had been a chaplain in the Marines. Uh, what'll you have after your tagliatelle? The saltimbocca?"

They were having dinner in Mike's favorite trattoria. De Vaere was studying the menu with a world-weary and somewhat cynical eye and had indeed not been paying too much attention to what Mike was saying. He didn't think his "scoop" could really amount to anything. It was just another one of Mike's wild ideas.

But Mike, squeezing his wine glass as if it would fly away, sputtered on.

"All right. Where were we?"

"In '54."

"Yes, that's right. At the time 'Monsignore,' well, John Flaherty—he wasn't a Monsignore yet—John Flaherty, having made a bundle in the lucky speculations I told you about, started dabbling in real estate developments. First there was the Rialto, in Southampton, remember? Well, it was promoted by a Varese company, in other words, by Flaherty. Over five hundred homes and apartments. In a part of Long Island that had very strict zoning laws covering new construction—but Flaherty got around them by building on pilings, which was something that wasn't covered by the law. There was a big stink, and a lawsuit—and as usual, he came out on top. Besides, the local artist colony was on his side, as well as the home-beautiful magazines, and the snobs. At the time they all were ecstatic over the off-the-ground buildings and the 'Venetian type' canals underneath. 'Just too, too divine, don't ya know?' But of course, after that the zoning laws were amended to keep any more such developments out. It's amazing how many rules and regulations have had to be rewritten since Varese and his, uh, gray eminence have been in business together. There's always a loophole, and 'Monsignore' is always the one who can find it! He can twist anything to suit his ends! I betcha if he wanted he could give America back to the Queen by finding some kind of loophole the Founding Fathers left!

"Now you understand why the Vatican called him in to help when they got into difficult straits. The Monsignori in the 'home office' suddenly remembered *Il Cowboy,* as old Tardini used to call him. So they figured, a guy who can pull stuff like that in the U S of A, where the laws aren't so easy to get around, ought to be a godsend here in Italy, the birthplace of *combinazioni.* Besides, he speaks almost perfect Italian, and knows the Curia inside out, and who knows what all else! So, they called him in, one day in '59. October I think it was, and after promoting him to being a prelate they showed him what stinking shape their books were in. This was just what he had been waiting for, apparently. He was getting bored with all the other deals he was into. The J&E Tower, Primabank, EMV, the Nassau Helicopter outfit, his Park Avenue apartment, his chalet at Squaw Valley, the

Cadillacs and formal dinners with Cardinal Spellman were old hat by now. He had made Holy Virgin the most prosperous parish in the state of New York: its extra-religious facilities were publicized all over the media. It had an indoor swimming pool, playgrounds, arts and crafts, choirs, free milk for all the neighborhood kids; you name it, they had it.

"But Flaherty is a born gambler, a guy who can't stand not taking a dare. He's been like that in everything in his life, I can assure you. He has to be on the trail of something new all the time, challenging himself, setting himself impossible goals. If not, as I said, he gets bored. So, De Vaere, you can imagine how he welcomed the opportunity. To lay his hands on the holy mess that the Holy See's finances were at the time —just what a guy like him would dream of! They were in desperate straits, nobody wanted to face their liabilities—not even that honorable Signore Micheli, whom they had called in as a consultant before they turned to Flaherty."

"Was Micheli involved with them?"

"Yep! The Vatican was really down on its uppers. They would have made a deal with the devil at the time. When he died, Pacelli had left almost empty coffers—why, is one of those goddamned mysteries that the Vatican is full of!—and Roncalli, who had been on the throne for less than a year, was spending money like a drunken sailor. At least, at the beginning. That's what that good old priest at Sant' Andrea dell' Orto that I told you about said: John XXIII was wildly generous. He gave to the poor, to charitable organizations, to the missions, to museums, to whoever needed money. So when the Secretariat saw bankruptcy staring them in the face—without a dime left in the ICC account—well, they panicked so that,

as I said, they would have made a pact with the devil!
But the devil would have been too smart to have any
truck with them!

"For a period of three months they tried every
crooked banker, every mafioso, every unscrupulous
lawyer, anyone who'd ever been near the Italian
Ministry of Finances, you know what I mean, 'all the
maggots that swarm over the manure heap of bankruptcies.' "

"Hey, that's not a bad phrase, 'all the maggots that
swarm over the manure heap of bankruptcies.' "

"Unfortunately, it's not original. But wait a minute, De Vaere. The funniest part is that every one of
those shysters and swindlers, to a man, said thanks
but no thanks! They tried to convince them with
promises of all kinds of indulgences, with *agnus dei*s
blessed by the Pope in person—but no one was having
any! Religion has lost its charms—even with gangsters!
The only one who saw where it could lead was him—
Flaherty!"

"But, Mike, didn't you say that at the start all he
handled was the Vatican police force and the secret
service?"

"That—well, that was only—shall we say?—the cover.
The few people who were in on the deal, that is, the
papal secretary of state, the surrogate, and old John
XXIII himself, didn't want to do anything the Sacred
College might take umbrage at. A young guy like
him—only thirty-seven—and an American, to boot!
You can imagine how jealous they would have been
and the spokes they'd have put in his wheels if they'd
known the real reason he was being called in! So, to
the rest of the Curia, he was simply the paratrooper,
the marine: the rough-and-ready prelate who was supposed to give some military bearing to the Holy See

and lay down the law to all those parallel police forces that overlapped inside the apostolic palace. Anyway, he did that job damned well, just as well as he did the other. At the time, the way it is after every conclave, there was regular gang warfare among the various prelates and cardinals. Like Chicago after the Valentine's Day massacre. Because the Vatican has a spoils system that makes ours in America look like peanuts! The minute the papal election is over, all the knives come out! And—if I can believe my informant, Father Farlari, who happened at the time to be father confessor to a certain number of the *Monsignori*—there were even a few cases of *borgiade* like in olden times."

"*Borgiade?*" De Vaere asked.

"Yes, just like in the days of the Borgias. It seems that the secrets of *elisir diabolico* or *aqua toffana* did not go to the grave with them. At Christmas 1958 there was a veritable little epidemic of strange illnesses at the Vatican: unexplained hemorrhages, sudden paralyses, and fits of lockjaw, all fatal, of course. To say nothing of epileptic fits among some young priests who had appeared perfectly healthy a few hours before."

"Mike, you're seeing things! This isn't the sixteenth century."

"That's what you think! Anyway, even if it didn't go quite that far, the fact is the palace was teeming with spies. You couldn't move a curtain without finding a hidden microphone behind it. First of all, Flaherty cleaned up that situation and straightened out the secret services. And then he reorganized the pontifical armed forces, modernizing the Swiss Guard's weapons and training. He taught them to use small arms the way the G-men do, and gave them close-order drill like the Marines'. That made them into the world's best soldiers—or so they claim. Then he became bodyguard first of John XXIII and then of Paul VI. This kept up the appearances, you see, De Vaere: to all intents and purposes, he was just His Holiness's paratrooper, a simple gorilla all-brawn-and-no-brains, but secretly he was already administering the Holy See's holdings and running the ICC."

"Already?"

"Yes, already—and don't think that that interfered with his numerous profitable private deals all over the world. That's what's so fascinating about him—his absolute frenzy of activity! He's able to run police, army, and finance all at the same time! He can be both a theologian and a banker. Did you know that he writes articles of exegesis or philosophy for the most arcane journals and the most learned? Recently he wrote a preface to a French psychoanalyst's book on the Mosaic myth. You see, he's a thinker, but *also* a sharpshooter, a boxer, and past his fiftieth birthday can still run a fifteen-mile amateur race—and come in among the first! He's an achitect as well, a collector, or rather an art lover—in the sense that that word was used in the sixteenth century, when they coined the word *amateur*—a lover of art and beautiful women!

"Just think of the lightninglike career he's had! It is reminiscent of the most famous highborn cardinals of last century: in '59 he became a prelate and in '62 an *in partibus* bishop; in '67 he fell from favor for a while because of the Micheli affair—but immediately afterwards he was called back to Rome, because the Vatican's finances had once again hit a new low. So back he came, stronger than ever—and now he didn't have to hide anymore. Then, in 1969, he got his biretta. So now he's a prince of the blood—and where did he start? In the slums of Brooklyn!"

"What do you mean by 'prince of the blood'?"

"Sure. Didn't you know that cardinals are considered princes of the blood and are entitled to exactly the same honors as royalty? De Vaere, just give a minute's thought to how far he came in thirty years, from being a Williamsburg ragamuffin. Yet, in the eyes of the Most Eminent and Most Reverend John K. Cardinal Flaherty, that still was not enough. So that same year he decided he had a better way to handle both his own deals and the Vatican's interests at the same time—by having a double life, two different personalities! As if just one life, especially one as crowded as his, wasn't enough for any man!

"Now, De Vaere, do you see what kind of fantastic character he is? Do you see the kind of series about him I could do for our feature section? Flaherty is best described as one of those *condottieri*-humanist princes of the Renaissance: a warrior, philosopher, statesman, banker, aesthete, epicurean, mystic, athlete, and stoic—all at the same time. And with an open-handedness, a generosity that's like the Medicis! He's John the Magnificent, that's it. I think that's what we ought to call the series, De Vaere, 'John the Magnificent'!"

De Vaere let Mike simmer down a little before he came back: "Now what about Cesare Tozzi? Remember Cesare Tozzi? Mike, I don't get you. An hour ago, all you could talk about was getting even for your friend, cooking the goose of that bastard, that murderer, that swindler, and what have you, Flaherty. And now you've built him up as a hero! You want to do a series on him and you've changed your mafioso into Lorenzo de' Medici!"

"Okay, okay." Mike was quite unfazed by the bureau chief's lack of appreciation. "All right! Nothing is all black or all white, all good or all bad. John can be both one and the other—like anybody else!"

"Oh, now you refer to him as John, do you?" De Vaere sneered. "Are you on that familiar terms with him?"

"Well," Mike stalled, somewhat crestfallen, "it's just that I've been fascinated by him. But that doesn't keep me from seeing clear. I'm a writer, De Vaere, don't forget that! A newspaperman. And what you just heard was the newspaperman, the writer, talking. All I was thinking of—"

"Was your 'scoop'!" De Vaere cut in.

"Go on! Make fun of it, if you want. But this series is just the thing that could avenge my friend Cesare! Because I'll tell it all—because I know it all now. I have the proofs: the murder of Farouh. Fuad. Varese. The HUELCO. The ICC. And why the Vatican's delegate tried to intervene at the UN. And the way all of those people are tied in with the CIA. And the Mafia. The only link that's still missing is what goes on at Via Sottocolle. But I'll find that out soon enough!"

"What's on Via Sottocolle?"

"I'm not sure yet. But I've got everything else I need, even the pictures. They're in my car, if you want to see them. Look, De Vaere, you don't seem to realize that this could be for the *World* what Watergate was for the *Washington Post*. This is an important story—and it means more dough, fame, something that all newspapermen can be proud of—maybe even the Pulitzer! Come on, De Vaere, admit this is as good as Woodstein."

Mike saw the son of the trattoria's owner, a four-

teen-year-old kid, going from one table to another
with the restaurant's only grated-cheese dispenser.

"Here, Gianni," he called, tossing him his car keys,
"go get me an envelope of pictures I left in my car,
will you? You know which one it is, the big American
one parked near the corner of Via Zanardelli."

Gianni nodded and ran out of the restaurant: he
knew he could expect a good tip from Signore Wyatt.

Mike took a breather, swallowed a long drink of
Frascati, and looking right into the bureau chief's
eyes, said, "Whatsamatter, De Vaere? Aren't you a
newspape—"

All hell broke loose. The restaurant windows were
splintered by the explosion, tables overturned, plaster
fell from the ceiling, people screamed in horror and
pain. The restaurant was half destroyed by the terrific impact.

It was hell.

But he wasn't dead. Mike was still able to crawl,
carefully, over the rubble and broken glass. No, he
wasn't dead. He wasn't even hurt. He was crawling,
and trying to get to the fresh air outside, like a diver
reaching for the surface when he suddenly feels he's
about to be asphyxiated.

Blinded by the dust, coughing his head off, bathed
in sweat, his heart pumping as if it would burst, he
kept crawling toward the street.

Outside, at the place where he had parked the Bel
Air, there was nothing but a deep crater in the pavement.

No car, no Gianni, nothing but a column of acrid
black smoke blotting out the starry sky.

7

"Go ahead, Joe!"

Jeffrey steered the Mercedes 600 into the left-hand lane of the rapidly moving traffic. The deluxe black sedan had already covered almost half the beltway called Raccordo Anulare.

"Are you sure that the call . . . ?" Eliah Varese was asking his son.

"Absolutely sure, Dad," John Kevin cut him off. "Our scrambling system is highly perfected. Besides, the faster the car is moving, the harder it is to locate who placed the call. It's picked up and relayed by all the wreckers in the area, the radio taxis, anything within six miles that has two-way radio. Even the motorcycle cops' radios!"

Eliah smiled with satisfaction as his son dialed the number on the radiophone in the armrest of the rear seat. Then John Kevin gave his father the other earphone.

At the other end, Gigi picked up before the end of the first ring and answered breathlessly, "Yes?"

"Mr. Barbieri? Do you have what we want?"

"Yes."

"All the files, and the tapes?"

"Yes, yes."

"Good. We'll call you back in an hour."

"But what about Maria-Pia? Please, I beg you. Is my little Maria-Pia all right?"

"She's just fine. You'll have her back tomorrow, if you don't try to pull any fast ones. Now, hang up."

John Kevin commented to his father, "For a Vatican secret agent, with CIA training, he's nothing to write home about."

"Maybe it's a trick. He may be acting dumb to lure us into a trap."

"No, Dad, you could hear it in his voice: he's completely licked!"

"Incidentally, how is Maria-Pia?"

"Wonderful. She's a cute kid. Never cries, eats whatever you give her, and tells you when she has to go potty. And she loves playing with the blocks I got her. The perfect hostage!"

Mike was yelling into the long-distance phone as if he expected to be heard on the other side of the ocean.

"Listen, Jim! Don't hang up, for Christ's sake! I need that lousy two thousand bucks. Hear? Two grand, Jim! What is two grand, after all? . . . All right, I can make it with fifteen hundred, Jim, and I'll split everything fifty-fifty with you! You know what that means? This is the opportunity of a lifetime!"

"Sure, Mike, sure. And then I get into my Capri to go to the races—and, poof! one widow and three orphans. These are tough times, Mike. Did you think about that?"

"Listen, Jim! Just don't hang up, old pal! If you can carry out your end as well as I do mine we can both end up managing editors, or better. Just like that!"

"Sure, just like that," Jim answered. "Or else, I can just kiss it all good-bye. If you see what I mean. I send you fifteen big ones and right away you'll spend fourteen hundred and ninety-nine on long-distance phones, the way you're doing right now! You say you've got everything worked out, but you didn't even think to reverse the charges! The Rome office is gonna be billed for this one, not us. An hour and a quarter on the line to New York, in tough times like this! You don't think De Vaere'll hold still for—"

"Oh, fuck him!" Mike cut in. "De Vaere! De Vaere! He seems to be all you can think of. Boy, if anyone—"

"Listen, Mike, if I was in his place, man! Can't even go out to eat dinner without getting buried under two feet of rubble! No wonder he's laying low."

"Oh, shit! You're all a bunch of pantywaists," Mike came back. "What the hell did any of you go to work for a paper for, anyway?"

"Look who's talking! Since when did you become a knight in shining armor? After all these years that you've been writing the same stories about Taylor and Burton and Mrs. Carlo Ponti's miscarriages, excuse me, Sophia's, to you pals of hers! So how about getting down from your high horse, huh?"

"You know what? The whole bunch of you are a pain in the ass!" Mike was shouting, now twice as loud. "Yep, a bunch of pains in the ass. Okay, I'll carry the ball by myself. I'll find someone to bankroll it. And you can shove your help up your ass! I'll sell my scoop to *Time* or *Newsweek,* and De Vaere'll be looking for a job—"

"Don't be so sure of that."

"What does that mean?"

"That he's not likely to be fired."

"Why?"

"Look, Mike, how naïve can you be? Why do you think De Vaere hasn't raised a finger to help you?"

"I wish I knew. Say, Jim . . . you don't mean—he's under orders?"

"Whoa, there, boy, me hear no evil, speak no evil. You're the one who said that, fella. Leave me out of it."

"Wait a minute, Jim. Tell me what you know. Don't hang up!"

But hang up was just what Jim had done in New York. Mike felt himself turning red with fury, almost losing control of himself. He let out a long low moan like a wounded animal.

Then everything else vanished from his mind as he envisioned the four-color cover of a mass-circulation magazine—never mind its name—with a boldface title of an article splashed across it. And he could read it, as if it were on display there before him:

CHRISTIAN CHARITY:
TWO THOUSAND DEAD IN THE NEAR EAST!
By Michael Wyatt

"Some lousy audience tonight," Honey Pie was thinking, as she went off stage to underwhelming applause. "What the hell do these bastards want? Do I have to show 'em my twat to get them interested?"

She kicked the door of her dressing room open with a vengeance.

"Aaahmmmhhh!"

Two masked men, hiding behind the door, had grabbed her and she was already passing out from the chloroform they gagged her with.

* * *

Lake Nemi. In ancient times it was called *La Bocca dell' inferno,* the Gates of Hell. Gigi knew this from having read it in the guidebook when looking for the road there, to deliver the valise with the ransom in it as they had demanded. "Very appropriately named!" he shuddered.

It was an old volcanic crater, etched deep in the rock. Not a light to be seen on the steep slopes, among the pine trees, but the black oily waters shone like blood in the moonlight. In the middle of the lake there was a boat, standing still, like the boat for crossing the Styx. And across the way, against the sky, the outline of the watchtower of the Ruspoli castle. Gigi was by himself, here at the end of the pier, where they had told him to come.

"An ideal spot for getting knocked off," he couldn't help thinking. What they called a pier here was, in fact, just a small wooden, very slippery footbridge, that extended some thirty meters out into the water, going nowhere. "Of course, *they*'ll come from shore, and if I make a step one way or the other, I'm in the water and I'm a goner."

While he waited, he crossed himself three times. Finally the village clocktower sounded 1:00 A.M.; *they* would have to be here soon now.

He could hear the water lapping at the wood beneath his feet and looked cautiously one way and the other.

Then, suddenly, a hand came up out of the water, scaring him so he almost cried out. Bubbles broke the surface, and then a head appeared, fearsome in its hood and the black rubber mask with the oneway glass over the eyes.

The frogman climbed up onto the tiny pier and spat the oxygen tube out. The wooden grating swayed under his flippered feet, and Gigi had to close his eyes, as the strength of the man's diving light blinded him.

"Gigi?" Because of the mask closing his nose, the man's voice came out pipey and muffled.

The Vatican secret agent quickly tried to open the valise he held in his hand, but he was trembling so that he had trouble working the combination.

"3–7–1," the frogman noted, then asked, "Everything in it?" His wet hand riffled through some of the file folders, counted the tapes. "Anyway," he said, "you don't get Maria-Pia back till we make sure it's all there."

Then he opened a zipper in his diving suit and took out a waterproof tarred-fabric bag, to which he transferred all the contents of the case Gigi had opened for him.

The delivery of the ransom didn't take much more than half a minute. Gigi was still openmouthed as he saw the waters close again over the stranger, who, with smooth strokes of his flippers, was heading out toward the boat in the middle of the lake—Charon's bark.

"Oh, Eliah, no! You shouldn't have! My love, you really shouldn't have!"

"Don't you like it, Claudine?"

"Of course I do, Eliah. But you already gave me that emerald yesterday! Oh, my love, my love, you're absolutely crazy!"

"Claudine! Claudine!" he murmured.

John thanked the Swiss guard with an affectionate clap on the shoulder. "Well, Franz, my son," he said, "I'm afraid I'm going to have to—"

The halberdier held his chin out, saying, "Don't

let that worry you, Your Eminence. Hit me real hard."

"Thank you, Franz. When the time comes—you know I won't forget—"

And without finishing the sentence, he delivered a solid uppercut that dropped the Swiss cold.

Then he adjusted his skullcap, made sure the gun the soldier had slipped to him was in place inside his broad scarlet moiré belt. And without any haste whatsoever walked calmly from his prison cell.

8

Two thirty tolled somewhere nearby. Between the obelisk and the north wing of the Bernini colonnade, an Autobianchi had been parked since midnight and no one had gotten out of it. Don Attilio, an old beadle at St. Peter's, had noticed that.

Somewhat intrigued, he went closer, followed by a dozen or so cats whining to be fed, and looked in the rear window. There was someone inside, and apparently that someone was alive.

Mike was feeling drowsy. He stifled a yawn and, his elbows on the steering wheel, lit a cigarette with trembling hands. He took a deep puff and stretched in order to loosen his muscles, which had become stiff from the long wait, and then closed his fist on the empty package of Muratis.

The radio was playing "Smoke Gets in Your Eyes" and he hummed along a while, then mumbled, "Why do they broadcast that kind of crap?"

Disgusted, he laid his head against the wheel and felt his way toward the glove compartment, from which his hand took a bottle of gin and unthinkingly uncorked it.

"Franz was very good about it all," John was thinking. "I'll have to remember him." He had not run into the slightest obstacle. The two men on guard outside "just happened" to be at the other end of the gallery when he came through. He had gone down the main staircase without meeting a soul, gone through two barracks dormitories in which the men were sound asleep, and by now was in the long narrow courtyard between the two wings of the guards' barracks.

At the end of the courtyard there was the little Sant' Ambrogio gate, which opened onto the Bernini colonnade. "Hardly anyone knows of its existence, except His Eminence John Cardinal Flaherty," he said laughingly to himself.

In the darkness, he could see only one Swiss guard in blue fatigues, but wearing a breastplate and helmet—a rather strange combination, he thought. The halberdier was sitting rather than standing guard, in a most slipshod manner, his back against one jamb of the doorway, his feet flat against the other, his long gangling body practically blocking the passageway. He was holding a tiny transistor set to his ear and listening to "Smoke Gets in Your Eyes."

John slipped noiselessly along the wall until he was close enough to give him a solid chop on the nape of the neck. The guard passed out without making a sound—other than that of his helmet and breastplate clanking against the grillwork.

The key was in the lock, so John stepped over the body, turned the key, listened as the door creaked open—and he was free.

Mike gave a start: he wondered what the clank of hardware had been, but could not be sure whether he had heard it or dreamed it. Yet when he saw a shadow cross between the columns, he knew it was what he was waiting for.

He quickly got out of the car, walked toward the colonnade, and stopped. A voice in the darkness asked, "Wyatt?"

It was half affirmative and half interrogative. Mike peered eagerly into the shadows but could distinguish nothing. He backed up, to take refuge behind his Autobianchi. He took a gun from his jacket pocket and aimed it at the shadows, but then soon dropped his arm. Everything was silent.

Finally, there was John's voice again: "Michael Wyatt, aren't you? What are you afraid of?"

"I—I—I'm not afraid," he stammered back, trying to sound disdainful. "Not afraid at all, Monsignore. If I was afraid, I certainly wouldn't have stayed here waiting for you half the night. I'm not afraid. You're the one who's afraid."

Spreading his arms to show that he was harmless, John came out into the light between the two front columns, and asked sarcastically, "Afraid of what?" Then walked calmly toward the Autobianchi, repeating, "Afraid of what?"

"You wanted to see me, didn't you?" he went on. "You wanted an exclusive interview. Quite a story: at three A.M. in St. Peter's Square, Flaherty, the shameless cardinal, tells all! Say, that would probably be the capstone of your whole newspaper career! What every cub reporter dreams of! Wyatt exposes the Vatican swindler! That's how you'd refer to me, isn't it? You must be a very good newspaperman, to have known I was going to make my break tonight!"

"I have my sources!" Mike retorted, meaningfully.

Now the two men were facing each other across the

Autobianchi, separated only by the top of the car. John, still mocking him, leaned nonchalantly on the gutter over the car door and, tapping his fingers on the metal, hissed, "Oh, probably my dependable Peppe! Good old Peppe! In the last letter I wrote, I told him to make sure and fill you in. And I told Father Farlari the same thing, over at Sant' Andrea dell' Orto . . ."

Mike was nonplussed, and grabbed at the door window so as not to fall. His fury at the man was at white heat. What was he? The devil incarnate? Mike could almost weep over how powerless he felt against him.

But the cardinal was going right on, unruffled, with broad smiles that revealed gleaming sharp teeth, but also with childlike faces that were charming, crinklings of the eyelids that were seductive—and, however much Mike resented it, he had to admit within himself that this man had gotten to him, that he was feeling his full power of fascination.

"To tell the truth," the cardinal was saying, "I had rather expected you here with paparazzi, and microphones, and everything necessary to break the story big."

"I'm not interested in breaking the story," Mike exploded, still able to stifle the sympathy the man evoked in him. "All I want to know is what you did with Honey Pie."

"Honey Pie?" John asked in unfeigned surprise. "Who is Honey Pie?"

But now Mike was pointing his gun at him and shouting, "You know who Honey Pie is, Monsignore! Don't give me that! You're the one who had Varese snatch her."

"Honey Pie?" John asked again. "I never knew she'd been snatched, as you put it."

Mike was now choking with hatred. "Of course not," he panted. "You never know! Not about that, nor the attempt to kill me, nor about the murder of Cesare, or the death of little Gianni . . ."

"Cesare? Gianni? Murder?" John repeated, each name and word more surprising to him than the last. "Wyatt, I have no idea what you're talking about. And I don't think Varese—"

"Yes, Varese," Mike cut him off. "Varese and you, both, you bastard! Bastard of a Monsignore that you are!"

John, hardly fazed by this outburst, wearily answered, "Look, you're beginning to get on my nerves. I told you—"

"Honey Pie! Where is Honey Pie, you bastard?"

Mike was shaking violently, with the gun still pointed at the cardinal. But the latter, instead of trying to reason with him, just opened the door of the car and got into the passenger seat.

Mike was bemused and shocked by such cool. John the Magnificent indeed! He hadn't known how apt the name was when he had come up with it. He looked in the window, and saw to his amazement that Flaherty was calmly turning the radio dial, trying to pick up a newscast.

"—est news bulletins," a newscaster was saying. "Here is the situation in the Near East: at Ahmat, the Haraoui rebels of the HNLM yesterday afternoon recaptured the fort at Al-Fahad, after five hours of bloody fighting."

Calmed down and, in a sense, overwhelmed by John's obvious unconcern, Mike opened the door on his side and got behind the wheel. John turned the radio off immediately and with a friendly smile asked, "Now, Wyatt, tell me. What is this fucking murder business you're talking about?"

"A plastic bomb was set on my car and a child was killed."

"Is that the Cesare that you—"

"No, the kid was named Gianni. He was the son of the restaurant owner where I was. Cesare was an Italian newspaperman who was investigating you."

"Investigating me?"

"Well, rather, investigating Harold Finnegan, if you prefer. He thought you were a Mafia capo!"

"A Mafia capo!" John burst out laughing.

But Mike saw nothing funny about it and snapped back, "Yes, and Varese had him knocked off!"

"I can hardly believe that Varese would do that! Eliah is no—well, never was, anyway. But I know that recently he has been acting mighty strange."

Mike, his hands tightly gripping the wheel, shot back, "I can prove it."

"Eliah?" the cardinal sighed, as if speaking to himself. Then, directly to Mike, with almost affection in his voice, he said, "Listen, I swear to you by all that's holy that I never had knowledge of any of this. Wyatt . . . Wyatt . . . Michael, listen. Listen to me, Mike. Eliah was my best friend. My only childhood friend. . . . And then I heard awful things about him that, at first, I couldn't believe. But, if you could prove to me that what you said is true—well, I'd be on your side. I'd help you. I'd help you get your revenge. Until the Good Lord avenges all of us."

"You mean . . . you really believe in God?" Mike hissed back at him.

"Just as much as you do, Mike," John replied affably. "No more and no less. I believe in God and I want to help you find your Honey Pie. Now, listen to me, Mike . . ."

Mike turned toward John and studied his face in the car's ceiling light. He wondered what the man was up to, afraid in his heart of hearts to trust him. Yet he seemed sincere enough.

John easily read the questions that were running through the younger man's mind and hit on the idea of taking the gun out of the moiré belt of his vestment and handing it to him.

"Here, Mike," he said, "take this as proof of my good faith. You can have it. But let me show you how to cock it. Before, when you aimed yours at me, you forgot to. That's very risky!"

Mike speechlessly handed the gun back to John, who took it and said, "I really like you, Mike. But I just can't get it through my head why you're in such a dirty business! Newspapering, phah!"

9

"It was in December '64," John was telling him. "I was in Bombay with the Pope; I was his bodyguard at the time, in charge of his immediate security. That morning, it must have been the fifth or sixth, it hardly matters, there had been High Mass on the Oval, for tens of thousands of the faithful, and in the afternoon everyone wanted to rest. But I wasn't tired; I never get tired—it's almost a sickness with me. I don't think I've really been exhausted more than two or three times in my whole life. Anyway, while they were all napping, I decided to go and see Sister Angelica of Bombay. You know who she is, Mike. The saint who opened the hostel where even the poorest could come to die in dignity when they were too far gone to need to be fed anymore. You can't imagine the horror of it all, Mike. The stench of rot took your breath away, to say nothing of the moaning and groaning of the dying. And their poor fleshless bodies—like skeletons!

"They were like all of us will be on Judgment Day. There were women carrying their dead babies in baskets, as if they had just gotten them at the market place. And in front of the pallets there was a sort of gutter in which everything flowed off, urine, blood, pus, bile, tears, sputum. Hell on earth, Mike—like the last circle of Dante's Inferno. And there was

389

Sister Angelica in the midst of all that, still offering them her love! Sister Angelica, still finding words of consolation for them!

"I was overwhelmed by it. I began to weep, and she even found words to soothe me with. I felt so horribly embarrassed; she wouldn't address me as Father, but only as Excellency. Mike, can you imagine? 'Excellency, this,' and 'Excellency, that,' and all the time I was thinking, 'God, do you allow this?'

"I didn't know what to do, I was so taken aback. On the way out, I realized that I had my checkbook with me, and one of the ICC's as well. I know it was ludicrous, but what else could I do? How could I show Sister Angelica how I felt about her? I wrote a huge check to her hostel—on the ICC account, and then I tore it up. And then I wrote one for the same amount on my own account. But I didn't know how to give it to her.

"I was afraid of offending her. You can see that, can't you? But one can never offend a Christian by showing charity. No Christian should be offended by that. And besides, I wasn't giving the fifty thousand dollars to her, but to her hostel. Finally, I folded the check and left it discreetly on a rolling infirmary table, between the bistouris and the scalpels.

"Well, Mike, once outside, looking back on this awful place, I heard her call to me: 'Excellency, you forgot something!' She had not understood, or had pretended she hadn't. So, I don't know why, I felt so mortified that I burst out sobbing. And you know what she did, then, Mike? She ran over to me to kiss my hand and apologize, saying she hadn't read how the check was made out. And I'll never, never know, whether it was true—or whether she was lying—out of pity for me."

John had taken off the cassock and skullcap that identified him as a cardinal. Mike was surprised to see that underneath he had on a plain Holy Year T-shirt and a pair of faded jeans that clung to his figure, with one of its pockets half torn by the sharp points of a set of brass knuckles. Only the heavy pectoral cross dancing on his athletic chest marked him as a cleric.

The Autobianchi was going along Via della Lungara, deserted at this time of night. John had asked Mike to drive him to Via Sottocolle. And now Mike would find out at last what this strange religious institute in the faroff street of the Trastevere was all about. What's more, the president of the ICC himself was taking him there.

Mike handed him the gin bottle and John took a deep swig from it, then sighed in a both mysterious and amused way.

"You know, I've known you for a very long time, Mike."

"Huh?"

"Oh, sure. Like forever, I've known you," John went on, reverting to an exaggerated form of his youthful Brooklyn intonation. "You gotta be from Brooklyn, too—or else maybe from Hell's Kitchen, or something like that, aren't you?"

Mike nodded.

"Just another lousy mick like me, crummy shanty Irish. Yep, I remember, there was even a Wyatt in my gang, when we were the Devils."

We are the same godforsaken breed. You, and me —and all the poor poverty-stricken slobs, the Jewboys and Catholics, guineas and micks—all the people from the ghetto. God's leftovers. And whatever happens later, I mean to say . . ."

But he didn't finish what he meant to say. They were at the Via Sottocolle.

It was a dark narrow street with terrifying shadows on the walls. As everywhere else in Rome, cats danced a regular witches' sabbath in the street in front of the car's headlights.

"Sinister looking," Mike said, as he parked the Autobianchi against the windowless wall of the palace which was the ICC's secret annex.

John opened the car door and set a foot on the street.

As he walked into the shadows under the archway, the echo repeated the sound of his footsteps and his breathing. Mike followed, no longer trying to fight off the strange fascination the "Monsignore" had for him: he had gotten to him and there was nothing Mike could do about it any longer. "John the Magnificent," he kept repeating to himself, aware that it was no longer sardonic, but reverent, and maybe even more. So what?

"Got a light?" John asked.

By the glow of his lighter Mike could see the glitter of the jewels in the pectoral cross. John turned it over; in its back there was a slit that held a small, flat key, which he pulled out with his fingernails.

"Besides," he was now saying to Mike in a low voice, "I can tell you now: your series would never have seen the light of day. The Institute owns about a third of the *World*'s stock. And De Vaere is on our pad—as most of the important bureau chiefs and foreign correspondents in Rome are."

"The bastard!" Mike grumbled.

But then, instead of feeling sore, he started to

laugh, and John knew he had just won; all resistance was gone.

He grabbed Mike's lighter and held it to the lock so he could see better. In its dancing flame, the man's face had something diabolical about it: his eyebrows were as thick as Mephisto's. Or at least they looked like that to Mike.

The old palace was sound asleep. They went through deserted galleries and corridors, a series of empty halls with torn drapery and broken flooring that creaked underfoot.

It was like a fairy-tale castle: here and there a few broken chandeliers with cobwebs hanging from them; over the mantels, mirrors whose silver backing was so eaten away that all they reflected was shapeless colored shadows; baroque candlesticks which, when electricity first came to the neighborhood, had been fitted with weak bulbs that had never been replaced; and warped doors that made ghostly sounds as their rusted hinges squeaked when they were opened.

Loose marble slabs shook beneath their feet as they went up the poorly lighted monumental stairway. At the first landing John pushed open a double door that led to a grand ballroom dully brilliant with its gilt stucco. Mike raised his eyes to a frescoed ceiling: at the four corners, the painter had represented Fortune rolling through the sky behind a four-in-hand of winged steeds and showering a rain of goldpieces down on the entire universe.

"Maybe he knew I'd set the ICC up here two hundred years later," John laughed.

Then, holding Mike by the shoulder, he guided him forward. And they went on through another series of parlors as run-down as the ones on the ground floor.

"Can you understand that they can't do anything to me? I am in possession of all the powers; I know all the secrets," John went on. "And I'm the one who turned the Institute into one of the world's greatest banks. They have to have me. Without me, they'd be lost."

He led Mike into a small oratory draped in red brocade, and there he lifted a fold of the drapery, behind which was hidden an electronic scanner, set into the wall.

Taking a plastic card from his back pocket, he slipped it into the slit and spelled something out on the digital keyboard. Under Mike's unbelieving eyes, an old wooden panel decorated with a pastoral scene began silently to slide back and disappeared into the wall.

The door, which was armored on the inside, opened onto a small aluminum-lined lock chamber that led to the computers.

All eyes, Mike stopped on the second threshold as the sliding door automatically closed behind him. But John was going right ahead with the familiarity of one who belonged.

In the bluish darkness, the terminal console was visible. Its control panel sparkled with an infinite number of luminous keys, and beyond the TV control screens it was obvious that there was a quadruple bank of computers with their quietly turning disks, stopping, going backward, then forward, and so on.

John ran his hand over an electric eye and the light went on.

Mike blinked, blinded by the glare of the tubes that shed a cold light: now he could see machines as far as the eye could reach.

At first he didn't understand. He thought he was so tired he was hallucinating. Then he whistled as he understood: John had set up the secret ICC computers in the old gallery of mirrors of the palazzo in the Via Sottocolle.

He watched him open a metal file cabinet with a numbered combination and take out sheafs of documents and lists. Wondering what it all was, Mike went toward the console, and bent over the teleposition screen.

Interrupting the sorting that he was doing among the papers before him, John laughingly hit four numbers on the keyboard, and said, "Were you wondering how big a bank account His Holiness has?"

Immediately, there appeared on the screen: 16 16 MONTINI GIOV CRED, followed by the amount in small green flourescent computer figures.

"What do you think of that, Mike?"

"Is that all?" he replied, disappointed.

But John told him, "Those aren't lire, Mike. They're dollars! Everything is figured in dollars here!"

"Wh-what? Wh-what?" Mike was stammering. "That can't be, John. It's just not possible!"

But John just nodded his head and laughed a mysterious little snicker which said better than words, "And yet it is!"

"Do you want to see the treasure, too?" John asked. "Want to see our Fort Knox?"

And Mike, excited as a kid who's been promised a wonderful adventure, slipped into the demagnetized vinyl coveralls that John handed him, as if he'd done so dozens of times before. Life was a dream now, but a waking dream: it was half past three in the morning, but he wasn't the least bit sleepy. On the contrary, he felt wider awake than he'd been in years. Suddenly he felt inexplicably serene, at peace with the world—like someone who had been looking for something and finally had found it. He understood! He understood that the real masters of the world are never the ones people think, never the ones you read about in the papers. No, they are the people like "Monsignore"! The revelation of this simple truth made him intoxicated, much more so than alcohol, he thought. Yes, he had just discovered an unsuspected world, unknown to all the rest of humanity—and the mystery surrounding this extraordinary place and man had him under its spell.

He was more than delighted when he heard John whisper to him, while he in turn was putting on a pair of coveralls, "You ought to come to work for me, Mike. A fellow like you doesn't belong in the newspaper business."

Then the two men went down a long concrete ramp leading to the cellar of the palazzo. In their lightweight transparent diving suits they looked to each other like the heroes of some slightly outdated sci-fi comic strip. John's voice was muffled by his plexiglass facepiece: "I'll give them a little time to forget about me. I'll go back and live in the States for a few months. But I know they'll call me back here soon enough. They need my know-how too darned much. There's too much at stake."

They had gotten to a metal door which also had an electronic scanner on it. John shoved in the plastic card he was holding, and a warning signal buzzed softly as the steel door swung on its hinges.

Then there was silence.

In front of them, the lock chamber's fire curtain noiselessly slid up into the ceiling.

"No!" Mike exclaimed as he stood stock still on the threshold.

As far as the eye could see, there were gold ingots piled upon shelving, sacred treasures arranged on metal display shelves, religious objects by the thousands: crosses, ciboria, reliquaries, statuettes, crucifixes, monstrances.

And John was going forward between these dazzling walls of precious metals and gems, saying, "Look, Mike, this is almost two thousand years of piety. Two thousand years of eternity, already. For eternity is here with us, Mike."

Having come to the end of a long lateral aisle about twenty-five yards long, he got up on tiptoe to reach a crucifix that was up above.

"Look, Mike," he said, coming back toward him. "Look at this!"

It was a golden cross with a Christ figure on it in ivory. His blood was a briolette-cut ruby. And his halo was a ring set with diamonds.

10

They began cutting up. First they finished the bottle of gin. Then they went parading through the empty streets of Rome, beneath the great starless sky in which light was starting to appear. Mike cupped his hands around his mouth, like a megaphone, and shouted in all directions, "Honey Pie, where are you? Come out, come out, wherever you are!"

John was as light-headed as a lad out on his first toot. Holding his cassock out like a matador swinging his muleta, he gave Mike a course in bullfighting right in the middle of the Piazza Navona. He stamped his heel on the ground as if to egg on an imaginary bull, and shouted, "Come on, Varese! Stand up and fight like a man!"

Then he burst out laughing and shook himself in an effort to dry out from the liquor he had drunk. But since he didn't feel he was truly sobering up, he ran over to the Fountain of the Four Rivers, in the middle of the square, and doused his head in the cool water.

"You coming along, you old lush?" he called out to Mike as he straightened up again, water dripping down him, but now quite sobered.

But all Mike could yell was "Honey Pie, Honey Pie, where are you?"

Then, as they kept walking, they finally got to Via Gregoriana, and were in front of the Residenza.

"The Zanti palace," John pointed out. And he told Mike about the strange prophecy of Maestro Abracadabra, the curse that hung over all the buildings that noble family had put up: "They will die by fire."

And the two friends went up.

They first saw a candlestick on an end table by the couch, a stick of incense that was smoldering out in a jade cup, as some sentimental music poured forth from the four stereo speakers. John pushed the door open but knew what he would see before he saw it: Claudine's body, lying on the velvet cushions, with her head in Eliah's lap.

He motioned to Mike to stay back in the Gallery of Cardinals and went on in himself.

Eliah gave a start and Claudine quickly jumped up. John pretended he had not noticed anything. He simply walked toward them. Eliah got up to greet him and give him an embrace.

"John!"

"Eliah!"

Then Claudine threw her arms about him and whispered, "Oh, my love, my love!"

Varese was already on his way to get the documents that had been extorted from Gigi, and brought them to him in a leather briefcase, which he opened for him.

John was a master of cool; he just smiled and said, "Still my faithful old Black Fangs, eh?"

Then he threw the tapes and the transcripts into the fireplace. Stooping and watching them burn, down to the last shred of paper, he took the poker to shove the twisting, turning plastic tapes under the logs, until nothing was left of any of it.

Suddenly he got back up, almost knocking over Claudine, who had been patting the back of his head. The hatred in him distorted his features; his mouth was twisted awry.

Mike was studying a Bacon portrait of a cardinal when he heard John shouting, "Come on, Eliah, don't try to deny it. You had one reporter killed off, a man named Cesare Tozzi. And you booby trapped another one's car, and a kid was killed by the explosion. What kind of dirty scum are you, anyway?"

"What do you mean? What are you saying?" the outraged Varese was replying proudly. "I did that all for you. Only for you."

"Eliah, where's that singer? What did you do with Honey Pie, Eliah?"

At which point, Mike broke into the room, gun in hand, taking a bead on Varese. Claudine shrieked with terror and fell, inadvertently knocking over the table with the candle on it. The candle set fire to the curtain, but none of them noticed it.

Eliah was backing away toward the terrace, shouting at John, "You mean, he was out there all this time, John? Wyatt? You mean you brought him up here? Are you out of your mind? Did you tell him? Did you give information to that little jerk? John, you've lost your marbles!"

But John just kept coming at him, and threatening him, while Mike, feeling superfluous, lowered his gun.

"Yes, I talked to that jerk, as you call him. Don't you know he's one of us, Eliah? A guy just like you and me."

He finally had Eliah backed against the bay window and landed a solid punch in his solar plexus. Varese fell.

"You're the crazy one," John was yelling, as if beside himself. "You're the one who lost his marbles! You've lost everything—every notion of fairness you ever had! Every notion of loyalty! You're the double-crosser, Eliah! Making a deal with Razzi! Going behind my back! Don't you understand anything at all? Not anything? Aren't you anything but a killer, a miserable little hired gun?" And turning to Claudine, who was still crying, "You, bitch, shut your trap!"

In his anger, he paid no attention to the second curtain which had just burst into flame.

Varese was coming to. Crawling painfully along on his hands and knees, he tried to sneak out onto the terrace. But Mike rushed over to him, pulled him savagely up, and shouted into his face, "Where is Honey Pie?"

Eliah, breathless, merely answered by suppressed moan, then backed a few steps more toward the pool. John meantime had grabbed his wrist and was twisting his arm behind his back.

"You heard Mike," he was saying. "Now, where is she? What did you do with Honey Pie?"

Gathering all his strength, Varese succeeded in landing an uppercut on John's chin and knocking him over.

"Where is Honey Pie?" Mike was insanely repeating.

He jumped on Varese and started pounding him. Eliah backed up some more—and fell into the pool.

"What about Honey Pie?" Mike yelled as he dropped his gun and jumped into the dark water, grabbing Varese by the throat just as the latter was about to get a footing. Their struggle was confused and deadly, each man trying to knock the other out as well as drown him.

John picked himself up. His jaw was broken. But he paid no attention to the living room which was now half invaded by the fire.

Claudine was surrounded by the flames and paralyzed with fear. She was not able even to yell "Help!"

"Where is Honey Pie?" John yelled as he too jumped into the pool to help Mike. He grabbed Varese from behind, clamping his forearm over Eliah's Adam's apple, and pressed as hard as he could, demanding, "Hurry up, Eliah! What about Honey Pie?"

Eliah was almost choking, but succeeded in getting out "Via della Nocetta, 36."

John let go. He pulled himself up on the diving board and extended a helping hand to Mike, half unconscious, below.

As he turned back, John saw that the living room was all ablaze, with Claudine in the middle of it, almost overcome.

Varese somehow pulled himself up out of the water on the metal ladder. He tottered over to the edge of the terrace, leaned over and, in a last desperate appeal, called to Jeffrey waiting below: "Hurry, Joe! Hurry up here!"

There was no more chance of escape through the blaze that had engulfed the living room.

John picked up a garden chair to use as a battering ram and smash one of the library bays. He held Mike up by the waist and helped him across the broken glass.

Behind the sliding partition to the living room the

fire was blazing madly. The lacquered panel of an old Japanese screen buckled with the heat and exploded just as the two men got to the Gallery of the Cardinals.

John had only one thought: to get to the Porsche or the Alfa-Romeo, Claudine's car or his, which were parked in the cellar garage. That was the way out.

And as the elevator door closed upon them, he could see the shadow of a man with a gun on the stairway wall: Joe Jeffrey, whom he had heard Eliah call to the rescue.

Mike connected the starter wires on the Porsche as John sat at its wheel. Then he closed the hood and jumped into the open car as it started up the garage ramp to Via Gregoriana and then sped noisily toward the Piazza della Trinità dei Monti and the Pincio Gardens.

John Kevin Varese was on guard in front of the Hotel Hassler. As soon as he saw the Porsche, he began to follow it and caught up with it in front of the Villa Medici. Seeing it start down into the hairpin turns of Salita Valadier toward the Piazza del Popolo, he got an idea. He jammed on his brakes and got out of the Innocenti Cooper.

In his hand he had his sawed-off Magnum.

In the telescopic sight, he could see the point of the obelisk in the foreground, then the head of the sphinx, the pavement, finally a wheel of the Porsche, its smoked-glass windwing, Mike's head, his ear, his nose.

At that point he pulled the trigger and could see his target's brain go flying.

The Porsche jumped out of control, spun around,

and with a tremendous crash went smashing into the bronze bars around the fountains before turning completely over.

The horn got stuck and kept blowing incessantly.

John Kevin put his right eye back against the sight: there was his godfather, splattered with blood and gray matter, crawling out from under the twisted metal. His shoulder was torn and he was also bleeding from the thigh. And yet, he succeeded in getting up and running limping toward the little church of Santa Maria del Popolo.

The young killer kept him in the hairline for a moment, but then could not bring himself to shoot again.

He lowered the gun. John had reached the doorway of the church, decked in the purple velvet of solemn holidays.

Today was Ascension Day: May eighth.

11

Suddenly, John felt that he was going to die—that he was dying already.

The tourniquet that he had made from a piece of his torn jeans was beginning to loosen, and he no longer had the strength to tighten it. He did not even have the will to look for that strength. His blood was pouring out through his femoral artery, and his life was ebbing slowly away, sticky and black.

It seemed to him that he was sinking into oblivion. Above him, the fine old stained-glass windows broke up the light like some huge constantly moving kaleidoscope. Now white, now yellow, then red, green, purple. And yellow again. And blue . . . The colors were dancing above the altar, and it seemed to him that the huge stone pillars were dancing too and then suddenly silently crumbled.

And he, who had always held it in supreme contempt, now began to be terrified of death. With a mad kind of intensity, as if to protect his eyes from its excessively bright glare, he put his hand to his forehead from which sweat was pouring, mixed with blood and with soot that had blackened his face when he fought against the apartment fire.

Then, slipping his hand under his soaked T-shirt, he felt for his heart. It seemed to have stopped. And then it started again—beating so hard it seemed it would burst.

"Oh, Lord, Lord, see how weak I am. Have pity upon me, you my savior. I am afraid, oh, Lord. I am dying, dying . . ." His broken jaw succeeded in mumbling the incoherent prayer. But soon the intolerable pain made him groan in agony, "I am dying, Lord!"

Was this the beyond already opening its gate to him?

He could hear an organ echoing through the arches, see strange very bright lights illuminating the nave and driving away the varicolored shadows. Was this the beyond?

"Or else maybe," he thought, "maybe it's just that ugly little old woman I saw coming into the church." Maybe it was the little old lady who washed the marble floor of the Chigi Chapel and was now cleaning the organ stand and making sure the lights on the Raphael frescoes were in working order.

Yes, that had to be it. Just that! What had he been afraid of? The discordant notes of an organ, a heavenly light that had suddenly fallen at his feet and engulfed him.

And despite his terrible pain, he had to laugh. The way madmen laugh, the way the simple-minded whom Jesus loved so dearly laugh. No, he would not die. God would not allow it. Not now! Not before he had gotten his vengeance. Not before he had caught up with Eliah Varese once more.

It was nothing. He had just fainted, felt a malaise. Soon, help would come. He would be saved. He would recover from his wounds. Help must already be on its way: He thought he could hear the siren of an ambulance approaching. Maybe it would be a Red Cross helicopter.

No! He couldn't die!

This was just a passing weakness. A very slight loss of consciousness. A forgetfulness.

But then, it was not really forgetfulness: As he let himself go, a memory came back to him, a very brief memory that he could not explain. He was inside one of the sacristies of St. Peter's, in front of a tall mirror in which he was watching the young priests, the deacons, the choirboys busying themselves as they dressed him in his luxurious episcopal vestments: the rochet, the amice, the alb, the stole, the beautiful gold-and-silver-embroidered chasuble, the miter sewn with precious gems.

Unctuously, reverently, they were all murmuring, "Monsignore . . . Monsignore . . . Monsignore . . ."

It had been the first time he had heard that delightful new title applied to him: "Monsignore"!

He was a Monsignore at last!

But then what had happened to him? And why? Why this—when it had started off so well?

They seemed answerless questions, desperately hopeless.

And then another memory flashed into his mind, a memory that gave a meaning to all the others—a meaning to all things: He was walking into that little seminary classroom for the first time and there, as he raised his eyes to the blackboard, he saw that sentence written in chalk, which as yet he did not understand:

ET EXPECTO RESURRECTIONEM MORTUORUM

while within its walls a voice was echoing, the teacher's without any doubt, saying, "Lord, O Lord, I await the resurrection of the dead!"

*Christ, O Christ, ever robbing
us of our energy . . .*

ARTHUR RIMBAUD

Mazes and Monsters

They had always had the best of everything. Kate, Jay Jay, Daniel and Robbie—four beautiful, bright, gifted young people. Their families had given them everything the American Dream could offer but they cast it aside for a darker dream. Together, they created a world of invented terrors, breathtaking adventure and glittering treasure. Alone, each stepped into the darkest part of his mind to discover forbidden places and to learn terrifying truths.

"Rona Jaffe's story telling instinct has sharpened over the years. Tension builds swiftly. *Mazes and Monsters* is a thriller with a heart."—*Philadelphia Enquirer*

A DELL BOOK   15699-8 $3.50

RONA JAFFE

author of *Class Reunion*

LUCIANO'S LUCK

1943. Under cover of night, a strange group parachutes into Nazi occupied Sicily. It includes the overlord of the American Mafia, "Lucky" Luciano. The object? To convince the Sicilian Mafia king to put his power—the power of the Sicilian peasantry—behind the invading American forces. It is a dangerous gamble. If they fail, hundreds of thousands will die on Sicilian soil. If they succeed, American troops will march through Sicily toward a stunning victory on the Italian Front, forever indebted to Mafia king, Lucky Luciano.

A DELL BOOK   14321-7 $3.50

JACK HIGGINS

bestselling author of *Solo*

The National Bestseller!

GOODBYE, DARKNESS

by WILLIAM MANCHESTER
author of *American Caesar*

The riveting, factual memoir of WW II battle in the Pacific—
and of an idealistic ex-marine's personal struggle to understand
its significance 35 years later.

"A strong and honest account, and it ends with a clash of
cymbals."—*The New York Times Book Review*

"The most moving memoir of combat in World War II that I
have read. A testimony to the fortitude of man. A gripping,
haunting book."—William L. Shirer

A Dell Book   **$3.95**   **(13110-3)**
